THE LOST GIRL

THE LOST GIRL

TANIA
CARVER

sphere

SPHERE

First published in Great Britain in 2016 by Sphere
This paperback edition published in 2016 by Sphere

1 3 5 7 9 10 8 6 4 2

A CIP catalogue record for this book
is available from the British Library.

ISBN 978-0-7515-5790-9

Typeset in Plantin by M Rules
Printed and bound in Great Britain by
Clays Ltd, St Ives plc

Papers used by Sphere are from well-managed forests
and other responsible sources.

MIX
Paper from
responsible sources
FSC® C104740

Sphere
An imprint of
Little, Brown Book Group
Carmelite House
50 Victoria Embankment
London EC4Y 0DZ

An Hachette UK Company
www.hachette.co.uk

www.littlebrown.co.uk

To Beth. As I promised it would be.

Snow Angels

*T*he house was supposed to be a safe one. That was why they were there.

She didn't know where 'there' was, exactly. Just followed what Mummy and Daddy said. Went where they went. Did what they did. But yes, she thought, it was safe. Or at least it felt safe.

Wrong.

It happened without warning. It had been a normal day. Or what had become a normal day for the family. Mummy, Daddy, her brother and her, all together as usual. It was snowing outside and she and her brother had wanted to go out, play in the snow. Mummy and Daddy had looked at each other, concerned. But the men who watched them, watched over them and kept them safe, Mummy said, told them it would be OK. They'd keep an eye on them. So she got ready.

Before that she had been playing with the new dolls she had been given. She didn't know what she was supposed to do with them, really. Their clothes, their hair and the little plastic things they came with were all different to what she was used to. She'd had dolls, of course she had. But they had been cloth and straw. They had smelled of natural things, of what they were made of. Like Belinda. Not like these. They smelled of things she didn't know. Didn't like. Plastic, her mum had said. And her mouth had twisted up the way it always did when she wasn't happy about something. She put the doll down, didn't want to play with it if it was going to upset Mummy. But Mummy saw what she was doing, smiled.

It's all right, she said. Play with your doll. It's fine. And she looked down at her and kept smiling. But when she looked up and away the smile evaporated quickly.

She didn't know how long they had been there. She remembered her life before the house. She remembered something that she thought must have been happiness. Safety. Security. She remembered smiling a lot and not worrying about things. Then one night, Mummy and Daddy had told her to be quiet, very quiet. Like they were playing a game. She had been allowed to carry one toy but that was it. She had chosen her favourite rag doll, Belinda. And that was it, they were off. Mummy, Daddy, her brother and her. Off into the night.

She was scared. Creeping along by a fence at what she thought must have been the bottom of the garden, still pretending it was a game for Mummy and Daddy's sake. Still trying not to breathe.

Eventually they came upon a hole in the fence. Daddy ran towards it, beckoning the others. She stopped, stared at it. Couldn't move. Mummy had seen her, stopped. Looked at her.

What? Come on.

It's a game, Mummy had said, her voice tight and hissing. *A game. Come on. You're with us. Everything'll be fine. We'll come back for . . . everything else. Come on.*

She still wasn't convinced but this was her mummy talking so she followed them.

They ran through some woods. Woods that until then she had only glimpsed the tops of from a distance. Now she was in amongst them, moving quickly.

They heard a sound from behind. Turned.

Come on, her daddy shouted and they all tried to run quicker.

This isn't a game, she thought. *This is scary. I want it to end. I want to go back . . .*

And then she saw lights ahead of them. Two. Blinking. On, then off. On, then off. And, pulled along by Daddy, they ran towards them, even faster.

2

It was a car. A big one with lots of seats in. Someone opened the back door and Daddy put her brother in then her. Finally he and Mummy joined them. They hardly had time to say hello to the driver and his friend before the door shut and they were off.

And then they came here. To the safe house.

Do this, said her brother.

He lay down in the snow, put his arms and legs out, moved them backwards and forwards. Because he was her brother and because he was older and she had been taught to always follow your elders and betters, she did the same.

What are we doing? she said after a few minutes.

Making snow angels, he said. Look.

He stood up, beckoning her to do likewise. He pointed at the ground where they had been.

See? It's like wings. He looked at her, smiled. He had hardly stopped smiling since they had arrived there. We've got wings!

She could see what he meant. And because he laughed, she laughed too. And they did it again.

The snow kept falling and lying all morning, so there was no shortage of it to play in. They played until she started to get tired and a bit hungry.

Going in, she said.

Her brother looked up from the huge snowball he had been rolling, intending it to be the body of the biggest snowman ever made. Aw, stay . . .

Coming back, she said, and went round the corner of the house.

That was when she saw it. The sight that would stay with her for the rest of her life.

At first she thought their two guards were playing snow angels too. But as she approached she noticed that their wings were red. And they weren't moving.

She didn't know what to do. She couldn't move. She looked

3

round, wanting to call for her brother, but the words wouldn't come. Eventually, she ran inside, heart pounding, needing Mummy and Daddy.

She found them. They were on the floor too, like the police had been. Covered in blood.

And then she was grabbed from behind.

She struggled, tried to bite, kick, scream, everything. Stop whoever it was doing whatever they had done to Mummy and Daddy. But she couldn't do anything. Whoever it was had her too tightly.

Stop struggling, you little fucker, a voice growled in her ear.

She smelled bad breath. Stale meat and cigarette smoke. She didn't stop struggling.

I said stop it, or you'll get what they've had.

The meaning of the words penetrated. She stopped struggling.

Good, the voice said. We're going to leave now. You're going to lie on the floor and not move. Keep your eyes and your mouth shut. Count to a hundred. Can you do that?

She didn't know if she could. She nodded.

Good. And when you've done that do it again. Or we'll come back. And you don't want that.

He threw her down on the floor. She kept her eyes closed. She tried to count to a hundred.

Eventually she opened her eyes. Stared. Her mummy was staring right back at her. She felt wet and picked her hand up. Mummy's blood.

She wondered what had happened to her brother, where he was. Didn't dare move to get up and find out.

So she lay there. For how long, she didn't know. Staring at her mummy's sightless eyes, letting her mummy's blood soak into her clothes.

Too scared, too numb, to even cry.

4

PART ONE

THE HANGED MAN

1

Claire held Damien's hand. Tight. Heart pounding, legs shaking. Other parts of her body quivering too. So excited. Barely able to believe what she was about to do.

Not her, they. *They* were going to do it. Finally.

She glanced at Damien. Caught his profile in the dying light. God, he was handsome. Maybe not everyone's idea of handsome, not classically good-looking, perhaps, but he did something to her. Moved something in her that no one else could move. Certainly not Gareth. He hadn't moved her for years.

She looked away from Damien, down at her feet once more. Moving slowly, the riverside sand still damp from the receding tide.

Behind her, the lane led to the main road where they had parked. Or as main a road as Wrabness could claim. North of Colchester, south of Ipswich, it barely counted as a village. Dotted houses, farms, a slice of beach sporting a few stilted huts and some overturned, rotting boats along the sandy, stony shore. That was it.

And a forest. A dark forest. The kind two people could get lost in. If they wanted to. And they wanted to. They knew what had happened out here. The murders. The madness. The babies. The stuff of nightmares, lurid true-crime books and prurient Channel Five documentaries. And there had been all three. They could have gone to a hotel like everyone else who had an affair, lain in a bed they would pay for but never sleep in, but where was the risk, the thrill, in that? They were transgressing. Where better to do it than in one of the most transgressive places around? The place had been the lair of a predatory sexual, cross-gendered serial killer. It just added an extra layer of excitement. A frisson of sex and death.

Claire used her free hand to pull her blouse back together. Along with her skirt it had been pulled about during their session in the car, their passion so great they could barely keep their hands off each other as they drove. Pulling in her blouse was just for appearances' sake, though, she thought. Just in case they bumped into anyone. Not that they would. Not down here. Not at this time of day. And if they did, she thought, breath shaking and mind giddy with what they were about to do, perhaps they might want to watch?

She looked round once more. No one about. Instead of keeping her blouse fastened she pulled it apart even more. Damien watched what she was doing. At her exposed black, lace-trimmed bra, the one she had worn specially for him, part of a set that he loved. That he had bought her. She saw the look on his face. Felt his pace increase.

Something in her own body responded to his increased pace. Something dark, hungry and primal.

She couldn't get into the woods quick enough.

'And this was where the body was actually found.' Malcolm pointed to the spot. 'Right there, ladies and gentlemen . . .'

He tried to put as much enthusiasm into his voice as he could but he sensed he was wasting his time. Seven people had turned up. That was it. And two had complained at having to walk so far. Three were texting while he was talking like they were in school and he was a particularly uninspiring teacher.

Despite what overly theatrical flourishes he could manage, the Colchester Murder Walk just wasn't the sure-fire success he had imagined it would be.

'Right there,' he shouted, feeling another theatrical flourish coming on, giving the buggers what they'd paid for, 'in front of the light on the lightship. The woman was naked. She had been attacked, mutilated. Almost split in two ...' Shouting the last two words as if he was a fairground barker in some Victorian penny dreadful. Giggles ensued. Not the response he had expected. He continued. 'Sexually assaulted. Her body riven by the effects of knives, chains, whips ...' He bent forward, eyes wide. 'And carved into her forehead, the word ... WHORE ...'

He kept staring. They just giggled.

Jesus, he thought. Pull it back, you're sounding like you're enjoying yourself too much. He sighed. Should have stayed at the library.

When the library service was cut Malcolm had been one of the first to go. That was when he had settled on the idea of the Colchester murder tour. He had been on a Jack the Ripper tour in London's East End and found it impressive. The guide knowledgeable but approachable, the crimes themselves explained in context to the times and the victims given a proper voice. Not sensational at all. A slice of living history, he had thought. On the train home he had got to thinking. Colchester had seen a rise in violent crime in recent years. More than its fair share of serial killers, too. Why not ...

And here he was, down on the quayside of the river Colne on a bleak, cold Tuesday night, dressed as flamboyantly as he could, trying to be a character, trying desperately to interest this tiny band of people. He felt like giving up and going to the pub.

'Any questions?' he asked.

'Yeah,' said one bloke. Big, shaven-headed, tattooed. The woman with him all fake tan and spike heels. Her legs looked sparrow-thin and every time she tottered Malcolm thought she was going to snap.

'Yes?' said Malcolm.

'What had happened to her?'

'I'm coming to that.'

'Only my mate used to have a burger van up that way.' The bloke pointed down the road. 'Said he helped the police, he did. Told me a few things.' The man smiled, relishing what he was about to say. 'He said that—'

'Well, that's great,' said Malcolm, cutting him off. 'For your mate. I'll tell you everything else that happened, don't worry. If you'll just follow me . . . '

He turned and walked along the dock towards an old, abandoned warehouse with a rusted crane beside it.

'Here's where the story really gets exciting,' he said, wishing he felt it.

Josh was glad of the darkness. It hid his fear.

Coming down this path, walking towards the house they were heading to, had been his idea. Kind of. It was a dare, something he felt expected to say. If he wanted to hang around with the cool kids, that was.

He looked at the other two. Kyle was small with perfect hair and a face that could look angelic but more often appeared manic and deranged. Eyes constantly waiting to be lit by a dark mischief. Tom was Kyle's best friend and acolyte. The archetypal follower, doing whatever Kyle said, walking behind him at school, coming to rest slightly behind his left shoulder, always sniggering as if he was constantly savouring a favourite punchline.

Josh wanted to get in with them. Why, he didn't really know. He hung about with the geekier kids. The scientists and readers. But Kyle and Tom seemed to have taken an interest in him, decided he was to be promoted to their ranks. Josh's friends had noticed too; they hadn't been happy about his new liaisons, had begun to withdraw from him. He was sad, of course, but someone else had taken their place. Hannah Cresswell. She liked the bad boys. And once Josh became friendly with Kyle and Tom, she had started paying attention to Josh. And Josh had boxed away his conscience, decided that the trade-off was worth it.

'So where is it?' asked Kyle.

'Just down here.'

They walked away from East Hill in Colchester, down a wooded path, the trees susurrating, whispering above them, all around them. A language Josh didn't understand. So many trees, so close to the road. Yet they couldn't see or hear the road. The noise made him feel uneasy.

Ahead was the river. Beyond that the allotments, an electricity substation and a path that led to their housing estate. Deeply shadowed and wildly overgrown, it was the preserve of muggers and rapists. Or so the local legends said.

But before all that was the house. The three houses, really, but there was only one that had their attention.

The house where the mad boy in the cage had been found. The cage made of bones.

It had been huge at the time, with a massive police investigation to go with it. People had died. Secrets had been exposed. But once that was over the house had been left alone, most of the cage still there. Due to be demolished but somehow never got round to, its dilapidated state had increased along with its legend.

'There it is,' said Josh, stopping and pointing.

The other two's eyes followed his finger. Didn't notice Josh shudder. The house was a ruin, the roof partly exposed and covered with black plastic sheeting, making it look like a huge, malevolent winged creature had perched on top of it. The walls were discoloured, crumbling brick. The back of the house had already been reclaimed by nature. In front of the house at the side of the path were huge metal mesh fence panels, sunk into concrete bases dotted with various signs threatening the unwary to keep out. There were still some streamers of old, dirty, faded police tape slapping against the mesh in the breeze. None of them moved.

Eventually, Kyle pushed Josh in the back.

'Go on, then,' he said, no dark mischief in his eyes now, only unacknowledged fear, 'you first.'

Josh turned to him. 'Thought we'd all go in together.'

'Hey, your idea. You wanted to come here. Said you'd show us what was there.'

'Yeah,' said Tom from behind Kyle's left shoulder. 'You said.'

Josh looked between the pair of them. They were as scared as he was. What had seemed like a good idea earlier at school, a brave thing to say in the daylight, didn't seem so good now.

'What you scared of?' asked Kyle, attempting to cast off his fear onto Josh.

Tom seemingly thought of backing him up but decided against it.

'Nothing,' said Josh, hoping he sounded as brave as he wanted to.

'Go on, then.'

'You said we'd all do it together . . .'

Kyle summoned up a laugh. It sounded like a harsh belch in the dark. 'Don't do it then. We'll tell everyone tomorrow that you were too scared.'

Everyone, thought Josh. He knew who that meant. Hannah Cresswell.

'I'm not scared,' he said, voice too loud and suddenly angry. 'I'm going in.'

He began to pull the fence away, try to make an opening wide enough to slip through. The other two just stared at him.

'You not coming?' said Josh.

'We'll wait till you've done it.'

Josh almost laughed. 'And then run home?'

Anger lit up Kyle's eyes. 'Fuck off, I'm not going to do that.'

'You scared, then?'

'I'm not fuckin' scared!'

Tom just looked between the pair of them, speechless.

Josh did laugh this time. The cool kids? They were nothing. Scared to even come with him. He and his mates had done this kind of thing before. Loads of times. They had explored all over the place. His mates. Real mates. He suddenly missed them.

He squeezed through, kept the fence pushed open. Let's get this over with, he thought. Then I can go and see my real friends again. Leave these losers behind.

'Come on then,' he said, holding the fence, 'haven't got all night.'

Kyle and Tom reluctantly followed him.

'Here,' said Claire, pulling Damien towards her, 'now.'

Her hands were all over him, pushing his jacket from his shoulders, pulling his shirt from the waistband of his trousers at the same time. Power surged through her, a primal hunger.

'Careful . . .' Damien tried to undo his shirt buttons, stop Claire from pulling them off. Fine thing that would be, he thought, if Joanne went through his dirty washing and came across a torn shirt. She could work the rest out for herself.

Claire gave up on Damien, letting him undress himself, and

13

began to pull her own clothes off. First the blouse which she had been opening as they walked, then her skirt.

She stood in her underwear and stockings and Damien tried to look at her in the fading light, admire the body that he had lusted after for so long, but she was moving so quickly that he didn't have a chance to savour the moment.

'Slow down, there's . . . there's no rush . . . '

She wasn't listening. She pushed him down onto the ground. The forest floor was damp with mulched leaves, uneven with broken branches and stones.

'This is it,' she gasped, 'I can feel it. Here. Now . . . ' Pulling at him all the time, hands on his body, clawing his clothes off.

Should have brought the picnic blanket, he thought, then followed that thought with: Now I'll have to have this suit dry-cleaned. He was beginning to wonder whether all this was just a lot of fuss for a little bit of pleasure, when Claire finally took off her bra and straddled his prone body. He looked up at her. Two kids, he thought, and her tits weren't even sagging. Well, not much. He felt himself stiffening, her hands on his trousers.

What the hell, he thought. Come this far . . .

He lay back. Let her do what she wanted to do. Tried to forget the discomfort and just enjoy it.

'Fiona Welch, ladies and gentlemen, that was her name.'

Malcolm was getting a sore throat from projecting his voice. Even the small number of people in front of him was difficult to reach. But then Malcolm had always had a problem making himself heard.

'And if you look up here . . . ' he pointed to the crane above them, etched against the gathering night sky by the quayside lights, 'this was where she fell to her *death*.' His hoped-for

14

dramatic crescendo on the final word was undermined by his voice cracking and croaking as he tried to project. ''Scuse me,' he said, hoping that the audience would laugh with him not at him, 'getting emotional.' He cleared his throat, continued.

'Fiona Welch. She was a psychologist, working with the police on a string of murders. But, ladies and gentlemen, as you may well be aware, that was all a smokescreen. Because it was Fiona Welch herself who was behind the murders.'

He waited for that to sink in, continued.

'She kidnapped women, young, single women, and imprisoned them in here.' He gestured to the warehouse. 'Kept in coffin-like boxes, wired up to electrocute them if they tried to move. Assisted by a shambling, mute monster known only as the Creeper.'

So much for giving voice to the victims in a non-exploitative way, Malcolm thought.

'Why did she do it? What did she hope to gain?' He looked round the crowd. Expectant now, waiting for him to relate the grisly, salacious details. He had their attention. Hooked. It was a novel, empowering experience. He couldn't disappoint them. 'Well, we don't know. These young women were tortured, mutilated and eventually murdered. All except the final victim. And she fought back. She was a heroine. But more on that later.'

He turned back to them, gestured to the warehouse.

'Shall we go inside? That's where the story continues.'

They eagerly followed him.

Malcolm smiled. He had them just where he wanted them. So what if he played up the exciting aspects? Give the people what they want. Oh yes.

There was no way his walking tour could fail now.

*

15

'Go on then, open it.' Tom stared at the door handle as if it would grab him back if he touched it. Josh, having spoken, just stood and watched. Waited.

Tom turned to him. 'You do it.' Even the darkness, sudden and deep, couldn't hide the fear in his eyes. It glistened like a timid flame.

Josh looked at Kyle but the other boy was saying nothing. He looked back to the door. He wasn't scared. Or at least not as scared as the other two. And that gave him strength. He almost smiled. 'You know what happened in here?'

The other two said nothing. Breathed hard. The trees had all but cut off the noise of the road. Beyond he could hear the movement of the river, ponderous and slow, like the water had come to a coagulated, stagnant standstill.

'Just open the door,' said Tom. Kyle seemed to have lost his voice completely. 'Open the door and let's get it over with.'

'Scared? Think the cage'll still be there? The cage of bones.' Josh continued, not giving them time to answer. 'I don't. People will have come in by now. Nicked bits of it, if the police didn't take it all away. But if there's some left, that'll be great, won't it? Get a trophy? One of the bones. Might even be a human one . . . '

Tom and Kyle were shivering now. Josh was enjoying himself.

'Let's go,' he said and opened the door.

He stepped inside, flicking on the flashlight on his phone. He swung the beam around. The place was a tip. From the trash, empty bottles and cans and calcified remains of human waste, someone had been living there. He moved slightly further in. Something crunched under his feet. He looked down. A syringe. Suddenly he didn't want to go any further. He felt for the first time that he was actually trespassing,

16

going somewhere he shouldn't be. Not because it was scary, not because of ghosts or anything, but because there might be someone there who could actually hurt him. Someone real.

He turned back, looked at the other two. They had tentatively followed him in. They were swinging their own phone flashlights around.

'Is that . . . ?' Kyle pointed to a calcified mass.

'Yeah,' said Tom. 'Shit . . . '

'We should leave,' said Josh. 'We've got this far, we should go.'

'I'm not afraid of some fucking tramp.' The other two looked at Kyle, surprised by the sudden anger in his voice. 'I'm not. Three of us, one of him. So what? Let's fuckin' have him.' Kyle swung his flashlight round, actually looking for someone.

Tom and Josh looked at each other. Both seemed amazed and taken aback at how suddenly allegiances had changed. It had been two against one all night. But now it was a different two, a different one.

Kyle stepped forward into the room. Floorboards creaked beneath him. 'Come on, let's find the fucker.'

He set off into the house.

Josh and Tom shared a look once more. From off inside the house, they heard the sound of Kyle descending wooden steps.

'Come on,' said Josh, 'let's—'

Kyle's scream silenced them.

Damien was lost to everything except his own pleasure, his own gratification.

Claire rode him hard, pushing right down, pulling right up again, and again, and again. And he loved it. All thoughts of morality, his wife and kids, his job, his life, were gone. Nothing existed outside of this moment.

He felt himself building up to his biggest finish for years. Eyes open, round, the irises totally circular. Most men closed their eyes as they climaxed, but not Damien. His widened. His wife had once said, before she stopped caring, when he came it looked like he died.

But now he was getting ready, eyes bulging, face contorted. Nearly there . . .

And then he saw it.

'Jesus . . . ' he screamed.

Claire took that as encouragement, rode him even harder.

Beneath her Damien squirmed, tried to get away.

'Jesus Christ . . . Jesus, it's . . . fuck . . . '

He put his hands on her, pushed her backwards. She resisted, not wanting to move, as into the moment as he was. She stared down at him, anger in her eyes. 'Wrong time to get a fucking conscience, Damien . . . '

He pushed her away from him, stood up. 'It's . . . ' He stood there, trousers around his ankles, rapidly diminishing erection, clothes stained and torn from the forest floor and, unable to move, pointed.

Claire, her underwear half pulled off, stockings ripped, with an expression that indicated she clearly wasn't happy with Damien, followed his gaze.

'Shit . . . '

Night vision had revealed it to them. Right beside where they had been and neither had noticed. The transgression Claire had desired, right above them. And suddenly she didn't want it any more. Neither of them did.

The body hung from a branch of a nearby oak tree. The noose tight, the head at an angle showing the neck had clearly been broken. Jeans, leather jacket, plaid shirt, boots.

18

That was what they saw. That was enough.

Barely pausing to gather up their discarded clothing, Claire and Damien turned and ran.

And didn't stop till they reached the car.

'If I can just get this door open, ladies and gentlemen . . .'

Malcolm pulled hard at the rusted, corrugated metal barrier at the side of the warehouse. It refused to budge, the brown, flaking metal sharp enough to dig into his hands. Tetanus, thought Malcolm. That's all I need.

'They said . . . they said they would leave it open for us . . . unlocked . . .'

One of the crowd stepped forward, the big guy with the footballer's wife type on his arm. He grabbed the door from Malcolm and, almost one-handed, pulled it open. The crowd gave a round of applause. The man bowed.

'Must have, must have loosened it for you . . .' Malcolm laughed as he spoke. The crowd laughed politely in return.

'Right, let's get inside.'

He stepped forward. They followed him, one by one. He spoke as he walked.

'It was in this very warehouse, ladies and gentlemen, that Fiona Welch kept her captives imprisoned. Boxed up, terrified to speak, to move, even. She fed them dog food to keep them alive.' A few reactions to that fact. Just what he had expected. He was beginning to enjoy this.

'If I can find the switch . . .'

He felt on the wall for a light switch, tried it. Nothing.

'Right, no power. Just as well I brought this . . .' He took out the most powerful torch he had been able to afford, switched it on, swung it over the faces of the crowd. 'Much more atmospheric, isn't it? Let's move forward.' He swung the torch ahead of him.

19

They all walked to the centre of the warehouse.

'As I said, it was here that the victims were imprisoned. And it was on that metal gantry that . . . '

He stopped talking, stared straight ahead. The torchlight dropped.

'Shit . . . '

The crowd looked to him, looked around in the gloom. Malcolm didn't move.

They began to get restless. Was this part of the walk? Was someone going to jump out of the shadows and scare them? Even box them away?

The big man who had opened the door stepped forward, touched Malcolm on the shoulder. Malcolm jumped and screamed. He pointed the light to where he had been looking, the metal gantry.

'Shit . . . '

The others followed the beam of light. Hanging from the gantry, a noose around his neck, was a man. Dressed in leather jacket, plaid shirt, jeans. The angle of his neck told them that he was long since dead.

'Oh God . . . oh God . . . '

Panic erupted from the crowd. People didn't know what to do. They milled, looked at each other. Scared, stunned.

'This is . . . this is not supposed to happen . . . '

Gradually their fear came under control as the crowd realised what they were witnessing. Someone suggested they call an ambulance. Someone else decided it was too late for that. The police, then. Yeah, the police.

Then began a discussion as to whether or not they were actually at a murder scene and should they touch anything?

Malcolm was no use. Whatever short-lived authority he had had was now completely gone. He just stared straight ahead. Lost.

Someone called the police.

And in the meantime the crowd, no longer scared but now strangely exhilarated by their accidental discovery, recovered enough composure to get out their phones and take selfies with the body.

Tom and Josh stared at each other, eyes wide with terror. They were both frozen to the spot, unable to move, not knowing whether to run away from Kyle's scream or towards it.

Kyle screamed again. And again the boys didn't move.

Then they heard the sound of footsteps, hard and clattering, coming up the wooden cellar stairs in an ungainly rush. They swung their torches towards the noise. Kyle came belting towards them.

'Get out ... out ... '

His words galvanised them and they turned, made for the door.

Out into the woods, away from the house.

They tripped over roots, branches, each other. They scrambled towards the metal fence, the safety of the path beyond, civilisation beyond that.

Once through the fence and on the path Josh found his voice.

'What did you see?' he asked Kyle.

The other boy didn't answer. Just stood there, staring straight ahead, breathing heavily.

'What was it?' Josh asked again.

Kyle looked between the two of them. Josh didn't think he had ever seen such fear in someone's eyes. He doubted he ever would. He hoped he never would.

'Kyle ... '

Kyle closed his eyes, shook his head. Opened them again.

'It ... it was a body ... a man ... just ... hanging there ...'

'Hanging? How? Like, like ... what?'

Kyle turned to him, spitting the words out. 'On a rope ... on a fucking rope ... round his neck, dead ... fuckin' hanging ...'

And then Kyle did the last thing Josh would have expected of him. He began to cry.

And neither he nor Tom blamed him.

PART TWO

NIGHTHAWKS

2

The three of them stared at the board. No one spoke. On the board were three pictures, blown up, copied photos. All showing identical images but none of them the same.

Each was an enlarged photo of a tarot card. The Hanged Man. And on it, written in the same black, block capital handwriting, a name. PHIL BRENNAN.

Before the board were three people. Detective Inspector Phil Brennan of the West Midlands Police Major Incident Unit. The MIU handled all the big cases. Their designated title changed with every departmental reshuffle but their intended objective remained the same. They were the murder squad by any other name. His superior, DCI Alison Cotter. And Marina Esposito, their criminal profiler and Phil's wife. None of them spoke, just examined the images before them. Studied them closely, hoped they would give up their secrets.

Cotter broke the silence. 'These cards have been examined over and over. Nothing. We can only match the handwriting if we have something to match it to. We don't. The same with DNA. Nothing there. No matches. Whoever placed them there wore gloves at the very least.'

'I've looked into the meaning of the card too,' said Marina. 'The Hanged Man. Number twelve in the Major Arcana of a set of tarot cards, if we're assuming it's based on an occult set used for divination.'

'What else would it be?' asked Cotter.

'Tarot used to be used for card games in Europe, decades ago. Now they're just for telling the future. The Hanged Man,' she said, pointing, 'is hanging from the tree of life. Upside down. His head in the roots of the world, the underworld, us, his feet in the heavens.' She looked at the other two, back to the pictures, finger gesturing. 'He looks calm, relaxed. Like he's there by choice, or at least the hanging's not bothering him. See here, he's attached to the tree by his right foot. His left leg is bent at the knee, tucked behind his body. His arms are behind his back. All done casually.'

'Is that supposed to mean something, him doing that?' asked Cotter.

'I think so, yes. Or at least readers can write something into it. But look at the colours, what he's wearing. That means something too. His trousers, leggings, whatever, are red. This apparently represents passion, the human body. Physicality. His upper half is blue, representing high ideals. And he's got a bright yellow halo around his head. Some kind of spiritual achievement? Holiness?'

'What a load of bollocks,' said Cotter.

Phil said nothing.

'Maybe,' said Marina, 'to you and me, but not to the person who placed it there. And there's more. It's the card of ultimate surrender. Of martyrdom, sacrifice to the greater good. Of getting rid of old patterns of behaviour, of change. Seeing the world from a different angle.'

'Well, you would if you're hanging upside down,' Cotter said.

'Want to know more?'

'Like what?'

'The card's ruling planet is Neptune, the planet of self-sacrifice and idealism . . .'

'I think that's enough for now, thanks.' Cotter, shaking her head, looked at the board once more, back to the other two. 'Of course, while we've found out what the card supposedly means and all that, interesting though it may or may not be, there's a massive elephant in the room we've not yet addressed, isn't there?'

Phil felt their eyes on him.

'Yeah,' he said. 'Me.'

3

'Three dead bodies,' continued Cotter. 'Males, Caucasian, aged late thirties. All dressed similarly. All found hanged. All with the same tarot card in their leather jacket pocket, the Hanged Man, and the same name written on it.' She fixed her gaze on him. 'Yours, Phil.'

'Yeah,' he said, not knowing what more he could meaningfully add.

'And I'm assuming the locations all mean something?' Cotter asked.

'They certainly do.' He gestured to the board. 'Want me to ...?'

'Please. Talk me through it.'

He stood up, walked over to the board that had been taken from the incident room and set up in the corner of Cotter's office. They were keeping this on a need-to-know basis. The rest of the team hadn't yet been informed. And they wouldn't be; not until they had more idea about what – or whom – they were dealing with.

There were photos of the three hanged bodies. One outdoors in a forest, strung up from a thick branch. One hanging from a metal strut in an old warehouse. One hanging from a crossbeam in a dark, cramped cellar. Multiple images showed their faces, bodies, clothes, in detail. All wearing

28

similar clothes to what Phil was wearing at that moment: brown leather jacket, plaid shirt, jeans, boots. All with similar haircuts to Phil's. Facially there was no resemblance. But physically there was. Same height, same hair colour. In the shadows they could have passed for him. Phil couldn't look at them for too long. It was unnerving, to say the least, seeing yourself hanging there. Dead.

'The first one, in the forest. It's Wrabness.' He looked at Marina. 'I don't need to tell you about that.'

Marina shook her head.

'You probably know about this already,' he said to Cotter.

'Well, obviously I've heard, but it's better if you tell me.'

Phil nodded. 'There was someone targeting full-term pregnant women. Cutting out their unborn babies and attempting to claim them as their own.'

'Jesus, that's . . . really sick.'

'Yeah,' said Phil, wincing, mind slipping back into the case. 'It was. And sad too, believe it or not. Tragic, really.'

'But you caught the perpetrator.'

'Oh yeah, or rather Marina did.'

Marina shuddered. Remembered the underground cavern, the desperate escape, the screwdriver as makeshift knife plunged again and again into her deranged assailant.

'Our first date,' she said, hoping humour could counteract the memory.

'So it's not just another case. It's somewhere that holds meaning to you,' said Cotter.

'Not just for Phil, both of us.'

Cotter nodded. 'And the next one? Which one is that, if we're going chronologically?'

'Here,' said Phil pointing to the body hanging in the warehouse. 'This one. This was where I encountered Fiona Welch.'

'Ah.' Cotter knew all about her. The psychologist who had attempted to try her torturously sickening theories out using a disfigured, rage-fuelled, psychopathic ex-serviceman.

'The real one,' said Phil.

Someone claiming to be her had recently broken free from a psychiatric hospital, gone on a killing spree then disappeared. But not before besting Phil physically and promising to see him again. But Phil knew it wasn't the real one. Because he had watched the real one fall to her death.

'And is this both of you again?'

'No,' said Marina. 'I had nothing to do with that. I was . . . away. Sorting something out.' She glanced at Phil, found his returned smile reassuring.

'So it's just you, then?' Cotter asked.

'Just me. And then there's the third one.' He pointed to the photo of the body hanging in the cellar. 'This is where we found a feral child, chained up in a cage made from bones.'

Cotter stared at the pair of them. 'Did you just come to work here for a holiday?'

'You think the stuff I've dealt with since I've been here counts as a holiday?'

Cotter nodded. 'Point taken.'

'There was an added layer to that one,' said Marina.

'Really?' Cotter raised her eyebrows. 'Can't wait to hear this one.'

'Involving Phil's background. His childhood.'

'Right.'

Phil nodded, not wanting to relive the unpleasantness. 'It was . . . a pretty harrowing experience. I don't want to go into it now.'

'What if it's relevant to the enquiry? To what's been done to these men?'

'Then I'll have no choice but to confront it again. And

I'll tell you all about it, don't worry. If I need to. But at the moment it's . . . well, I hope it's not relevant.'

'Fair enough,' said Cotter. 'But this was targeted at you. I think we're in no doubt about that now. So if needs be we'll have to start looking into your childhood.'

Phil nodded once more, clearly unhappy, but knowing it was necessary.

'The question is,' said Cotter, 'what do we do next?'

4

'I presume I should go over there,' said Phil. 'Back to Colchester and see what's happening. Someone's clearly trying to get my attention.'

'It's not safe,' said Marina, an edge of hysteria creeping into her voice.

Phil looked at her. He knew why she was so upset. Shared her misgivings.

'Look,' she went on, 'we know these deaths are no coincidence. And let's be honest, we know who's behind this.'

'Marina, we don't—'

'Yes, we do, Phil. You might not want to admit it, but you do. You know as well as I do.'

They stared at each other. Cotter broke the silence.

'I take it you mean this is the work of the woman calling herself Fiona Welch?'

'Who else?' said Marina, pleased that the name, the supposition, was out in the open, hoping that by speaking it aloud it would be robbed of its power. 'It's her. It has to be. She's . . . '

'Insane?' suggested Cotter.

'I don't know what she is, or what she wants. But she made it more than clear last time we met her that she was going to come back for Phil. And this seems like her way of getting his attention.'

'Well it's worked,' said Phil. 'Whoever it is.'

'Let's hope it is her,' said Cotter.

They both looked at her.

'We don't want another one as mad as her running around now, do we?'

'True,' said Phil, with some reluctance. 'And if it is her, that's all the more reason I should go. Get it over with. Find her, stop her. Get rid of her once and for all.'

'But she's dangerous,' said Marina. 'Really dangerous.'

'And that's my job.'

Marina shook her head. Stood up, walked about the room. She stopped, turned to face Phil. Spoke to him as if Cotter wasn't there. 'You can't go.'

'You see those bodies?' Phil gestured to the board. 'The names? I think I have to.'

'It's a trap. She's waiting for you. Trying to get your attention, trying to get you to . . . '

Phil crossed to her, placed his hands on her shoulders. She shook him off.

'Don't go. She's waiting for you. Anticipating you coming. If this is what she's done to get your attention, what's she going to do once you're over there? No. It's not safe.'

'Nothing's safe. Life isn't safe. Come on, we've discussed this. We can't live our lives in the shadows. We've got to stand up, confront her. Get it over with.'

Marina stared at him, said nothing. He continued.

'Look, I know. I've thought all this myself, as soon as I heard about it I knew who it would be. And you're right. She's dangerous. And this is just what she wants me to do. But I have to do it. And you know it. I think you know it.'

Again, she said nothing.

'I can't just ignore it, can I? We can't ignore it. None of us in this room. What would happen if we did that? Would she keep trying to get my attention, do something more in retaliation? Something even worse?'

'What would be worse?'

'I don't know. How many more lives would she take just to get my attention? What could she do to them? Don't know. Don't want to think about it. And I certainly don't want to find out.'

Marina stared at him. She knew he was right, no matter how much she didn't want to hear him say it. And deep down, she knew she agreed with him.

'Well,' she said, the words drawn from her with great reluctance, 'if you have to go, then at least let me come with you.'

'No,' said Cotter stepping in, 'I can't allow that. I know you've become a very valuable part of our team but you're still a civilian.'

'Then I could just go with him. There's nothing to stop me from accompanying my husband on a trip to where we used to live.'

'No there's not,' said Cotter. 'But the police at the other end would have orders not to involve you. I'm afraid you'd find yourself incapacitated there.'

Marina's expression was incredulous. 'You mean under guard?'

'Not exactly.'

'Not *exactly*?' Her voice was getting louder. 'What *exactly* do you mean, then?'

'Marina, please,' said Phil. 'I know it's difficult. But ... please.'

'You'll need a psychologist. You'll need me.'

'I don't even know if they'll need me, Marina. I'm just going to advise. You know I won't be able to get involved. Not directly. That's my name on the bodies. I'm too personally involved already.'

Marina fell into a sullen silence once more.

'Please,' said Phil, his voice low, his tone conciliatory, 'Josephina needs at least one of us to stay with her. And it won't be for long. At least I don't think so. I'll just go over there, see for myself what's happened, give them as much help and information as I possibly can and then come back. That's all I can do. The rest is up to them. Let Franks and his team deal with it.'

Gary Franks was Cotter's opposite number in Colchester.

Marina, reluctantly, nodded.

'You'll be given round-the-clock protection,' said Cotter to Marina. 'You and your daughter. Ring of steel. Nothing will get through.'

Marina nodded once more, not making eye contact with either of them.

'I've spoken to Franks,' said Cotter, 'and he said he'll send over someone to escort you there.'

'I know the way to Colchester.'

'I'm sure you do, but this officer is firearms trained and is to be your bodyguard. Just as a precaution. You'll be perfectly safe.'

Phil said nothing.

Marina gave one more try. 'What d'you hope to achieve by this? It's a trap. You know it is. She's targeting you for a reason.'

'Yeah, I'm sure she is. And I'm sure that's what she intends. But as long as I'm there and protected, I'm in a good place to find out what she wants, what's going on. And the sooner we know that, the sooner we catch her.'

'And the sooner we can all relax,' said Cotter.

'Exactly.'

Marina said nothing.

5

Josephina Brennan couldn't have been happier. She sat with her parents, surveyed the bowls of food before her. There was barely a centimetre of the table uncovered. She smiled, looked up at them.

'Did I tell you this is my favourite place?'

'Only about a hundred times,' said Phil, smiling. 'Today.'

It was a treat. They had picked her up from school, brought her down to the Las Iguanas restaurant at the Arcadian. The lighting was dim in the chain restaurant, with palm trees and faux, unspecific South American tiki décor. Josephina loved the place. It was a glimpse of a different, exciting world, miles away from her own home and school and playing with friends. And she loved the food. Especially the tapas menu.

Quesadillas, *gambas* and *champiñones*. *Pata taquito* and *albondigas*. Plus empanadas, crayfish salad and beer for the grown-ups. Nachos to share.

'Can I start?' she asked, barely able to restrain herself.

'Go on,' said Marina. 'But don't forget your manners. We're in a restaurant. There are other people here.'

Josephina rolled her eyes, hoping her mother wouldn't see. Phil tried to stifle a grin. Couldn't begin to explain, even to himself, just how much this seven-year-old girl meant to him. Josephina began eating. Phil's grin faded to sadness. Like he had already gone and this dinner just a memory.

He looked up. Marina was watching him. She raised her eyebrows.

'Sorry,' he said quietly, shaking his head.

Marina said nothing. She felt the tension coming off him. Shared it herself. Knew what he was about to say, dreaded it as much as him.

He waited until Josephina was well into the meal before speaking. Let her have a brief bit of pleasure first, he thought.

'Listen, Josie, I've got something to tell you.'

Josephina looked up, eyes round, expectant. Trusting. The look of creeping apprehension on Phil's face began to remove the trust from hers.

'It's nothing,' he said. 'It's just . . . I've got to go away. Only for a couple of days, though.'

Josephina stopped eating. She looked between her parents, trying to find some kind of clue as to what was about to happen next.

A parent going away, even for a couple of days, shouldn't be a big deal for a child. But given all the things that Phil, Marina and Josephina had been through over the years, the suffering they had undergone both separately and as a family, every item of news such as this had to be carefully couched, sensitively explained. Even though past memories were receding, Josephina still had nightmares about ordeals she had been through. Growing more sporadic but still there. They couldn't afford to do or say anything to her that would upset her too much. Especially now that she was at an age where she could understand the truth. Or most of it. She still had to be protected, brought up as safely as possible.

'Is it . . . ' said Josephina, eyes still darting between one parent to the other, 'is it like before?'

'Before?' asked Marina.

Josephina nodded. 'When I had to go and live in the flat

37

with Mummy and not see you,' she said, uncertain eyes settling on Phil. 'When you wouldn't speak to each other?'

'It wasn't like that,' said Marina, her voice as soothing as possible.

'Yes it was,' said Josephina. 'You know it was.'

'It was ... difficult,' said Marina. 'But we never stopped loving each other. You knew that. I told you that.'

Josephina still didn't look convinced. Before she could answer, Phil spoke.

'Mum's right,' he said. 'This is different. Not like the last time.'

He could barely look at her as he spoke. Their separation had been through Marina's fear of what the woman calling herself Fiona Welch could do to them. The punitive action she might take against them. Against their daughter. She hadn't believed Phil – or his department – could adequately protect them as a family. So she had taken Josephina away. And now this. He had to make his daughter understand the truth of the situation, but only as it concerned her. Namely, that he was coming back.

'No,' he said, as emphatically as he could, 'nothing like that at all. This is just a work thing. That's all. Just a couple of days. Get it sorted out, and then I'm back.'

Josephina stared at him. 'Promise?' Part of her wanted to believe in her father's words. Another part of her didn't dare to.

'Promise. Just a couple of days for work. That's all.'

Marina smiled. 'We just wanted to tell you so you wouldn't get worried tomorrow. Get home from school and Daddy's not there.'

Josephina looked between the pair of them once more. Then down at her food. 'You're definitely coming back?' she said once more.

38

Phil found a smile. 'Definitely.' He leaned forward. 'You think I want to be without you?'

Josephina smiled.

'Good,' said Phil, still smiling but out of relief now. 'Right, then. What shall we do after this? Who wants to go to the cinema?'

Josephina put her hand up.

Phil kept smiling. He couldn't look at Marina. Just had to keep staring straight ahead.

6

'Detective Inspector Brennan?'

Phil opened the front door to his house, looked at the man in front of him. Well over six foot and solid with it. A rugby player's frame that his suit was barely able to contain. His flattened and reset nose seemed to back that initial impression. Hair cut close to his scalp, heavy boots.

'That's me,' said Phil.

The man stretched out a hand, all muscle and meat. 'Detective Sergeant Beresford, sir. DCI Franks sent me. I'm your lift to Colchester.'

Phil shook it. Powerful, and Beresford knew it. No crushing finger games. Not needed. Phil would have hated to be on the receiving end of it. He almost smiled. Franks wasn't joking when he said he'd send him a bodyguard. 'Of course you are.'

'D'you need to get anything?' asked Beresford, pointing back towards the door.

'Yeah, give me a minute. You want to come in?'

'I'll just stay here, sir, if it's all the same to you.'

Barrel of laughs, thought Phil. The drive to Colchester's going to fly by.

Phil went back into the house. Marina was at work, Josephina at school. He had filled a holdall with enough stuff to last two or three days. He didn't think that the investigation would be wrapped up in that time, but he didn't intend to be there longer than that. At least not initially. He had made a promise to Marina on waking and he intended to keep it.

'I'll be back as soon as I can. I won't stay there longer than I have to.'

'Promise?'

'Promise.'

'I know you,' she had said, a resigned smile on her face. 'You'll get drawn into the investigation. You won't be able to help yourself but you will.'

'I won't. I promise. Franks can sort it out. I'll give them what I can then come straight back.'

They had held each other longer than they had for ages after that.

He grabbed his bag, slung it over his shoulder. Took a last look round at his home, went out, locking the door behind him.

A big, heavy Vauxhall was parked in the street. An Insignia. Silver and powerful-looking, it screamed unmarked police car. Before they reached it, Phil stopped, put his hand on Beresford's arm. Beresford stopped moving, looked at him.

'Before we go any further, could I see some ID?'

'Sure,' said Beresford, putting his hand into his pocket. He drew out a warrant card, handed it over. Phil took it, examined it, turning it over in his hands. He knew the things to look out for, how to spot a fake. But this wasn't it. This was genuine. He handed it back.

'Can't be too careful,' he said.

'I'd have been disappointed if you hadn't asked to see it, sir.'

'Quite right.'

Beresford took the holdall from Phil, swung it into the boot of the car. Straightened up, looked at Phil. Quizzical.

'Something wrong, DS Beresford?'

'Well, it's probably not my place to say it, sir, but DCI Franks wanted you to go straight to the station.'

'And that's where we're going, isn't it?'

'Yes, sir, but . . .'

'But what?'

'I just assumed from your clothes that . . . I mean we just won't have time to go to your hotel first for you to change. DCI Franks likes his officers to be suited at all times.'

Phil smiled. 'I'm sure DCI Franks has seen a man in a pair of jeans before. He'll get over it. Let's go.'

Beresford didn't reply. They drove away.

Out of Birmingham city centre, onto the M6. Then from there, the M1 to the A14, the wide featureless expanse of motorway giving way to something more scenic. Or it would have been had the road not been shrouded in fog and drizzle. Beresford all the while driving cautiously but not timidly. With restrained power. Like there were several more gears he could step up through if needed.

Phil's initial thoughts had been proved right. Beresford wasn't one for conversation. The radio had been playing when he'd started the car but he'd turned it off immediately. Some right-wing phone-in host berating his callers.

'You can keep it on if you like,' Phil said. 'I don't mind.'

'Better not, sir.'

And that had been that. Phil wished he had insisted on taking his own car. At least that way he could have played music as they drove. His own choice of music. God only knew what Beresford would have listened to.

Phil took out his mobile, texted Marina.

Been picked up. On the way. Love you. Xxx

Pressed Send, put it away again.

On the A14 Phil tried to talk once more.

'How's the investigation going, then? Into the three dead men?'

Beresford frowned, as if he didn't know whether he should answer. Or indeed which answer to give. 'It's progressing, sir.'

Phil gave a small laugh. 'You're exploring several avenues and examining every lead, right?' He shook his head. 'Come on, DS Beresford, I'm not a punter. I'm just asking how it's going.'

Beresford thought for a while before answering. He gave a quick, unreadable glance towards Phil then turned back to the wheel, keeping his eyes fixed on the road ahead. 'It's . . . we don't have many leads as yet.'

'Have you identified the victims?'

'Not yet. It's proving difficult. We've contacted MisPers, sent out descriptions. No matches yet.'

'PMs? Forensics?'

'Lots of alcohol in their bloodstreams, it looks like. The one thing they all had in common. Some evidence of drug use. They're still looking to see how much and how long ago that was.'

'And no one saw anything.' A statement not a question.

'Only the people who found the bodies. We checked their backgrounds out. Nothing to link them to each other, nothing in their backgrounds to link them to the victims.'

'So far as you know.'

'Yes, sir. But we've shown them pictures of all three victims. None of them know any of them.'

Information given, Beresford fell silent once more.

Phil settled back in his seat. Wondered what exactly he could add to the investigation.

It was going to be a long journey.

7

Work. That's what Marina thought would take her mind off things. Work.

She sat at her desk in her office at Birmingham University, the once temporary arrangement now looking more permanent. Dark wood bookshelves covered the walls, initially filled neatly, now overflowing and haphazard. Framed photos of Phil and Josephina rested on desk surfaces. Journals, periodicals and magazines accumulated in piles all around. The room looked slightly chaotic but still managed to retain a kind of academic order to it. Framed prints hung in between the bookshelves, mainly Edward Hopper. Marina thought she had been expected to put something on the walls that reflected her subject, psychology. Something like Escher or even Magritte. Something that could become a talking point for the students who visited, get them revealing layers of meaning in the work, become some kind of symbol or metaphor for the study of the mind. But Marina wanted Hopper.

He wasn't a great painter, she thought, not in a technical photorealist way, but something about his sketchy, almost blankly realised characters stuck in often bleak environments while the light, usually luminous and penetrating, fell somewhere else, invited constant questions. Who were these people? Why were they drawn to that particular spot? What was their relationship with the other characters in the paintings?

Nighthawks, his most famous piece, showed disparate figures sitting round a diner counter at night. None of them touching or close to the others. *Office at Night* showed a man at a desk and a woman at a filing cabinet. Light came in from somewhere, missing them both. Marina liked to imagine what went on before and after the moment Hopper had captured them. The psychogeometry of the spaces in between them. The lives they lived, the values they held, what they meant – or didn't mean – to each other. If that wasn't a psychological view of painting, and a valid reason for hanging them on her walls, she didn't know what was.

But she wasn't looking at them now. She had marking to do. Piles of essays from second-year students on reinterpreting and modernising Jungian archetypes. Get them to think creatively but constructively. She tried to get involved in their arguments, correct and question with a light hand where possible, condemn and contradict only as a last resort. She had hoped that doing this would take her mind off Phil and his journey. And it did, intermittently. But something she would read, or a random thought would spark within her and she would find herself thinking about him again. Wondering. Hoping.

Her phone, beside her on the desk, pinged. She glanced at it. Smiled. A text from Phil.

Been picked up. On the way. Love you. Xxx

She read it twice, the smile not moving from her face. Tried to break it down, squeeze every last item of information, both real and imagined from it. He was on the way. In a car. Franks had sent a driver. Someone he could trust, someone who would keep Phil safe. So there was nothing to worry about. Nothing.

45

She went back to work, resolved to become as involved as she could with the essays.

She did, not noticing another hour slip away.

Until her phone rang. Her office phone.

She picked up. 'Dr Esposito.'

'Marina? Alison Cotter.'

Marina immediately sat up straight, asked what she could do for her.

'It's Phil. Just wondering where he is.'

Marina frowned. 'What d'you mean?'

'Well, I've just had a call from Gary Franks telling me the officer he sent to pick him up, DS Beresford, couldn't get his car started. Developed some kind of problem, apparently. I went looking round the building for Phil but couldn't find him. I've tried your home number but no reply. Same with his mobile. Any ideas?'

Marina froze. Thought of the previous text.

'I'm coming in. Right now.'

She ended the call, went straight to the door. Passing a Hopper print on the way: *House by the Railroad*. Bleak and forlorn. The model for the Bates Motel in Hitchcock's *Psycho*.

8

'So you got a first name, then, DS Beresford?'

'David,' grunted Beresford. The word, grudgingly given, seemingly excavated from his body.

'David. Right.'

'But everybody calls me Dave.'

'Dave.' Phil nodded. 'Sure they do.' He checked his watch. 'You thinking of stopping soon?'

'DCI Franks told me to get you to Colchester as quickly as possible.'

'I'm sure he did. But didn't he say anything about coffee stops or toilet breaks?'

Beresford acted like he hadn't heard.

'DS Beresford.' Phil slipped a blade of authority into his voice. 'I want to stop.'

Beresford didn't reply, nodded.

They drove in silence until he found a Little Chef on the A14, pulled the Insignia off the road, parked up. Turned to Phil. 'Quick as you can, please, sir.'

Phil got out of the car, made his way to the restroom. Finished up, made his way to the café. Queued. Saw that the coffee was instant and picked up a bottle of water instead. There weren't many things Phil couldn't abide but instant coffee was one of them. No excuse, he thought, this day and age, for instant. No excuse. He paid for the water, went back to the car.

Beresford looked like he hadn't moved. He started the car, not looking at Phil, and drove away.

'So,' said Phil, once they were on the road and had gone some distance, 'you got any hobbies, Dave?'

Beresford shrugged. 'Play golf. That's about it.'

Phil nodded, wished he hadn't said anything. Nothing worse than a golf bore. Thankfully Beresford didn't feel the need to expand on that. Phil went back to looking out of the window.

He may have nodded off. In fact he was sure of it. He sat up, looked around. Still on the road. He leaned over to the back seat where he left his jacket, felt inside for his phone, thought of checking for emails or texts. Couldn't find it. Tried his jeans pocket. Not there either. Felt around on the seat. Nothing.

'You seen my phone, Dave?'

Beresford kept his eyes on the road. 'No, sir.'

Phil checked once again. 'You sure?'

'Sure, sir.'

Phil frowned. 'Must have put it in my bag.' He thought back, tried to remember. He had texted Marina. Put the phone back in . . . his pocket. He felt again. No phone. Had he left it in the Little Chef? No. He didn't take it in with him. He tried looking round, seeing if it had fallen out underneath the seat.

'Do you need it, sir?'

Phil straightened up. 'I just thought I'd check my work emails. That's all.'

'Won't be long now, sir. We'll be there soon.'

Phil nodded. Glanced across at Beresford. The DS was sweating. Despite it not being particularly warm.

48

Phil began to feel uneasy. He didn't know why, couldn't explain. Just a feeling. But it was the kind he had come to trust over the years.

'Can you stop, please, DS Beresford? I need to find my phone.'

Beresford didn't reply.

'DS Beresford? Hello?'

'I'm sorry, sir,' said Beresford, sweating even more now, his voice shaking slightly, 'I can't stop.'

'DS Beresford. I'm ordering you to stop. Right now. Pull over and stop.'

'I . . . I can't, sir . . . '

Beresford pushed harder on the accelerator. Phil looked round. Something wasn't right. Seriously not right.

'DS Beresford. Stop right now. I'm commandeering this vehicle.'

Beresford ignored him.

'I'm your superior officer and I'm telling you—'

'Just don't move . . . ' Beresford shouting now. But not angry, just like a pressure cooker about to blow. 'Stay where you are . . . '

Keeping one hand on the wheel and increasing his speed, he reached into his jacket and produced a taser. Pointed it at Phil.

Phil just stared. Open-mouthed.

'Listen, sir,' said Beresford, not able to look Phil in the eye, 'I really don't want to use this. Not on a superior officer. Just do what I tell you and don't give me cause.'

'Why would I give you cause, DS Beresford?' Phil tried to keep his voice calm and steady, despite his heart hammering away. So fast he was sure Beresford could hear it. 'What would I do that would make you use that?'

Beresford increased the speed of the car. 'Just keep your

hands where I can see them. Don't make any sudden moves. I really don't want to use this ...'

'Who says you've got to?'

Conflicting emotions appeared on Beresford's features. 'She ... I really didn't want to, sir, especially not a fellow officer, but I had no choice. She's ... it's my son, sir. I have to ... have to do this for ...'

Beresford's words confirmed all of Phil's fears. He felt his heart sink as he tried to find the right words – any words – to say. 'Look,' he said eventually, 'you don't have to do this, Dave. You don't. Just stop the car now, give me the taser and we can sort this out. OK? Just do that and we can sort this out.'

Beresford stared straight ahead, some kind of struggle being waged on his features.

Phil kept on. 'Your son, that right? She's threatened your son?'

Beresford nodded. 'More than that.' Moisture appeared at the corners of his eyes. Tears or sweat, Phil wasn't sure which.

'That's ... that's understandable. Your behaviour – this – is understandable. If we're talking about the same person then I know what you mean. She threatened my daughter too. And my wife. But I didn't let her win. I can't let her win. And you ... you can do the same, Dave. Can't you? Just ... just stop the car, hand over the taser and we can make this all go away.'

Beresford didn't reply.

'Come on, Dave, you can do it. We can do it.'

Nothing.

'We can sort this together. Stop her together. That's ... that's what I'm here for.' Phil waited, kept staring at him. Tried to ignore the countryside as it rushed past in a blur, tried not to look at the speedometer. 'Come on, Dave ...'

Beresford's face was stone. Phil took that as encouragement, that his words were breaking him down.

'That's it,' said Phil, expelling breath he wasn't aware he'd been holding. 'That's it. Just stop the car and we can get this sorted. We'll protect your son. We'll get her. We will. Just . . . '

Beresford started to laugh. An alien sound, like an old battery cranking into life one final time, a death rattle. 'You've got no idea, have you?' he said. 'No idea at all . . . '

'Look, Dave . . . '

'Sorry, sir, mind's made up.'

Phil's words ended in a scream then trailed off to silence as Beresford tasered him.

Phil jerked, spasmed, fell unconscious.

The car sped on. Away from Colchester.

Castles Burning

*S*he wouldn't play with dolls. Not any more. Not after the centre. Or whatever it was called.

She had been taken there from the unsafe safe house. When they found her they thought she was dead. Lying beside the corpses of her parents, not daring to move, to breathe, in case the sweaty men with the meat breath came back again. Feeling the blood – Mummy's blood – thicken and harden on her hands. Not knowing where her brother was. Hoping he was alive, somewhere. Waiting for him to come back and save her. Waiting for anyone.

It was the police at first. A man in a blue uniform had tried to touch her and she had just screamed. And screamed and screamed. Eventually a woman with a soft voice had come, talked to her and helped her up. Mummy and Daddy were taken away. She never saw them again.

They took her to a place where people tried to be kind to her. But they were also scared. She could tell. She saw something in their eyes when they tried to talk to her. Scared of her or scared for her, she didn't know which. Maybe one, maybe both. But scared.

The room they gave her was brightly coloured, paintings and pictures of smiling animals and things on the walls, filled with equally brightly coloured stuffed animals and plastic toys. Belinda was long gone and she felt sad about that. Nothing like she had been used to. Like they had belonged to another child entirely.

She kept having nightmares. Couldn't have the door closed or the light off. She kept seeing the man, smelling his breath, feeling Mummy's blood all over again. She woke up screaming. Night after night after night.

Then one day another lady appeared. A different one. Call me Caroline, she said. All smiles. And you are? She said her name. Caroline nodded, like it was a test and she had given the right answer.

Then Caroline had more questions. She took a doll out of her bag, handed it over. Do you want to play? she asked.

She said nothing, made no movement. Caroline kept her hand extended, the doll still there. It didn't look like Belinda. It had arms and legs, eyes and nose, but no mouth.

Here.

The girl took it.

Now, said Caroline, let's imagine. This doll is you, right? It's got your name. Yes?

The girl nodded.

Right. So what I want you to do is think about where you used to be. When you were with your Mummy and Daddy, back before the safe house. Can you do that?

Caroline was wrong. This wasn't playing. But she said nothing. Just nodded because that's what she thought Caroline wanted to see.

OK, good. Now. She handed her a black pen. Here. I want you to draw your mouth on the doll's face.

She stared at Caroline.

Were you happy? Were you sad? Would you have been smiling then or frowning?

She thought. Back before they escaped. Was she happy? Had any of them been happy? She didn't know. It was just what it had been. Her life. There had been things that upset and things that didn't. So she didn't know what to put on the doll's face. Then she thought of Mummy. Daddy. Her brother. Saw Mummy's blood all over her hand again. Thought back to before the safe house. Drew a smile on the doll.

Good, said Caroline. She took a cloth, wiped the smile off the doll's face. Now how were you at the safe house?

She started to draw another smile then stopped. Snow angels, she said.

Caroline frowned. Sorry?

Snow angels. We were playing snow angels. I saw my wings. Then the men came . . .

Right. OK. Just a few more questions, and then we can play some more.

And Caroline kept going. She had other dolls with her. Some to make her feel happy or safe, some to make her feel scared. Or so she could tell when she was feeling scared and what scared her. Caroline wanted to be her friend, she said. To help her. To tell her things so she could make her happy again. And she wanted to be happy. She wanted to see Mummy and Daddy and her brother again. So Caroline asked her about the men. And what they had done and said in the house.

Show me with the dolls, Caroline said.

She did so. Moving the dolls, making them talk, doing the voices and the actions.

Good, said Caroline when she had finished. Well done. Then she looked serious at her. Did it make you feel like crying? When you played with the dolls?

She looked at the dolls, lying on the table beside her. No, she said.

Didn't it upset you, thinking about it again?

She thought of Mummy's blood, thickening and drying on her hand. Of lying still, as still as death, trying to count to a hundred and then trying to count to a hundred again and again, her mouth moving fast, the numbers whispered, like a spell to keep the men from coming back again. Of lying there even longer when she had stopped counting, fallen asleep. Woken up and started counting again. Knowing she had wet herself and still not getting up. Feeling colder than cold from the door being open and the winter getting in.

Thought of all those things. Thought there was a before that and an after that. One girl had died and another was born. They just looked a bit the same.

No, she said.

Eventually they told her she was moving and she came here. This house. With Mr and Mrs Wignall. They were old and they were used to having a lot of children there, they said to her when she arrived. She would be no trouble. They were kind, she thought. Or they were trying to be.

Mrs Wignall cooked and looked after them. Mr Wignall had to take it easy. His heart, he said. Doctor's orders. Yet she still heard Mrs Wignall being pretend angry with him sometimes because he kept drinking from a bottle on the sideboard in the back room.

And she was happy there. Or as happy as she could be. She stopped asking about her brother. No one told her about him any more. Except to say that he was gone. And there were other children to play with. But she mainly played on her own.

The castle. That was what she liked best. Not dolls. She had had enough of dolls.

And she sat there now, looking at the soldiers she had put on the battlements. Behind the walls. They could keep anything out. Keep anything safe. That's all she had to do. Be like the soldiers.

Even if it meant killing.

PART THREE

RAINSFORD HOUSE

9

Marina wasted no time, straight over to the station on Steelhouse Lane, right into Cotter's office.

'So where is he?' Of all the questions rising inside Marina, that was the first one to break. She felt impotent even asking it but knew there was nothing else she could ask.

'We don't know,' said Cotter. She had stood up from behind her desk on Marina's entering and seemed reluctant to get behind it once more. She remained standing in the centre of the room alongside Marina. The action seemed to give the whole conversation greater urgency.

'Have you heard from him?'

Cotter shook her head. 'You?'

'I tried his phone in the cab all the way here. Nothing. Straight to voicemail.'

Cotter nodded, her face drawn into a grim mask. 'Same.'

'Can't you put some kind of GPS trace on him?'

'Not if his phone's switched off.'

Marina sighed. She felt suddenly exhausted, wanted to sit down, rest, but resisted the urge. 'Perhaps he's . . . ' she began, then gave up, the words dying on her breath.

Silence fell.

'I think we have to assume the worst, Alison.' Marina's voice sounded small and broken. Acknowledging those words she felt a dark dread move into her heart. But the words had to be said. The situation to be faced.

Cotter nodded. Her voice was resigned. 'If it were anyone else in any other situation I'd say wait. But not this. Not with what we know. Or rather don't know.'

'So who . . . '

'Sperring and Khan are busy on another case.'

'Right.'

Cotter walked to the door, put her head round it, called to the person she wanted.

Marina felt a sense of relief as DC Imani Oliver entered. They had worked together before. Had a good rapport. She trusted her.

'Thanks for stepping in, Imani,' said Cotter. 'Something's come up.'

Imani looked between Marina and Cotter, frowned, a question forming on her lips.

'I'll fill you in,' said Cotter.

She did so.

'Let's sit down,' said Cotter once she'd finished. 'Coordinate.'

Marina wanted to shout out that she didn't want to sit down, that she wanted something done immediately, but she swallowed down what would have been grossly unprofessional behaviour and took a seat.

Cotter had a small table and four chairs in her office for meetings. She moved over to it, followed by Marina and Imani.

'Right,' Cotter said, once they were settled, 'plan of action. Imani, I want you to get over to Marina's house straight away. Take a couple of uniforms with you. Go door to door. I want to know if Phil was seen this morning, getting into a car or otherwise. I want to know if anyone else was there with him.'

'Maybe he drove to Colchester himself,' said Imani.

'Not likely,' said Cotter. 'He knew someone was coming for him.' She turned to Marina. 'Was his Audi parked on the street?'

Marina felt that impatience rise within her again. 'Yes, but—'

Back to Imani. 'Check that it's still there.'

Imani made a note.

'And then what?' asked Marina, barely suppressing her distress.

Cotter turned to her, about to answer. Marina continued. 'This is all ... pointless. We know he's gone. You should get a description issued, get out on the roads, check CCTV, just ... ' she sighed, ' ... be doing something ... '

'We are doing something,' said Cotter. 'This is where we start, what we do. We work methodically. You know that.'

Marina said nothing.

'I know how you must feel. And I want him back as quickly as possible too. But let's not abandon all sense of procedure just because it's one of our own. That should be all the more reason to follow it. Speed, not haste.'

Marina slowly nodded. She knew Cotter was right. That what she was implementing was the way forward. She just wanted confirmation that Phil was safe. And she knew she wouldn't get it.

'Perhaps there's something you could do, Marina?' asked Imani.

'Like what?'

'Well, if this is OK with the boss ... ' She looked over at Cotter who nodded. 'If this is who we think it is, checking out Fiona Welch's background. Going over the case notes from the woman who claimed to be her. See if there are any similarities, things we might've missed. Corresponding behaviours.

61

Anything that might give us a clue, a break. Look at it from a psychologist's point of view not a police officer's.'

Marina nodded. 'OK.' She knew it was work that needed to be done and she was the best person for it, but she felt it was being given to her just to keep her busy.

'Good idea,' said Cotter. 'But I only want you doing this if you feel up to it. I realise it's uncomfortably close to home but I don't want that clouding your judgement. Can you do it?'

Marina, her face impassive, unreadable, said, 'I can do it.'

'Good.' Cotter looked at Imani. 'Right. Get to work. Let's find him.'

10

Phil opened his eyes. Blinked. Again. Looked round. He was home.

Confused, he tried sitting up. Couldn't, something was stopping him. He fell down again, on his back. He was warm but couldn't move. He tested his limbs once more: restrained, wrists and ankles. And he was naked too. A duvet covered him, pillows behind his head. He looked down the length of his body. The print on the duvet was the one he had at home.

He looked round the room once more. *His* room. *His* bedroom. The one he shared with Marina in Moseley village. And it was dark, the curtains closed. The only light coming from the bedside light on his bedside table. He blinked once more, confused. Checked himself over again.

He hurt. Down one side. His right. Why did he . . .

Then he remembered: he had been in the car. Passenger. With Beresford. On his way to . . .

Beresford.

The taser. Was that what it had been? Or some kind of stun gun? Something like that. Speeding up, going faster, couldn't get out, his questions were . . . Then the look on Beresford's face – an apology? Was that right? Then . . . Nothing.

Then now.

He looked round the room once more. His room. But . . .

How was here? How was he back in his bedroom? And

63

where was everyone else? No Marina, no Josephina ... And how did it get so dark so suddenly? He thought. No. He must have been out of it for some time. Long enough for day to become night. He had been found, brought home. That was it. But even thinking that didn't feel right. Didn't bring him any comfort. Too many unanswered questions. And then there were the restraints.

No. He looked round the room again, closer this time. Something was wrong. Something was off. Yes, it was his room and it was dark, but that wasn't what was wrong with it. Looking hard, scrutinising the place, he tried to focus, make out what was there. Work out what was wrong.

But he couldn't see it properly. He kept blinking, wondering why the walls, the wardrobe, the chest of drawers, why none of it would come into focus properly. He looked again at the wall opposite, the wardrobe. Blinked. Screwed his eyes tight, opened them wide. What ...

Then he knew. He had it. The mirror on the wardrobe cast no reflection. He couldn't look into it. There was no depth. It was flat. Not just the mirror, the wardrobe, the walls, but everything. The wallpaper the same as the wardrobe, as the window. Flat. His bedroom, yes, but in only two dimensions. Nothing stuck out. Apart from the bedside tables, the bedside lights, nothing was real. But it looked real ...

He got it. Photorealistic. Like his bedroom had been photographed and blown up to life-size. Like a theatre set or movie backdrop. So ...

He realised what he had just thought.

His bedroom had been photographed.

Someone had been in his bedroom with a camera, taking their time, studying. *In his bedroom.* Not to mention the time taken to set this all up, the expense. Someone had been in his room.

He shivered. Now he knew who was behind this. No more guessing.

Her.

He pulled at his restraints once more. Frantically this time. Had to get away from here. Wherever here was.

As he struggled he felt his chest tightening. *No . . . no . . . not now . . .* Harder, harder, stopping him from taking in a whole lungful of air, removing the strength to expel it. Restricting him even worse than his restraints . . . No . . . His body shaking, chest palpitating . . .

He lay back on the bed again, unable to move.

A panic attack. Hadn't had one for ages. Now of all times, it chooses a reappearance.

He tried to trick his body into breathing again. Pretended to not care, not to feel it, hoped his hammering heart rate would drop, allow air inside him once more.

It worked. Slowly, he began to breathe freely again.

And then the door opened.

He froze, stared at it.

A figure stepped through the doorway. Medium height, dark hair. A very familiar silhouette.

Marina.

Phil felt relief at first but that soon gave way to puzzlement.

The figure stepped completely into the room, crossed to him in the bed. Looked down on him, smiling.

'Hello, Phil. Remember me?'

He stared at her. The hair was perfect, the clothes just right. But the face . . .

Not Marina. But he knew who it was.

'Yeah,' he said, his voice drying up, fading. He needed more breath. Didn't have it. 'I remember . . .'

She sat on the edge of the bed. Still smiling. Unspeaking.

He stared at her, scrutinised her. She was different to how

he had last seen her. Not just the hair and the clothes but the body shape. Like she had remade herself in Marina's image. Or a grotesque parody of Marina.

She kept staring at him. Eventually the smile faded to be replaced by a puzzled expression. 'I thought you remembered me, Phil.'

'I do,' he said reluctantly.

'So why don't you say my name?'

'Because I don't know your name.'

She leaned closer to him, mouth right next to his ear. She spoke in a whisper. He could feel the warm air on his neck. 'Oh yes you do . . .'

Phil felt something in his chest dislodge, turn over. He knew she was waiting for him to ask the question. He wouldn't give her the satisfaction. And he didn't want to hear her response.

She waited. Realising he wasn't going to ask, she leant in even further, her mouth right on his ear.

'You know who I am. I'm your wife. Marina . . .'

Phil felt his body stiffen in revulsion.

'And you're mine, Phil.'

He felt her hand move over the duvet, make its way down his body.

'Mine . . .'

11

Imani knocked on another door in Phil and Marina's street in Moseley village. Old Edwardian and thirties houses, substantial and solid, a suburban part of Birmingham but with enough character in pubs, restaurants, non-chain shops and residents to still justify calling itself a village.

She hadn't expected much and so far she hadn't been disappointed. Most of the houses on the street were empty. People at work, school runs done and off into town, or just not answering the door. The only ones who had answered her had been elderly and lonely. They invited her in, made or offered her tea. Tried and tried to think if they had seen anything, willing an image or a memory to mind, not wanting to disappoint this young and attractive woman, to prove they could still be of some use, but ultimately had nothing to tell her. Imani didn't hint, didn't lead in the questioning, didn't want them to pick up on something she said and confirm it just to make her happy. She offered no clues. They gave her no answers. But she was fairly well versed on the occupations and spread geography of their offsprings. The two uniforms she had with her were, she presumed, making a similar lack of progress.

She knocked and waited at the latest door. Idly checked her watch and found herself agreeing with Marina. Yes, this was procedure, yes, it was to be followed. But all the while she

67

was doing this, whoever had taken Phil – and that was looking increasingly likely – was getting further away.

Further thought was stopped. The door opened. There stood an old woman. Here we go again, thought Imani.

She held up her warrant card. 'I'm Detective Sergeant Imani Oliver.' She put the card down, smiled. Reassuringly, she hoped. 'We're doing door-to-door enquiries in this area. Could I ask you a few questions, please?'

The woman immediately became suspicious, glancing behind Imani, up and down the street. 'What about?'

She took a photo from her pocket, showed it to her. 'Have you seen this man?'

'I don't have my glasses on . . . ' The woman picked up the photo, scrutinised it. 'Wait a moment.' She turned, left Imani on the doorstep. She returned quickly with her glasses, resumed looking.

Imani watched her. Eventually the woman looked up, pointed to the photo. 'He lives over there.' She looked quizzically at Imani. 'Is he in trouble?'

Imani ignored the question. 'Have you seen him this morning?'

The woman looked up at Imani. 'Yes,' she said. 'Getting into a car.'

Imani felt her heart thud.

'Could I come in, please?'

Imani sat on the sofa, the woman opposite in an armchair. An open book lay on the arm of the chair. Imani tried to read the spine, make out what it was. Some non-fiction history. Not the cheap supermarket romance she had been expecting. And she hadn't been offered tea, either.

'Joan Harrison,' said the woman by way of an introduction. Imani smiled in turn.

'Joan – d'you mind if I call you Joan?'

The woman shrugged. 'It's my name.'

'Joan, what can you tell me about the man you saw this morning?'

'He was getting into a car.' Her voice didn't betray her age at all. Clear and lucid, just like her eyes.

'Can you describe the car?'

'Large, silver. Looked expensive. Big and powerful. Cars aren't my strong point, I'm afraid.' She gave a small smile. Like she was testing how it would fit her features. 'If it had been a hansom cab or a sedan chair or litter, then I might be more help.'

She continued, answering Imani's quizzical expression. 'Historian. Retired, unfortunately.'

'I see.'

'But I'm not one of those busybodies with too much time on their hands, who spend the day curtain-twitching.' The statement was more like an admonishment, thought Imani. *Don't expect me to answer all your questions.*

'Right,' said Imani, smiling. 'It's good to keep active. I don't suppose you saw the make or model of the car?'

'Big and silver. Sorry.'

'Or the registration number?'

Another smile. 'As I said, I'm not a professional curtain-twitcher. I happened to look out of the window when I opened the living room curtains, here.' She pointed to the bay window. 'I saw the man from over the road getting into a car. I didn't know I was going to be tested on it. If so, I'd have taken more notice.'

'I understand. You're being helpful, though, thank you.'

'May I just ask one question before you proceed further?'

'Certainly. If I can answer it.'

'What is the man from opposite supposed to have done?'

'Done?'

'You're a policewoman. You must be interested in him for some reason. Is he a criminal?'

'No. He's not. He's a police detective. He works with me.'

'Really?' The woman's eyebrows raised in surprise. 'Is he undercover?'

'Why d'you ask?'

'His clothes. He dresses more like a labourer.'

Imani returned the smile, shook her head. 'You're not the first to say that.'

Before the woman could speak further, Imani continued. 'Did you see anybody else? Was someone driving the car?'

'Yes. A big man. Bald. Or shaven-headed. It's so hard to distinguish these days. A lot do it instead of having to comb over what hair they have that remains. I don't suppose I could blame them, really. Although it does make one look like some kind of street thug.'

'Absolutely. Did you catch what he was wearing, by any chance?'

'Not really.'

'A suit? Casual clothes?'

'A shirt. And tie. Like he'd taken his jacket off. He helped the man from opposite with his luggage.'

'Luggage?'

'Put it in the boot. Then the man opposite got into the car with the bald man and they drove off.'

'What time was this, exactly?'

Another smile. 'Around nine o'clock. I'm afraid I can't be more accurate. As I said, I wasn't expecting to be quizzed about it.'

'Thank you,' said Imani. 'Just one more question.' She reached into her bag, drew out a photograph of Beresford that had been printed off from the email Franks had sent over. She showed it to Joan. 'Was this the man driving the car?'

'Well, as I said, I wasn't watching closely but yes. Yes, it could very well have been.'

Imani stood up to go. Heart racing, tingling now. 'You've been very helpful. By the way – did the man from opposite look like he was being coerced to get into the car?'

'Not at all. They even shook hands.'

'Thank you.'

Imani hurried out, phone already in her hand, dialling Cotter.

'It's me, ma'am,' she said, getting behind the wheel of her car. 'I've got a witness who saw Phil getting into a car this morning.'

'What kind?'

'Big and silver. Driven by a big, bald man. What kind of car does Beresford drive?'

She heard papers being moved in the background. 'A Vauxhall Insignia. Silver.'

A shiver ran though Imani.

'I've got what could well be a positive ID on DS Beresford being the driver from a witness.'

Cotter didn't reply.

'I'm coming back to the station. Right now.'

12

Marina knew how it ended. She had been there.

Fiona Welch falling to her death from a crane gantry by the old Dock Transit Company building on the River Colne in Colchester. Phil Brennan up there beside her. She didn't need to bring up reports or old files to remember that.

Sitting at a desk, going through things as Cotter had suggested, trying to take her mind off what was happening. Or what might be happening. She could have been back in her office on campus. Almost.

Because this wasn't a way to forget. All Marina did was remember.

Fiona Welch. PhD student. Murderer. Killed three women and one man – a police officer – that they knew of. Her self-justification: an attempt to demonstrate a transgressive lifestyle. To show superiority to other humans. In reality: self-deluded jealousy. The victims were all ex-girlfriends of her boyfriends or, in the case of the police officer, her lover.

Marina knew all that. What she didn't know was the woman's life story. Where she came from. What caused her to grow into the monster she became?

She looked at the screen, rubbed her eyes, ran another search.

Names appeared. Photos. None of them right. She didn't want Fiona Welch the business analyst whose LinkedIn profile said hailed from Cardiff. Or the Fiona Welch who, according to Facebook, was a second-year Classics student at Manchester University and was planning a trip to Glastonbury. She redefined her search parameters. Added *Murderer* to the list. That did it.

A collection of true-crime articles appeared. She leaned forward, read the titles of each one, checked on their provenance. It was what she had expected. Some were erudite, psychological in approach, attempting – or claiming to attempt – to understand what had formed her, made her behave the way she had. Others were more predictably lurid, their prose sensational, making no attempt at understanding, just glorifying and amplifying her violently murderous career.

Marina realised she should have been looking at the reports with a degree of professional detachment but since it was her own husband who she was trying to find she found it increasingly difficult. Especially after reading the tabloid reports.

My husband has been taken by *that woman* . . .

She shook the thought out of her head. Not that woman. *That* woman was dead. Another woman. One who she needed to find. Hoped this would help her to do so. Head down again, she tried to continue. She read everything, attempting to ignore both the tabloid prurient descriptions of crime scenes and skipping over the broadsheet pseudo-psychology behind her motivations. Just the facts. All she wanted. Facts. From them and more official reports and associated databases she managed to piece together Fiona Welch's early life.

Fiona Welch had been brought up in various care homes in Chelmsford, Essex. Marina made a list of the ones noted. Foster homes were also mentioned but she could find no specific details of them. She had attended various schools in Chelmsford, not lasting very long at most of them. Marina leaned forward. It was becoming interesting. The schools she

73

attended all spoke of an initially disruptive pupil who, with time and effort, settled down and began to apply herself to work. Such an achievement in itself shouldn't have been a surprise, thought Marina, but children from care and foster homes always struggled, always started on a lower rung to children from happy homes. She immediately felt guilty for thinking that. Her husband Phil had had a similar background, brought up by foster parents who had eventually adopted him. Phil's adoptive father, and possibly the greatest male influence on his life, had been a police detective. And that was, even after all this time, something she still couldn't work out about him.

Phil, Marina had often observed, was the last person most people would think of as a police officer. She had watched, amused, as he had introduced himself to friends and colleagues at the university. His dress sense, hair and general manner all suggested another lecturer, possibly English, maybe History or even Drama. Then she would see their faces change when he told them who he was and what he did for a living. Apart from the fact that he was good at catching criminals, Marina wondered whether he wouldn't have been happier doing something else. But then she also wondered if Phil would have thought he'd be letting the memory of his adoptive father down. That was why she believed he had joined the force. Not that he had ever said as much. Not even to her.

She put those thoughts from her mind, concentrated once more on the task at hand.

Essex University in Colchester was next. Then secondment with the police while she was a PhD student. The murders. Then her demise. Marina didn't need to read about that again.

Marina sat back. Looked at the screen once more, at her notes.

Children's homes. Foster homes. Something to go on. She

knew – or strongly suspected – that Cotter had given her this job just to give her something to do, to feel like she was contributing in some way. Keep her from worrying.

Marina hoped that wasn't true. She wasn't a frontline detective but she had skills that could catch this woman, could find her husband, skills that most police officers often didn't possess.

She kept staring at the notes. Yes, Cotter would follow it up. But no matter how urgent the job of finding Phil was, she would be hidebound by procedure and protocol. And every second counted. But Marina had no procedure or protocol to follow. Nothing to stop her from investigating this herself.

She smiled. And she knew just the person to ask to help her.

13

'Get your bags packed,' Cotter had said, 'you're off to Colchester.' That was how Imani found herself on the A14 driving as fast as she could, ready to hopefully make some headway in the hunt for her missing DI.

She had gone straight back to Steelhouse Lane after phoning Cotter. Passed on the neighbour's information to the DCI.

'So he did leave,' said Cotter. 'We have to assume as much. And we can't get in touch with him.'

'And the description matches the one Colchester gave us for DS Beresford,' said Imani. 'Even the car fits. This isn't random. Definitely. There's some planning been put into this.'

Cotter nodded, thought. 'I'll get Sperring and Khan looking into it from this end. Get Elli to check CCTV in the area, uniforms to get out looking for a Vauxhall Insignia. Perhaps he's even matched the number plate.'

'It seems likely,' said Cotter. 'Or something similar. Muddying the water, perhaps?'

'Could be. Sending us on a wild goose chase.'

The drive was largely uneventful. The road was single track in parts and although Imani became frustrated when she got stuck behind someone who didn't share her sense of urgency she refrained from using the lights and siren of her unmarked. The slower pace actually helped her, forced her to take in the surroundings, look for any signs that Phil hadn't arrived at Colchester, had taken a detour somewhere along this road. She sighed. That could be anywhere.

She looked at her hands on the wheel. Her knuckles. Steady. No shaking. She hadn't been back on frontline duties for long. A remarkable recovery, the psychologist said, considering what she had been through. Nearly nine months ago now. But it was still hard to forget. Watching a colleague being killed in front of her, a colleague who perhaps could have become more than a friend, was one thing. Being tasered, kidnapped and imprisoned by a murderer who planned on killing her slowly and making her suffer purely because she was a woman who had bested him was something else entirely. Something she wouldn't – couldn't, didn't – forget easily.

If it hadn't been for the support shown to her by her colleagues and family she didn't know what would have become of her. Especially Marina. She had worked hard to bring her back to some semblance of normal. Hours of ranting, screaming, sobbing, holding. And eventually a small chink of light through her darkness, a light that expanded and grew until she felt confident – safe – enough to walk in it. Marina was brilliant. She understood what Imani had gone through. After all, she had been there herself.

Whatever doesn't kill you, her dad had said during that time when she had returned to the small family home to feel safe, trotting out the old Nietzschean cliché (not that he had a clue where it came from), makes you stronger. His bluff way of showing concern. She smiled at the memory. If it didn't concern Aston Villa he was useless at expressing emotion. The smile faded. Imani had never agreed with the sentiment. If something didn't kill you straight away it didn't necessarily make you stronger. It could also kill you bit by bit. She hoped that wasn't the case.

The afternoon was more empty than full when she eventually arrived at Queensway station in Colchester, satnav pinging that this was her final destination. She looked at the building before her. It was totally unlike Steelhouse Lane. She always considered her place of work to be like some kind of Gothic schoolhouse, all red brick, turrets and crenellations. This was completely the opposite. Low and spread out, a kind of bland, beige box. She could almost feel her hair lifting from the imagined static coming off the nylon carpets inside. It could have been anything from an office block on an anonymous provincial industrial estate to a low security prison. In a way, she thought, it was both of those things.

She locked the car, went to the desk, asked for DCI Gary Franks.

She didn't wait long. A red-headed, red-faced bull of a man came barrelling down the corridor towards her. He wore his suit grudgingly, as if he'd lost a fight with it. He gave a grim smile, extended his paw of a hand.

'DCI Franks.'

'Detective Sergeant Imani Oliver.' She shook. His eyes looked like they had seen bad things and learned from the experiences.

'Come this way.'

He beckoned her along the corridor. She followed.

Despite the beige trappings, the station was the same as what she was used to. Same smell. Same feel. Same atmosphere. Same people doing the same job.

He directed her to his office, closed the door behind her and gestured she take a seat. She did so. He took his jacket off, ripping it away like it was some kind of parasite that had wrapped itself round his body, and sat down behind his desk.

'Quite a day,' he said. She noticed, for the first time, his Welsh accent.

'Yes, sir,' she said.

'Quite a few days, really.'

'How is that going, sir? I presume you mean the hanging bodies?'

'I do,' he said, sitting back.

She took the opportunity to glance around the room; through it, take some impressions of the man himself. There was a kind of near-military discipline to the place. Framed photos and citations on the walls. Everything neatly placed. Rugby trophies, handsomely mounted.

Franks continued. 'We're still working on them. As yet, no one's come forward with anything. No missing persons that fit the description. But we're working. We're looking. Our top priority.'

She nodded.

'I take it there's no sign of DI Brennan yet?'

'No. We were hoping you had some news.'

Franks shook his head. 'Incredible. Just incredible.' A ghost of a smile passed his lips. 'Mind you, if it would happen to anyone, it would happen to him. Magnet for trouble, that man. Murder rate's dropped since he left. Bet it's gone up where you are?'

Imani wasn't sure how to answer. 'I . . . I'd have to check, sir.'

He did smile this time, but it didn't stay very long on his features. 'Only joking, DS Oliver.' He sighed, all business again. 'You say someone answering Detective Sergeant Beresford's description was seen at DI Brennan's house? And that he got into the car with him and off they went?'

'That's right. Even the car, make and model, matched. Same with the description. I'm sure Phil—' she corrected herself, 'DI Brennan would have asked for identification. There's no way he would have got into that car otherwise.'

'Phil,' said Franks, nodding. 'Still big on informality. But yes, you're right. And DS Beresford couldn't go anywhere because of his car.'

'Does he have his warrant card with him?'

'Of course.' Franks sounded insulted at the suggestion.

'I'm sorry, sir,' said Imani, 'but I have to ask. I'm sure you've done the same thing. Even if he is an officer of yours.'

'True. And I have done. DCI Cotter and I have been sharing information all the while you've been driving here. I know what's happened and I've questioned DS Beresford. I'm satisfied he told me the truth.'

There was a knock on the door.

'That'll be him now.'

Franks shouted to whoever it was to enter. A huge, bald man came in. Imani stood up. DS Dave Beresford looked just like his photo. He crossed to her, smiled. Shook hands.

'DS Beresford.' He smiled. 'Dave.'

He had an appealing smile for such a large man. Charming, in fact.

'DS Oliver,' she said. 'Imani.'

'Right,' said Franks, while Beresford pulled up a chair, 'you've had your pleasantries, let's get down to it. I assume DCI Cotter's sent you here to see how we're doing, that right?'

'And to assist in any way I can, sir.'

'Right. Well.' He looked to Beresford and back to Imani. 'We've got a lot to do. Hope you can think on your feet.'

'I can, sir.'

'That's it then. Welcome aboard, DS Oliver. Here's to a successful investigation.'

She smiled, nodded. Aware all the time of Beresford's eyes on her.

14

At least she had stopped touching him. That seemed to be the best he could hope for at the moment.

Phil still couldn't move. Every time he pulled against the restraints they just seemed to tighten. But at least the woman had left him alone.

Terror had crept up on him when she had started stroking. Her hand firmly brushing over him, working its way down the length of his body. All the while smiling at him, holding eye contact. Waiting for him to flinch, move, respond, anything. Phil struggled hard to keep as still, be as passive as he could. Not let his body make any kind of involuntary responses to her touch. In any way.

Seeing that her fingers weren't having the response she had hoped for she had stood up, laughed and left the room. He was alone once more. His head reeling with questions.

He once again tried to work out what he knew, rationalise the situation. He was in trouble, yes. More than that: danger. She had killed before. Clearly she had no compunction about killing again. But he didn't think she wanted to kill him. Or at least not yet. She wanted him for something else. She had gone to all this trouble, killing three men, even getting a serving police officer to kidnap him. Or who he presumed was a police officer. She wanted something. Something he hadn't yet given her. Something that, in her twisted mind, it seemed like he was the only person who could provide. That was the one good thought he clung on to, the one thing that kept him going. That meant that, no matter how slim, he still had a chance.

He looked round the room once more, trying to find some clue as to where he was. His eyes fell on two little capsules on his bedside table. Blue and white, just lying there. He didn't know what they were, but he was sure they weren't good.

But he didn't have time to dwell on anything further as the door opened and she entered once more.

'Had a little rest?' she said. 'Good. Build your strength up. You're going to need it.'

'What for?'

She didn't reply. Just gave him another smile. 'Dinner will be served soon. One of your favourites. Pork and chorizo goulash, is that right?'

Phil couldn't answer for a few seconds. She was right, it was one of his favourites. He often made it himself since it was one of his signature dishes, as he had once laughingly described it to Marina – that and spaghetti bolognese.

'I know you like to make it yourself,' she said, 'but I do hope you'll enjoy my recipe. I've followed yours as closely as I could.'

More questions than Phil could articulate. Before he could seize on one of them, she sat down on the bed, looked at him once more.

'Thought we might have a little chat before dinner.'

'Where am I?' asked Phil. 'And why have you got me here like this?'

She sighed, looked disappointed. 'I thought you'd be more original than that. Really, I expected better of you.'

'Who are you, then? How about that one.'

She gave a smile reserved for the most patronising of nurses. 'You know who I am, darling.'

'No I don't.'

'Look at me.' She sat back, flung her arms wide, cocked her head to one side. 'Who do I look like? Who am I?'

'You're not Marina. You know you're not Marina.'

She leaned forward once more, talking as if explaining something to a slow child. 'No. I'm not Marina. But I'm more than her. Much more.'

'Like what, who?'

She leaned even further in. 'I'm the person who knows you best, Phil Brennan. I'm the only person who understands you.' She sat back again, smiling, waiting for his response. A manic, self-satisfied glee dancing in her eyes. 'Really, truly understands you.'

'No you don't. Don't talk bullshit. I don't know you.'

She looked mock-appalled. 'No need for that language, lovely one. You know there isn't. Now.'

She leaned forward once more, her hands upon him. He stiffened, tried to pull away from her touch. Couldn't. She smiled.

'Just relax. You're not going anywhere.'

He said nothing. Stiffened his body even more, clenched his teeth together.

She continued. 'Phil, I know what you're really like. I mean, really, really like. Underneath it all. I know the real you.'

She still hadn't moved her hands. He couldn't keep still forever, hold his breath forever. He exhaled. Tried to relax, concentrate on her words. Remember his training. Try to engage her.

'This is the real me.'

She shook her head. 'No it's not.'

'Then who, or what, is the real me?'

'The one who's underneath . . . ' she gave an expansive ges-ture, flicked her wrist at where the wardrobe was supposed to

83

be, ' . . . all this. The clothes. The attitude. The outlook, that carefully cultivated outlook that puts you at odds with everyone else you work with. Even your own team. Especially your own team. The thrill you get from trying to be . . . different.'

'I don't try to be different, I just . . . I am who I am.'

She laughed. 'Nō. You think you know who you are. Don't you? You believe the lies you tell yourself. You get up every day, look at yourself in the mirror and think, what can I do that's different? What can I wear that'll make me stand out at work? What opinion shall I have that's contrary to everyone else's? That's what you do, Phil. Each and every day.'

'Bullshit.'

'Language, please.'

'Fuck off.'

She sat back once more, stared at him. There was no playfulness in her eyes this time. Just dark, angry blackness.

'Don't say that to me again, Phil. I won't tolerate it.' Her voice low, quiet even, carrying an unmistakable threat. 'Keep speaking to me like that and I'll make you sorry. I don't care what you mean to me. No one talks to me like that. Not even you.'

Phil glimpsed the madness inside her. He didn't want to antagonise her further. But he still couldn't bring himself to apologise to her. So instead he said nothing.

She waited to see that he wasn't going to say anything else. 'That's better.'

He glanced to the capsules on the bedside table. 'What are they for? Suicide pills, are they? Or something to help me sleep?'

She smiled. 'All in good time. You're not ready for that yet. I'll let you know when you are. You've a long way to go.'

'Have I?'

'Oh yes. Now. As I was saying. You get a thrill from being

transgressive. There's no point denying it, because if you do that you're denying a basic part of yourself. You get a thrill from being different. Don't you?'

He listened to her this time, let her words penetrate. He had to admit, grudgingly, she was right. He liked to dress differently for work. He couldn't abide the opinions that the majority of other officers held. No matter how much some of them pretended otherwise, they would always come down on the opposite side to him. He knew they joked about him, called him a bleeding heart liberal, but he didn't care. He was. That was one of the main reasons he had gone into the police force in the first place.

'Don't you?'

'Yes,' he said.

She grinned, like she had just scored an important point. 'I knew it. I just had to get you to admit it, that's all. But I know you are. Because guess what? I am too. We make quite a pair, don't we?'

Phil said nothing.

The smile dropped. A look of mania danced in her eyes once more. She leaned towards him, her mouth by his ear. He could feel her breath on his cheek. 'Oh yes, I am too. Never forget that. But with me, it's everything.'

She sat back once more. Phil found his voice again.

'It isn't like that with me. I'm not like that. Yes, I like to dress differently at work. That's one thing. But transgressive? I'm the least transgressive person I know.'

'No you're not.'

'Yes I am. And all this? About me? You're just guessing. That's all. You don't really know anything.'

'Oh I do, Phil. More than you know. More than you realise.'

'Oh really? Such as. Go on, give me an example.'

She looked at her nails as if what she was about to say wasn't a big deal. 'Oh, I know about the darkness inside you, Phil. That real, harrowing darkness that you keep hidden. From everyone. That darkness you can barely acknowledge.'

'Bull—' He stopped himself. 'There's no darkness.'

'Yes there is. So deep, so hidden that you daren't tell anyone. Not even the sainted Marina.'

'Prove it, then.'

'I will.' She leaned forward towards him once more, her mouth close to his ear. She cupped her hand round it, so as not to let any of the sound spill out.

And she whispered two words.

Then sat back, staring at him. Eyes dancing with a sick triumph.

Phil couldn't move, couldn't speak. His heart was pounding faster than a stampede of bulls. He was frozen.

'Right,' she said, smoothing down the front of her dress, 'ready for dinner yet?' She produced a taser. 'Sorry. Necessary precaution. Till I know you're not going to try anything stupid. Till we get to trust each other.'

She put it to his chest, fired. Phil screamed, shuddered, collapsed.

Blackness.

15

One. Two. One. One. Fast. Two. Slow. Uppercut. One. One. Jab. Hard. Harder.

Anni Hepburn was in the gym, gloved up, focused, eyes steely and feet positioned. Strong. Pounding the bag for all it was worth.

She blinked sweat from her eyes, kept pounding, hitting. Felt pain in her chest, her arms. Cramp. The jarring of her fists, even against padded polymer, sent shockwaves up her arms, jangled the joints as they went. Her response was to hit harder, jab faster. Make each punch count. Let each one hurt.

She knew her opponent wasn't real. She knew her opponent couldn't feel. But that wouldn't stop her from trying. Because *she* could feel. No matter how much she tried to block it out, she could still feel.

She paused, let her arms drop to her sides. Exhausted. More tired than she had felt for ages. But she wasn't done yet. She picked up her towel, wiped away most of the sweat. Squared up against the bag once more. And raised her leg to strike.

Boxing. Kickboxing. It had become her life. Her obsession. Punching and kicking the pain away. Keeping the loss at bay. Keeping her anger contained. Directed.

Over six months since she had left the police force. Since she had realised she just couldn't walk into the station any more, couldn't face the rest of the team staring at her while they were pretending not to. At least that was what it had felt like.

She had tried. At first. Once she had gone through sessions with the psychologist, counselling for grief and anything else that came up. Tried to force herself to believe that she was stronger than her faults, that her emotions wouldn't get the better of her. That she was in control. The sessions went as expected.

Screaming out the name of her dead partner, Mickey, Detective Sergeant Philips, her partner on the force and in life, asking why him, why not her, why not anyone but him. And hating the woman who had done it. The woman who had called herself Fiona Welch.

Eventually she had run out of hatred, leaving herself numb. That, she considered, was progress. Or as much progress as she thought she could accomplish.

And gradually she began to pull herself back together. She refused medication, tried a different way. Exercise to release her body's endorphins. Then more exercise. Then more. Now, her body was a small, compact walking muscle. Like she was wearing her own-grown armour.

Eventually she returned to work. Light duties at first, which she hated, then frontline work. Which, she was shocked to learn, she hated even more. She couldn't cope. More than that, she didn't care. And she had always told herself that when she stopped caring then it was time to leave the force.

But the staring. The whispering. The judging, either real or imagined. That was worse. That was the deciding factor.

So she left. And, pragmatically, turned her fitness obsession into a career. She worked as a personal trainer in one of Colchester's many health clubs. It was fine. She worked part time, still had her police pension and they allowed her to come in and train as much as she liked. And she did it a lot. Worked her body, tired herself out. It stopped her from dwelling on the past, on the future, on herself. Stopped her from thinking too much.

She needed a rest, couldn't ignore her body this time. She walked away from the bag, reluctantly, and headed for a seat. Changed her mind at the last minute and sat at one of the machines instead. If she was going to rest she could be working on her arms and upper body while she did so.

She took a drink of water, gulping it down from her bottle, exhaled once more. Her arms were shaking from the exercise, her legs likewise.

And then her phone rang.

Her iPhone, attached to her arm in a gym strap, used only for her fitness and training programme, for music to listen to when she needed to zone out completely. She had almost forgotten it could take calls. Hardly anyone called any more.

She took it from her arm, looked at the display. And kept looking. Staring all the while, her body now shaking from more than the workout. Just staring. Seeing that one name staring back at her.

Marina.

Her thumb hovered between the green and red buttons. It kept ringing. She pressed red. It stopped.

Sighing, closing her eyes, she began to return it to her arm strap. Just that one name had sliced through all her carefully fortified defences. And everything came tumbling back. Work. Phil. Marina. Her old team. And especially Mickey. His smiling face there in her mind once more.

They had tried to help her and she had been grateful for that. But she couldn't see them any more, couldn't talk to them. It was too painful, brought back too many memories. When she spoke to Phil or Marina she kept seeing the after-image of Mickey standing next to them. An unremarked-upon ghost. She knew they meant well. And they were her friends. But there was some part of her, one she hated to acknowledge, that blamed them for Mickey's death. She knew it wasn't true when she looked at the facts logically, but still the thought persisted. They were all tied up together. And Anni had found it better to just cut herself off from all of them.

Her phone rang again. Her heart flipped. She knew who it would be even without looking.

She took it from the strap, checked the display once more. Marina. She had been right.

And again her thumb hovered over the red and the green. Red and green. Stop, go. So easy. Press red and that would be it. The end of it. So easy . . .

She pressed green.

Placed the phone to her ear. Her fingers trembling from more than just physical exertion.

'Anni?'

'What d'you want?' Her voice as brusque, as emotionless as possible. Use it as a barrier. Keep everyone out.

'Oh.' Marina was clearly taken aback by Anni's response. Anni felt guilty about that. Shamed at the response to her friend. But she still wouldn't change her tone. She had to do what she had to do to get by. That's what she always told herself. Her mantra.

'What d'you want?' Anni barely lifted the words, turned the question into a statement.

Marina sighed. Seemed to accept that this was the way the conversation was going to go. 'I . . . I was . . .' Another sigh. Anni knew Marina was trying to find a way to make pleasantries, to ask how she was. She had cut her off. There would be none of that. And even if Marina did manage to ask anything, did manage to try and break through, she would just cut her off again. Tell her she was fine.

90

Marina continued. 'I need your help, Anni.'

Anni said nothing, waited.

'It's . . . it's that woman. The one who called herself Fiona Welch.'

Anni's stomach flipped over once more. And kept flipping. She couldn't breathe. Her legs shook. She was thankful to be sitting down.

'What . . . ' Her voice seemed to have deserted her. 'What about her?'

'She's back again. She's . . . she's killed three people. Men. You . . . you might have heard about it. One in Wrabness, one in the Dock Transit building, one in that house at the bottom of East Hill, the one where we—'

'I know what we found there. I've heard about this.'

'Right. OK. Well, it's worse than that. She's . . . she's got Phil.'

It felt like Anni's heart had stopped.

'She's taken Phil. And I need . . . I need help. I don't think that the police at my end are doing enough or will do the right thing. I need someone to help me. Someone who knew him.'

Marina stopped talking. Anni picked up on it. She had spoken about her husband in the past tense.

Marina stumbled over that, kept going. 'She's taken him. Abducted him. And I . . . ' Another sigh. 'I need to find him. I need your help, Anni. Please.' She seemed to struggle to keep the pleading from her voice. Failed.

Anni felt her defences being breached, her heart being touched. She couldn't allow that to happen. If she did, if she stopped protecting herself, she might just fall apart. And she didn't how long it would take to put herself together then.

'The police can help you. I can't.'

'But Anni—'

'Sorry.'

91

She hung up while Marina was still pleading with her.

She held the phone in her hands, looked at it. Sighed. Turned it off. It was only a temporary measure, she knew that, but it would stop any more calls for the time being.

She took a deep breath. Another one. Felt her body still shaking. Knew she had to do something about it, knew she couldn't allow herself to dwell on what had just happened.

She walked towards the bag once more, strapping her gloves back on as she went.

Started punching as hard as she could.

Rebuilding the Castle

*T*he window was dirty. It had been cleaned, just not enough. But it would take a lot of scouring to rid the glass of all the grime and dirt that had accumulated and gathered over the years. Like the glass had pores and the dirt was stuck in them. And no amount of rubbing would make them clean again.

She knew that was stupid. Knew glass didn't have pores. But that was what it looked like. She took a finger, stuck it in her mouth until it was good and wet, tried wiping the dirt off. She ended up with a dirty finger and smeary glass. She wiped her finger on her jeans. Didn't try that again.

She spent a lot of time at that window, looking out. Not that there was much to see. A railway line. An industrial estate. Beyond that, a road. People came and went. Nobody stopped for long. Except her. And the other children. They never went anywhere.

The worst thing that could have happened, happened. Mr Wignall had had a stroke. Mrs Wignall said it was inevitable, the way he kept on eating the wrong things and smoking and drinking when he thought she wasn't looking. Mrs Wignall was angry when she said it, angry at him for what he'd done, but also sad. Sad for her and him. And, when she'd stopped thinking about her and him, sad for all the children.

She didn't know what Mrs Wignall meant by that: sad for all the children. The children were all right. None of them had suffered a stroke. None of them had eaten the wrong things or smoked or drank. Well, a couple of them might have smoked, but that was all. But not as much as Mr Wignall. Not yet, anyway. So the children were all right.

But they weren't.

I can't look after you any more, said Mrs Wignall. She had called them all into the living room after they'd come back from school that day. I would love to. But I can't. Since Mr Wignall had his stroke I have to look after him. And it's a lot of work to look after him and all of you. And I love you all but I'm afraid I can't keep looking after you. She looked round the room, into all of their eyes and cried when she spoke. Some of the children cried too. Boys as well. But most of the boys just balled up their fists and made faces to stop the tears. None of them looked at each other.

But she didn't cry. She didn't know what she would be crying for.

She had enjoyed her time at the Wignalls'. But now she had to go somewhere else. She understood that. And inside her something small felt sad. Something small felt like crying. But she had tried to hide that. Like the castle she used to play with, put what needed to be defended in the heart of something, then build the biggest, strongest set of walls around it that she could. Let no one in there. So no one could hurt what was there. Not even herself.

She still saw Caroline from the centre but less and less. She had come to see her at the Wignalls' to ask how she was doing. Fine, she had said. Good. Are you making friends? Yes. Who? She had thought. James. Good, said Caroline. This seemed to have been the right answer. And Melanie. Caroline had nodded. I'm very pleased to hear it, she had said. She had said the right thing. That was good. And are you happy? Oh yes. I'm happy here. And she had tried to look happy when she said it. She knew what happy was. She had heard the other children talking about it. And she had watched the way they looked when they said it and tried to imitate them. She thought she had got it right.

Nothing had made her smile since she had built her castle wall. Since she had decided no one was going to hurt her any more. But she couldn't tell them, couldn't let them know that that was what she had done. So she watched. Learned. Pretended to think the way the others did, feel the way they did so they wouldn't leave her out. She was clever. It was easy.

Caroline had gone away happy. It had worked and that was good. She wouldn't be calling back any more, making her go over sad and unpleasant things once again. Getting inside the walls.

She often wondered what the thing that she kept locked up, the sad and happy bit of her, looked like. She thought she knew. Her old doll. Belinda. She even called it that, the thing inside her. Belinda. As good a name as any.

And so Mrs Wignall said goodbye to them all. She had seen Mr Wignall before she left. He looked like he'd got old. Really, really old. He stared at her funny. He dribbled things and blew spit bubbles from the side of his mouth. Some of the other kids were upset, even appalled by it. She was just fascinated. How someone could change so much. Go from being one person to another. Just like that. Snap. Something to remember.

They moved her to a children's home. Some of the other children went on to other foster homes. The happier ones. The easier ones. But not her. She was in this home now and the castle walls around her had grown even stronger.

The other kids all looked at her funny. Like they were angry with her when she hadn't done anything to make them angry. Like they didn't want her there even though they couldn't understand why. But she could see that the anger hid something else behind their eyes. Fear or something. It didn't stop them, though. Just made them worse.

One girl in particular was bad. Collette. Collette said she couldn't have the bed she wanted. It was too near to Collette and Collette had the best bed in the room. Then Collette said she smelled funny and that she was a nasty little whore. Collette had friends who stood behind her and laughed at what she said when she told them to.

She said nothing. Just ignored them. Kept those castle walls strong.

She liked going to school. That was one thing. Liked the lessons, the reading, the learning things. She was clever, liked to know things. She asked for books that had facts in them. Spent time on the internet looking things up. She got homework and enjoyed doing it. But others didn't like her doing that. Collette didn't.

One night Collette came over to her. She was sitting at the table, the room still smelling of the food they had eaten, the TV on loud. And she was doing her maths homework. She had her compass out and was drawing a circle, ready to make a pie chart of it.

What you doin'?

Homework.

A snort from Collette. Homework. You're a fuckin' pussy, aren't ya? Doin' homework. She looked around, ready for her gang to take their cue and sneer and laugh. They did so.

Collette kept on. About what type of girl did homework. About what was wrong with her. And more. And more. About her parents being dead. Poor little orphan. Poor little smelly, stinking orph—

She had had enough. She yanked Collette's head back as far as it would go, pulling her hair so tight some of it came out by the roots, twisting the girl's body round to get her face where she wanted it. Then she calmly picked up her compass and, still without saying a word, stuck it into Collette's right eye.

Collette screamed, her gang screamed. They ran. Collette couldn't go anywhere. She held her eye as the blood fountained out. She watched, fascinated. And something inside her felt warm. For the first time in years, she smiled for real.

*

96

She got Collette's old bed after that. And Collette's old gang, if she wanted them but she didn't. She didn't need a gang. Didn't want a gang. There was just her. But she had a feeling she wouldn't be there for long. She knew they would take her somewhere else. Or thought they would. Because of what she'd done.

She had been called in front of the home manager to explain herself. She remembered what children did in situations like that and cried. Said Collette had been bullying her and she'd had enough. Just lashed out, didn't know what she was doing. Found the compass in her hand, didn't realise . . .

The manager seemed to accept that. Even though she also said that some of Collette's gang had been scared when she did it, that she hadn't shown any emotion. I was frightened, she said, crying again. Wailing. That seemed to be enough. She hadn't got away with it, don't think that. What she had done was very serious. But at least she understood why she had done it.

Then the manager had leaned across the desk, hands out, sighed. Come to me next time. Before something like this happens again.

She said she would.

So now she stood at the window looking out. Not knowing if they would take her somewhere else or let her stay here. Not caring, really.

But she had learned something. She had learned that fear wasn't something to be kept hidden away.

It was a tool, to be used.

And she was just beginning to understand how to use it.

16

'D o we start off in here or get out and go looking?'

Imani was still in the Queensway station with Beresford. They had left Franks' office and entered the incident room. The case was on the way to a high classification so there were plenty of officers working on it with the promise of more coming in. At the moment Beresford was in charge of the case. And Imani wanted to know what they had so far.

'Start here,' said Beresford. 'Have a look at what we've got so far, get yourself up to speed.' He gave a grim smile. 'Shouldn't take you too long.'

'How d'you mean?'

'We don't have a lot,' said Beresford, leaning over his desk, grabbing a pile of files. 'That's most of the paperwork. Some is still on computer.' He gestured to his desk. 'Be my guest.'

She sat down. Her presence in the room had drawn attention. It seemed that Beresford didn't intend to make a formal introduction so she would have to do so as she went on. She also noticed something else: she was the only black person in the room. A couple of brown faces but no black ones. Sometimes she forgot how non-diverse other parts of the country were.

She opened the first file he had given her, read. Crime scene report with photos. She scanned the photos, seeing a body hanging in a wooded area. Read the forensic report, the CSI report. Looked up.

'Nothing there,' she said.

'I know,' said Beresford. 'Nothing that could identify him. Some tattoos, and that's what we're going on. But we can't match him to anyone else in the system. No mispers match, nothing.'

'What about DNA? A PM?'

Another grim smile. 'Still waiting on the results.'

Imani frowned. 'But it's been . . . '

'Yeah, I know. Should have been almost instant. But the lab we use have got a backlog. Apparently there's been so many unsafe convictions recently involving evidence supplied by this lab that they've got to be thorough now. Double-check everything.'

'Use another lab.'

Beresford shrugged. 'Politics, best practice . . . '

'Right. And the PM?'

'Same thing. Backlog.'

'So in the meantime, nothing.'

'Yep. No name, no match. No DNA, no match. Nothing beyond what he looks like.'

'And presumably you've done media appeals?'

Another nod. 'Nothing as yet.'

She looked down at the report again, read. 'The tarot card. Anything on that?'

'Deck of Thoth, apparently. Aleister Crowley's. The Great Beast, and all that. Pretty common in those circles, available from all good hippy-shit stores. The pen that was used, a Sharpie. Again, not uncommon. We're getting tests run on them, but the results won't be any time soon.'

'And the location?'

'Wrabness. Where DI Brennan was involved with a very high-profile case. Better known now for some art thing put there by that gay artist.'

Imani frowned.

'The one in a dress.'

'Grayson Perry?'

'That's him.' A smirk. 'Her. Whatever.'

'I don't think he's gay.'

Another shrug. Beresford clearly didn't care one way or the other.

'Right.' She looked at the next file. 'And this one?'

'More of the same, really. Body found in the cellar of an old house at the bottom of East Hill in town, just by the river. Exactly the same thing, and another location where DI Brennan was involved in a major investigation. You're welcome to look. Feel free.'

She did so. And found the same paucity of information as in the previous file. 'And no DNA,' she said.

'Same reasons.'

'Is it worth me looking at the third file now?'

'You're welcome to. But . . . '

'I get it.'

She put the file back on the desk, looked round the room. Eyes flickered up, caught hers, then down again. One held her gaze for slightly longer than the rest. A young male detective. Must fancy me, she thought. Then castigated herself for being so arrogant. No, she thought. Don't even think that. Remembered what happened last time you allowed yourself to get involved with someone on the same case. Look what happened to him then. She went back to the report, scanned it, glanced up again. He was no longer looking at her. At least not obviously.

'All these people,' she said.

'Yeah?'

'In the room, on this case. All these people. And not one single, solid lead?'

Beresford flushed slightly. A look of anger swept across his eyes. He clearly didn't like having his professional integrity brought into question.

'So what? Some cases are like that. You should know, you've probably worked on plenty.'

'Yes I have.'

'Well, then. You know what it's like. All you need is that one spark to ignite it, that one thread to pull and the whole thing starts to unravel. It'll come.'

'Have we got time for that, though? Phil Brennan was abducted this morning. By someone answering your description driving a car exactly like yours. You were here, you say. Fine. But I think we need to cultivate a sense of urgency, wouldn't you say? Step things up a bit?'

That anger was back again. 'What d'you mean, "You say"?'

Imani sighed. 'Sorry. I didn't mean to be confrontational. I just want to get things moving a bit faster, that's all.'

Beresford nodded.

But before he could reply, a voice called from somewhere in the room.

'Boss?'

They turned. It was the detective who had been staring at Imani moments earlier. He became aware that all eyes on the room were on him now.

'I've got something,' he said. 'Think we've got a name.'

Beresford turned to Imani before crossing the room. 'That quick enough for you?'

He went over to the other detective.

Imani was about to follow. But she couldn't shake the feeling that she had glimpsed – just glimpsed – something in Beresford's eyes on the announcement. Anger? Fear? Which one?

She followed him across the room.

17

Pork and chorizo goulash. Just as she had said. And it was good, too. He wondered where she got the recipe from – or rather how she had obtained it – because it tasted the same as if he had made it.

She sat opposite him, staring at him, watching him eat. Still dressed in a facsimile of Marina's clothes. Her face eager, expectant. Waiting to be praised for the good she had done, seemingly needing that acknowledgement.

He had found himself in a wheelchair, coming round after the tasering. He was sitting in a copy of his dining room but again the lights were low, even lower than he had them at home and that was so low that Marina always complained. In the darkness he could make out the walls, the door. Everything looked flat, lifeless. Near to his house, but not quite.

The table that he sat at was different too. It was a copy of the real one but not right. The one in their house in Mosley came from a store that had gone under in the credit crunch and no one had stepped in to take their place. No one made furniture or furnishings like that shop any more. A good copy, then, but not perfect. A detail that jarred.

But the cutlery, the plates were all the same. They might have been his.

There was one other thing in the room. A doll. The same shape and size as his daughter. Dressed like his daughter.

Sitting at the other end of the table, half in shadow. A dish of food in front of it.

A mad woman's idea of a complete family.

He thought it best not to mention it.

'Well?' she said eventually, eyes gesturing towards the food. 'D'you like it?'

'Yeah, it's good.'

A satisfied, even smug, smile appeared on her face. For only a few seconds, then it was replaced by doubt.

'Good? That's it, is it? Just good?'

'Yeah, good. It's pork and chorizo goulash, what more would you like me to say?'

'Is it the best one you've ever had? Better than Marina's?'

He put his fork down, stared at her. 'I thought you were Marina.'

Anger flashed in her eyes. Anger and an unhinged malice. 'Don't get clever, you know what I mean. She's gone. Old and worn out.' A smile. Still with the same unbalance in the eyes. 'I'm here now. And I'm her. But I'm so much more than her. So I'll ask you again.' She picked up a knife as she spoke, began idly toying with it, caressing it. 'Is mine better?'

'Yes,' said Phil, becoming afraid of arguing, 'yes it is.'

She sat back, beaming once more.

'Though to be fair, she never cooked it. It was always me. My dish.'

Her eyes stared at him once more. Unblinking, unmoving. Unreadable. But not good. He knew that.

Eventually she regained her composure. 'Well,' she said, 'from now on it'll be me cooking it.'

He said nothing. She smiled once more, head to one side.

'I want to make you happy, Phil. I want to give you everything you love.'

'Right.'

'I understand you, Phil. Like no one else on this Earth. I understand you.'

Phil said nothing. Just ate in silence.

He had one hand free. The other was strapped to the arm of the wheelchair. As were his legs. It must have been quite a struggle to get him into it from the bed, he thought. And then to get him into this room. Did she have help to negotiate the stairs? Were there any stairs? Was there a lift? Too many questions.

And then there was what she had said to him, whispered, in the bedroom. Those two words had stunned him. While he ate he had thought about them, tried to rationalise her knowledge. Anyone could have discovered that, he tried to convince himself. Anyone. That wasn't so special. But there was something in the way she had said it, the look in her eyes. Like she knew what she was talking about. Like she had been there . . . And that was something that terrified him. He had to get away from her as soon as possible. He definitely wasn't safe.

But he didn't think he would get answers by being confrontational. Despite the creeping fear he was experiencing, he knew the best thing to do would be to tamp down his rising hysteria, go along with her, find out what she wanted. Then hopefully identify her weak points and exploit them.

And hope – somehow – that in the meantime Cotter and her team were looking for him and would find him. Before it was too late.

He finished the goulash, put down his fork. She was still sitting there, staring at him, face expectant. She needed something from him.

'Great,' he said. He tried to remain calm, despite the pounding in his chest. But it seemed he had said the right thing.

'Now,' she said, getting up, 'don't worry about the dishes,

105

leave all that to me.' She looked down at him. 'Am I going to have to taser you again to get you back to bed?'

'Do I have to go back to bed? I've just eaten.'

She frowned, thinking.

'It's not what I would do at home.'

She didn't even say *You are home*, he noticed, so busy was she thinking. She was taking his words as a test, proving to him that she knew his routine.

'No,' she said eventually, 'let's go into the living room.'

'Good idea,' said Phil. Careful not to antagonise her, but also demonstrating to her that she knew what he did with his evenings. He hoped she would find the gesture – at least on the surface – respectful. Then he tried to push the point. He nodded towards the doll at the end of the table.

'What about her?'

The woman glanced at the doll, back again. The expression on her face was of incomprehension. 'She'll stay here. She doesn't leave the table until she's finished her dinner. And then she can go to her room.' She smiled. Back in control. 'Leaving us alone.'

'Right,' said Phil. 'So into the front room we go.'

'Yes.'

'And you can tell me more about this darkness you think I have inside me.'

She froze. Turned to him. Her eyes as icy as her voice when she spoke. 'I'll decide when we talk about that. I'll decide when you're ready.'

'Same with those little pills.'

'Exactly.'

Phil managed what he hoped was a shrug, which was a struggle when all he was feeling was increasing despair. He had been counting on getting her to open up, find out more about her. He would have to be patient. Hope that she didn't

106

get tired or bored and do something deranged in the meantime. 'Fair enough,' he said, trying to make his voice light. 'Let's go.'

'I'll have to blindfold you first, though.'

She didn't wait for him to speak, just pulled a blindfold from somewhere on her person and tied it tight round his eyes.

'There.' He heard her voice beside his ear. She smelled like Marina. Or rather almost like Marina. But not quite. A flawed copy. 'Exciting, isn't it?' She giggled. He said nothing. Gave no indication that he had heard her or would respond.

He felt her pull him away from the table, manoeuvre him across the floor. He tried to work out where the door would be, if he was heading towards that. He was. Then, with a slight bump, he was pushed over the threshold. Immediately the air changed. Became colder, dank almost.

Then the air changed again and he was turned to a stop.

'There now.'

His blindfold was removed and he found himself in a facsimile of his living room.

She spread her arms out, smiled once more. 'You like?'

'It's . . . ' He looked around. Again it was too dark, again flat and two dimensional. 'Lovely,' he said. 'Homely.'

'Oh it is, my love, it is. And you'll be very happy here. In your new life. Your *old life* and with me again.'

Phil said nothing. She walked over to the wall where he had his hi-fi equipment. Music filled the air. She turned to him once more, almost jumping up and down with joy.

'Like it? It's one of your favourites, isn't it?'

It was. Band of Horses. Their second album. 'Yeah,' he said, still feigning enthusiasm, 'great.'

'And I've got you this.' She passed him a bottle of beer. 'Your favourite as well. Isn't it?'

'Well, it used to be.'

She had been quivering with emotion, at getting things right. Now she stopped dead. Like a marionette left hanging without a master. Phil said nothing more, knew he had made a mistake. He waited.

The room held its breath, Band of Horses singing about funerals and monsters.

'What?' she said. Her voice was flat, the word intoned. Not a question, a warning.

'I just . . . I don't drink that any more. Lager. I've gone onto craft beer now. That's all.'

Nothing. Just those unblinking eyes.

Phil was beginning to feel fearful. 'You weren't to know. Don't worry.'

'I wasn't to know.' The same dead monotone. 'I wasn't to know . . . '

She began advancing towards him.

Phil looked round, realised there was nowhere he could escape to. He was still bound to the chair, only one arm free.

'*I wasn't to know . . .*' Low and chilling.

'It's . . . no. Don't . . . it's no big deal . . . '

She stopped directly in front of him, stared down. Breathing like she was trying to keep something under control. Phil felt fear. Real fear. He couldn't move, couldn't escape.

'What about the darkness in me?' he said, desperately. 'I need to know about that . . . You can't . . . I need to know . . . Please . . . the words you said to me, I have to know about that. About how you know about that.'

She ignored him. 'Anything else?'

'What?' Phil was genuinely puzzled.

'Anything else you think I've got wrong?' The words dripped with disdain.

Emboldened now by a sudden hopelessness, by the thought that he had nothing to lose he said, 'That table.'

'What?' Hissed at him.

'The dining room table. Close, but . . . '

She swooped down on him then, plucked the beer bottle from his hand, raised it above his head.

'Just . . . no, wait . . . '

He tried to lift his arm to protect himself. It didn't work.

The bottle came down, glancing across his head. The pain was immediate and immense. He tried to cry out, to reason with her, but she was beyond that.

'Can you . . . wait, I'm—'

Down again. Beer frothing and raining everywhere. Glass connecting with skull. More, even deeper, pain.

'Please, I—'

She swung the bottle again. This time he tried to react, to move. Using his free arm he propelled the wheelchair forward with as much speed as he could manage, aiming for her legs.

He made a sloppy connection, but it was enough. He unbalanced her and she dropped the bottle, losing her footing and stumbling backwards.

She righted herself, stared at him. Didn't speak.

Phil held his breath and, through the pain, waited to see what she would do next. Fearful of what she would do next.

He didn't have to wait long. She came forward, grabbed his free arm and secured it to the arm of the wheelchair with the same thick leather straps his other arm was held by.

'No, wait . . . '

She ignored him. Stood back, stared at him.

'Goodnight.'

She turned, left the room. Flicked the light switch off.

Phil was left alone in the darkness, only the throbbing, debilitating pain in his head for company.

Biting Back

*S*he had thought she was immune to flattery. She was wrong.
He was older than her. Obviously. And he knew a few of
the girls at the home. Came to pick them up, take them out. She
could guess what they were getting up to. And she was jealous. Just
a bit. No. Not jealous. That wasn't right. Curious. That was a
better word.

Sex was something she hadn't tried. Hadn't even had much of
a desire to try. She was happy with her studies and the way the
other kids treated her. With respect. Or rather fear. But for sex
she didn't have any feelings that way at all. And it didn't bother
her. If she was meant to have them, or going to have them then
she would. But she knew about it. They all did. Some of the older
girls, leaving the home and trying to get a place at the YMCA
already had kids of their own, or they were on the way. Some had
contracted STIs. All of them claimed to know everything there
was to know about it, from the best way to orgasm to the most
perverted way to do it. Their talk made her curious, nothing else.
Especially because she didn't believe the girls knew what they were
talking about. But it was something else to learn, to experience. So
when this older boy started paying attention to her, her curiosity
was piqued.

He had a car. He would pull up outside the home and she
would watch him letting out one of the girls. Or a couple of them,

sometimes. They always smiled, looked a bit lost, stumbled as they walked. Drunk. She could tell that. Or on some drug. And they were dressed in short skirts and high heels, neither of which they could walk in. Michael, who was running the centre, always said the same thing to them as they came back in.

Told you not to go with them, they're bad news.

Shut up, Michael, one of them would say, you're just jealous.

Not up to me what you do, just be careful. But she could tell his heart wasn't in the words. She could tell he didn't really care one way or the other what they got up to.

But these girls all had money. And new clothes. And presents from their boyfriends. So they told Michael where he could stick his concern.

And then one day, one of those girls came up to her.

Tel fancies you, she said.

They were sitting in the TV room. Hollyoaks was on. For some reason most of the kids liked it. She didn't. But she pretended to so they wouldn't think she was weird.

Who's Tel?

In the car. And Dev. He said he likes you an' all.

She didn't know what to say to that. So she said nothing.

The other girl, Ellis, stepped it up. So d'you wanna come out with us? He's comin' round later.

This was her chance, she thought. To satisfy her curiosity. See what it was all about.

OK, she said.

Ellis sat back, looked at her funny. That wasn't the response she had been expecting. But then this kid was a weird one. Fine. Let you know when he's here.

The car was low on the road with a noisy engine, big wheels and tinted windows. Ellis seemed impressed by this so she pretended to be as well.

She got in the front seat, Ellis and Dev in the back. Tel was driving. He wasn't particularly handsome. But he seemed to find her attractive, judging by the way his eyes travelled all over her, looking down her top as well.

What's your name, then?

She told him.

Good, good. Here. Have some a'this.

He handed her a bottle with clear liquid in it. Vodka.

No thanks.

He laughed. Go on, you'll like it.

She took it, took a sip. It burnt. She coughed. The others laughed at her.

Got to get used to it, ain't you?

She took another sip, a larger one this time. Didn't cough. Held it down.

Good girl, said Tel. Let's get going.

Where? she asked.

You'll see.

They drove off.

The music was as loud as the car. Behind her, Ellis and Dev were touching each other in between swigs of vodka. Tel laughed. Fancy a bit o'that?

She shrugged. It didn't look that exciting.

Dev passed round a joint. Again it made her cough. Again they laughed. Again she silenced the laughter on the second attempt.

Here we are, then, said Tel, pulling the car up in front of a large house. It looked a bit like the children's home but more anonymous. Cars were parked in front of it. Lights were on inside.

Come on, then, said Tel.

They got out. Went to the front door. It was opened by a well-dressed man. He looked Tel over, then at her and the others. Told them to come in.

They entered.

The house was more stylish and opulent than the home. Whoever

112

lived here had money. There were men, all older, some very old, in the front room. There were girls about her age with them. Some boys, too. They all looked interested at the young arrivals. One came up and stood in front of her.

This her? The new one?

Tel nodded.

Never been touched? Guaranteed?

Guaranteed. Tel stood there as if waiting for something.

We'll sort it later, said the man. He turned to her once more, smiled. It wasn't pleasant. Hello there, what's your name?

She told him.

Very pretty. Come along, my pretty thing. Let's get going.

He grabbed her arm, pulled her away.

She turned round, frightened now, trying to twist away. Looked at Ellis for an explanation.

Who just laughed. Sorry, she said. If I didn't bring you it was going to be me. And I ain't up for that again. Have fun. She waved and laughed again.

The man dragged her away. Her heart was beating fast, too fast. Faster than it had done since all those years ago at that not safe safe house. This was one of the men. It had to be. Or someone like him.

Please . . . stop . . .

But he didn't.

You going to beg? Oh good. I like it when they do that.

Terror. That was what she was feeling. Pure, stark terror.

The man kept talking, telling her what he was going to do to her but all she could hear was a voice, asking her to count to a hundred. Can you do that?

He dragged her to a room. Slammed the door shut and started to undress. Then he turned to her.

She closed her eyes. She wasn't curious any more. She just wanted this to stop. All of it. She tried to think of something happy.

113

*Thought only of the Wignalls. Was that it? Was that happiness?
She tried again. Snow angels.*

And that just made her angry.

*But she didn't have time to think about that because the man
had forced her down in front of him and was pushing her head
towards him.*

Go on . . . that's it . . . you little slut . . . go on . . .

*And then she couldn't breathe. This horrible, stinking hard thing
in her mouth. And he was pushing her, pushing her . . . up and
down, up and down . . . and she couldn't breathe, and couldn't
think and was starting to gag . . .*

Snow angels.

That's what was in her mind once more.

Snow angels.

And anger.

*For all those times she had thought of what happened. All the
times she imagined it coming out differently.*

Count to a hundred. Can you do that?

*And she had. But she had heard those words and counted to a
hundred more times than she could remember over the years. And
sometimes something different happened. Sometimes someone burst
in and saved them. Sometimes it was her parents, sometimes it
was her brother. Sometimes it was her. Those were the times that it
hurt the most. The ones when she had fought back, jumped up and
grabbed the gun, started shooting. Killing them, saving her parents,
her brother. Those were the ones that hurt the most. Because she
hadn't done that. Hadn't fought back.*

But here she was. With a chance.

*Anything can be a weapon. She had read that in a book, seen it
in a film. Anything. And what did she have? Herself.*

*The man was groaning and sweating, pushing her head harder,
his hands rougher. Faster. And that was when she did it. Used her
weapon.*

Bit down as hard as she could.

The man screamed. She kept biting. He screamed some more. Tried to pull away from her. She held on to him. Snarling. Growling. Not letting go.

Eventually others came running to the room and managed to get her away from him. The man was led screaming and crying from the room. She never saw him again.

She looked up at the others, staring down at her. There was Tel and Dev. And Ellis too. All staring at her in horror. In fear. And she loved it. Because this was the last time she would be someone else's victim.

Ever.

Ellis had kept her distance after that. Word had gone round once more that she had done something scary and the rest kept their distance too.

They had wanted to punish her. Teach her a lesson in some way. But all of them, staring down at the half-dressed child, mouth and chin covered in dripping blood, hadn't known what to do. So they had sent her back to the home.

And as the time passed she watched. Ellis took other girls away. Plenty. And yes, they got presents and nice clothes and all of that. But she noticed something different about them. Like a light had gone out in their eyes. They drank. They took drugs. Trying to fill that hole inside them that the men had hollowed out. They disappeared, never heard from again. One of them killed herself. Several others tried. And she knew what they all were.

Victims.

That wasn't going to happen to her. Oh no. She kept telling herself that. Never. Never.

But still, the car kept arriving and the girls kept going. And it was a constant reminder to her of what had happened. Of how scared she had been. The ghost-like victim girls drifted around the *home, haunting her memories. And she couldn't have that. So she decided to do something about it. Nightmares had to be faced. So she would confront this one head on.*

One night she heard the car outside. Ellis got up, ready to go. She stopped her.

I'll take over now, she said.

Ellis stared at her. What d'you mean?

My job. I find the girls. I bring them over. I take a cut.

Ellis stared at her, terrified. She wanted to say something, assert her authority once more, but the look of steel in her eyes stopped her.

She walked out to the car. Tel saw her coming, looked as scared as Ellis had.

I'm taking over from Ellis. I'll supply the girls. You get paid, right?

Yeah . . .

And now I do. You're just the driver. I do the work. We split the money.

They won't like it . . .

Let's ask them.

But Tel didn't want to do that. And he was so scared he agreed. And that was that.

It was a good arrangement. She made money. She had to pay off Michael at the home like Ellis had done, as she had suspected, for turning a blind eye to what was going on but that was OK. And the girls became victims, not her.

And everybody was happy.

Until she met a girl called Fiona.

Marina stared out of the window. It was clean, a double-glazed unit in a uPVC replacement frame. The view: a railway line, an industrial estate and beyond that a road. In the middle of all that, on a patch of reclaimed brownfield land, had been built a relatively recent housing development, all small orange boxes, and adjacent to that were the beginnings of a shed-based retail park. It still looked like somewhere Marina wouldn't want to live. She couldn't imagine anyone would look forward to coming home there.

'Gorgeous, isn't it?' said a voice behind her. 'It's the view that sells it.'

Marina turned. Caitlin Hennessey, the current manager of the children's home, was behind her. Tall, her blonde hair artfully mussed, dressed in various combinations of florals, denim and wool with a pair of brightly coloured, neo-designer DM boots on her feet. Just what Marina would have imagined. But she also displayed a core of compassionate steel and a no-nonsense protective attitude. Not what Marina would have imagined this time but, given what she did for a living, what she would have hoped to see.

'I'm sure it's always the first consideration in council-run homes,' said Marina, smiling.

Caitlin nodded. 'Of course. And then they make sure

there's no expense spared in providing for the kids we have to look after.'

After the abortive and, if she was honest, heartbreaking call to Anni, Marina had called Rainsford House, the children's home on the outskirts of Chelmsford in Essex where Fiona Welch had spent the majority of her adolescence growing up, and got straight through to the manager, Caitlin. After explaining who she was and what she wanted, Caitlin had said it would be better to talk face to face rather than on the phone and was she anywhere nearby? Marina said she would be there as quickly as she could.

So, deciding not to check in with Cotter, fearing her response if she knew what she was about to do, she had phoned her work colleague and friend Joy, asked her to pick up Josephina from school, and drove straight from Birmingham to Chelmsford.

She had felt guilty at leaving her daughter with friends, no matter how reliable and trustworthy they were. She had given her word to Josephina that everything was going to be all right and while she was sure she wasn't the first adult to tell that lie to her own child, it didn't make it any easier to bear. Josephina had yet to discover her father was missing. Another confrontation she was dreading.

The car journey there had been full of such thoughts. Guilt had lain oppressively on her. Not just Josephina but also Anni. She should have realised how traumatised her friend still was, still grieving over Mickey. The last person she should have asked for help. Especially without giving anything in return. All she had thought about was Phil. Finding him. Getting him back safely. And then: neutralising this woman once and for all. In whichever way possible.

She had turned the radio up as loud as she could bear it in the car, tried to let the aural wallpaper of Radio 2 wash away her guilt, compartmentalise her feelings. She could feel hurt later. She had work to do.

It was now dark. The light from the room reflecting on the glass, turning it into a mirror, letting Marina see her frazzled reflection. Professional, she thought. Look and act professional.

The room had four beds, each placed at corners, all trying to give the impression of individuality and personal space. Different coloured duvets, a small set of shelves adjacent to each bed personalised by the owner's own belongings, a cheap self-assembly wardrobe.

'We try and provide a home,' said Caitlin, sensing what Marina was thinking. 'Or at least a safe and happy environment. The kids come to us for all different reasons. Parents can't cope, parents in prison, no parents ... all sorts. We don't generalise. We do what we're meant to do, by law and inclination.'

'Looks like you're doing a good job.'

'We try.' Caitlin gave a wry smile. Marina knew that wry needed only two letters to become weary.

'So,' said Marina, putting her back on track, 'Fiona Welch.'

'Yes,' said Caitlin. She looked at Marina, scrutinising her. 'What did you say this was concerning? And which police force are you with?'

'West Midlands,' she said. 'And I'm not an officer; I'm a consulting psychologist working on an investigation. I can give you the name of the DCI in charge if you'd like to check.'

'You already did on the phone. And I've already checked.'

Shit. Marina held her breath.

Caitlin smiled. 'DCI Cotter said that given the nature of the investigation she wasn't surprised that you were on the way to see me.'

Marina breathed out. 'That's good of her.'

119

'Now, shall we go to my office?'

They did so, walking through the rest of the home as they went. Marina was impressed by how Caitlin was running it. It had a good feel to the place: the staff and residents seemingly getting along fine. They had taken this forbidding old house on the edge of Chelmsford and turned it into somewhere less imposing, more welcoming. She could see the children were well looked after and cared for. They behaved just like regular teenagers. But Marina knew from experience how much of that was bravado. She tried to imagine Phil in a place like this. Couldn't.

They reached the office and Caitlin made them comfortable. One of the teenage boys was given the job of making tea for the pair of them.

'This should be an adventure,' said Caitlin.

The tea arrived eventually and the door closed.

'Fiona Welch,' said Caitlin.

'Yes,' said Marina. 'She was here . . . when? Late nineties?'

'Round about then. I don't have her exact details to hand. I could get them sent on to you.'

'But you remember her?'

'I remember the case, obviously. The news. Doorstepped by the tabloids. Not an experience I want to repeat.'

'Quite,' said Marina.

'And I also remember because of what happened while she was here.'

'What did happen?'

Caitlin paused. 'You have to remember something. Each and every generation and the theories and practices of that generation tend to come as a reaction against the previous one.'

'Same in my line.'

Caitlin nodded. 'Right. But I'm not saying everything done then was wrong and everything we do now is right. There's good and bad in both. And that's what makes – or should make – good practice.'

'So what happened here then that was so bad?'

'This place used to be badly run. Very badly run. The Dark Ages, we call it now. At around the time Fiona Welch was here the management was lax. Drugs were allowed on the premises. As was alcohol. As was sex. Now we know that sometimes happens, all these teenagers with raging hormones, course it does. And we have to try and legislate for that as realistically and honestly as possible. But there were people here, in charge, who weren't always as stringent as that.'

Marina felt a sense of dread at what was coming but still had to ask the question. 'How d'you mean?'

Caitlin looked at her, her eyes weighing up what to say. Eventually she continued. 'All I can tell you is what's a matter of public record. If you're in a hurry it may speed things up. Otherwise you'll need to come back with a court order. Sorry, but that's the way it has to be. I have my position and this home to protect.'

It was less than Marina had hoped for but about what she had expected. She nodded.

'Right. You know all those old scandals about children's homes? Letting pimps prey on the most vulnerable? Renting the kids out to rich paedophiles? All those tabloid headlines.'

Marina nodded.

'Well, it pains me to say it, but this was one of the worst. When Fiona Welch was here. She was right in the thick of it.'

'Oh,' said Marina, sitting back. 'She was one of the victims?'

A smile crept across Caitlin's features.

'Not quite.'

19

'Jason Lansdowne. Local bloke. Address in Essex. He matches. Result.'

Imani – and the rest of the room – looked at the young officer who had just made the announcement. The atmosphere had changed in the room, the surge of energy palpable. Like they'd all suddenly taken a jolt, become electrified. She knew what they were all thinking and feeling: breakthrough.

'Brilliant work, DC Matthews,' said Beresford, then turned to the room. 'Let's keep going. DC Matthews, come and tell me what you've got.'

Red-faced, he stood up, walked to the front of the room. Imani noticed just how young he was, how small. No, not small, compact. Neat. Everything in proportion, just waiting for life to fill him out. His suit was uncreased, sandy hair short and conservative, no stubble on his smooth face. He looked as if he didn't know whether to be embarrassed or arrogant about his discovery.

'Right,' said Beresford, sitting down at his desk and looking up, 'let's be having it. What you got?'

He didn't introduce Imani so she did so herself.

'Detective Sergeant Imani Oliver, West Midlands. Here temporarily.'

'Detective Constable Simon Matthews.'

They shook.

'Waiting,' said Beresford.

Matthews cleared his throat. 'Jason Lansdowne. Address 46 Holloway Crescent, Leaden Roding. That's in Essex, sir, near Chelmsford.'

'I know, DC Matthews, keep going.'

'Apparently he's been missing a few weeks now. His wife notified the local force but because they live on the border with Hertfordshire there seems to have been a mix-up and the information went there.'

'Why?' asked Imani.

'He, er . . .' Matthews was flustered. 'He worked in Bishop's Stortford. Over the line. He spent most of his time that way. His wife said he'd probably be there. It was only recently that we got involved.'

'Has he vanished before?' asked Imani.

'He's got a history of it, apparently. Gets drunk and disappears for a few days. At first his wife didn't think anything of it. But when he'd been gone for longer than a week she called it in.'

'Tolerant woman,' Beresford commented. 'Has she been contacted?'

'Not yet. We'll have to inform her.'

Beresford sighed. 'Hate informing the families. But I suppose as senior officer in charge—'

'I'll go,' said Imani.

Beresford frowned. 'Why?'

'Well, you'll be needed here. I could take DC Matthews with me. I've got to do something to be useful. May as well be that.'

Beresford actually looked disappointed, Imani thought. Usually a copper would jump at the chance not to have to be the bearer of bad news. So why did he seem so put out?

She studied him further. Something about him made her

123

uneasy. A few minutes earlier, when the rest of the team had been adrenalised by Matthews' discovery, she had glanced at Beresford and he didn't seem to be sharing in the exultation. His reaction was more of trepidation, she thought. And that couldn't be right. He had hidden it well, but from his expression it seemed as if he hadn't wanted the information to be discovered and was putting a brave face on it.

She dismissed the thoughts as ridiculous. She was imagining it.

And yet he had wanted to do the death knock . . .

'Fair enough,' Beresford said, although his eyes said a different thing. 'Off you go.' He glanced at his watch. 'It's getting late. Once you've done that, call it a day. I'll want you in here bright and early tomorrow. You got anywhere to stay?'

'Haven't had time to sort it. I'll find a B and B on the way back.'

Beresford nodded. 'Go on, then.'

Imani turned to Matthews. Smiled. 'Get your coat, mate. You've pulled.'

It was worth it just to see his expression.

Matthews drove. His car, some kind of Toyota, Imani noted, seemed as shiny and compact as he did. Even though it wasn't new it seemed to have a new car smell. Same as Matthews, thought Imani, then felt slightly guilty. But only slightly.

Off they went down the A12. Patches of countryside were interspersed with industrial estates and railway lines. At times the railway ran alongside the main road, as if the cars were being invited to race the trains.

Matthews had asked her why she was there, what was her part in the investigation.

'Phil Brennan,' she said. 'He's my boss over in Birmingham. He disappeared this morning.'

'So I heard. You think there's a connection between that and the case we're working on?'

'That's what I'm here to find out.'

They drove on. Matthews had the radio tuned locally. An Essex-accented DJ playing songs that should have been in a nursing home. She tuned out. Matthews held the wheel rigidly. It seemed like he hadn't exhaled since he got in the car.

'What's he like?' asked Matthews eventually.

'Who?'

'DI Brennan. He was before my time. But we heard a lot about him. Made a name for himself. One way and another.'

'Bit of a trouble magnet, you mean?' Imani smiled.

'Yeah,' said Matthews, relaxing slightly.

'As a boss? Good. Really good. Encourages you to think outside the box, you know? Be creative. Follow procedure, but not slavishly. Be inspired. And he's a nice guy, too. As far as I know him.'

Matthews nodded. Said nothing.

'How's Beresford?' asked Imani.

Matthews hesitated before answering, seemingly choosing his words carefully. 'He's . . . well, he doesn't sound much like DI Brennan. Quite the opposite, actually.'

'Not much of a maverick?' said Imani, smiling again at her choice of words.

Matthews barely smiled. 'By the book, all the way.' And said no more. Though from his expression, Imani guessed there was more he wanted to say.

Eventually they turned off the main road, went round winding, tree- and bush-lined country ones. The satnav directed them.

They pulled up in a small cul de sac of red-brick houses, fifties, Imani guessed, all looking ex-council, now with uPVC windows and front doors. A fair few of them had white vans parked outside them.

'Thought that was an urban myth about Essex,' said Imani.

Matthews frowned.

'The white vans,' she pointed out.

'Lot of blue-collar workers live round here,' he said, straight-faced. 'Electricians, builders, that sort of thing.'

'Right.'

He turned to her. He still hadn't loosened his seat belt, she noticed. 'Can I say something?' He looked concerned.

'Sure,' she said.

'Before. In the office.'

'Yeah?' Imani had no idea what he was on about.

'"Get your coat, you've pulled." I just wanted you to know that I'm married. That I . . . I don't do things like that.'

'Fine,' said Imani, not knowing whether to actually laugh out loud.

'I'm sure you meant it as a joke, but I just . . . didn't want to get off on the wrong foot. That's all.'

'Fine by me, and yes, it was a joke.' She pointed to the door, opened it. 'Shall we?'

He looked at her once more. This time there was fear in his eyes. 'Can we just stay here a few minutes and go over what we're going to say? Please. I don't . . . I . . . this is a bad time for his wife. He may have a family. I just want to get this right. I want to make sure they have as little distress as possible.'

He looked really worried. Imani closed the door again.

'Sure,' she said. 'Let's get it right.'

20

Marina waited for Caitlin to continue.

'Fiona was – according to the reports – a bright girl. Exceptionally so, in fact. It was picked up on straight away.'

'What does that mean?'

Caitlin studied her mug, looked back up again. 'Even the bright ones don't always make it. Not from here, or places like it.' She leaned forward, eyes imploring. 'This is off the record, of course.'

'Of course.'

'I mean, we do what we can. And there are success stories. But sometimes intellect isn't enough. Heart isn't enough. Drive isn't enough. For most of the kids who go through care homes just making it to adulthood, getting a regular job, having a planned family is a result in itself.'

Caitlin's eyes drifted away past Marina. Past the room.

'And Fiona Welch?' prompted Marina.

Caitlin blinked, back with her. 'Exceptional. Like I said. She loved school. Couldn't wait to get there.' A small laugh. 'Something else that marked her out. We did all we could to push her. Encourage her. And it was going well.'

Caitlin stopped. Marina picked up the cue.

'Until?'

Caitlin's tone changed. Harder. What warmth there had

been when talking about the hope for Fiona Welch now all but gone. 'There was another girl, apparently.'

Marina nodded. 'A disruptive influence? Always the way.'

'Not disruptive, no.' Caitlin searched for the correct word. 'More ... malign. Yes.' She nodded. 'Malign.'

Marina leaned forward. A surge of excitement ran through her. This was it. She was on to something. This was what she had come to this place hoping to hear. She tried not to let her excitement show too much in case it led Caitlin, made her sense the way Marina wanted to hear the story, tailor it that way. Even unconsciously. She had known it happen before – experienced it – and the testimony ended up being worse than useless. 'Malign? A kind of leader–follower thing? Like one wouldn't have turned out the way she did if she hadn't met the other one?'

Caitlin frowned, looked at her mug once more. As she looked up she caught Marina with a grim smile. 'This is the trouble, isn't it? The unreliable narrator.'

Marina was slightly taken aback by the words. Not what she had expected to hear. 'What? I would never have called you that. I'm sorry if I've ... '

Caitlin shook her head. 'No, no, I didn't mean it that way. Not you. Or me, for that matter. Well, all of us actually. I was speaking generally. We try and summon up the past, pull out our memories, thinking we've got a perfect grasp of the facts as they happened, we've remembered things perfectly. Our memories haven't been coloured by our emotions. But they have. Or we've allowed the emotions of others to do the colouring. So everything's subjective. We're all unreliable narrators, really. In our own way.'

'But if you're ... I don't get it. If you're worried about telling me something that may turn out to be incorrect, why not just check the files?'

'I don't have them. All I have to go on is the rumours and stories that did the rounds at the time of Fiona Welch's death.'

'Where are the files, then?'

'Child Services. At the council offices. I'd have to check with them, see if they'd would allow those files to be released.'

Marina took a deep breath. Saw Phil's face swim into her vision. Felt a tremble within her as it did so. An urgent reminder of a ticking clock. She damped it down, continued. 'Could you phone over? See if I could look at these files?'

'Why is that so important?'

Marina scrutinised the woman opposite her. Wondered how much she could trust her with. Came to a decision. Tell her. That way she might put her in touch with someone who could help or . . . 'There's been a woman impersonating Fiona Welch.'

Caitlin leaned forward, interested now.

'She . . . long story short. She's killed and . . . and abducted someone.' Marina paused. She didn't need to know everything. Just enough to get her onside. 'And I'm part of the investigation looking for her. Fiona Welch was seen as a way in.'

'Right.' Caitlin nodded, taking the information in. 'Right. I'm sorry, but I'll have to put in an official request. No way round it, I'm afraid.'

'But this is—'

'I'm sure it is. But we can't just let confidential records out to everyone who asks for them. There are protocols. Even in cases like this. Especially in cases like this.' She glanced at her watch.

Marina picked up on the signal, sensed she was losing her. She leaned forward, made one last attempt. 'Is there anything, anything at all you can remember?'

Caitlin sighed. 'Wish there was. Sorry. As I said, most of this was before my time. My information was second-hand.'

'Who did you get that from? Could I talk to them?'

Caitlin stiffened. 'I'm afraid not.'

'Why not?'

'Well . . . it's difficult, I'm afraid.'

'In what way?'

'He . . . left under something of a cloud. He was in charge when Fiona Welch and the other girl were here. We've been instructed, collectively again, not to have anything to do with him. You'll have to find some other way to communicate with him.'

Marina started to protest. Caitlin checked her watch again. Stood up. 'I'm sorry, but . . . '

Realising she would get no more, Marina took the hint and left.

On the way out, Marina noticed a woman trying to pretend she wasn't looking at her. Older than Caitlin, she looked like she worked there. Marina didn't know whether to take any notice of her or not. The woman made her mind up for her.

'Wait,' she called, glancing round as Marina reached the door, checking no one else was in earshot.

Marina turned, waited for the woman to catch up with her. 'Yes?'

'You been in there with Caitlin? Asking about Fiona Welch? You looking for Michael Prosser?'

'Who?'

'Used to run this place.' She smiled. It was even more weary than Catlin's. 'I worked here then, an' all. Should have been me you talked to.'

'Why, what would have told me?'

'Michael Prosser's address.'

A shudder of excitement ran through Marina. 'Was he the one running the home when Fiona Welch was here? Caitlin said he left under a cloud.'

130

Another laugh. 'Putting it mildly.'

'And he can help me? Where can I find him?'

'Here,' she said, slipping a piece of paper into Marina's hand. 'Address.'

'Thank you.' Marina frowned. 'Why are you helping me?'

'Because I want you to give him a message.'

'OK. What?'

Another laugh. 'Tell him Mary hopes you rot in Hell, you fucking paedophile cunt.'

And with that she walked off.

21

'Mrs Lansdowne? Judith Lansdowne?' Imani held up her warrant card, introduced herself. 'Could we come in, please?'

She watched as the features of the woman in front of them ran through a whole range of emotions. Confusion ramped up to hope, wavered towards doubt, then finally plummeted to despair. All in a few seconds, all before she had spoken. Imani had been unfortunate enough to have witnessed it plenty of times before. In fact she expected it. Would have been surprised if she hadn't done it.

Judith Lansdowne was large, long dark hair, wearing velour sweatpants and a T-shirt. Her eyes looked tired, her skin sallow. She looked like she had given up hope and was bracing herself for something bad to happen to her long before they had arrived.

'It's Jason, isn't it?' she said, nodding, confirming her own words.

'Could we come in, please?'

The woman opened the door fully, allowed them to enter. The house looked fuzzed with dust and dirt, like it hadn't been cleaned or looked after for quite a while. A smell of frying on top of stale fat came from down the hall. A clatter of music from the TV came from the living room. She went into that room, hurried a teenage girl out. The girl turned and looked at Imani and Matthews as they entered.

'Go upstairs, Rhiannon.'

The girl looked between all of the adults, reading expressions. Wanting to speak, wanting to stay. Wanting to know what was going on but probably guessing.

'Just go upstairs, I said.'

The girl reluctantly did so.

Judith Lansdowne picked up the remote, turned off the TV. Threw it on the sofa, turned back to Imani.

'It would be better if we all sat down,' said Imani.

They sat. Imani and Matthews on the sofa, Mrs Lansdowne on the chair.

'What's happened, then,' she said, more statement than question. 'You don't come round here mob-handed if it's good news, now, do you?' Her voice, although sounding naturally quite loud, was beginning to shake. 'Would just be a phone call, wouldn't it? Congratulations and all that.'

Imani looked at Matthews who was sitting on the edge of the sofa, hands between his knees, eyes wide. Clearly not going to stop her talking. Down to me then, she thought, going back on what they had agreed in the car.

'I'm afraid, yes,' said Imani. 'It's your husband. We've . . .' No easy way. Straightforward was best in the long run. 'We've found a body we believe to be his. We . . . I'm sorry, Mrs Lansdowne, but you'll have to come and identify him.'

Judith Lansdowne seemed to deflate at the news. Like all the bones had been suddenly removed from her body and the rest of her just melted into a pool on the armchair. Her head dropped.

They sat in silence while she took the news in.

'I'm sorry, Mrs Lansdowne.' Matthews spoke.

Judith Lansdowne started to nod then, kept nodding, agreeing to something only she could hear, something she had told herself a while ago. Wheezing and sighing as she did so.

They waited for her. Tried to emotionally absent themselves from the room, give her the time and space she needed.

Eventually she looked up, spoke. Her eyes looked wet but no tears had fallen.

'Where?' she asked, still wheezing, like the air was having trouble leaving her body.

'In Colchester. The old Dock Transit building. We think . . . we're treating his death as suspicious.'

She looked up then, glance sharpening. 'What d'you mean, suspicious?'

Imani gave a nod to Matthews. His cue to speak. 'You might have heard, there've been a series of deaths, suspicious deaths, murders, we're treating them as, in Colchester and the surrounding area. You might have seen it on the news.'

He stopped. Just keep going, thought Imani, silently urging him.

'I saw . . . yes,' Judith Lansdowne said, 'I saw something about that.' She thought for a few seconds. 'He was one of them?'

'He was.'

'They said they was . . . they was all hanged . . . '

'I'm afraid so, Mrs Lansdowne,' said Matthews.

And then those tears, long pent-up, came for Judith Lansdowne.

Matthews made them all tea. Seemed glad to have something to do. The teenage girl, Rhiannon, had been listening on the stairs, had heard her mother crying, come to investigate. She now sat with her on the arm of the chair, as they both held each other up.

Imani had told the two of them all they knew about finding her husband, her father. But she still had questions to ask, blanks to fill in. A job to do while wading through another's grief. The part of the job she truly hated. A lot of coppers tried to get it over with quickly, do the questions by rote or wait until later, just get out and hand it over to Family Liaison. But not Imani. She knew that these minutes were often important. When the next of kin would say something unguarded that could present a lead.

'We're actually a little unsure as to when he was . . . ' She looked at the daughter, found an angry challenge in the girl's eye. Like she didn't want to be treated as a child, wasn't afraid to hear what had to be said. Imani, emboldened by that, continued. 'When he was killed. We just wondered if you could tell us how long he had been missing.'

Judith looked up. 'How long?' She gave a snort. 'Told you, didn't I? Went to see you, reported him missing. You didn't do nothing about it.'

'When was this, Mrs Lansdowne?' Imani could sense the anger building up in the woman. First grief, now anger as she digested the news, looked for someone to blame.

'Nearly three weeks ago. And what did you do about it? Nothing, that's what.'

'To be fair,' said Matthews, chiming in somewhat unexpectedly, 'when you reported him missing you did tell the desk sergeant at Bishop's Stortford police station that he had done this before. That your husband had a history of disappearing for a few days then returning with his tail between his legs, some wild stories for his mates and an almighty hangover, isn't that right?'

Imani said nothing but was secretly impressed. He had been paying attention.

Judith Lansdowne fell silent. Imani saw an opportunity.

'What did your husband do, Mrs Lansdowne? For work, I mean.'

'You mentioned in the missing person's report that he could be away for long periods of time,' said Matthews.

She nodded, slightly chastised after her outburst, more cooperative. 'Photographic reproduction. Screen printing, that kind of thing. But large-scale, you know? Conventions, stuff like that.' She put her head down, stared at the floor.

'How d'you mean?'

She looked up again. Spoke listlessly. 'Like if someone wanted some billboards at the O2, something like that. His company would print them, transport them, then rig them up. That kind of thing.'

'Right. So he was away for long periods of work and also ...'

Judith Lansdowne hesitated, looked at her daughter but something in the girl's expression said she knew what her mother was going to say next.

'He ...' She sighed. 'Rhiannon knows this. No secrets now. Things weren't right between us. Between Jason and me. Hadn't been for a long time.'

'In what way?' asked Imani. 'Money worries or ...'

'He wouldn't come near me, wouldn't ...' She snapped the words out then fell silent, sighed. 'God knows what he got up to when he was away. That's why I wasn't ... He always sent money, made sure we were taken care of. And we didn't get it. That's when I thought something was wrong. When I reported him missing.'

'So,' said Matthews, 'you've no idea where he could have been, what he could have been doing that led him to that warehouse?'

'No idea at all.' She sighed, looked suddenly tired as she spoke.

Imani looked at her, really looked at her. Seeing her for the first time. Not someone who was a potential source of leads or an unpleasant duty to perform but a woman who was heading towards middle age, losing her looks, gaining weight, stuck at home raising a child, dependant on the money of a man who roamed all over the place. And now he was dead and Imani understood what the tears had been for earlier.

Not for his death.

But mourning for a husband she had lost a long time ago.

22

It was late, it was dark and Marina knew she shouldn't have been there. But she couldn't help it.

The address the woman Mary had given her was for a block of flats in what Marina judged to be the less exclusive part of town. Well-maintained thirties and forties semis had given way to more recent buildings. Low, red brick, two and three storey, arranged in L-shaped courtyards like prison wings. Cracked concrete pavements and selective street lighting. Maze-like roads that seemed to never come out at the same destination twice, all choked full of parked cars making navigation if not near impossible then certainly difficult. The kind of place that seemed designed to discourage outsiders.

Marina tried hard not to feel discouraged.

She had checked Michael Prosser out as soon as she got back to her car. A simple Google search was all it took. There was plenty there. He had been in charge of the Rainsford House children's home during the time Fiona Welch had been there. The Dark Ages, Caitlin had called it. It wasn't hard to see why. He had started by turning a blind eye when the girls – and some of the boys – in his care became victims of child sexual exploitation. This progressed to actually procuring and enabling this to happen. Even picking to order.

Eventually he had been reported, there was a trial, a custodial sentence and he had been released. Living quietly at an undisclosed location, as one report had it. However the location wasn't that undisclosed. He was found and became the victim of a particularly vicious attack. And that was the last she had on him.

The more she had read, the more she had become disgusted with him. She could see why Mary wanted her to deliver the message. She even wondered whether she had been behind the attack.

Putting that all to the back of her mind, she parked her Prius as near to the flat her satnav had sent her to as she could, locked it, checked again that she'd locked it. Then walked towards the flat.

A narrow alleyway confronted her. The streetlight was out. Trying once again not to ask herself what she was doing there she walked on. Something crunched underfoot – broken glass, broken pavement, she didn't know – and the sound echoed round the walls like sonar announcing her location.

She came through the alleyway, found herself in a courtyard. The weak yellow streetlight showed up a square of patchy grass decorated with old fast food wrappers, crumpled tabloid pages and selected discarded household appliances. She thought she had stumbled onto the set of *The Wire*.

Except this was no set. This was real.

She walked round the perimeter of the square, heading towards the flat she wanted. She saw no one but felt eyes on her constantly.

She reached the outer door, opened it. A timed light came on inside as she did so. A black rubberised floor covering felt sticky beneath the soles of her boots. It shone dully and deeply and would have looked more at home in a fetish club. The hallway had a textured ceiling with fake miniature stalactites dripping down. The walls were a colour that she could only describe as 'functional'.

She walked up the stairway to the first floor, found the flat she was looking for. Checked her watch. Probably too late to be calling but also late enough for him to be at home. She knew immediately which door was his. It had been vandalised with graffiti and painted over. And it had been reinforced after what looked like signs of forced entry. She found a buzzer. Rang it.

No reply.

She tried again.

She could hear a TV from inside. Eventually there was a shuffling sound as someone made their way to the door. She waited.

'Who's it?'

'It's . . . my name is Marina Esposito. I'm . . . Caitlin Hennessey sent me.' She thought that name rather than Mary's would help her get in.

'Why?' No curiosity, more of a statement.

'She . . . I'm working with the police. Could I . . . could we talk please?'

'What have I got to talk about?'

'If you open the door I'll tell you.'

Nothing.

'Please, Mr Prosser.' As she spoke she found it hard to keep the tiredness from her voice. 'I've come a long way, I've had a hell of a day and I'm very tired. And I need your help. Please just answer my questions and I'll leave you alone.'

Silence. Eventually she heard the door being unlocked, chains being removed and it opened.

'Five minutes,' he said.

She summoned up a smile. 'Thank you.' And entered.

She walked down a hallway to a living room. There was a bookcase full of books but they looked old and unread for a long time. Some DVDs rested beside them. A TV, big but aged, occupied one corner. Old, sagging furniture sat around like tired squatters. An off-brand laptop was open on the floor, screen grey with dust and greasy finger smudges. The lighting was low, a couple of ancient occasional table lamps, nothing else.

'Sit down, then.'

She turned, getting her first real look at Michael Prosser. He was a big man, like he had been fit once but had run to fat. His stained sweatpants and old jumper needed a wash or perhaps burning and replacing. But it was his face she was drawn to. She knew she shouldn't stare but also that she couldn't help it.

Where his left eye should have been there was just a rough pink crater that resembled a lunar surface more than skin. The terrain spread towards his hairline, down to his jaw. She tried to look away but he had caught her.

'Acid,' he said, sitting down. 'You've probably read about it. Not everyone gets public sympathy and a rebuilding job. Not everyone can be a pretty fucking model.'

'What happened?'

'Someone threw acid at me,' he said, his voice aiming for matter-of-fact but unable to hide the bitterness beneath, 'fuck d'you think?'

He snapped the TV off. The room fell to silence. Prosser looked at her. She couldn't read him.

'What d'you want, then?'

'I'm part of a murder investigation and I'd just like to ask you a few questions, if that's all right with you.'

'You're not a copper. Don't look like one. Or act like one.'

'I'm not. I'm attached to the investigation. I'm a psychologist.'

He smiled. His face split, cracking unpleasantly. 'Another

one. Just what we need. Seen enough of them in my time. So what's this investigation, then?'

'Fiona Welch.'

Prosser froze. Marina was sure she saw fear in his one eye. 'What about her?' His voice low.

'Someone's been pretending to be her. Calling herself by that name. This person has killed . . . well, we don't know how many people she's killed. And now she's abducted someone. We have to find her.'

'Abducted?' He snorted. 'You'll never see them again.'

Marina's heart skipped. Both from his admission and what he had actually said. She was onto something. But she needed to move quickly. 'So you know who she is, then?'

Prosser's mouth clamped shut. 'Didn't say that.'

'But can you—'

'You're not a copper, you said?'

'No. I'm not.'

'So I don't have to say anything to you. Legally.'

'No, you don't. But—'

'Then fuck off.'

Marina stared at him. 'Mr Prosser, please.'

'I said fuck off. Get out. Now.'

Marina took a deep breath, another. This was a chance. A real chance to get a solid lead on Phil's whereabouts. He needed to be handled with finesse. Coaxed into giving out the information. She tried a more personal approach.

'Mr Prosser, please. The person who's been abducted is my husband. A police officer. This woman has threatened my family before and thinks she has some kind of hold over him.' She leaned forward, her body language begging. 'Please. We need to find her. We need to stop her. And I need to find him.'

Prosser stared at her without speaking. Marina waited, holding her breath. Eventually he smiled.

'No.'

Marina stared at him, opened her mouth to make another entreaty. He got there first.

'Your old man's a copper, yeah? Hope he gets what's fucking coming to him.' A malicious glee dancing behind his one eye.

Marina felt anger rising within. Couldn't stop herself from speaking. 'Is this because you lost your job? What you were doing in the children's home, how you were running it?'

He stood up, moved towards her, his face now red with anger.

She continued. 'Or rather what you were running it as.'

He stopped, stared at her. 'You cunt.' The words spat at her.

Anger spiralled out of control now. 'You can't blame anyone for that acid attack, can you? Apart from yourself.'

'Fuck you.'

'I'm sure the people here love having a nonce for a neighbour.'

He was on her then. She tried to get up but his hands found her. She could smell him, the sourness of his body, his clothes. She nearly gagged. She struggled, tried to get away, but he had her.

'I don't know who fucking sent you or why but you're out, now.'

Saying that, he grabbed her hair with one hand, her shoulders with the other and marched her down the hall towards the door. Her feet fumbled and dragged, she caught one ankle with the other, nearly went over. Would have done if he hadn't been holding her upright. She tried to speak, explain. No words would come out.

He opened the door, threw her outside. She lost her footing, stumbled, fell down on the landing.

The door slammed behind her. She lay there unmoving.

And hating herself for what she had done. Embarrassed for the outburst.

Stupid, stupid, stupid . . . Should have waited, should have seen him in the morning. Should have . . . should have . . .

She felt suddenly exhausted.

She picked herself up. Her ankle was throbbing. She made her way slowly and painfully towards the stairs.

23

Phil opened his eyes. Still clamped to the chair, his body unable to move or even relax. He felt pain down from his neck through his back, along his legs. Stiffness from sitting in the same position combined with rigidly cramped muscles resulting from the tension in his body, the fear, the uncertainty in his mind. And the more purely physical pain: his head still throbbing and aching from the attack.

After the woman left the room, the first thing he had done was give in to the pain. He knew that was the wrong thing to do, like sleeping after a concussion, but his body gave him no choice. The pain, combined with his terror-filled situation, caused his body to close down, to either sleep or pass out, he didn't know which. He didn't care. The numbness, the absence of being, came as a relief.

But now he was awake again. Disorientated, alone. His body felt like it had been on a long-haul flight with an economy airline and not allowed to move for the duration of the trip. It screamed out for movement. But, try as he might, straining and pulling against the leather straps, he just couldn't provide any.

He tried to calm himself down, quell his rising fear. Take deep breaths, focus. Calm. *Calm*. Think about what he knows, try to put it in order. Try to formulate some kind of plan. Don't give in to despair or helplessness. Don't have another panic attack. Not now.

Focus. How long had he been in the chair? He didn't know. Could he tell from the way his body was feeling? Unlikely. Several hours, it felt like, judging from the pain in his muscles. No other way to judge what time it was.

What can you see? Nothing. No, wait. That wasn't quite true. His eyes had adjusted to the darkness and could make out vague shapes and shadows in his surroundings. He was still in the facsimile of his dining room, could still make out the features on the walls. Light, faint and small, must be getting in from somewhere. But he had no way of knowing whether it was artificial or day.

Close your eyes, listen. What could he hear? Nothing around him. Silence in the building – wherever and whatever the building was. Listen harder, expand his reach: still nothing. No TV, music, no traffic beyond, no noise from anywhere apart from his own movement, his own breathing.

No trace of the woman.

What else? He needed the toilet. His bladder was aching.

Phil sighed. He had rarely felt so alone.

He shook his head. The throbbing increased. He tried to ignore it. No. No. Don't give in to despair, to self-pity. He was alive. He had hope. He had to assume that Cotter had worked out what had happened, that she would have a team out looking for him. That Beresford – if it was, in fact, him – had been brought in for questioning and given him up.

Hope. That was all he had. And he couldn't give up on it.

In the meantime, he thought, if he was alone, he should try and turn that to his advantage. He looked round the room, eyes now as accustomed as they could be to the darkness. What did he see? What could he use? And then he saw it.

The door.

Yes, he was strapped to a wheelchair, but there was a door in front of him. A working door that the woman had used. Turned the handle, gone in and out. It closed, it opened. And there had been no sign of a lock on it.

Something small fluttered inside him. Hope. There it was again. He tried not to let it build too much, take on unworkable aspects, false properties, but he didn't dismiss it either.

Feeling the aches in his muscles diminish as adrenalin pumped through them, he wheeled his way towards the door. It was slow going, his bare feet, strapped at the ankles, being his only method of conveyance, his stomach muscles cramping as he used them to push too.

Gasping and grunting, he eventually reached the wall. He stopped moving, allowing his breath to return. The movement had left him light-headed. Black stars danced before his eyes, took away sections of the room from him. He tried to ignore them. Breathe deep. Concentrate. Just try to get out of that room.

He was up close to the wall now, able to see it closely. When the photographic images of his house had been enlarged the colours had leached away to near black and white, the sharpness of the small image now blurry. But he could still make out details.

He pushed himself round the perimeter of the room, examining those details, trying to work out, from what he could see, when the photos had been taken. Within the last year, he concluded. Not too recently because there had been certain additions to the room – ornaments, books on shelves, small things of that nature – but nothing large enough or specific enough to resonate in his memory. But it meant that someone had been in his house. With enough time to catalogue every room. And the worst thing of all, they had done it without him knowing or even suspecting it.

He kept moving, slowly, agonisingly slowly, until eventually he reached the door. Like the walls, it was a photographic representation of his dining room door, the one leading off to the kitchen. He didn't know where this one would lead but wouldn't have been surprised if his kitchen lay beyond, or at least a photographic facsimile of it.

The door handle was real. Three-dimensional. A copy of his, of course. Not quite perfect for close scrutiny, but good enough to be taken as the real thing from a distance.

Phil didn't care about that right now. All he wanted to do was open the door, get to the other side. See what lay beyond, negotiate his way to freedom.

He was facing the door. He tried to reach out, grasp the handle, but couldn't. The restraints held his hand too tightly. He would have to try it sideways. Grab it that way. He pushed back the wheelchair with his bare feet, agonisingly slowly once more, feeling even worse than when he had started because the handle was so tantalisingly close.

He tried to move the wheelchair sideways into the wall, found it wouldn't go. So he had to move it slowly backwards and forwards, incrementally, like trying to parallel park a large car in a too-tight space when he couldn't see the kerb.

Eventually he managed it. He was sweating, gasping for breath and again seeing stars once more when he came to a stop beside the handle. But he ignored all that. He had made it. He had done it. He was one step closer to freedom.

The handle was near his left hand. If he could reach out and pull it down then push his weight against it while still holding it the door would open. It had to. He thought again. Had it opened inwardly? Had she come through that way? A tremor of doubt ran through him. If that was the case his

148

plan wouldn't work. He thought once more. No. Outward. From the dining room, into the kitchen. Yes. He was sure of it.

He took a deep breath. Another. Tamped down his nerves. Grasped the handle.

And screamed.

24

Marina felt the cold of the late evening almost as keenly as she felt the pain in her ankle. The stairs had been a challenge for her but now, trying to make her way as quickly as she could through the estate and back to the car, she couldn't help shivering. She tried to use the cold to her advantage, concentrate on it, hope that by doing so it would take her mind off her foot. She hoped she had just twisted or sprained it. If it was broken she wouldn't be able to move for weeks. And that, she thought guiltily, desperately, meant she could play no further part in looking for Phil. And that wasn't something she was prepared to face.

The door slammed behind her. Upstairs, she thought, Michael Prosser was watching her leave. She had no idea what he was thinking but knew it wouldn't be good. She was still angry with herself for the way she had behaved with him. Unprofessional. Letting him wind her up like that. She had to rein her emotions in if she was to get anywhere doing this. Treat it as another case. Yeah, she thought. Because that isn't impossible.

She again ignored the square of scorched earth in the centre of the quadrant, walked round the outside. Kept to the light. Or what there was of it. Then she reached the narrow alleyway. She could see her car ahead. Only a few metres to go. But she was thinking so much on the way she had behaved with Prosser, so wrapped up in her own thoughts, that she wasn't aware of being followed.

It wasn't until she had set foot in the alleyway, walked away from the buildings, that she noticed. She was grabbed from behind, a strong, heavy arm wrapping itself round her throat, another arm round her midriff.

A muffled voice: 'Scream and I'll fucking cut you.'

She looked down. Her attacker had a knife against her throat. She didn't scream. Instead she spoke.

'I've got ... I've got money ... Here, take, take my bag, it's ... it's just under here ...'

She moved against the arms, heart hammering away, trying to get her bag out.

'I've got ... cards, my cards, credit cards are in there ...'

'I don't want your fucking money,' the figure said.

Because of the fear, the adrenalin and blood pounding round her system, deafening her to everything but her wildly running heartbeat, it took a few seconds for Marina to process the words she had heard.

'You ... what?'

The figure gripped her even tighter. She felt the air huff out of her lungs, her throat constrict. Couldn't get enough air into her body.

'What did you want with Prosser? What did he say?'

'He ...' She gasped, unable to breathe properly. Not enough air to speak with. 'We talked ...'

Tighter again. 'What about? I'm not fucking about here.'

'I ... we ... can't breathe, please ...'

The figure didn't relax its grip. Just pushed the knife against the skin of her throat. 'Answer the question.'

Marina felt wetness on her neck, a small stab of pain. The blade had broken skin. Her body now trembling she tried not

151

to move, barely to breathe. 'I . . . ' Focus. Concentrate. 'I asked him some questions. He wouldn't tell me anything.'

She felt the knife push harder against her skin. Tried to gasp, breathe her neck away from it. Couldn't.

'What kind of questions? Who about?'

'About . . . about . . . Fiona Welch . . . ' She didn't think it was a good time to lie. Or even attempt to negotiate. Do nothing to antagonise her assailant, inflame the situation. That was all that was running through her mind.

'And what did he say?'

'He . . . nothing. He said nothing. Wouldn't . . . talk to me.'

The figure didn't reply.

She could still hear the ragged breathing in her ear, smell some kind of aftershave on the scarf he was wearing. But no more words. Tentatively, she tried to speak.

'Look, just . . . just let me go. Now. I'll not . . . not report this, not say anything to anyone about this. I swear. Just, just . . . please let me go . . . '

'Shut up, bitch.'

Tighter again.

Marina made another attempt to reason. Perhaps her last one, for all she knew. 'Michael Prosser told me nothing. Now please, let me go . . . '

She didn't know what the reply would be. Because at that moment another figure appeared at the end of the alleyway, blocking out the light, cutting off Marina's view of the relative safety of her car.

She opened her mouth, attempting to scream to this new-comer, taking her chance, but she had no time. Because the figure, small, compact and all in black, began to move along the alley at speed, building up momentum as it reached Marina and her attacker.

The figure shouted four words. 'Close your eyes, Marina . . . '

Too scared, confused and numb to think actively and coherently, she mutely obeyed. She heard a sound, then a scream. And felt air flood her lungs once more.

She fell to the ground, opening her eyes as she did so.

This new figure had pepper sprayed her attacker in the eyes. She had then followed this up by taking out an extendable nightstick and bringing it down hard on the attacker's wrists and arms. As Marina watched, the attacker turned and, blinded and injured, ran as fast as he could.

Instead of giving chase, as Marina had expected the newcomer to do, she found herself being helped up from the ground.

'You OK?'

'Yeah, I think so. Thanks, I . . . '

Something about that voice made Marina turn. Took in this new person for the first time. All dressed in black Lycra and running shoes like a cat burglar or an athlete. With a black wool beanie cap pulled down low. The figure pulled it off revealing spiked peroxide hair, illuminated against black skin. The figure smiled.

'Can't leave you alone for five minutes, can I?' said Anni Hepburn.

Fiona

*I*t was the eyes that got her first. Big, sad. Not that that was unusual in itself; lots of the kids here had big sad eyes. Most of them tried to hide the fact. Put angry screens in front of them. Or funny. Or brave. The ones who didn't became the stragglers of the pack and got the sadness bullied and beaten out of them. But this one was different. Something about that sadness in those eyes that connected. In a big, big way. In a way that no one had ever connected with her before.

Yes. She could remember what she was doing the first time she saw Fiona. Nothing. Waiting. It was all she ever seemed to do there. Michael ushered the girl into the common room.

This is Fiona, he said. Look after her, treat her well. She's coming to join us. Live here. She's one of us now.

And off he went, back to avoiding whatever it was he was supposed to be doing.

Kids gathered round her. Hoping to project whatever they wanted of themselves onto the new arrival. Those wanting friends hoped they saw a friend. Those wanting a victim hoped they saw that. But what did she want when she looked at Fiona? She didn't know.

She saw a girl, a little underweight, her hair cut in an unfashionable style. Wearing clothes that were old but that she could sense she still had pride in. That must make her feel good to wear them. But it was what she saw in her next that broke her heart.

Damage, vulnerability. But deep, intrinsic to her. Not the kind

154

she could exploit, make worse. The kind that made her want to protect this new girl. Nurture her. This was a new sensation and she didn't know how to cope with it.

She went up to the girl. You're Fiona, she said.

Fiona nodded.

She gave Fiona her name.

Fiona nodded again. But this time reached out. To do what? Shake hands? Touch her? She didn't know. But she was glad Fiona did. Because as soon as Fiona's fingers touched her, it felt like an electric charge had been put through her body. She looked at Fiona. Right into her eyes. And knew that Fiona felt it too.

Responding, she placed her arm round Fiona's shoulder. Looked round the room. The rest of the children knew what that meant. Fiona wasn't to be touched, harmed. Fiona was protected.

And she felt so good about it.

Weeks passed. They became inseparable. Fiona enjoyed school and work too. They shared the same interests in music, TV shows. The fact that it was different to everyone else's just bound the two more tightly together. They even started to dress alike. She shared her money from pimping out the other girls with Fiona. It was one of the first things she had told Fiona she was doing.

They're weak, she said. They need someone to take care of them.

Is that taking care of them? Letting men do . . . She couldn't say the word . . . what they do to them?

It's either them or us, Fiona, she said, stroking the other girl's hand. If I wasn't doing that to them, one of them would be doing it to me. To us. D'you want that to happen?

Fiona thought. Shook her head. No.

No. Exactly. This way I make sure it doesn't happen. I keep you safe. And I get money to buy you things. She smiled when she said the last bit.

Why? asked Fiona. Why d'you want to buy me things?

155

Why? Because ... She knew the answer, the words, but she didn't want to say them. Or rather couldn't bring herself to say them. Even with Fiona. Because everything that had happened before meeting her was still part of her. That castle was still inside her. The walls thick and strong. But she had to say something – or do something – to show Fiona how she felt, what she meant to her. So instead of words she grabbed Fiona by the back of the neck, moved her head towards her own, and pushed her lips on to hers.

The kiss was returned.

The kiss was beautiful.

And just the start. After that there was no stopping them. The other kids knew what was happening. It wasn't the first time something like that had happened in the home but it was the most intense. And Michael knew too. But he didn't dare interfere or stop it or even, as he had done on other occasions, threatened to inform on the kids unless they allowed him to watch. So they were left alone. In their own world. Population: two.

She had never been so happy. Fiona's body, like her mind – her soul – was a beautiful, wonderful thing to explore. And Fiona felt the same in response. She could tell.

Fiona began to blossom then. There was still that damage, that pain inside her. But it started to fade as her happiness grew. She began to look beautiful. Smile. Have confidence in herself. And that just made her love Fiona even more.

But some of the other children began to notice the new, confident, even beautiful, girl. One of the boys in particular. Jack was an arrogant boy. Or at least full of bravado, bluff and boasting. She hadn't let him near her, but he had fucked (nearly) all the other girls in the home. And a few outside. He was dealing drugs. He was going to nightclubs and working for local gangsters. He was all of that. And he was keen on Fiona.

At first she found it quite amusing how Jack would flirt with

Fiona. How Fiona would have nothing to do with him. Belittle him and make him look stupid in front of the rest of the kids. But he kept at her. And gradually, Fiona began to respond. In her own small way. Flirting back with him, teasing him instead of traducing him. And she didn't like that. Didn't like that at all.

So she seethed, hated. She had never felt like this. It was the flipside of what she had felt like with Fiona at first. That gnashing and gnawing inside no longer pleasurable, just hateful. She didn't want to feel like this any more. So she confronted Fiona.

What are you doing with him? Why are you talking to him like that?

Fiona looked confused, then smiled. Oh, Jack. It's just fun. That's all. Nothing serious.

Well, I don't like it. I don't like you talking to him like that. He'll get the wrong idea.

What would the wrong idea be?

He wants to fuck you. And you'll let him.

Fiona smiled again. So what? It might be fun. I might enjoy it.

She couldn't believe what she was hearing. Not from her Fiona. I don't care, she said. You're not doing it.

Why not?

Right up close to her. Breath to breath. Because you're mine, Fiona. Mine.

And again, a smile. More crooked this time. I'm not yours. Really. What we've got together is great. But it's not everything. If Jack wants to fuck me, I might let him. And there's nothing you can do to stop me.

She stared at Fiona. At that still smiling face. And she realised something. She had misjudged the girl. Badly. The damage she had seen within her, that she had recognised, went even deeper than she had thought. There was something in her that was unreachable. That was wrong. Even more wrong than the damage inside herself.

She stepped back. Knew she had no control over Fiona any more. That she never really had. All the time she had been fucking Fiona, Fiona had been fucking with her.

It felt like her whole world was ending.

Fiona fucked Jack. She said she enjoyed it. But Jack didn't. Whatever she did to him scared the boy. Seriously scared him. So much so that he wasn't as loud-mouthed after that. But Fiona was happy. Happier than she had been since she arrived at the home.

And she desperately hoped that Fiona would come back to her now. That everything would be as it was before. She would forgive her – of course she would. If Fiona would just come back.

And she did. Kind of.

She got into bed with her that night. Looked at her.

What you do with the girls, she said. How you pimp them out to men.

She waited.

I think I'll join you. I think I'll help you.

She was so desperate to keep her she said yes.

And then lay awake all night.

PART FOUR

SEASON OF THE WITCH

25

'**M**orning, lover.'
    Phil slowly opened his eyes, didn't know where he was. Or why he hurt so much. Focused. Saw a pair of huge eyes, made-up, a face smiling at him. His first response was to return the smile. Then he slowly, and with a shuddering lurch inside him, remembered where he was. And who was smiling at him.

'Pleased to see me, handsome? Course you are.'

Phil's headache immediately started again. He felt tired, aching. Like he hadn't slept. Or if he had, hadn't rested. Then his memory slotted in more pieces. The dining room, the wheelchair. The escape attempt. The pain. Then . . . nothing. Here.

'How did I . . .'

'I put you to bed, silly. Had to take you to the toilet first.' She giggled. 'That was interesting.' She was wearing something else of Marina's. A black silk dressing gown. It was clear from the way her body moved, although Phil tried hard to avert his eyes, that she was naked beneath it.

'All that nonsense last night . . .' She got on the bed alongside him, then reached over to the bedside table, picked up a mug. It looked like one of Phil's own mugs from home. Part of a range Marina had bought. The detail unnerved him. He tried to rationalise it away, think that anyone could get mugs from Designers at Debenhams if they knew the ones they were looking for. But he failed. That detail had unnerved him. More than he wanted to admit to himself.

'Drink this,' she said, putting it to his lips.

He looked quickly to the bedside table. The two capsules were still there. She caught his gaze. Smiled once more.

'Not yet,' she said. 'You're not ready for that yet.'

He tried to speak, argue, but she didn't give him the chance. The drink was pushed to his mouth, the mug upended. Tea, he managed to taste between forced gulps. Warm.

She replaced the mug on the bedside table once he had drained it. She looked at him again. Smiled. Her mood playful, coquettish.

'What am I going to do with you, eh?'

Phil tried a shrug, a weak smile. 'Let me go?'

A flash of anger appeared behind her eyes. This time she controlled it, rode it out. Smiled once more.

'Go where, darling? There's nowhere for you to go to. You're home. Here. Now. With me.'

She stood up, locking her eyes on to his the whole time. Placed one knee on the bed. Began to slowly undo the belt of the silk dressing gown. Her tongue appeared at the corner of her mouth. A wicked grin appeared around it. Her lips bright red, an open, fresh wound.

Phil felt his heart racing. This couldn't be happening. It couldn't be.

'I've forgiven you. For last night. Because . . . ' An exaggerated shrug. 'That's what married couples do, isn't it? That's what being married is all about. Compromise. I mean, if I got upset at the tiniest little things that you said, where would we be?'

She waited as if expecting an answer. Phil wasn't even listening to her words. His mind had slipped a gear. Even after everything he had been through since he had arrived at this place with her, all the torment both mental and physical, he still couldn't believe this was actually happening. Not here, not now. Not to him. Definitely not to him . . .

'But seriously. Don't do it again. I might not be so forgiving next time.'

She pulled the belt apart, and with it the dressing gown. She slowly, and what she presumed was seductively, pulled the belt from the gown, let it drop at the side of the bed.

'I could have used that to tie you up with,' she said, giggling. 'If you weren't already restrained, that is.'

Phil tried to pull against his bindings. He was tied firm, the leather thick, unyielding.

'Please. Don't do this. Please . . .'

She leaned over, placed a finger delicately on his lips. 'Shhh.' A whisper. 'Don't talk. Don't say a word.'

She slipped the gown from her shoulders. Let it drop where it fell. Knelt on the bed beside Phil, legs apart. Proudly displaying her body. Eyes still locked with his, smiling all the time.

Phil's heart was hammering. He didn't know what to do. What he could do.

And then he felt something. His body began to betray him.

He was getting an erection.

She noticed, laughed.

'That was quick. Mind you, I put enough of those little blue pills in your tea so I'm not surprised. But just in case . . .'

She reached over him to the bedside table once more. He closed his eyes as she did so. Kept them closed as he felt her hands on him. Then felt a tightness round his genitals.

'There, that should keep you nice and big. You won't be going anywhere in a hurry now.'

He looked down. She had placed a small elastic band round the base of his cock. He lay back. Unable to comprehend what was happening, nearly unable to cope.

'Please . . . ' His voice so weak he didn't even know whether he had actually spoken the words aloud.

She ran her hands down her naked body, lifted her breasts towards him as if for inspection. He turned his head away.

'Playing hard to get? Got a headache?' She giggled. 'That's supposed to be my prerogative.'

She pulled back the duvet, slid into bed beside him. Pushed her body up against his.

'There,' she said. 'Isn't this cosy? Just a normal husband and wife having a lie-in. No kids, Josephina's with her grandmother, no work because it's a Saturday, so all we have to do is have a lazy time together.' Her hand moved along his body. 'A long, lazy time . . . '

He felt like he was about to have a heart attack. Everything was totally beyond his control. He had never felt more completely helpless in his life.

She stopped stroking, stared right into his eyes once more. 'It's all about that darkness, Phil. The darkness inside you. You see, I have to show you who you are. Who you really are. Only then can you understand who I am. Really, really understand. And when you do, you'll love me. Love me like you've never loved anyone in your life before. And then we can be together forever. But first you have to open up. Explore it. Welcome it. I'm here for you. Here to explore it with you. Show you your real self. So don't be afraid . . . '

He screamed, thrashed, pulled against the restraints, tried to avoid her caresses, her body's closeness. But nothing he did had any effect.

Slowly she swung one leg over him, straddled him. Looking down she smiled once more.

'I love you, Phil. So, so much.'

And lowered herself down on to him.

26

The morning briefing was, thought Imani, the same the country over. The surroundings might be different, the faces too, but the types were similar, even if there were fewer of them than she was used to on a major investigation. But the goals, the ultimate outcome, she expected, would be exactly the same.

Result. Resolution. The bad guys punished.

She perched herself on the front of Matthews' desk, making sure he had space to see round her. She felt she had succeeded in fitting in with the team. Or at least by not standing out. That was something. Even if, she thought, they weren't used to seeing too many black faces on this side of the country. At least not on this side of the thin blue line.

She had booked into a B and B just off Maldon Road the night before, preferring that to an anonymous budget hotel like she would normally have had to endure. She had had a good night's sleep, being so tired that she had just about collapsed on hitting the bed. Waking up had been different though; a sudden, startled awakening when the alarm sounded, a panicked glance round unfamiliar surroundings, heart palpitating, stomach lurching. For a few seconds she had thought she was back in that apartment at the mercy of the madman who had tried to murder her. A few deep breaths, a few minutes to reorientate and she was all right. Or as all right as she could be. She doubted she would ever be truly all right from it again. She never voiced those fears aloud, not even to the counsellor whose sessions she had been obliged to attend. But she felt the trauma was still inside her, still waiting for a moment to manifest itself. She just hoped that when it came, as it inevitably would, it wouldn't be too bad. That was all.

The noise in the room hushed as Beresford took to the floor.

'Good morning, everyone, let's get down to it.'

He had the room's attention. Imani looked at him, puzzled. His eyes looked sore. Red-rimmed, puffed up. Every time he blinked he winced slightly. Movement seemed to be causing him discomfort too. He smiled, apparently reading her mind.

'Sorry for my appearance,' he said, 'had an argument with a can of wasp spray last night. You think this is bad, you should see the wasp.'

Polite laughter from the room. Imani smiled to show she was joining in even though the line sounded like it had been prepared.

'Moving on,' Beresford said, then pointed to Imani. 'What did you and Matthews get from the victim's next of kin yesterday?'

Imani glanced at Matthews who looked back at her, gesturing that she should speak. Imani appreciated the courtesy. She stood up, referred to her notebook.

'We visited Jason Lansdowne's wife, the widow of the second body to be discovered. Gave her the news. Naturally she took it badly. She told us he was away a lot, didn't think too much of his absence at first.'

'He worked for a company that did large-scale screen printing for events,' said Matthews. She couldn't immediately decide if he was backing her up or anxious not to give her all the limelight. 'Went away a lot for work.'

'And was also,' said Imani, feeling suddenly competitive,

'from what we could gather, a bit of a lad. Had other women. He didn't seem to treat his wife with much respect.'

Beresford nodded. 'So not much there, really.' He smiled, gave a brief nod. 'Thank you, DS Oliver.'

Imani was taken aback. She hadn't finished. 'Sorry, sir, but there's quite a bit we can do on the back of that.'

Beresford folded his arms. 'Such as?'

'Well, talking to his co-workers. Seeing if they knew any of these women he was supposed to have been seeing. Names, a description, even. Getting a list of places he'd visited recently for his work. Then seeing if anyone saw him near the building he was found hanging in.' She stopped talking, aware that the whole room was staring at her. Apart from Matthews who had found something on his desk absolutely fascinating. 'Well, that's what I would do.'

Beresford gave a smile as false as a *Strictly Come Dancing* tan. 'Thank you, DS Oliver, for your contribution. We're very grateful.' He turned away from her. 'Right. Moving on . . .'

The briefing continued. The longer it went on, the more Imani's sense of unease built. Beresford, she noticed, seemed to be talking a lot but, when she broke down what he was saying into what had been done and what the plan was to take the investigation forward, not actually achieving much.

The meeting broke up. She looked at Matthews. 'So, what do we do today?'

Matthews shrugged, kept looking at his desk. 'Get on with things. Keep doing what we were working on.'

Imani looked round, made sure they weren't being overheard, leaned in closer to him. 'What d'you think of Beresford?' Her voice hushed, her face showing a slight grin in case anyone watching thought they were just sharing a joke. 'I mean really.'

Matthews looked up, a wary, startled look in his eyes. 'What d'you mean? He's the CIO for this case.'

'Yeah I know that, but he doesn't seem to be actually doing anything.'

Matthews didn't reply. Imani felt that she had to continue.

'I gave him all those potential leads to follow up, all the things we discovered yesterday, and he didn't seem interested.'

'Well, we can follow them up.'

'Yes we can, Simon, and we will. But don't you think it's usual in a case – any case, not just this one – for the CIO to be eager to follow up any lead that comes in? How else are the team supposed to make progress?'

Matthews looked away from her once more. When he spoke, his voice was a mumble. 'I'm sure the boss knows best.'

Imani stood directly in front of him. Determined to make eye contact. 'Are you? Really?'

He looked round, nervous, as if everyone in the room was listening to them. No one, as far as Imani could tell, actually was. Most people seemed to be getting on with work.

'I mean,' she went on, 'I read the report yesterday. Where was the PM on the three bodies? Held up, Beresford said. Why? Has anybody checked for them?'

'DS Beresford. Says there's still a hold-up.'

'The same with forensics. I mean, how long does it take for a report to arrive here? Are they sent by carrier pigeon? And what was all that about with his eyes? Wasp spray?'

Matthews said nothing.

Imani made her tone less harsh. 'Sorry. Getting a bit carried away. I don't mean to sound like I've come from the big city and we're used to having everything done for us. I just . . . well I hate to say this, but he seems to be a bit incompetent, that's all.' She shrugged. 'Sorry. I know he's your CIO and everything. Your work colleague and all that.'

Matthews looked round the room once more then back down to his desk. He seemed to be battling something internally, fighting to come to some kind of conclusion. Eventually he looked up. Eyes locked with Imani's.

'Let's go outside. Let's get a coffee.'

27

Marina and Anni had talked the night before. And talked and talked and talked. Eventually they had fallen asleep, Marina exhausted by the events of the previous twenty-four hours.

She opened her eyes, shook her head, realised where she was: Anni's spare room in her flat in Colchester. She immediately threw the duvet back and got up, pulling on yesterday's clothes before leaving the room.

She looked down at them, at the dirt and tears in her skirt, and remembered. The attack. Shuddered.

That had been the first thing she had said to Anni, stunned as she had been to see her there in Chelmsford.

'What are you doing here?'

'Followed you,' Anni had said.

Marina had thought for a few seconds, taken aback by the answer. 'You didn't know where I was.'

Anni had shrugged. 'Easy enough to find out. Knew you wanted help, followed your trail. Used to be a detective, remember?'

They had hugged then, Marina expressing her relief. She had kept hugging her friend as she thought about everything that had happened to her recently and began to break down.

'Hey, hey,' Anni had said. 'None of that here. Let's get away first.'

They had looked round for Marina's assailant but there was no trace of him.

'Still,' said Anni, 'he's going to have hell seeing tomorrow. That's something.'

'You should have run after him. Not stopped for me.'

Anni put her hands on her hips, spoke in a mock-hurt voice. 'That's the thanks I get for saving the damsel in distress.'

Marina managed a laugh. 'Oh shut up.'

They had then driven back to Anni's apartment in Colchester. Talking all the while.

'Sorry,' Anni had said once they were under way on the A12.

'What for?'

'You came to me for help. I didn't give it. I should have.' Eyes on the road, straight ahead, the whole time.

'No, it was wrong of me to ask. To just phone up and expect you to be there. Drop everything for me. Wrong. And selfish. Especially after everything you've been through.'

'I'm here, aren't I?'

'Yeah, but . . .'

'So shut up, then.'

More silence, more miles. Eventually Anni spoke once more.

'Doesn't matter, you know.'

'What doesn't?'

'How long we've been apart. How long it's been since we've spoken. None of that counts. Not really. Friends – good friends, proper friends – can just pick up where they left off. Or should be able to. No matter how long it's been or what they've been through since. So, you know. I'm here now.'

Marina nodded. 'Thank you.'

Anni tried a smile again. Marina knew it was covering real emotion. 'Thank *you*,' she said. 'Needed to get out of the house.'

From beyond the bedroom door, Marina could smell coffee. She ventured out in search of it.

Anni was in the kitchen area. Her flat was open plan, all straight lines, highly lit and modernist furniture. The direct opposite to Marina's place which was all curves, deep colours and old. Vintage, as she liked to call it. Hippy shit, as Anni often described it.

'You're awake,' said Anni. 'Thought I'd let you sleep for a bit.'

'What time is it?'

'Nearly half ten.'

'Jesus, we'd better get going. Why'd you let me sleep that long?'

'Because you were exhausted and you needed to rest. You'd be no good today without the sleep you've just had.'

Marina sat down on the sofa. Despite having angles that could have been measured with a set square, it was surprisingly comfortable. 'You not at work today?'

'The gym can do without me for a while. The unfit of the parish will just have to exercise on their own.'

Marina smiled, took the coffee Anni offered her. 'Thank you,' she said again.

'You don't have to keep thanking me.'

'I meant for the coffee.'

'Whatever.'

Marina took out her phone, checked for messages. Still holding the forlorn hope that Phil might have been released, come home. Called her. Nothing from him. But a few missed calls from Cotter. She played the several voicemails the woman had left. They all ran along the same lines. She was angry with Marina for just taking off like that and not telling her where she was going. If she had any solid leads she should have shared them with the team not gone out as a maverick on her own. She wasn't helping anyone like that, least of all Phil. And then a later one, more conciliatory in tone. Just call me. Please.

Anni looked at her. 'Cotter?'

'Yep. Wants me to call her.'

'You should.'

Marina looked at her phone. 'Maybe later.'

She had told Anni everything she had discovered the night before. About Fiona Welch's children's home, the other girl, Michael Prosser.

'You think that was him that attacked you?' asked Anni.

'I thought so at first, but I don't now. The person who grabbed me didn't smell like Prosser. And after being alone with him in that flat, I should know what he smells like. And it's not something you forget in a hurry. And then there's the pepper spray. He only has one eye. Doubt he'd have been able to run off like that.'

'Then who?'

'No idea. The only thing I can think of is that I was on to something and someone wanted me stopped.'

Anni nodded.

Marina drained her coffee mug, stood up. 'So what are we going to do today?'

Anni just looked at her. 'Get you in the shower, for a start. Then get you something to wear. Then you're going to phone your daughter and Cotter. Then we're going to do a bit of hunting round ourselves.'

'Couldn't we just—'

'No. In that order. You look like the wild woman of Wongo.'

173

'What?'

'Never mind. Just get a shower.'

Marina stared at her old friend. It felt like no matter what she said, who she talked to, there was only one word in her mind, one picture in her head: Phil. Find Phil. An overriding imperative.

'Look,' said Anni, as if reading her mind, 'I know you want to get going. But believe me, it'll be better if we do things my way.'

'Where are we going? To see Franks?'

'Franks was good to me, didn't want me to leave. But was very understanding when I did. I like to think I could rely on him. And I'm sure he's running this investigation. But I don't think I can just walk up to him and tell him to give me what he's got, I'm running my own investigation with you.'

'No, you're right. Any other friends on the team?'

'Virtually all new. No. You get your shower, I'll make a few calls. I know a couple of people who might be able to help us.'

Marina just stood there.

'Well, off you go. Day's a-wasting.'

'Hey, Anni.'

'Yeah?'

'Thank you. I really ... really ... '

Anni kept her face down, attention on her coffee, expression unreadable.

'Go and get your shower.'

28

Michael Prosser had seen it all, watching from his window.

That nosy psychologist bitch, the one who'd pretended to be nice because she wanted something but had ended up screaming at him when he wouldn't play along with her, insulting him, vile fucking bile, her. He had seen what happened to her. In the alleyway.

His first thought had been to call the police. His immediate, gut response. In fact his body had started to do just that, stomach lurching at witnessing the sudden attack, an involuntary reach for his phone. But he had stopped himself. Or something had stopped him. Instead he had just stood at his window, watching. He saw the man pull a knife on her. Hold it to her throat. He didn't hear what he said but he was sure it was something unpleasant. Good, he had thought, his cracked lips curling into a smile. What that bitch deserves.

He'd felt something run through him at that point, like a rusty sword piercing points within that he hadn't experienced feelings from for ages. Years, even. And he had discovered his hand reaching for the phone once more.

But again he had stopped himself. No. Don't do it. The reason had changed. In such a small space of time, the reason had changed. He wouldn't make a call. Not because of who that bitch was and how she had talked to him. But for another reason altogether. Fear. Of what, he didn't know. Or wasn't sure. But fear was enough. His last few dealings with the police hadn't been positive. There was no reason to expect this one to be. They would ask what he was doing at his window, why he was watching that woman, what she meant to him. And then he would have to tell them that she had been here, talking to him, asking him questions. And they would want to know what the questions were about. And he would lie. About everything, all of that. And then they would do a bit of digging and find out about him. And what he had done. And what had happened to him. And then they might forget about the person he had seen and turn their investigation on him. And he couldn't have that. He wouldn't have that. So he left the phone where it was.

And left whatever it was he was feeling alone inside him.

Yet still he had watched. And then something had happened that he wasn't expecting.

A tiny ninja girl, her clothing as dark as her skin, had rushed forward, attacking the attacker. Spraying him with something, making him scream and stagger off. And he had smiled once more. But this time there was no cruelty to it. Just a sense of justice being done. And a fluttering of something else inside him. An emotion he hadn't experienced for a long time. So long he couldn't name it, didn't dare put a name to it.

And he watched them walk away, arm in arm, while the attacker fled.

But that had been enough.

After that he had tried to go back to his life once more, or what passed for his life. But he couldn't relax, couldn't settle. The whole evening had upset him. In more ways than he wanted to think about.

It wasn't just that woman's visit. Or what – or rather who – she was asking about. It was more than that. Because he had seen the attacker. And he knew who he was. Oh yes. Someone like that wasn't easily forgotten. Who they were and what they were capable of. And because of that, he knew why the attacker wanted to silence that psychologist woman.

He had kept away from the window after that. The whole thing had set him thinking.

If he had attacked that woman then he knew she had been to see him. And if he knew that, then he must have been watching his flat. And if he had been watching his flat and hadn't got what he wanted from the woman, then he knew who would be next for a visit.

Michael bloody Prosser, that's who.

And if that was the case then things must be serious.

Deathly serious.

So Michael Prosser sat in his flat, emotions tumbling about inside him. He had tried to keep them quiet with whisky but it was just some cheap supermarket knock-off brand that burned rather than tasted. But even that was better than thinking, than feeling.

His hand went absently to the side of his face, to the angry red craters that were once his skin. A reminder. And a warning.

He could remember the name of the other emotion. The one he didn't want to acknowledge. Guilt.

But right now, the only emotion he would allow himself was the one he could not only name but readily embrace.

Fear.

29

'Well, I have to say, Simon – can I call you Simon?'
Matthews nodded.

'Simon, that this isn't the kind of place I expected you to bring me.' Imani smiled. 'Or any copper, for that matter.'

Matthews looked slightly uncomfortable, mumbled something about clichés. Imani looked round once more.

The Daisy Cup Flower Café on St Isaac's Walk in Colchester seemed to have a permanent smile, bright, cheerful and welcoming, if a café could be said to do that. A flower shop on one side, the café had blond wooden flooring, a fake turf counter and wall, mismatched but colourful armchairs and painted wooden furniture. Old forklift truck pallets had been painted white and turned into sofas stretching along one wall. It looked inviting and relaxing, off-beat and slightly bohemian for Colchester. And all the more incongruous because of the two police officers sitting in two mauve armchairs at a low table away from everyone else. They had walked there in silence, Imani's anticipation increasing to know just what Matthews had to say that was so important. Wondering if it would match her developing suspicions.

'At least I doubt we'll see anyone else from the station,' said Imani.

'That's the idea.'

Imani sipped her flat white. Just the right ratio of sweet milk to bitter coffee. Good.

'You come here often?' She hadn't meant it as a joke but a serious enquiry.

'When we're out shopping on a weekend. Hannah and I often pop in. It's a nice place.'

Something almost defensive yet apologetic behind his words. Imani didn't probe further. She felt Matthews was feeling he had opened up enough about himself and his private life for one day.

'So,' she said, leaning forward, 'what did you want to talk to me about?'

He gave a furtive look around as if he was a bad spy in an even worse spy movie. But still he didn't speak. She suspected she knew what he wanted to say, or rather who he wanted to voice his concerns about, and it didn't come easily to a man like him. A rank and file follower. Even for the greater good.

She decided to nudge him along. 'It's about Beresford, isn't it?'

He looked at his coffee. Nodded.

'About the way he's running this investigation?'

Another nod towards the coffee. A sigh, struggling to allow the words out.

'Well,' said Imani, realising she was going to have to start, 'I don't think our CIO is running this investigation very effectively. Do you agree?'

'Yes,' he said, the word tumbling out like a great weight had been lifted from his shoulders.

'The way he treated the information you discovered, the work we did yesterday, the way he dismissed what to do next, it's like he doesn't want this case to go anywhere. Is he always like this?'

'No,' said Matthews, eventually finding his voice, 'he's

usually good. You know, on the ball, taking decisions, good on intuition too. Knows the right way to take an investigation. Follows up all the leads. But not this time, for some reason. It's like he's ...' Another sigh. 'Oh, I don't know. I don't like talking about him like this. Feels disloyal. Not only that.' He leaned forward even further. Drawing attention to himself rather than deflecting it. 'This goes against everything I believe in, telling you this. My job's on the line here. I'm up for promotion. Higher grade, bigger pension, everything.'

'I know what you mean. I'd feel exactly the same if it was my boss. Totally disloyal.' She locked her eyes with his. 'But it's my boss we're trying to find. And I have to say, I'm not too impressed. Not by you, I mean. Beresford.'

Another nod from Matthews.

'I mean,' Imani continued, 'there's no PMs for any of the victims yet. What's the excuse for that?'

'Backlog, the boss said. You know that. It hasn't yet been given priority so we can't expect to get them quickly.'

Imani couldn't believe what she was hearing. 'Is he having a laugh? Three murders all with the same name in the pocket and it hasn't been given priority? And the person whose name they all have has gone missing? And he's a copper? Nope. Don't buy it. Not for one second. That would have gone straight to the top of the pile.'

Matthews chose that moment to become defensive. 'Maybe we don't have the resources that you have in West Mids. Maybe we have to make do with what we've got.' His voice unexpectedly fiery.

Imani drew back. Knew he was finding this difficult. Decided to continue in a more conciliatory tone. She wanted him onside, after all. 'Sorry. That's not what I meant at all and I apologise if it came out that way. All I meant was that

Beresford doesn't seem to be running this investigation in a way that'll get results. That's all. Like his eye's off the ball. Not looking where he's supposed to be looking.'

He said nothing. She continued.

'And I think you feel the same way, Simon. You wouldn't have brought me here for this chat if you didn't, would you?'

Another sigh. 'It's ... I don't like grassing on a senior officer. Especially one I respect and admire and have to work with when you've gone back to Birmingham. It's difficult for me. You have to understand that.'

'I do, Simon. Really I do. And like I said, I'd feel exactly the same if it was my boss. But I'd also think of myself as a good enough copper to be able to voice those concerns. Especially if the investigation was being put in potential jeopardy. If lives were at stake.'

He nodded once more. Not in defeat, but understanding.

'So what d'you suggest we do?' he asked her.

Imani looked round once more. It would be tempting to stay in this café, she thought. Drink another flat white, have some chocolate thing with it. Relax. Put aside all my suspicions and think that everything was going OK. But she couldn't. She had never run away from a challenge in her life. No matter what the outcome. When she was a kid growing up around Aston, being one of the smartest in the class wasn't the way to make friends, not the kind of classmates she had. So if she wanted to have friends she had to make sure her body was as sharp as her mind. Because everyone thought the class nerd was an easy target. And she was determined to prove them wrong. And she did. It cost her bruised knuckles, sore ribs and black eyes, but she achieved it. Her father had always told her that if she believed in something then it was worth fighting for, no matter what anyone else said. And she had lived by those words all her life.

She looked at Matthews, saw he was still waiting for answer.

'What would you do, Simon? If you thought an investigation was being handled wrongly? If you thought that certain procedures hadn't been followed?'

He shrugged again. 'Follow them.'

'Exactly what I would do.' She stood up, reluctantly relinquishing all thoughts of a second cup of coffee.

'Right,' she said. 'Which way to the morgue?'

30

'Malcolm?'

Malcolm Turvey turned when he heard his name, teacup nearly at his lip. He replaced it in its saucer, surprised to hear it being said aloud, more than anything. Especially in the tea room he was in where the clientele were aged and conversation never rose above a murmur.

He saw a small black woman with a shock of spiked blonde hair and a taller woman accompanying her. She was a looker: dark, curly black hair, strong Latin features and a figure that could make anything good. Even the jeans and hoodie she was wearing.

He then felt guilty for thinking that way. That was no way to think about a woman. Had a lifetime of working amongst books and reading the *Guardian* taught him nothing?

The tea room was one of a number on Sir Isaac's Walk in Colchester, an old building, all visible beams, supports and struts, with old-fashioned crockery and menu to match. The perfect place for beige-jacketed retirees to gather for lunch.

He recognised the black woman immediately. Beckoned them over. Stood up. Remembered his manners.

'DS Hepburn,' he said, his voice not as loud as Anni's had been. 'Please, come and join me.'

He moved the files, notepads and books he had scattered over the table into one central space and scooped them up, placing them in his oversized messenger bag, dropped it on the floor.

'Just . . . just preparing for another walk.' He smiled. 'Keeps me off the streets.'

The two women sat down. Looked at him. He noticed Anni staring at him for rather longer than he would have expected. Still got it, he thought. Then realised he should have squeezed that spot on the side of his nose this morning.

'Well, this is an honour. What can I do for one of our most distinguished ladies in blue?'

'Ex-lady in blue,' said Anni, pulling out a chair and sitting down. 'Retired now.'

'Oh.' He hadn't been expecting that. Somehow the lustre of being greeted by Anni Hepburn – Ms rather than DS now – was tarnished slightly. A lessening of the thrill he usually felt at meeting her.

Not that he was a police groupie or anything, oh no. He would never admit to that. Or having some unhealthy fascination with crimes, criminals and catchers. No. It wasn't unhealthy. Far from it. He saw it as making a study of important work. You can tell how civilised a society is by how it treats its criminals, he always said. At least he wasn't a collector of stuff, like other people he knew. Well, not much stuff. Comparatively.

'So, erm . . . to what do I owe the pleasure?' He tried not to look at the attractive woman too much. Didn't want to make her feel uncomfortable, so just had to content himself with casting surreptitious little sideways glances at her.

'Still work, Malcolm. Still something you might be able to help me with.'

Malcolm tried to stop grinning. *Help. Me.* If he had known this was going to happen to him today he would have worn a clean shirt under his anorak. Or at least a cleaner one.

'Anything. Anything. I'm at your disposal.'

Anni indicated the other woman. 'By the way, this is a friend of mine, Marina Esposito.'

Marina nodded in greeting.

Malcolm stopped moving, as if suddenly frozen. Had he heard correctly? 'Marina Esposito? *The* Marina Esposito?'

'Erm ... yes. I think so.'

He looked at Anni once more. Beaming. 'Oh thank you. Thank you. For bringing ...' He stuck out his hand, then retracted it, wiping the remains of raspberry jam on the side of his khakis, stuck it out once more. 'I'm a huge – *huge* – admirer of yours. Please ...'

He took her hand, shook it. Kept eye contact all the while. Smiling. Eventually Marina tried to remove her hand from his. He let it go, slightly ashamed at his actions. 'Sorry. Sorry. I'm just ...' He sighed. 'I've heard so much about you.'

He noticed Marina share a glance with Anni but couldn't tell what it meant.

'So, Malcolm. Help.'

'Yes. Of course. Anything. How may I assist?'

'How's the walk going?'

Malcolm stopped dead in his tracks, mouth hanging open. The walk? That was what they wanted to talk about? 'Ah. Well. It's ... fine. Actually, yes. After what happened it's been going great. Twice a week now. Make hay while the sun, and all that.'

'Good. I want you to tell me – and Marina here – what it was you discovered. Exactly what it was.'

'Well ...' He settled in, ready to give his spiel.

'Just the facts, please. Thanks.' Anni smiled. 'We're not punters.'

'No. Quite. Well. I walked them round the usual haunts, gave them the story, all of that. Then we reached the old Dock Transit building. I'd been on to the company that owns that building, asked them to leave it open. They hadn't done so, so I had to get one of the punters to pull open a door.' He laughed. 'Don't tell Health and Safety.'

They smiled politely. He continued.

'We all went inside. The lights weren't working – again, I'd been assured they'd be left on – so I had to improvise. Lucky I'd brought a torch with me. Then I started my story.' He paused. 'And then we found the body.'

'Hanging?'

He nodded. Swallowed. Excited to be telling them this now. 'Yes. From the gantry.'

Marina, listening, frowned. 'That's a high gantry. Must have been a lot of rope.'

'Oh yes. Indeed.' Nodding, eager to tell them everything. Give his own observations, if necessary.

'Did it look like it had been there a while?' Anni asked.

He frowned, actually thinking. 'If you mean were there any marks, signs of the body decomposing, not really. It just looked like a man.'

Anni leaned forward. 'Did you see anyone? Hear anyone?'

Malcolm shook his head. 'Like I said, we were just coming in. Just finishing that part of the walk.'

'You didn't see any shadows or figures as you were approaching?' Marina this time.

Malcolm blushed as he looked at her. Marina Esposito, asking him a question . . . him . . .

'Malcolm?' asked Anni. 'Think we lost you there.'

'Yes. Sorry. Right.'

He closed his eyes. Thought back to that night. Tried to go over everything again. The big man and his footballer wife girlfriend. The texting kids. He let his eyes scan the ground once more, tried to see anything . . . The . . .

'Yes.'

He opened his eyes. They were both staring at him. Waiting.

'I . . . don't know.' He looked away from them both, not able to hold their eye contact.

Marina leaned forward. 'What d'you mean you don't know?'

'Well . . . ' He couldn't tell them. Not here, not now. Even if it was Marina Esposito. 'There might have been a man, hanging around. It was dark. I couldn't be sure.'

'A man? Tall? Small? Wide, thin?'

Questions being fired at him, trying to think, trying to do what they had asked of him, trying not to tell them what he was really thinking about . . . 'Erm . . . tall, I think. Big.'

'Did you tell this to the police?' asked Marina.

'Er, no.'

'Why not?'

'Well, I er . . . I don't know. Like I said I, I maybe didn't see him. I don't know.'

Anni and Marina shared another look. Again he couldn't read it, but it was different from the first one, he knew that much.

'So what's happened since that night, then? The investigation.'

Malcolm just stared at her. 'I wouldn't know.'

Anni smiled again. 'Oh come on, Malcolm. I know what you're like. You'll have been all over this investigation like a rash. Exciting enough that this all happened in Colchester, but you finding the body? You won't have let this one go. So what's happened?'

Malcolm didn't know whether to be pleased or offended at Anni's words. But since she had come to him for information – and brought Marina Esposito with her – he decided to be pleased. Flattered even.

'Well,' he said, leaning closer, conspiratorially, 'nothing.'

Anni frowned. 'Nothing? What d'you mean?'

'Just that. Nothing. They're getting nowhere. No information, nothing to go on, the investigation seems to be grinding to a halt.'

'Who's in charge?'

'DS Beresford.'

Marina looked at her. 'Know him?'

'Little bit. Was just coming in as I was going. Full of himself. Self-described alpha. You know the type.'

Marina nodded.

'And he's not getting anywhere?'

'No PMs? Forensics? Nothing like that?'

He closed his eyes again. He really wanted to help, wanted to find the missing clue that would put the whole puzzle together, solve the crime. Him. Malcolm, solving the crime. He'd be a hero. Famous. He—

'Malcolm?'

He opened his eyes again.

'Lost you again.'

'Oh. Sorry. No. No, I can't think of anything more.'

'Well, thanks, Malcolm, you've been a great help. If you think of anything else . . . '

'I've got your number.'

Anni nodded, her expression once again unreadable.

The two women stood up to go.

'Thanks for your time,' said Anni.

'Thank you,' Marina echoed.

'Oh.'

Malcolm stood too. They both looked at him. Waited.

He looked at Marina, gave what he hoped was his most winning smile.

'Could I . . . could I have your autograph, please?'

A Thin Line

*T*hings were never to be the same again. She knew it, even as *she was saying yes to Fiona. Yes to everything. Yes. Yes. And the more she agreed with her, the more desperately she clung to her, the more she felt her heart weaken. Like Fiona had infected her with a terminal disease. A heroine from an old Gothic romance, diminished by love to waste away to nothing.*

Love. That's what it was. Not infatuation or a phase. Nothing like that. Love. The fortress walls she had worked so hard to keep in place all those years now well and truly breached.

And even knowing all that, she was powerless to do anything to stop herself.

Fiona had her. Any and every way she wanted her.

She tried to tell herself that it was an equal partnership. That Fiona and she picked the girls together, decided who to single out, how to nurture them. When to turn them out. And Fiona was right. Always right. The girls she chose were always the most damaged, the saddest, yet the most willing. Fiona could size them up straight away. She revealed a natural talent for turning suffering into money.

And Fiona seduced them in ways she had never done, couldn't have even thought of doing. Not just sexually – although that was involved too, a surprisingly gentle, nurturing and caring weapon in Fiona's arsenal, at least at first – but in other ways too. Kinder ways. Ways that made it even worse for the girls in the long run.

Making them feel beautiful, wanted. Special. Important. All of that. Usually for the first and sometimes only times in these girls' lives.

Why d'you do that? she asked Fiona after a while. You don't have to do all that. But she suspected she knew the answer before she'd spoken. The real answer.

Makes it easier for me to control them when I have to, she said in reply. Less trouble. Then I can move on quicker.

I, she noticed. Not even We. Not any more.

The real answer? Because Fiona enjoyed it. Got a kick out of seeing them fall so far. Watching hope die in their eyes and knowing she had been responsible for that. Manipulating them. Her human puppets.

And she could understand that. Because it was something she had got a kick out of herself when she was in charge. But Fiona enjoyed it so much more. Got off on seeing that damage be removed, replaced by a thin sliver of hope, then removed once and for all, the damage brought back tenfold. Fiona thrived on that dark energy.

When she was in charge. Yes. She had actually thought that.

Because she knew what had happened. She wasn't stupid. And eventually had to admit it to herself. Fiona had taken over. Yes, Fiona still kept her alongside, but that was, she felt, more because she turned up and stayed and not because she particularly wanted or – the really hurtful part – needed her there.

Fiona didn't need her. That should have made her want to walk away, leave the girl alone. Get on with her life. But she couldn't. She had an addiction to the girl that was stronger, more all-devouring than any drug. She was in love, in lust, in EVERYTHING with Fiona.

She didn't know what to do. For the first time in a very long time she was absolutely helpless. She thought of approaching Michael, telling him what was going on. But never did. What could he do? He took his cut – which had gone up since Fiona took charge – looked the other way, smoothed over things officially if need be. He wouldn't help her. He was happy the way things were.

At school they were studying King Lear. A king who's no longer a king but still wants to behave and be treated like one. She knew exactly how that felt. But she knew that Lear's fate would not be hers. At least she hoped not.

At night, when Fiona was asleep or even sleeping with someone else, she reached deep within herself. Tried to touch that hard, angry centre she had nurtured for so many years. Tried to consciously rebuild that stone wall. Brick by brick, night after night, through insomniac, heartbroken tear after insomniac, heartbroken tear. Or at least she tried. Come morning she hoped it would give her the strength to get through another day.

It always did. Because at the end of that day she'd be in the same place again.

It was getting time for them to leave the home. Forever.

The thought of leaving, of losing Fiona, gave her even more pain than actually being with her. So she tried to talk to her. Convince her that they were still a couple. That they would still be a couple. Their A levels done, the summer stretched ahead of them. But it was what lay beyond that worried her most.

Which uni you going to, then? she asked Fiona, one day when they were both lying on their backs out in the fields near the new Homebase superstore. The sun was blazing, they had weed and vodka and it should have been perfect. She kept trying to convince herself that it was.

You know. Portsmouth. They do the course I want.

What if you don't get your first choice? What then?

Fiona looked at her, smiled like there was something about her only she knew. There seemed to be nothing left of that shy, damaged girl she had first met. The one she had fallen in love with. This Fiona was altogether different. But still so, so desirable.

I'll get my first choice. The confidence in her voice unshakeable.

She propped herself on one arm, looked directly at her, smiling a completely different smile to Fiona's previous one. Head spinning from the weed and booze, the sun looking like it was oozing into the sky, spreading heat and warmth and goodness. Why don't we go together?

What d'you mean?

Portsmouth. I'll go there too.

Why?

She didn't understand. How could Fiona ask that?

So . . . so we can be together.

Oh.

She waited.

Well?

Go where you like. I'm going to Portsmouth.

She lay back down again. Stared at the sky. The sun was a cracked, rancid egg, broken over the horizon.

That was it. The moment when everything came to a head. The moment she snapped.

She sat up, looked down at Fiona.

You don't want me any more, do you?

Fiona barely looked at her. Want you? What d'you mean, want you?

Want me. Like I want you.

Fiona sighed. Things change. People change. We're not who we used to be. I understand that. You have to understand that. Spoken almost as a sigh. Breathed as an afterthought.

Look, said Fiona, continuing. We're here. Right now. We're together. Let's just enjoy what we've got. Everything ends. Everything that lives dies. Just enjoy the living bit.

She nodded. Hung onto that small glimmer of hope. That small shard of love. Lay back on the ground, gripped it tight as she clung to the spinning Earth, hoping never to fall off.

*

192

She had thought that meant Fiona would be spending the summer with her. But she was wrong again. Because Fiona got herself a boyfriend.

Sean, his name was. A local boy from Chelmsford. Tall, dirty blond hair, good-looking. And he seemed to be devoted to Fiona, a fact she was well aware of.

Fiona took every opportunity to parade him in front of her. Ostentatiously kissing in public, letting him feel her up while her eyes locked onto hers, issuing challenge after challenge with just a smile, a tip of the head, a parting of the lips. A quick gasp of ecstasy.

And she hated Fiona for it.

That was it. Hate. And it felt so good to admit it.

And with that acknowledgement something changed inside her, almost immediately. She became focused, fixated on Fiona once more. But in a different way this time. Because she knew what Fiona was doing with Sean. Trying to provoke her. Hurt her. And she knew what she must do in return. Hurt Fiona. Really hurt Fiona. Purge her from her system. Make sure she can never hurt her again.

That thin line between love and hate. She was ready to cross it.

31

The music coming out of the closed doors was both funereal yet beat driven. Imani wondered how that was possible. Mournful guitars, viola and piano soared over pounding rhythm, topped by a dark, rumbling voice, by turns angry and melancholic, that sounded like it belonged to an Old Testament prophet. The fact that he was singing about death and murder just added to that. She shouldn't have liked it. It shouldn't have worked. But she did, and it did.

She opened the doors. A man dressed in scrubs hovered over a dead body on the table. Thin and bald, he looked like a resurrected cadaver. Imani guessed who he was. She had heard Phil and Marina mention him. Nick Lines.

'Dr Lines?' She spoke from the doorway.

He looked up, startled to find someone there. Peered over his glasses at them. His look wasn't welcoming. Matthews flinched, retreated behind Imani slightly.

'Yes?'

'DS Oliver,' she said, raising her voice over the music. 'Can I have a word?'

He looked irritated to have been disturbed. Ready to refuse her request. Imani played what she hoped would be an ace of a card.

'I'm working on the Phil Brennan case.'

It was like the clouds disappearing after a particularly dreadful downpour.

'Come in.' He pointed at Matthews. 'You look familiar.'

Matthews nodded. 'Detective Constable Matthews. I've—'

'That's right. Yes.' He turned to Imani. 'Who'd you say you were, again?'

'DS Oliver.'

'Not from round here, DS Oliver.'

'No. West Midlands.'

Nick Lines raised an eyebrow, left the table, turned the music off. Silence. 'Nothing makes the time fly by like a Willard Grant Conspiracy death ballad,' he said. 'What can I do for you?'

The room was cold and smelled of death, decay and disinfectant. Most police hated morgues, Imani had discovered, but that wasn't the case with her. She had always been fascinated by them. Like a butcher's shop staffed by high-end graduates. But then, she thought, her dad had always said she was a weird one.

'It's the Phil Brennan case.'

'Those three bodies, you mean?'

'Well, it's kind of more than that now.'

Nick Lines stared at her, still frowning. Waited.

'Phil Brennan's disappeared,' she said.

'Disappeared?'

'On his way over here to join in the investigation of the three bodies. He left, never turned up.'

'Right.' Another frown. 'And you think I know where he is?'

'Do you?'

'No.'

'Didn't think so. No, we just want to talk to you about the PMs on the three dead men.'

'What about them?'

'Well, I know you're busy,' she said, gesturing to the table, 'but since DI Brennan's actually disappeared we need every bit of help we can get.'

'I'm sure you do.' Nick folded his arms, leaned his head forward. 'So what d'you think I can do for you?'

Imani shrugged. 'Hurry along the PMs.' She looked at him, still frowning. 'Please.'

He held her in a hard, unblinking gaze. Matthews had warned her about him on the way over. Doesn't suffer fools gladly and all that. Doesn't suffer anyone gladly. That was all right, she thought. She didn't like to put up with idiots either.

She held his gaze. Eventually he walked away, sat behind his desk, started clicking at his screen. Found something, invited her over.

'Here. Three post-mortems for you to look at.'

It was Imani's turn to frown. 'You've done them?'

He nodded.

'You had them all this time?'

'I don't know what you mean. These were sent over to DS Beresford as soon as I'd done them. A matter of priority.' He pointed to the table with the half-dissected corpse on it. 'Luckily that day wasn't busy. Hospital death, that one. Always needs a PM.'

Imani and Matthews shared a look. Or at least she attempted to: Matthews couldn't hold her gaze.

'DS Beresford said he didn't get them. Some kind of hold-up at your end, apparently.'

Nick Lines bristled. His professionalism was being questioned and he didn't like it. 'I don't know why he would say that. I sent them over straight away. He had them on his desk within twelve hours. I worked overtime to get them there. And I'll invoice for it.' The last sentence dripping with the indignity of it all.

It felt to Imani like having suspicions confirmed. Unpleasant suspicions. She didn't have time to think about that now. There was something more pressing.

'Could I have a look at them, please?'

'By my guest.'

She moved round the computer until she stood at his shoulder. Matthews followed meekly.

'Talk me through them.'

Nick Lines barely stifled a smile. 'Police are the same the world over,' he said and pointed at the screen. 'All three bodies were found hanging from the neck. Obviously, the first thought would be that this was what killed them.'

'But?'

'But. I knew better. Lividity, body temperature, not to mention burst capillaries in the eyeball all told me that wasn't the case. The bodies had been deliberately placed there to give that effect.'

'Any idea who placed them there?'

'Yes, of course. We also handle clairvoyance in this department.'

'I meant a physical description. Any indication. Big? Strong? Man? Woman?'

'Yes, all of that,' he said, shaking his head.

'I mean was there any damage done to the bodies that would have been consistent with them being hung there? Any bruising, something that might give us an idea of the height of the person, the build?'

'Not really. The bodies were, for the most part, unmarked. Normal wear and tear.'

'So was there anything else?'

'Patience, please. I'm getting to that.' He clicked on the mouse. The images on the screen changed. Three backs of three necks. 'See here?'

Imani moved in closer, squinted at what he was pointing at. 'What am I looking for?'

'Here,' he said, irritation in his voice. 'Look. Punctuation marks.'

Imani kept squinting. 'How can you tell?'

'Because all three have them in exactly the same place. Not nearly the same place, exactly the same place. A pin prick in each.' He looked up at her, smiled. 'Not everyone would have found them. But I'm not everyone.'

Imani found herself – somehow – warming to this cadaverous egoist. 'Indeed.'

'Which led me to my next discovery. Some kind of poison was used. An opiate, as best as I could deduce. I've sent trace amounts off for analysis.'

'What was it meant to do?'

'Paralyse. That, in conjunction with the hole in the skin, which I assume was made by an acupuncture needle, is what killed them.'

'Poison?'

'In conjunction. The needle was stuck in one of the main nerves running along the spine. A gifted practitioner could almost paralyse a person instantly. The poison would doubly ensure that. And then they would slowly choke to death.'

Imani stood up, thinking about what he had just said.

A voice from the door brought her out of her grim reverie.

'You've not lost your touch, Nick.'

All three of them looked up. There in the doorway stood Marina and Anni.

32

Michael Prosser had done nothing all day. Barely moved from his seat, and then only to get tea, cigarettes or relieve himself. Yes, he had told himself what he was going to do, how he was going to do it and when, but somehow that hadn't translated into action. So he'd just sat there staring numbly, the inane babble of the TV white noise mercifully disguising his thoughts from himself.

Because he was scared now. Really scared. Doubt and fear his prisoners once more.

It was her. He knew that. Her. And yes, the argument went, he should stop her. Or try to. But, the other argument went, what could he do? And more importantly why? His hand went to the side of his face. Stroked the rough, dead cratering where once he'd had taut, tingling skin. She had done this. Taken everything from him. Why should he try to stop her taking everything from someone else?

He hadn't recognised her at first. Or that was what he'd told himself that night. The one he had replayed and replayed in his head over and over for years, analysing it in the minutest detail, wondering if there was anything he could have done differently, anything that could have changed the course of what happened in the night's aftermath. Yes, he had decided. Never spoken to her in the first place. But if he hadn't there would have always been that niggle, that doubt. Was it really her? Was she really offering ... what she had been offering? To him? Honestly, there was no way he wasn't going to find out. No way.

And every day he paid for that mistake.

A night out in a bar. Years ago. But not too many. Just enough. A Chelmsford city centre bar, one by the bridge over the river. Posher than Yates's, but not by much. Still with the same kind of clientele. And Michael liked it that way. They came out in packs, got easily and quickly smashed on their three WKDs for a tenner, then became easy prey. Stand at the bar, watch. Chat to a few people, look like you belong. Watch. Like a lion sizing up a pack of gazelles, he had always thought. Don't go for the strongest, prettiest, most attention-grabbing one. No. Go for the one who looks vulnerable. Who might need a helping hand home from a familiar face, someone they've seen all through the evening. He couldn't be bad, could he? He's a friend of the barman's. He's chatted to him all night. Or at least it looked like he had.

And that had been his Saturday nights. Watch. Observe. Pick off a straggler – or two, it had been known to happen, although not very often – and become a friend. And from that ... Bingo. Free sex. Didn't even have to pay to get her drunk. Someone else had done that for him.

And that was what he was doing that one Saturday night when he met her.

Straight away he knew there was something different about her. He just didn't know what. She was alone. And she was rebuffing the attention she had attracted. And she was attracting a lot. But something attracted him to her. He couldn't say what it was – apart from the obvious – but something just clicked. A connection. Like he already knew her, or something. But that was impossible. He'd never seen this young woman before in his life.

200

Again, how wrong he was.

So he moved over to her, asked her if he could buy her a drink. Gave her the kind of lines that only ever worked on drunk, easily impressed girls. But, incredibly, she seemed to respond to them. That should have been a warning but he ignored it and kept going.

One thing led to another – very quickly, if he remembered correctly, and he soon found himself back at her hotel.

'I grew up around here,' she had told him. 'Just back in the area on business. Catching up on a few old sights.'

That suited him just fine. A great fuck – and looking at her perfect body, her filthy smile, he knew it would be – and then off she went in the morning. What more could he want?

She was dominant, that was the first thing he learned about her. Which was OK by him. If she wanted to put all the effort in while he just lay there, who was he to complain? She stripped him, lay him on the bed, then stood at the foot of it, slowly undressing, eyes locked with his the whole time. He couldn't take his eyes off her. A dream come true.

'Wait,' she said, before finally removing her dress. 'Don't want you to run away when you see me naked.'

'No chance of that.'

'Nevertheless . . . '

Swiftly and expertly she grabbed his arms, pulled them over his head and tied his wrists together.

'Hey, wha—'

'Shh,' she said, tying his wrists to the side of the bed, then quickly spreading his legs and doing the same with his feet. She stood at the foot of the bed again, looked at him once more. 'Hope you don't mind,' she said and there was that filthy grin once more.

'No, not at all . . . ' Even less work for him. Result.

'I didn't think you would, Michael.'

She took off her dress, revealing her naked body beneath. He was almost salivating. She was much better than the usual ones he managed to get. A real cut above. Almost like a model—

'Wait, what did you call me?'

'Michael.'

He frowned. 'But I . . . ' He had given her a false name. He was sure of that, he always did. 'I'm . . . '

'You're Michael. No matter what name you might have given me.' She smiled again. It was no longer filthy this time.

He stared at her again, really studying her this time. Really trying to see her properly. And then, with what felt like rusty chainmail dredging his heart, he remembered. He did know her.

'It's you.'

'Hello again.'

He closed his eyes, tried to unsee her. Couldn't. 'Oh God . . . '

'Certainly is. So.' She moved closer. 'I'm all grown up now, Michael. Do you still fancy me?'

'No, no. This is, this is all wrong.'

She stopped, gave a mock frown. 'Why? Am I too old for you, is that it? Did you only like me when I was younger?'

'Stop, just, just stop it . . . '

'Why?' She moved closer, a hand sliding up his naked leg.

'Please, just . . . let me go. Now. Just let me go now and I'll . . . I'll forget this ever happened. Pretend we never met.'

'Oh, but we did meet, Michael. And here we are.' Her hand at the top of his thigh.

He couldn't speak. Couldn't believe how something he had wanted so much so recently had gone so wrong.

'I said I was in town to catch up on a few of the old sights. Well, you're certainly one of them.'

He could hardly breathe. 'I know . . . I know what you did.'

She shrugged. 'I know you do. And I don't care. You see, since we last saw each other, I've been busy. Turning a hobby into a career, you might say. It's been very lucrative.' She waggled an enticing finger at him. 'You, Michael, were the one that got away. The one I had to come back for. My unfinished business.'

And, with a feeling of absolute dread, he knew what she meant. What she was going to do to him.

'Please, oh please . . . '

'Are you begging? Seriously? That's not like you . . . '

Her hand slowly stroking its way towards his penis.

He closed his eyes.

'You've wanted this for years, haven't you? Wanted me for years? Here. Now. Like this. Except I'm sure that in your fancy I'm the one tied to the bed. The one you want to play your power games on.'

No reply.

'Michael, and this is a serious question, just how have you got away for so long with being a paedophile in charge of children?'

He found his voice. Or a smaller version of it. 'I'm. . . I'm not . . . not a paedophile.'

Another mock frown. 'You like to fuck children. You like to watch children fucking. You even took a percentage for pimping children out to be fucked by other paedophiles.' She seemed to be struggling to keep her voice steady. 'I'd say that makes you count as one in my book.'

'I don't . . . I've never fucked kids. Never.'

'Never?'

She stared at him. He eventually relented. Blinked. Answered.

'I like, yes I like my, my sexual partners young. On the young side. I admit that.'

'Young?' She gave a harsh laugh. 'That's an understatement.'

He felt anger welling inside him at her words. 'Yeah? Who made you so high and fucking mighty? Who gave you the power to tell me what's what? You know what?' He tried to gesture, couldn't because of the bindings. 'You're a fucking hypocrite, like all the rest of them.'

'Oh really?' She sat back. 'Do explain. This should be worth listening to.'

'You listen to music? Rock music? They were all at it, all of them. Groupies aged fourteen. When they were nineteen they were past it. And you know who used to pimp them out? Their mothers. Yeah, their mothers. So their daughters could fuck rock stars. And what about the tabloids? All anger about paedos on one page then showing photos of twelve-year-olds in bikinis, saying how they're developing nicely. And what about the time that tabloid did a daily countdown until it was Charlotte Church's sixteenth birthday and she was legal? Remember that? No. Bet you don't. But I do. So yeah. I like my girlfriends younger. Big fucking deal.'

She stared at him. Features unmoving, giving nothing away. He didn't move, hardly breathed.

Eventually she stood up, undid his bindings.

'Get up,' she said. 'Go.'

He stared at her. 'What, you're—'

She turned to him, eyes alight with sudden, raging fire. 'Just go . . .'

He didn't need to be told twice. He knew what a lucky escape he had had.

Or thought he had had.

For weeks nothing happened. He never heard from her, never saw her again. And he began to relax. Think he had got away with it. A life lesson, well learned. Don't make that mistake again. He didn't even go out on a Saturday night any more. Well, not for a few weeks. Then he started going back to bars again. But he was always more careful. Always kept to the script.

And he got on with his life. Forgot about her.

Another mistake.

One night there was a ring at his door. Unusual, he thought, but went to answer it. He didn't get a chance to see who it was.

'Paedophile!' someone shouted at him and then his face was melting with a pain he had never experienced before.

Acid attack.

He lost his job, his house, everything. Because word had gone round about him. The paedo in charge of the children's home. There were testimonies from ex-kids, a lot of them. He was a hate figure in the tabloids. And eventually, with only half a face remaining, he had to move to the flat where he was now, shunned and hated by all of his neighbours. They knew who he was. More importantly, they knew what he was.

And he knew who had been behind all this. Oh yes. She had got her revenge on him all right.

So he sat where he was, not daring to move, barely daring to think. She was back.

And maybe it was time for someone else to stop her.

33

Simon Matthews felt like a guest at the wrong party. As if his invite to participate in the investigation he was currently working on had gone astray and in its place was some kind of free-for-all that he hadn't been expecting.

Marina Esposito had turned up, alongside Anni Hepburn. He knew Anni Hepburn, at least by reputation. She had been part of the department but the death of her partner had sent her off the rails. At least that was the word around the station. She had walked out, blaming everyone for what had happened. In fact, it had been her leaving that had created a space for him. So, if he was honest, he hadn't been sad to see her go.

Nick Lines seemed to have brightened up considerably, too, since the others arrived. Or at least as bright as he ever got, which wasn't saying much. But Matthews could tell the difference.

Introductions had been made. Imani had taken the role of hostess, the central hub around which the others all orbited. Matthews noticed a kind of reluctance or a reticence from Hepburn when she was introduced to him. Likely it was because of who he worked for and what he did and he was pleased, deep down, that he didn't have to work with her.

Lines was explaining his findings to the two newcomers. Pointing to the report to back his work up.

'So that was the same for all three of them?' asked Marina.

Lines nodded. 'Exactly the same. Once I'd spotted it on one body I checked for it on the others. The first had been difficult to find. The other two less so. I knew what I was looking for.'

'So have you found this on any other bodies?' asked Anni.

Nick Lines shook his head. 'Not that I'm aware of. At least not round here. Not in connection with this investigation. Just these three.'

Marina sat down. Matthews couldn't help but notice that she looked tired, strained. He felt some compassion for her; after all it was her husband they were all looking for. Another thought struck him. Why was she here? Why was she part of the investigation along with an ex-copper?

Marina looked up at him, smiled. Almost reading his mind. Or at least reading the puzzled expression on his face.

'I suppose, DC Matthews,' she said, 'that you're wondering what I'm doing here? What Anni is doing here too?'

He shrugged, tried to regard it as no big deal. 'The thought had crossed my mind.' It felt like the most politic thing to say.

'I'm sure it has. We're a different part of the investigation. Tracking down different leads.'

'Coming at it from another direction, you might say,' said Anni.

'But you're still civilians,' Matthews said. 'You have no real jurisdiction here.'

He felt the whole room turn and look at him. It wasn't a comfortable feeling.

Nick Lines almost smiled. 'Actually, Detective Constable, this is my workplace. I could say that about all of you.'

Murmured laughter. Good-natured in origin, but Matthews didn't take it that way. He felt they were all getting at him. Needling him for his relative inexperience. And because he didn't know them and hadn't known them for years, he wasn't one of the gang. He tried not to blush. Failed.

'All I was saying,' he said, trying to stand his ground, 'was that this is a police investigation. And it should only be current serving officers dealing with it.'

'You don't want to pool resources, then?' asked Anni.

'Why, what have you found?'

Anni smiled. 'So you do, then.'

He didn't answer. Just felt his blushing increase.

'Well actually,' Anni continued, 'it's us who should be asking you things. From what we've heard, you're getting nowhere. Why is that?'

Matthews shared a wary glance with Imani. It wasn't returned. 'We may as well share,' she told him. Matthews still wasn't convinced. Imani smiled. 'I trust these people. I know Anni, and Marina and I have worked together. We can share.'

Matthews looked from one to the other. If they were going to share, his expression said, he wasn't going to be the one to do it.

Imani turned towards Anni and Marina. 'We've been getting nowhere because the investigation seems to be getting nowhere. We managed to put a name to one of the victims yesterday, thanks to Simon here.'

She indicated Matthews. He appreciated the gesture. It was meant to be inclusive. He searched her features for signs that she was patronising him, could find none.

Imani continued. 'We still don't know how he actually ended up as one of the victims yet though. That's to be discovered. And we just heard about the manner of death minutes before you two turned up. So that's about where we are, really.'

Anni frowned. 'Why has so little progress been made? You'd think this would be top priority.'

'It seems that Beresford – the DS in charge – doesn't seem in any great hurry to reach a conclusion.'

'And would this be the same Beresford that was supposed

to have been seen driving Phil away from our house?' Marina knew the answer but placed the question for context.

'The very same,' said Imani. 'Although he denies he was ever there. Car's in the garage, apparently.'

'Have you checked?' asked Marina.

That was too much for Matthews. 'Sorry, but are you questioning the integrity of the CIO for this investigation?'

All eyes turned towards him again. No one spoke. In the absence of sound, he felt the need to continue, to justify his outburst.

'I mean … what are you suggesting? That's he's in on it? That he's, I don't know, deliberately trying to lead the investigation astray?'

'I don't know,' asked Marina quietly, getting slowly to her feet. 'Is that what it sounds like?'

Matthews bit back the response he had been about to make. Settled for a shake of his head instead. 'Yes, I've checked. About the car. I phoned the garage. DCI Franks asked me to. I spoke to the owner and he backed up DS Beresford's story.'

Imani – all of them – stared at him. Eventually Imani spoke.

'Well, something seems to be going wrong with this investigation. Leads haven't been followed up, facts have been, shall we say, obscured. And it all seems to lead back to DS Beresford.'

'Or DCI Franks,' said Anni.

'I don't think Franks would deliberately do this,' said Marina. 'And he's not incompetent. No, he's many things but, deep down, he's one of the good guys.'

'Very deep down,' muttered Anni, semi-audibly.

'So where does that lead us?' asked Imani.

'With a job to do.' Anni thought for a few seconds. 'We need someone to follow up this PM. Find out if anyone else on the database – nationally, not just in the area – has been reported as dying in this manner. We need to pool our resources about Fiona Welch's background and childhood, what we've found there. I think we should take another crack at Michael Prosser. And also, we should do a bit of digging into this DS Beresford. See if he checks out.'

'I'll do the database checking,' said Matthews, making for the door as he spoke.

'OK, fine,' said Imani. 'I'll see you back at the office.'

Matthews had had enough. Now they were taking orders from someone who wasn't even on the force. She worked in a gym, for Christ's sake. A *gym*. And here she was dishing out orders. That was the final straw.

He would find out what was happening with this investigation, but, he thought, reaching the open air, he would do it his way.

34

Phil was staring at the ceiling. Or what passed for the ceiling. Staring up at the darkness where he thought a ceiling was. Or should have been. He had been asleep again. Or unconscious. One of the two. He didn't know what time it was, what day it was. He barely knew who he was any more. Or if he was dreaming or awake. Either way, the nightmare he was enduring was so unreal it felt more than real.

His mind was spinning, warping in and out of what passed for focus. It kept skipping, reversing over what had happened. The memory thudding back to him like a wrecking ball. Apt. A wrecking ball to his psyche.

She had raped him. *Raped* him.

He wouldn't have thought it possible. Not physically or mentally possible. Yes, theoretically, maybe so. But not something that would have ever happened to him. Could have ever happened to him. An event so far out of the bounds of logic and experience that he couldn't have even imagined it. Ever. Well, now he didn't need to. It was there. It was real. It had happened.

He sighed, the weight of depressing reality on him like a physical thing. He wanted to run, scream. Throw himself against the wall just to see if he could still feel. Anything but lie here. Immobile; his mind running marathons through hell while his body remained bound. Or even just have the ability to curl up into a foetal ball. Put his hands over his head, keep the world and all its hurt out. Close his eyes, make it all go away. All the while his stomach was lurching, threatening to spew bile from his body like his head wanted to expel horrific memories. And he was helpless. *Helpless*.

The door opened. A hand felt the wall, put the light on.

Phil blinked at the sudden change. Kept his eyes closed until they gradually accustomed themselves then opened them fully.

'What . . .'

The room had changed. It was no longer his bedroom. Or not the one he shared with Marina, at any rate. He looked around, stared at it. It still looked familiar but he couldn't place it. Like a memory that was running out of synch with his mind.

Then he looked at the woman who had entered. She no longer looked like Marina. Her hair was shorter, lighter. Her clothes more conventional, those of an older woman. Her bearing was completely different. But something about the smile was exactly the same. That kind of gleeful madness couldn't be disguised.

'Good morning, Phil. Sleep well?'

He just stared at her, mouth open. Still trying to process this sudden change. No . . . no . . .

She stopped what she was doing, stared at him. 'What's the matter, Phil? You look confused. Don't you recognise your own mother?'

'My . . . What? Mother?'

She shook her head as if she couldn't believe what he was saying, laughed. 'Are you still asleep, is that it?' She came over to him, sat on the edge of the bed. Took his hand in hers. 'Yes. Your own mother. Eileen. Don't you recognise me?'

Phil recognised the room now. It was the one he had been brought up in, when Don and Eileen took him in, adopted him. His old childhood bedroom. The first one that he had been able to truly call his own. He glanced at the bedside table, knew immediately it wasn't really his old room. The same two capsules sat there.

He couldn't bear to look any more. Either at the room or her. Kept his eyes firmly closed. Just felt the stroking of her fingers along his hand.

'Why,' he said eventually, his voice as broken as the rest of him, 'why are you doing this to me?'

'Doing what, Phil?' Her voice all innocence.

'This. All of . . . this. Why? What d'you want? What d'you want from me?' Tears forming in the corners of his closed eyes.

'Want from you, Phil? Nothing. Want to give you,' he felt her body move closer to his, 'yourself.'

He opened his eyes. She was right next to him on the bed.

He groaned. No . . . no . . . not again. 'Please, no . . . Don't touch me . . .'

'What d'you mean?' Again, all innocence. 'I don't know what you mean by that. I'm not going to do anything again. I'm your mother, Phil. Or what passed for your mother.'

Her words triggered something. He found his voice. 'Eileen was my mother. Not biologically, but families are more than a matter of biology.'

'Oh, I couldn't agree more.'

'You're not my mother. You're not Eileen.' He was gripped by a stunned, impotent anger. 'So stop playing games and tell me what you fucking want . . .' The last few words shouted as loudly as he could.

She stared at him, not blinking for a length of time that he found unnatural for a normal person. Then stood up, her face

213

as featureless and composed as marble. He held his breath, slowly realising what she had shown herself capable of until this point. Not knowing what she would do to him next, what indignity, what pain she would inflict. And that uncertainty scared him. More than that: terrified him.

She kept her face hard, still stared at him. Eventually she spoke. Her voice calm, measured.

'I'm here to help you, Phil. Everything ...' She leaned in to him, hissed the word. '*Everything* is for your benefit.' She straightened up once more. Continued. 'Your life was going nowhere. Meaningless. You'd gone wrong, Phil. Badly wrong. Misguided, shall we say. To put it mildly. You'd lied to yourself. About who you were, who you are. What you're supposed to be. All of it. Oh I know it's easy to do, I'm sure you didn't start off being like that, none of us do, but it's how you ended up.' She smiled. 'So don't worry. I'm here to put all that right.'

He just stared at her. Was she insane? Or was that him? His mind was spinning, out of control. He couldn't grasp the thoughts that flew past, couldn't hold on to them.

'How?' he asked eventually, his voice sounding rusted over. 'How will you put me right?'

'Rebirth,' she said, her eyes shining. 'I'm going to take you back to the womb. Show you where you went wrong. Show you who you really are, Phil.'

'I know who I am.' But as he spoke, he knew he didn't believe the words. That he was lying, even to himself.

She picked up on that. Gave a small laugh. 'You sure about that, Phil? You don't sound too sure.'

'I know who I am ...' Said with even less conviction this time. The words drying up as he exhaled.

Another smile, this one pitying, indulgent. 'It's sweet that you think that. But you honestly aren't convincing me. You're not even convincing yourself.' She sat back on the edge of the bed. 'I'm your mother, Phil.'

'You're . . . you're not . . . my . . .'

She shushed him to silence. 'I'm your mother, Phil. I'm your wife, I'm your . . .' She smiled. 'We'll have to wait for that one. Your everything, Phil. I'm everything to you as you are to me. I'm taking you right back to the beginning. And you're going to walk away from this a new man. Hand in hand with me.'

'I . . . I don't even know who you are . . .'

'Yes you do, Phil. Yes you do.'

Those unhinged unblinking eyes staring into his own damaged ones.

'D'you have nightmares, Phil? Do you?' She seemed to be genuinely waiting for an answer.

He supplied her with one. 'I'm having one now . . .'

She shook her head, dismissing the last sentence, concentrating on his answer. 'You're not. This is all real. But I know you have nightmares. About where you come from? About who you are?'

Still those eyes staring at him. He looked back into them, shocked at her words.

Since he made no sound, she kept searching his eyes for answers. She found them. 'You do, don't you? About your childhood. About what happened to you. About what it was like before you came to see me. And Don. God rest his soul. All the horror, the fear, the darkness you had in you then. Still gives you nightmares, doesn't it?'

He had no choice but to answer. 'Yes.'

'I know. I know it does.' She stood up. 'I'm going to leave you for a little while. Give you some time to think. But I'll be back soon. And I'll show you a mother's love like you've never experienced before.' She stood there staring down at him, like a private school matron to a sick boy. 'And I'll make those nightmares go away forever. You'll see.'

And she was gone.

Phil lay there, staring at the newly closed door. Thinking about her words.

Not knowing whether they brought him comfort or made him more afraid than ever.

Pulling the Cord Tight

*She plotted. She planned. She subsumed her feelings about
Fiona, kept them locked tightly inside, only letting them out
when she was sure she was alone. Unobserved. A hard thing to do
in a home. She took long walks. She went to private places, open
spaces and screamed at the air till she was exhausted.*

And plotted. And planned.

*A housing estate was being built near the home. Beige-bricked
and boxy, curling in round ribbons of conformity. But not quite
there yet, still all scaffolding, breeze blocks and cheap cavity insu-
lation tufting out. It became the new playground for the kids in the
home. They kissed, they had tentative sex, they smoked whatever
and drank whatever. The mesh fence and fierce dog signs were no
barrier.*

And that was where she decided it would happen.

*Fiona didn't want to go, initially. For the kids, she had said.
Nothing for us there. She had a kind of detached amusement about
the place. A smug, superior grin. But she insisted.*

*Come on, Fiona, we should go there. It's fun. We'll make it fun.
On and on, wearing her down until eventually Fiona said yes.*

Plotting and planning. All leading up to this.

*Through the mesh fence, creeping along unconstructed roads.
Distant streetlights casting long shadows in the darkness. Fiona
laughing all the while, saying, Can you imagine what it would be*

like to live here? How dull and boring would you have to be to buy one of these houses?

She didn't answer. Part of her would have loved to live in a house like this. Small, yes, but comforting. Comfortable. And secure. Lock the door, keep the world at bay. But she laughed along with Fiona, agreed with what she said.

In here, she said to Fiona, pointing to a half-built house. It had an upstairs but only wooden roof joists above. The clear, summer night sky moving slowly above.

Fiona looked up. How romantic, she said, her voice a sneer. So why have you brought me here? Are you going to declare your undying love to me again?

Fiona sat down on the bare, dusty boards, looking up, waiting for an answer. Challenging for an answer.

I hate you, she thought. I've never hated anyone the way I hate you. Not anyone ever. Not even the killers of my parents. You. Just you.

But she didn't say any of this. Instead she just smiled, knelt beside Fiona.

I wanted you here . . .

She fumbled in her pocket. Got closer to Fiona.

I wanted . . .

Body against body, readying for a lover's embrace.

I . . .

And then she was on her. The cord, tight woven silk, bought from the market, round Fiona's neck. Pulling tight on either end, like she'd seen them do in films.

No words. Just staring at Fiona, all the hatred she felt for her coursing through her hands, her wrists, knuckles and fingers white, pulling as hard as she could.

And then she stopped.

Fiona hadn't responded. Just sat there, not even put her hands to her throat. Just stayed still as she was choked. And her eyes.

Locked on, staring. And calm. Calm. And her face. Still smiling that smug, superior grin.

Go on then, said Fiona. If you're going to do it, do it.

And then the last thing she expected to hear.

Fiona laughing.

She couldn't do it after that. She let her hands drop, the cord loosening at Fiona's throat. She sat back. Looked at Fiona.

Fiona smiled. Is that what you brought me here for?

She said nothing. She couldn't speak.

Fiona stood up. Said nothing. Went down the stairs, out of the house.

She watched her go. Felt all sorts of things she couldn't even begin to name. But one overriding emotion she could recognise: love. After all that, she still loved Fiona.

She avoided Fiona after that. As much as she could. She felt ashamed. Not because she had tried to kill her, but because she had failed. And in failing, let Fiona win.

But soon, that familiar feeling re-emerged. That hatred. Just seeing Fiona walking around, talking, unaffected. Enjoying herself. So she started again. Plotting. Planning. Loving her so much she wanted to kill her.

Or at least hurt her. And she thought she had found a way of doing it.

Sean. Fiona was still seeing Sean. The tall, good-looking boy was a constant presence at her side. And he seemed to genuinely make Fiona happy. Or as happy as she was capable of being.

That was it. That was the way to hurt her.

She tried to seduce Sean. Back to the housing estate, back to the house with no roof. Come and see something, Sean. I've got something to show you.

That something was herself.

Sean seemed eager at first. She made the first move on him,

touching him, kissing him, and he responded. Green-lit, she moved up a gear. Have me, Sean. I'm better than Fiona, have me . . .

Yes, said a voice. Have her. See what you think, Sean.

They both stopped, turned to the stairs. There was Fiona, smiling.

She looked at Sean, expecting to see him look mortified, start to apologise to Fiona. Allowing herself to feel a slight sliver of hope. But Sean didn't respond that way. He smiled too. Then laughed.

He stood up, went to join Fiona.

Did you think it would be that easy? asked Fiona. Did you really think Sean would fall for you? When I can do this to him?

Fiona started on him. He responded.

Just watch, said Fiona. Don't move. Just watch. Watch what he can do to me that you can't. That you never could.

So she did. And it was difficult to decide which of the three of them she hated more at that moment.

She needed to do something more. Be cleverer.

She took herself off, alone once more. Tried to connect with the cold, steely part of herself. The way she used to be before Fiona came along. And sapped her of her strength. That part of her that ran the home before Fiona turned up. That turned all that damage outwards and kept herself intact. That would be the part of her to hurt Fiona through Sean.

So she watched them. Didn't allow herself to become angry at the sight of them together, just used it as information. Material. She studied their movements. Made plans. She would do this properly. No room for error. No room for humiliation. No chance of her failing now.

Love wouldn't get in the way. Just hatred. Pure, channelled, streamlined hatred.

And this time she would win.

35

Imani followed the satnav. Couldn't help hearing Anni Hepburn's words ringing round her head again as she drove.

'You sure he's OK, young Matthews?'

'Yeah,' she had replied. 'Why shouldn't he be?'

Anni gave her a look. 'You mentioned Beresford. Looking into him, seeing if he checks out. Might that not be a conflict of interest? Might he not want to give his boss a heads-up?'

'It's a legitimate line of enquiry.'

'No doubt, but it's still his boss.'

'We had words before coming here. He's OK, he's onside.'

Anni didn't look convinced. 'Let's hope so.'

And that had been that. The three women had left Nick Lines to his work, gone their separate ways. Promising to keep in touch, keep each other informed, liaise later. And now she was driving around Colchester, looking for Prentice's Garage.

So far, all she had done was battle a one-way system that could rival Birmingham's for fiendishness. Even the satnav appeared to be giving up. She had passed the same section of Roman wall three times before she found the turn-off she needed. She spun off the roundabout an exit before the one she had taken the last two times and headed up towards the New Town area. She didn't know why they called it that. It seemed to be composed of red-brick terraces, all auditioning for *Coronation Street*. She followed the satnav further, heading down streets undesigned for vehicles, lined on both sides with cars and vans, negotiating blind junctions and tiny looping crescents. None of the houses looked uniform either. Some had been extended and refitted with varying degrees of pride and expense, some left to rot, some turned to the ubiquitous student accommodation. And then she found what she was looking for.

Prentice's Garage was easy to miss. Between two rows of houses was an open doorway that went up two storeys. Inside it was the Tardis: long and narrow but with space for ramps and lifts, with three cars currently being worked on. She pulled up on the opposite side of the road, locked her car, went over.

'Hi,' she said to a trim, grey-haired, bespectacled man wearing a set of grey overalls. 'Mr Prentice?'

'Yes?'

Apart from the grease and the work clothes, she thought, he had the thoughtful bearing of an accountant.

'I'm Detective Sergeant Oliver,' she said, flourishing her warrant card. 'Could I have a word, please?'

Immediately he became suspicious. Those shrewd eyes narrowing behind the glasses. 'What about?'

'Oh, nothing to worry about. You're not in any trouble, nothing like that. Just wanted to ask about a car you've had in.'

Now he looked more irritated than suspicious. 'A car?'

'Yes.' She looked round. Saw an office up a flight of wooden steps in the rafters of the building. 'Should we go up there or are you happy here?'

Give him the option, she thought. Put him at his ease with the illusion of choice.

'Here's fine,' he said. 'Unless I need to look something up.'

'It was a car earlier this week. Yesterday, perhaps. A Vauxhall Insignia. Belonging to DS David Beresford.'

'Dave Beresford?' Prentice asked surprised. 'He's one of your lot.'

'He is indeed. I just need to check whether his car developed a fault and you brought it in this week.'

Another suspicious look. 'Why don't you ask him? You work with him, don't you?' Then another look appeared on his face. Fear. 'Can I see your warrant card again, please?'

She showed him it.

'West Midlands. You're not from round here.'

'No, I'm not. I'm working on an investigation in conjunction with Essex Police here in Colchester. It involves the disappearance of one of our senior officers. So could you tell me whether you've had DS Beresford's car in here this week and what, if anything, was wrong with it?'

Prentice seemed to be the kind of person who didn't act, think, or speak rashly. He mulled over his reply before answering her. 'Before I say anything else, I just want to say that Dave Beresford is a good customer of mine. He's brought me in other custom too, word of mouth. I had a little spot of bother a few years ago – nothing serious – and he helped me out with it. So I count him a good friend. If he's in trouble I think I have the right to know.'

It was Imani's turn to mull over her reply before speaking. Deciding whether to tell him everything or just as much as he needed to know in order for her to get an answer. Get creative, she thought.

'His car may have been involved in a kidnapping. That's not to say that DS Beresford had anything to do with it in any way. I just need to know whether his car was in this garage for any reason this week. Can you tell me that, please?'

He kept his steady gaze on her, didn't answer. Imani tried to work out what his little spot of bother could have been. Her first thought, given his neat appearance, was accounting trouble of some kind. Financial mismanagement of some sort. But not necessarily. His neat appearance, even in a set of overalls, could have meant anything. Alcohol, gambling problems? Not her place to ask. Just curious. Something big enough to get the police involved though. But something big enough in order to lie to cover up for a detective you owed a favour to? She didn't know. She sensed she was about to find out.

'I've already had a call about this. One of your lot. Young lad, it sounded like.'

'That's right, I'm working with him.'

'So,' Prentice said, measuring the words once more, 'if I were to call DS Beresford would he be happy for me to release this information? Again?'

She was starting to tire of this man. Time for her to remind him of her job description. 'I don't know, Mr Prentice. I do know that if needs be I could get a warrant to have your books turned over to us and go through them. Obviously I don't want to do that. It's a lot of fuss. And as I said, this is a kidnapping I'm investigating. And I'm sure you realise that in cases such as these time is of the essence.' All said while smiling and seeming reasonable. Imani thought that was some achievement.

'Fine. Right. I see.' Prentice nodded. He sighed.

Get on with it, she thought. Even Sophie in *Sophie's Choice* didn't take this long to make her mind up.

'No,' he said eventually.

'No what?'

'No. Dave Beresford's car hasn't been in my garage this week. Haven't had it in since I did his MOT last March. I've seen him socially, of course, since then. But not as a customer.'

'So did he contact you to say his car's been here when it hasn't? Was that why you said earlier that was?'

Prentice looked like it was a difficult question to answer.

'I'd ... I'd rather not say. Not without proper representation.' He looked straight at her, fear once again furrowing his features. 'Will I need representation?'

'I doubt it, Mr Prentice. As long as you've told me the truth.'

He nodded, more vigorously than the admission needed. 'I have. He's a friend, but ... ' He shrugged. 'Debts have to be considered repaid sometimes.'

She nodded, told him she understood and returned to her car.

Not knowing if that feeling inside her was elation or dread.

36

'Well, this is an unexpected surprise,' said Malcolm Turvey. 'But a good one, though,' he added hastily, should there be any doubt.

Anni Hepburn smiled at the man. It was clear he didn't get many visitors, especially female ones. His house was in New Town – part of the same warren of streets Imani was currently negotiating – and it wasn't one of the added on or added to ones in the street. It had the look of a house that was cleaned and painted only when absolutely necessary, did its primary job without any adornment. Not because the owner couldn't manage the upkeep – although the two dead hanging baskets, one at either side of the front door, said there may be some truth in that – but because he had other, more important things on his mind. It was a house belonging to someone who believed the life of the mind was more important than the physical one. And that, clearly, excused a lot.

Anni kept smiling, hoping to be asked in, dreading a little what state she would find the inside of the house in.

Malcolm seemed to be having similar thoughts. 'Was there … can I do something for you?' Looking round as he said it. Hoping the neighbours saw this pretty young black girl on his doorstep while simultaneously hoping they didn't think she was there to arrest him.

'Need your help, Malcolm. Can we talk inside?'

'Yes. Obviously. Certainly. Of course.' He stepped out of the way, showed her inside. 'Come in, please.'

She did so. He closed the door behind her.

The house was small, the front door opening on to the living room. The first thing she noticed was the gloom. The curtains were drawn, keeping what daylight was left firmly out. From the dust grooves on them it looked like it had been a while since they had been opened. And the furniture didn't suggest a normal living room either. Bookcases in the alcoves were overflowing with texts. Two old metal filing cabinets stood against one wall where a shabby old sofa was pushed up against them. A TV, the front greasy with fingerprints, was pushed up against the curtains and a desk and wooden dining chair with a frayed, dirty cushion on it was in front of the blocked up fireplace. On the desk was a computer. Black and complicated-looking. If this is the living room, thought Anni, she would hate to see what the bedroom was like.

She shuddered. Hoped Malcolm didn't catch it.

'Tea?' he asked. 'Or coffee?'

'Whatever's easiest.'

He stood there looking puzzled.

'Tea,' she said, making his mind up for him. She smiled as she said it.

He went off to the kitchen to make it. Once the kettle was filled and on he re-entered the room.

'Sorry. It's probably not what you'd think of as homely,' he told her.

'That's fine.' She perched on the edge of the sofa. She looked at the filing cabinets. 'Your work?'

'Ah,' he said, face lighting up. 'Yes. Real work, I mean. Well, what I think of as work. You know. Not the library work. Not like I used to do. Real work.'

'Which is? The crimes?'

'Absolutely.' He sat on the wooden chair, swung his body towards her.

He really didn't look healthy, she thought. Unkempt grey hair, a red face that could have been from alcohol, bad diet or a combination of both, a spreading paunch and wearing a sweater and khakis, both of which had dodged the washing machine for a few weeks longer than they should have done.

'My work,' he said again. 'A complete catalogue of all the major crimes in the area. All of this century and the majority of the last one too. Everything from discovery and investigation through to prosecution – or not in a few unfortunate cases – and imprisonment. I've even tried to find out what happened to the perpetrators on release. Fascinating. It really is. I always say,' he continued, getting really into his story now, 'I always say you can take the cultural and moral temperature of a society not just by the crimes it commits, collectively, but just as importantly in how we deal with and punish those crimes.'

'Absolutely right. The one I—'

'That's the kettle.'

She waited while he pottered in the kitchen, returning with two mugs that despite a vigorous washing couldn't disguise the immovable tannic scale on the insides, an open plastic bottle of milk and a teapot decorated with a picture of Prince Charles and Lady Diana.

'Here you go,' he said, pouring.

Anni did her best to look enthusiastic about it, took a sip, declared it too hot, left it on the floor beside her foot.

'So what can I do for you?'

He seemed almost too eager, she thought. But continued.

'Fiona Welch. The fake one.'

'I thought so,' he said nodding. 'I thought so.'

'Her victims. I'm sure you've got all the details.'

He jumped up, almost upsetting his tea in the process, and crossed to the computer, moved his mouse to turn it on. 'Got them right here. Modern stuff is all on computer now,' he said, a note of sadness in his voice. 'Much prefer the filing cabinet.'

'Can't beat the old ways,' said Anni, suspecting she was expected to say something.

'Quite. What did you want to know?'

'Everything, really. Who they were, how they met her, all of that.'

He turned to her, frowning. 'Don't you have all this stuff?'

'Well, I did, but then I left the force. They didn't let me keep it.'

'No,' he said, turning back to the screen, 'suppose not.' He scrolled through information. 'Here we go,' he said eventually. He turned to her once more. 'You're not drinking your tea.'

'Too hot still. What you got?'

'Right.' He read from the screen. 'First victim, Michael Duncan. University student, worked nights behind a bar.'

'Which one?'

'The Castle. Down the High Street. Beside the Castle, strangely enough.' He read on. 'Had a girlfriend but started to try and change her. Got her to grow her hair long, dye it dark brown. Black. Bought her dresses from Monsoon.'

'On a barman's wages?'

'And a student as well, don't forget. No, I think it was discovered later that the woman claiming to be Fiona Welch bought them for her.'

'Weird.'

'Yeah. That's just the start. Apparently he wanted her to start calling herself Marina.'

229

'Oh, I think I remember this now.' She nodded. Getting more than just a memory of the case. Remembering Mickey too. The last case they had worked together before his death. Before she had killed him.

She tried to hold it in check, concentrate on the facts. Remember her training.

'And then he killed her. Once she'd done all that for him.'

'How?'

'Strangled.'

'Right. And the next one?'

'Same. Everything the same. Glyn McDonald. Student, had a girlfriend that he tried to change, call Marina. Worked in a different bar, though. Still in the city. The Purple Dog. Know that one?'

'Yeah. So how did she meet them? Through the bars?'

'Difficult to say. They were all studying something different. The third one, Tom Houston, fitted the bill exactly. But he didn't work in a bar. He worked in a coffee shop.'

'But still in the service industry. So she could have met them all as a customer.'

'The bars and the café were all quizzed at the time. None of them could remember seeing her. At least, not the woman who was then taken into custody calling herself Fiona Welch. But she may have changed her appearance by then.'

'And all of these three confessed to the murders, if I remember.'

'Absolutely. Not just confessed, they were proud of it. Happy to confess. Said they'd done it for her. All three of them.'

'She was easy to track down, wasn't she?'

'Like she was waiting to be caught. Or at least catch the eye of someone.' Malcolm became bashful. 'Marina Esposito. That's who. And you brought her in.'

'We did. We had to. She was waiting for us. We didn't know

230

what to do with her so she was put in the special unit.' Anni sighed. 'And then everything turned to shit.'

Malcolm just nodded.

Anni looked up, determined not to give in. At least, not in front of Malcolm. But another part of her thought she should. Let it go. Let him witness the anger, the pain, the grief, at first-hand through her. Let him see that crime had consequences, that it wasn't something that could be carefully filed away, just a story to extrapolate morality from. Let him see the real cost of it.

But she didn't. She held it in. Professional once more.

'So where are they now, these three men?'

'In the system. Doing time. I don't think any of them will be out any time soon. None of them have shown remorse. The only remorse they seemed to have shown was in not seeing this woman again.'

'That's some hold she had on them.'

Malcolm agreed.

'Have you any photos of them?'

'Of course.' A few more mouse clicks, then the sound of the printer. He gathered up the images, handed them to her. 'In order. Michael Duncan. Glyn McDonald. Tom Houston. There you go.'

Anni studied the images. They weren't what she had been expecting. She was expecting a likeness of Phil Brennan. But yes, she could see there was something about them that did resemble him in a kind of generic way, they did all share similar qualities. They all looked alike. They all look like someone, she thought, just not Phil.

She stood up. 'Well, I won't take up any more of your time. Thanks, Malcolm. Really appreciated it.'

Malcolm blushed once more. 'Oh. Thank you. Anything, anything I can do to help. Any time.'

Smile in place, she made her way to the door.

'Oh,' he said as she stepped foot outside, 'you haven't finished your tea.'

'Next time,' she said and hurried back to the car.

As she went she remembered something she hadn't asked Malcolm: What had he been keeping from them when they spoke to him in the tea room?

The First

*S*ean. *That was how she would get at Fiona. Sean. And not like she had done it last time, all love-clumsy and driven by her emotions. No. This time it would be done cold. Planned properly. Like she used to do with the girls. Back before Fiona came along.*

Fiona. Anger rose at the very mention of her ex-lover's name. She pushed it down, ignored it. Channelled it. Use it, don't let it use her.

So she concentrated on Sean instead. Sean. Sean. All about Sean. Where he lived, who he lived with. How old he was. Who his friends were. Where he worked. Studied him. Analysed him until she had a full dossier on him.

He was nineteen, lived with his divorced father in a small ex-council house just off the Moulsham area of town. He worked for the council as a gardener but was in danger of being laid off due to cuts. Most of his friends were boys he'd been to school with. None of them were academic, all of them had stayed in the area they had been born in. They drank together regularly, usually on a Friday night. Saturday night was for taking out Fiona.

So that was Sean. His whole life. All she had to do was find a way to get to him. Do something to him that would make Fiona know what she was up against. Take him away from her. One way or another. Make Fiona fear her. Make Fiona hurt.

More planning. More plotting. Google became her best friend.

Then, eventually, she hit upon it. A way to get to Sean, back at Fiona.

She started to lay tracks. Smiling at Fiona, being nice to her. Showing her she wasn't upset by her previous behaviour, that she was over her now. So over her. And Fiona responded in kind. By ignoring her.

Or so she thought. But, she surmised in hindsight, what Fiona was actually doing was only pretending to ignore her. In reality – always a tricky word to use in relation to Fiona – she was hurt, angry even, that she seemed to have no more control over her. And nothing she could do would change it. Flaunting Sean no longer worked. Public displays of affection were ignored. Bragging was met with a shrug. Even taunting her about not joining her at university was met with indifference. She was sure Fiona was becoming angry at all of this. But she also knew she could never express that. So while Fiona seethed silently, she secretly gloated.

Then remembered she had to be calm, controlled. Cold. No gloating. Plenty of time for that later.

In the meantime she had to strike at Sean. And it was even easier than she had thought it would be.

She became more friendly with the other kids in the home, especially the ones that were due to leave that summer. They started going out together, bars and clubs in the town centre. Sean and Fiona were often there. And Sean was starting to get a taste for drugs. Weed, obviously. Everyone did that. It was nothing. So they decided they needed something a bit stronger, a bit more targeted. Ecstasy was the obvious next step. And the same dealers could supply it. Along with coke, MDMA, whatever they wanted. Perfect, she thought.

Sean had a job, Fiona had saved enough money from pimping out the other girls so money wasn't a problem for either of them. But then she had money too. So she became friendly with the dealer.

Asked him to supply her with something that the others didn't want. Rohypnol. At first the dealer just laughed at her.

What d'you want that for?

Got something in mind. Something special. She tried smiling when she spoke, the kind of smile that she hoped would turn him on, or at least get him a bit excited, interested. Didn't really work.

I could get done for that, you know. Really land me in trouble. Pills, skunk and weed is one thing. That's another. If I knew how you were going to use it, supplying that could leave me open to a rape accessory charge.

Ah, she said, but you don't, do you? You don't know how I'm going to use it. Or who on. Or what for.

He studied her. She knew she unnerved him. Good. But she intrigued him as well. Even better. He gave in. Supplied her.

Now all she had to do was let him have it, wait for an opportunity to present itself.

Which was easier than she had thought it would be.

One night at a club, all of them there, Sean laughing and joking with his mates, all of them drinking pints. And she was no longer seen as a threat or even an irritant. Almost too easy.

She checked her handbag. Knife. Tape. Pills. All there.

Not that she was going to kill him. No. Of course not. That would be stupid. And dangerous too. That could really backfire on her, get her in trouble. What would be the point of that? All people would think was that she actually was jealous of Fiona, jealous enough to kill her boyfriend. And that wasn't how she wanted people to see her.

No. Hurt him. That was all. Scare him. Cut him, maybe. Or threaten to cut him. Get him helpless. Get him alone. Take away his hope. Frighten him away from Fiona. Yeah. That was all she was going to do. That would be enough. And then when Fiona asked her if she had seen Sean, heard from him, she could tell her. I told him to leave. I told him you were better off without him. I told him you wanted me. And then ignore her the way Fiona had done to her.

Yeah. That would do it.

But things didn't quite go to plan.

Getting him separated from the herd was easy. She just talked to him, laughed with him. Said she was sorry for all that earlier shit with Fiona. Said they were really good together. Sean, simpleton that he was, took her words at face value. Even said yes when she offered to buy him a drink to show there were no hard feelings. That was his mistake. It was an easy matter to slip the Rohypnol into his drink. Hand it to him. Watch him drink it. Perfect. Too easy. Now all she had to do was lead him away from the rest of them, get him past Fiona, wherever she was.

And that was when things went badly wrong.

Sean started to feel woozy, couldn't stand up straight. That was what she had been expecting. So far so good. So she tried to lead him away from the crowd, take him somewhere quiet. In the plan she had formulated, that was outside to the taxi rank and away in a cab to the housing estate once again, where she could use the other two implements on him. But she didn't get that far. Because Sean collapsed before he had left the club.

This wasn't right. She knew that. He wasn't supposed to have such a violent reaction. And not so quickly, either. But there was nothing she could do. He just passed out right in front of her and everybody witnessed it.

The doormen came running over, thinking him drunk. They soon saw that wasn't the case.

What's he taken? the biggest doorman asked.

She played dumb, said she didn't know. Didn't think he had taken anything. He was just drinking lager. Bottled, that's all. Eyes big and wide. Innocent.

From the corner of her eye she saw Fiona come running up. She looked concerned. She was stunned: that was the first time

236

she had ever seen her display such deep, unaffected emotion. As she approached she looked down, saw Sean, dropped to his side. Screamed for an ambulance. Then looked up.

The innocent mask dropped. A smile took its place. Devious. Challenging. But above all, victorious.

And Fiona didn't like that. Didn't like that at all.

Sean died a couple of days later. An allergic reaction, the official report said, to something he had taken in the club.

She was questioned by police, played the wide-eyed innocent again. It worked. They weren't interested in her. Then they spoke to Fiona. And for once the shock of Sean's death must have really affected her because she didn't have time to put her mask back in place. They became interested in Fiona. Very interested. And, after Sean's death, that was the best thing that could have happened.

Eventually Fiona was released without charge. She hadn't supplied the drugs that killed him. They didn't know who did. And since he seemed to have taken whatever it was voluntarily, they had nothing else to go on. Death by misadventure. Case closed.

It was time for them to leave the home. Fiona was avoiding her. When she did happen to bump into her, she couldn't keep eye contact. Would look shamefully, fearfully, away.

She made a point of speaking to Fiona on the last day. Surprised her in a corridor where she couldn't escape.

Just wanted to say good luck at uni.

Fiona mumbled some kind of thanks, tried to get past.

Must be hard without Sean in your life. Tragedy, really. Must really, really hurt.

No response, just an attempt to move past.

Of course, she said, moving in closer, someone must have really hated him to give him that when they knew it would kill him.

She didn't know how the lie would be taken, but Fiona looked up sharply.

Buoyed by the response, she continued. If only they knew who had hated him that much. Or who hated his girlfriend enough to do that so she would be alone and hurting.

She smiled. And Fiona, staring straight at her, understood. And hurried away.

And that was the last she ever saw of Fiona.

At least, while she was alive.

37

Marina had turned a corner of the Art Café opposite the library in Colchester's Trinity Square into a makeshift office.

She remembered the place from when she had previously lived in the town, taught at the university. Had pleasant memories of it. She would meet other lecturers here on free afternoons, put the world to rights – or at least the department – over coffee and cake. Maybe buy a few handmade greetings cards or perhaps occasionally a piece of jewellery too. But she tried not to let any of those memories take over today.

Now she sat in a corner, table to herself, papers and laptop spread out before her. The coffee and cake was still evident but somehow it didn't taste as good as it used to. But then, the state she was in, screaming emotion being hopefully channelled into useful professionalism, nothing did.

She had as much information as she could have possibly found about Fiona Welch in front of her. Even remote access to Home Office files not normally open to the public. Anni had showed her how to do it. Said a computer hacker had taught her in exchange for leniency. It was a good trade-off.

Now Marina knew where Fiona Welch had been kept and for how long. As a child at least. She had then gone to Portsmouth University to study psychology. From there a PhD at Essex in Colchester. And from there her death.

She had also looked into her childhood pre-children's home. It wasn't good. A typical tale of abuse and family breakdown with the small girl taking the brunt of it. An absent, alcoholic father. A mother who let her various boyfriends take turns on Fiona until Social Services intervened and placed her in care. There, apparently, she came under the influence of another girl. Marina felt that familiar frisson when she knew she was getting somewhere. She knew who this would be. Or thought she did.

She read on, expecting to find out about this other girl, but there was nothing further about her. No name, no place of birth, nothing.

She sat back, frowned at the screen. Why? Why no information? There was plenty on Fiona Welch, plenty on all the other children in care alongside her. But why nothing on this particular girl? That just made her all the more curious. All the more certain that this was the girl – now woman – that she was looking for. All she had to do now was find out more about her. A name would be a good place to start.

But before Marina could do anything about it, her phone rang.

She took it from her bag, stared at it. A number she didn't recognise. She shuddered at that, her heart and stomach flipping and diving and immediately she was in turmoil. Her first thought: Phil. Or his kidnapper. Phoning to gloat. Or taunt. Second thought: the police. Phoning to say they'd found a body. Neither a good option.

But she had to answer. She had no choice.

She did so. 'Marina Esposito.'

'Yeah,' said a voice, then nothing more. Male, she knew that much. And familiar too. Slightly. But recently.

But not Phil. Not the woman.

'Hello,' she said again. Waited.

A sigh that turned into a cough. She waited for the attack to cease. Listened.

'It's Michael Prosser.'

Now she recognised it. But it still didn't answer her questions. Just confused her even more. The last person she had expected to hear from.

'Hello, Michael,' she said, hoping her voice remained low and calm, 'what can I do for you?'

A sound that she presumed was a laugh. 'Bet you didn't think you'd hear from me again, did you?'

'No, I didn't.'

'Not after what you called me. Not after how you left.'

She waited. Should she apologise for what she had said? It was the truth, after all. Maybe she should. At least for the way she had said it.

'Yes,' she started to say. But she stopped. Unable to bring herself to apologise. 'So what can I do for you, then, Michael?'

'Saw what happened to you when you left me.'

Another shudder ran through her.

'And before you start, it was nothing to do with me. At least, not directly.'

'What d'you mean?'

'You've been asking questions. About her.'

'Who?'

'Don't insult me by going suddenly thick. You know who. That woman. The one who's got your old man.'

'You know her? What's her name?'

Another noise that she interpreted as a laugh. 'Steady on. It's not that simple. Never is, though, is it?'

'I suppose not,' she said, humouring him. Keeping him talking. Waiting until he asked her for something in exchange for information.

'I mean what you said to me the other night. What you called me. Never that simple. Never that clear-cut. Nothing is.'

'Then if I was wrong, I apologise.' Trying to keep calm, keep her temper.

'Oh, thank you very much, your fucking majesty,' he said, sarcasm dripping through the phone. 'But that's not the point. Well, not the only point. If you see what I mean.'

'Not really, Michael,' said Marina, trying to hide her exasperation. 'Perhaps you could explain it to me.'

'Respect. I've been thinking and that's what I've decided I want. Respect.' A deep breath, ragged and rattling at its nicotine-stained edges. 'For starters. You see, I wasn't going to call. Was going to let someone else deal with it. You, probably. Let it all go away. Have nothing to do with it.'

She listened, decided that he wasn't used to speaking so much to another person. The years of living alone in his self-righteously imposed exile had left him unsocialised, unable to follow his thread of conversation. As long as she made the right kind of encouraging noises, she hoped, he would continue. Maybe even reach his point.

'So what changed your mind?'

'I'm not one of the bad guys. I'm not.'

She wondered whether he was speaking to himself now.

'I saw what happened to you. And I know who it was.'

'Who?'

'Not the question. You have to ask why. And what for.'

'Because I was asking questions about that woman, you said.'

'Right. Well, now it's all about respect. I'm not one of the bad guys.'

'No.'

'So don't fucking treat me like one. I'm trying to help here.'

242

'And for that I'm very, very grateful. So how can you help me? What can I do?'

'Come back to see me. At the flat.'

'You can't leave it to meet me?'

'What d'you fucking think?' Bitterness in his voice now. She didn't push him on it.

'So you've got something to tell me.'

'I've got everything to tell you.'

'Couldn't we just do it over the phone?'

'Don't be so fucking stupid. Course we couldn't. You've got to come over here and bring something with you. Respect. Like I said.'

'I'll certainly come with respect for you, Michael. You have my word.'

'I want more than that.'

'What d'you mean?'

'Respect doesn't come cheap.'

She had been expecting that. She just nodded to herself. 'How much?'

'I'll decide by the time you've got here. Give me a chance to think. I want my side of the story heard. Properly. And I want some compensation for all the shit I've had to put up with.'

'Fine, I'll bring my chequebook. What time?'

'Just get over here.'

The connection was broken. Marina stared at the phone.

Was he for real? Was this the breakthrough she had been waiting for? Or was it some kind of trap, a way of getting revenge on her for the way she had treated him. She didn't know.

But there was only one way to find out.

38

S imon Matthews had surprised himself.

He had driven back to Queensway, taken his place at his desk, started work. At first he was angry, full of bitterness and resentment towards Imani Oliver and her friends. Really annoyed at the way he had been sidelined. But, as he worked, he thoug.ht. He hadn't been sidelined. Not really. He had asked to do this job, volunteered for it. The more he thought about it, the more he realised that no one else had stepped up and asked to do it. Only him. So really, the logical part of his brain said, he had nothing to complain about.

And yet . . .

It still gnawed at him. The way they had all greeted each other, old friends. Leaving him out. Well, not leaving him out, not as such, just feeling left out because he didn't have the shared experience they all had. If he was honest, that was what had annoyed him. That they had all been part of something and he hadn't. And that in turn opened up a whole lot of other thoughts.

Because he hadn't found his place in the squad. Not yet, not really. He was a fairly recent addition and, although he seemed to be building respect among his peers, he wasn't yet at the heart of the group. And that hurt him more than he would normally admit, even to himself.

So he had come back to the office, hoping, if he was honest, to impress both groups with his work.

And he was already surprising himself.

He had entered details into the computer, scanned county-wide at first. And received two positive results. The first from a Holiday Inn just outside Colchester. Seven years ago. A four-day convention of fireplace retailers. The mind boggled at such boredom, he thought, then remembered he was sitting inputting data at a computer. But at least he seemed to be getting somewhere. Andrew Murray. Forty-eight years old. Married. Apparently last seen talking to a group of people in the bar. He'd had dinner (steak) and plenty to drink (beer, wine, whisky). At first it had looked like a heart attack. But his wife hadn't believed it. He played tennis, she had said. Golf. Kept himself fit. Was training for a triathlon. Simon Matthews knew a mid-life crisis when he read about one, the intimations of mortality creeping close. But he was glad of it. Because of the wife's insistence another post-mortem was performed. And that was when the puncture wound to the back of the spine was located. Not only that, but Andrew Murray had withdrawn quite a large sum of money the same night, transferred it into an account bearing his name, then had it emptied and closed that same night.

Then it became a murder inquiry. Everyone that could be contacted from the convention was questioned. All of them said the same. He was seen chatting to a lot of people in the bar the night he died. No one in particular. A couple of people did say he may have been flirting with a younger woman but there didn't seem to be anything serious going on. Attempts had been made to locate this woman. A dead end. It was assumed she was just another fireplace retailer.

The investigation was still, officially, open. But that was seven years ago. No leads, nothing.

Matthews cross-referenced further. Southend-on-Sea was the next one. Five years ago. No convention this time, just a single man staying at a waterfront hotel. Graeme Parker. Divorced and down in Essex for a few days hoping to see his children before his ex-wife emigrated to Canada and took them with her. Last seen that night in the bar unsuccessfully trying to order hot food after the kitchen had closed. After that he had apparently got into a conversation with another guest, a female one, and they had disappeared off together. The next morning he had been found dead.

Attempts were made to locate the woman he had been talking to but without success. She hadn't shown up on CCTV and there was no record of anyone answering her description staying there that night. And that was another thing. Her description. No two people could agree on it. She seemed to be young, or fairly young. Pretty or plain. Unmemorably dressed. No one could remember her.

That was enough to order an in-depth post-mortem. And that was when the puncture mark was discovered. Toxicology showed something but it was dispersing fast. Traces of Rohypnol, or a derivative, it looked like. And again, a large sum of money had been transferred. This was again traced but reached a dead end. An account had been opened and closed on the same day. The name and all information given was that of Graeme Parker. The account, like the previous one, had been cleaned out.

Matthews sat back. Barely able to hold his excitement in check. This was what he loved most. Not the physical side, chasing down criminals, getting a few surreptitious fists in before carting them away, the adrenalin rush that comes with it. No. He loved this side. Chasing down information, watching patterns emerge from it, webs of data spun tighter and tighter the closer he got to the centre, helping to trap some villain who had thought themselves too clever, too untouchable to get away with it. This was his adrenalin rush. This was what he had signed up for.

He decided to widen his search, take in a few more counties, keep seven years as a parameter.

And there it was. Another one in Kent. This time—

'Having fun?'

Matthews jumped, looked up startled. DS Beresford had appeared at the side of him, was looking over his shoulder, checking his screen. He laughed.

'Feeling guilty, DC Matthews? You nearly jumped out of your skin.'

A few others nearby laughed too. Matthews didn't know if it was with him or at him. He reddened.

'Sorry, sir. I was . . .'

Beresford was peering at the screen. 'What's this?'

'We went to see Nick Lines, sir,' he said, running on adrenalin and enthusiasm before he could stop himself. 'He gave us the PMs for the three men who we found killed.' Matthews stopped speaking, remembered Nick Lines' words. About giving the information to DS Beresford. And Beresford saying he hadn't had it. He tried to look at his screen, aware Beresford was looking at him.

'Oh, you did, did you?' Beresford asked, a studied attempt at breeziness. 'Whose idea was that?'

'DS Oliver, sir.'

Beresford nodded, his expression unreadable.

Matthews felt he should explain some more. 'You told me I had to extend her every courtesy, sir. I was just doing what you ordered.'

Beresford looked at him. Fixed a smile in place. 'Very good, DC Matthews.' He pointed to the screen. 'And this?'

Matthews explained about the wounds found on the three

bodies and how he had decided to look for any historical cases where the same thing had happened.

'I've found three so far. And I've only just started.'

'Good police work, DC Mathews. Excellent.' Beresford's smile had atrophied on his face. He looked round the room, checked no one was listening to them and leaned closer.

'How is our friend from the north?'

Matthews looked confused. 'Sir?'

'DS Oliver. North, West Midlands, same difference. How you getting on with her?'

'Fine, sir.'

Beresford nodded. Brought himself even closer still.

'Just want to remind you, Simon, that DS Oliver is only here temporarily. She'll be gone soon. But you'll still be here. And so will I. Understand me?'

Beresford locked eyes with Matthews. Bored right into him. Matthews blinked, flinched. He knew what his superior officer was intimating. He was reminding him who was boss. But more than that.

'So with that in mind, she doing anything I should know about?'

'I'm . . . ' He pointed to the screen. 'This, sir. I'm working on it.'

'Good. Anything else?'

Matthews didn't reply. He knew what Beresford was asking him to do. Rat out a fellow officer. But Imani had talked with him. Assured him that if she looked into some of the lapses in Beresford's handling of the investigation, then it wasn't a question of disloyalty. It was all about getting the job done. Getting the right results. No matter who was in charge.

But . . .

There was also the question of how excluded he had felt by

248

Imani and her friends. Yes, he had rationalised it away. He also felt excluded here in the office.

But . . .

'DC Matthews? Anything you want to share with me?'

Matthews stared at his screen.

'Because if this officer from another force is coming into my investigation and has something to say about it, I'd like to know. More than that, I've got a right to know. Wouldn't you say so?'

Matthews nodded.

'So go on then. There's something you want to share with me, isn't there? She not happy with the way I'm doing things? Just remember, DC Matthews, like I said she'll be going home soon. But you'll be staying here. With me.'

Matthews nodded once more.

'So?'

Matthews looked round. No one was listening to them or looking at them. Or they were all doing a damned good job of pretending not to.

'She's . . .' his voice low, unsteady, 'not happy with the way you're running things.'

'I see. Specifics?'

'She thinks . . . she suspected you may be withholding things from the investigation. Like the PMs.'

'Right. Anything else?'

'I . . . I don't know. Sir.'

'Come on now, DC Matthews . . .' Beresford unable to hide the threat in his voice.

'I don't know. She . . . that's all she told me. There's others working on this with her. Anni Hepburn who used to be here. And Marina Esposito. Phil Brennan's wife.'

'I know who she is. And what do all of them say?'

'I . . . I don't know. I came back here to work on this.'

'So where is she now?'

'I don't know.'

Beresford stared at him.

'Honestly, sir, I don't know.'

Beresford laid a huge paw of a hand on Matthews' shoulder. Squeezed hard. He straightened up. 'Well done, DC Matthews. You did the right thing. Loyalty is a rare commodity these days. A highly prized one. Even amongst such as ourselves. And you've just demonstrated it. Well done, lad.'

Matthews kept nodding until Beresford had walked away.

He tried to go back to work. But couldn't concentrate on the screen.

39

Phil was dreaming. That was the only answer. Had to be. He had had dreams like this before. But the familiarity of it wasn't comforting. Part of his mind knew how it would end. But try as he might, there was no way to change it. Like a runaway train stuck on a track, no way to make it go forwards or backwards or even turn off, just stick with it until it crashes or derails.

He was a boy again. A small, young boy. And he was alone. And scared. There were shadows all around him. Dream logic told him that they were both metaphorical and real. And he was supposed to be doing something. Going somewhere. Or getting ready to go somewhere. Hoping the shadows would disperse and allow him to do so. Let that small boy in darkness emerge into the light.

Boy Phil was putting his clothes on. They felt new, unfamiliar to him. Scratchy in a different way to his old clothes. But soft as well, like his old clothes had never been. And well-fitting. His own. Not someone else's that had been mended, altered and given to him to make do with. His own.

He saw smiles in the darkness, in the shadows. Comforting smiles. Or they should have been: there was something behind them. A tenseness, worry. Fear. Just call it fear. That would cover everything.

The older he got, the more he revisited the dream. The more he revisited it, the clearer things became. Fear. That was what everything was about. Fear. And love.

There were words to go with the smiling faces. But these had been lost down the decades. Now he just watched the lips move, felt the emotion behind them. Two of them. Always two of them. The same two. The same comforting words. Or supposedly comforting.

But something else this time. Some*one* else. Standing behind the two comforting faces. Just out of focus. Small. Female.

Mouthing something, saying two words . . .

His heart shuddered and he begged himself to wake.

He stayed asleep.

This was it, he dream-thought with the familiar dread that this particular nightmare had taught him to expect over the years. This was what happened to his biological parents. And . . .

The other person. Just out of focus.

He closed his eyes, hoping to wake up, hoping for the dream to change. Willing, begging himself to wake.

Nothing happened.

The two faces kept smiling. That was how he remembered them. In dreams. And only dreams. His real mother and father. Just before they were killed.

Along with his younger sister.

Noise behind them. Their pursuers had found them. Screams. More screams. More noise. And then . . .

Here it comes . . .

The screen went red.

And Phil woke up.

Screaming.

*

252

'What was it, love? A nightmare?'

Stroking his face, cradling his head to her bosom. Eileen. No. Not Eileen. But enough like her to actually want to believe it. Wanting comfort. Needing it. Desperately craving someone to chase the nightmares away. Tell him everything was going to be all right.

Phil nodded.

She hugged him all the harder. He let himself be hugged.

He needed someone to. And she was there. He allowed her lies to be truth. Just for a few seconds. That was what he told himself. Just for a few seconds. A few long seconds.

Some comforting shushes. Rocking gently backwards and forwards. Telling him it was all right. Everything was all right.

He believed it. Just a few seconds. Or minutes. What did it matter?

'So what was it about, your nightmare?' Hushed voice, asking so she could give answers not because she wanted details. That made him want to talk.

'The usual.'

'What's the usual?'

'My recurring one. My . . . mother and father. My real ones. We'd left the commune but they'd tracked us down. The last few seconds before they find us. Their last smiles.'

She stopped rocking him. He noticed. She kept going.

'Right. Just your . . . your mother and father?'

Phil didn't answer straight away.

'Phil? Was someone else there?'

How did she know? How could she possibly know?

'No,' he said. His voice sounded shaky. A house with no foundations ready to topple in a strong breeze.

'Who?' She moved around, seemingly excited. 'Who else was there?'

253

Phil kept his eyes tightly closed. The dream played behind his eyelids.

She waited for his reply.

'My ... sister ... '

He felt her stiffen. Her hands clutch him all the harder. Nails digging into his bare flesh.

'Oww ...'

She realised what she was doing, became all gentleness again.

'Your sister?'

He nodded.

'Do you dream of her often?'

He shook his head. 'Only this ... dream. Not often. Only sometimes. Sometimes, most times, it's just my mother and father. And their smiles. And their fear.'

'But this time it was different. Wonder why?'

'Don't know.'

She held him tighter once more, resumed rocking him.

'It's a good sign, Phil. That you dreamed of her. A really good sign. It means your past life is coming through. You're starting to remember.'

'It's never far from me ... never forgotten, the nightmare. This time ... she was there.'

'I think it's more than that. I think you've had some kind of mental breakthrough. And that's wonderful, Phil. It really is.'

'Why?' Genuinely confused. Her words like a calm, murmuring brook.

'Because you can move on to the next level, that's why. I told you, didn't I? The darkness inside you. It has to come out. This is it working itself out.'

'No ... guilt ... grief ... anger ... grief ... that's all ...'
Tears on his face. Couldn't wipe them away.

More shushing, more rocking. Then he felt her arms move.

'Come on. I know what you need.'

Her fingers, hands moved about and the fabric against his cheek, now wet from his tears, disappeared. His face was resting on bare flesh.

'This is what you want. This'll make you feel good . . .'

Her hands guided his face towards her breast, moved his mouth towards her nipple. Phil made a show of resisting.

More shushing and she stroked his cheek. Her hand stronger this time, holding his head in place. 'Come on, Phil. This is what you need. I know best. Mother knows best. You've had a shock. A bad dream. But you've got to get better. And I'm here to help you.' She gave a small laugh. 'I mean, if you can't trust me, who can you trust?'

Phil said nothing. Just moved his mouth over her exposed nipple.

Sucked.

40

Imani found herself once again in the Daisy Cup Flower Café, alone this time.

She needed somewhere to go, to think, to process what she had discovered about Beresford and how to proceed. This place was as good as any. And she still didn't know her way around Colchester. So she sat at her table, notes spread out in front of her, getting anxious looks from the staff behind the counter. She was the last person there. They wanted to go home.

She had called Anni, no reply. Likewise with Marina. They all seemed to have missed calls from each other, though. But she had no idea where and when they would meet up and swap information. So meanwhile she sat in the café.

Outside, the day slipped into its crepuscular transition into night. Commuters hurried past on their way home, the shops were closing up. Light, real and artificial, fought vainly against dark. The town seemed tired, ready to retreat for a few hours the ways towns and smaller cities do before the evening brings out a different kind of denizen. Or the same ones, just dressed up differently.

Imani studiously avoided eye contact with the staff. It wasn't just that she wanted to work and be left alone, she had nowhere to go. Apart from an empty rented room in an unfamiliar town.

She wasn't one for going out by herself either. She had friends back in Birmingham, a few at least, and she sometimes went out with them. Bars and restaurants. Cinemas, occasionally. Birthdays or been-too-long-let's-catch-up get-togethers. But all her friends were in relationships now, most of them serious, some married with kids. And there she was, still on her own. And because of that, conversation with the rest of them was becoming strained. Not deliberately, not because they wanted to exclude her or because they didn't all get on, they did. But they were all talking about different things to her. Different things in common. And always referring to themselves as half of a couple. Not ostentatiously, just through habit. Or as mothers. And she felt like the hold-out, the group spinster.

Any effort to ingratiate herself into those types of conversations just felt stilted and awkward. And it worked both ways. She couldn't talk to them about her day either. While they were telling each other about the latest cute thing Josh or Hildie had done, or the skiing holiday Damien had booked for them both, or some office scandal involving people she neither knew nor cared about, she could say nothing, contribute nothing. And when they did ask her about her life, her work, there was nothing she could say.

What did I do today? Watched my partner get fatally shot while I was abducted, stripped naked, assaulted and tied to a rusty old bedframe while some psychopath waited to kill me. Yeah. That would go down well.

Now when they called about a get-together, she was always busy.

Imani watched people walk by. Noticing, as a lot of single people do, how many couples there seem to be in the world. She could work out which stage they were at in their relationships, just by watching them for a minute or so. A skill

257

the police force had taught her, or so she told herself. That couple there, mid-thirties. He worked at something manual, she worked in retail. Been together for years, no longer needed to hold each other's hands to know the other was beside them. Off to get something for dinner, off home. And that couple there. Older, or at least he is. Wearing clothes too young for him, but holding hands, laughing and smiling. Him nuzzling her neck. Her giggling. Second-time-arounders or mid-life crisis. One of the two. And them. Young, early twenties. Him with a protective arm around her like he's frightened to let go of her in case she wanders off or has an independent thought. Behaving how the films have told him to behave. The look on her face: tolerant. She's having independent thoughts all the time.

She sighed. Looked down at her nearly empty mug. She felt lonely. And it was difficult to admit that to herself.

It wasn't just looking through the window where she saw couples. It was everywhere. Marina and Phil, for instance. She had barely met a couple more in love. But not just that, totally in sync with each other. A perfect couple, she thought, but not in the schmaltzy way that phrase was usually used. Perfect in the way that they had been though all sorts of shit and found a way to still be together. Because they knew they were meant to be together. That was what made them so perfect.

And even Anni with her lost Mickey. She hadn't known them well but it had still been a massive shock when he died. And she could see she wasn't over him yet. Didn't know if she ever would be.

And then there was herself. She got hit on occasionally, she was an attractive woman. But most of the men who did that were colleagues, usually married ones at that. So she didn't have a very high opinion of dating other coppers. But DS Ari Patel had been different. Not that anything ever happened between them, but she was sure that something would have done. If he hadn't been killed. And she still wasn't over that. She knew how Anni must feel. But she still hadn't come to terms with just how close to death she herself had been. Even with the therapy she had undergone, she doubted she ever would.

Maybe I'll get a cat, she thought. Something to come home to. Something to look after. No, she then thought. That way definitely lies spinsterdom. If she got one cat she'd want another. And another. And then, without quite realising it, she'd become the kind of mad, lonely cat lady who would die alone and have the police break down her door after several weeks when the neighbours complained about the smell, to find her lying on the kitchen floor with half her face eaten off by the cats. No, she thought. Not for her.

The coffee was gone now. She had to make a move.

All her dad's fault. That's what she often told herself. Work hard, yes. Got it. Don't take shit from anyone. Yep. Done that. Get a good job, take pride in it. Tick, tick. Her job. If she didn't have that, then she really would have nothing in her life. Make him proud, he had said. And she had done. Or hoped she had. But it makes me lonely, she wanted to say.

She looked up. Saw the waitress's expression. She had said it. Aloud.

She gathered her papers together, stood up.

And her phone rang.

She didn't recognise the number but that meant nothing. 'Detective Sergeant Oliver.'

'Hello?' A hesitant voice, but a recently familiar one. She couldn't yet place it.

'Yes, how can I help?'

'It's Roger Prentice here. From the garage?'

'Oh yes, Mr Prentice. What can I do for you?'

'It's . . . well it's . . . '

She waited, let him get to it. She felt a shudder. The tone of his voice told her this would be important.

'Yes?' she said, spurring him on.

'I need you to come to the garage. Now. Tonight.' Blurted out.

'Why, Mr Prentice?'

'Because I . . . ' He paused. She thought she had lost him but he returned. 'I've . . . found something out. About Dave Beresford. And his car. Discovered something.'

'Can't you tell me over the phone?'

'No,' he said quickly. 'No, I can't. You won't believe what I've discovered.'

She stifled a smile. Sure he didn't know he was talking like a cheap clickbait website. 'Straight away?'

'Yes. Please. Now.'

He hung up.

She quickly phoned Matthews, to ask him to accompany her. No reply. She pocketed the phone and made for the door.

That shudder she had felt was getting bigger.

41

Marina pulled the car up at the same spot she had previously. Looked round, nervous. There was the alleyway. It seemed to have lost a bulb or two in illumination since her last visit, the shadows deeper, wider. Or it was just her imagination?

She closed her eyes, opened them again. Tried to see things in perspective. View the alleyway itself as something no more foreboding than the person she was going to call on. After all, there wouldn't be someone waiting for her again. Would there?

She looked round, tried to make out another route to Michael Prosser's flat. Couldn't see one. No. It would have to be the alleyway.

But this time she would be armed. She checked her bag. Rape alarm. Pepper spray. Would it work a second time? It would have to. And something else. She felt under the seat. Found what she was looking for. A black heavy metal American police torch. Phil had told her to carry one. It couldn't be regarded as a weapon – not legally, anyway, since it had a practical purpose – but it was heavy enough to do some real damage.

She got out of the car, locked it. Turned towards the alley. Torch in one hand and pepper spray in the other, she set off.

Slowly, cautiously. She made her way down it towards the flat, eyes ever vigilant, alert to the slightest noise.

She made it through unscathed. Let out a breath she

wasn't aware she had been holding. Made her way to Michael Prosser's flat.

It didn't look any better the second time. The same walk up, the same filth and graffiti greeting her arrival. Pocketing the pepper spray and putting the torch in her handbag, she knocked on the door.

And waited. Eventually she heard movement from the other side.

'Who's it?'

'Marina Esposito. You called me.'

A hesitation then the door was opened.

'Come in.'

She did so. Walked down the hall, straight into the living room. She looked round. It was, if anything, even filthier than her last appearance. The air was filled with a sour human odour and the ashtray looked like he had been having a smoking contest against himself and he had won.

'Sit down,' he said, entering behind her and closing the door.

Closing the door, she thought. Was that a bad sign?

She sat on the sofa, perching on the edge. He stayed standing. Right in front of the door. His one eye roved the room, settled on anything but her. He looked anxious, like he was building himself up to something.

Something wasn't right with him, Marina thought. She felt a shudder of dread run through her. Wondered if she could make it to the door before he did.

'Right, Michael, I'm here.' Her voice calm, as neutral as she could make it. Let him do the talking. Make the offer.

No reply. He just rocked on his feet, backwards and forwards, humming slightly to himself.

'Michael? I'm here. What would you like to talk about?'

'Respect ...' His voice barely above a whisper. A hard, cracked, dry whisper.

'Respect. OK, then. Maybe we got off on the wrong foot last time. I apologised for that. Let's put it past us and move on.'

A snort. It could have been a laugh or a cough. 'Put it past us, move on . . . '

Rocking more violently now, fists clenching and unclenching.

'You talk like a . . . like a . . . social worker. Probation officer.'

'Or a psychologist, Michael,' she said, engaging him, standing her ground, but not doing anything that might enrage him. He seemed volatile enough. 'And you should know what a social worker talks like. You used to be one.'

Her words prompted him to look at her. His one eye red and angry, staring like an enraged Cyclops. 'Yeah . . . look where that got me . . . '

Don't antagonise him further, she thought. 'Michael, please. You called me, asked me to come here. Told me you had some information for me, for a price. That the respect you want costs. Well, I'm here to pay. So let's start talking or I'll just have to conclude that you've got no information and leave.'

Having found her face he kept staring at her. Breathing heavily, each long ragged inhalation and exhalation sounding like a bull waiting to charge.

Eventually he found his voice.

'This is unfair. You know that? Unfair.'

She said nothing. Waited for him to continue.

'What happened to me. All of it. All unfair.'

Again she didn't reply. She wasn't sure what to say, how to engage him. She waited to hear more, get a sense of where he was going. Find some words then to defuse him.

'It was her, not me. Her. I just . . . I did . . . I did nothing. Her. All her.' Looking away from Marina as he spoke. Looking all round the room as if seeing ghosts.

'All who, Michael?'

263

He found Marina's face again. Gave another snort. 'You just want the name, don't you? Just give you a name and then you'll go. Pay me like a whore. And all that bullshit you told me'll be just that. Bullshit.'

'Help me here, Michael. Please. Tell me what you're talking about. Who you're talking about.'

'You know who . . . ' The words roared at her.

Marina jumped, startled. And also scared.

'No respect . . . no fucking respect . . . '

Marina stood up. 'I've had enough of this, Michael.' Hoped her voice was stronger, less fearful, than she felt. 'I'm going.'

She made a move towards the door.

And with a speed he didn't look like he possessed, he was on her.

'You're not going fucking anywhere . . . '

His hands round her throat, squeezing hard.

Marina felt the room going black.

42

Daylight was completely gone, darkness in full force when Imani pulled up outside Prentice's Garage in New Town. The place wasn't lit, the double doors closed. It confirmed her bad feeling: it didn't look right.

Still, she got out of the car and made her way over to the doors. Wary, looking round all the while. She reached them, placed her hand on one. It opened. A good sign or a bad one? She didn't know. Nervous but trying to hide it, remembering her training, she pushed it open and, with a final look up and down the street, entered.

The garage floor was in darkness. She could make out a light in the overhead office, a desk lamp, she thought, given it was small and localised.

'Mr Prentice?'

No reply.

She looked round, her eyes becoming accustomed to the gloom, able to pick out shapes, grey against darker grey. There was a car in front of her on the hydraulic ramp. It seemed to be higher at one side, the other flat on the ground. She moved forwards, stumbled over two wheels which she hadn't seen.

'Mr Prentice?' she called again.

Again, no answer.

Right, she thought, turn around. Walk away. Get backup.

Something's happened here. She didn't know what, but she knew it wasn't good.

She stepped backwards and slipped, almost falling over. She reached out, steadied herself against a work bench, took out her iPhone, operated the flashlight. Pointed it downwards.

Her heart skipped a beat. What she assumed was oil, the substance she had slipped in, wasn't. It was as thick but more congealed, a different colour. Blood.

Right. Definitely get out of there.

She should have done. But she had to have one more look around. Perhaps Prentice had hurt himself, needed her help. Accidents happened.

She swung the flashlight again. And saw what was holding up the car on the hydraulic lift, what was making it appear lopsided. A body was trapped underneath it. She couldn't make out much but it was wearing the same overalls that Roger Prentice had been wearing.

'Oh God . . .'

She stepped backwards, trying to avoid the pooled blood once more, thinking: crime scene. Preserve it. Get out. Call for backup.

'I'm afraid Mr Prentice won't be joining us. He had a pressing engagement.' Then a laugh. Loud. Hard. 'Sorry, couldn't resist. I know I shouldn't make jokes and that but . . . what can you do?'

She looked to where the source of the voice was coming from, knowing immediately who it was even without seeing the speaker.

'Beresford.'

'Yeah.' He stood at the top of the steps in front of the office, body silhouetted against the dim light, making him seem bigger, more intimidating than he actually was. Or that's what Imani told herself. Beresford was already big and intimidating.

266

'You're cleverer than I thought, DS Oliver. Or maybe just more suspiciously minded. But you're also thicker too.'

'In what way?'

'You came here, didn't you?'

Her heart skipped a beat. Part of her couldn't believe this was happening. The man was a copper. Had he really killed a garage owner?

'Did you do that?' she asked, pointing to what was left of Roger Prentice.

'Yes it was me. No point lying now. He should have kept his mouth shut like I told him to. Should have said what I told him to say.'

'That your car was in his garage.'

'Yeah.' He nodded, the light glinting off his bald head. He made no attempt to come downstairs. 'Dunno what he was playing at.'

'So you killed him.'

'I didn't mean to. But we got into a conversation. Well, an argument, really. And he said he would do it again if he had to.'

'You had some kind of hold over him. Helped him out with something?'

'Yeah. He's a bit of a lad, is our Roger. Likes them young, shall we say. Got into trouble a few years ago. I made it go away.'

'He was a paedophile? And you covered for him?'

'Greater good, and all that. He was a good contact to have. A good informant. Let me know what was going on in his shitty little world. He wasn't as bad as some of them. Didn't act on his impulses. But he passed on quite a bit of stuff.' He looked down at the body. Sighed. 'Shame, really. Could have used him a bit more. But needs must, and all that.'

Imani stood still, taking everything in. It was like her world had tilted, tectonic plates shifted and the ground wasn't where it used to be. She tried to rationalise, focus. She turned, looked at the door. It was still slightly ajar. She could make a run for it. Find Matthews, tell him everything. Franks too. Get everyone—

Matthews.

'He told you, didn't he?'

'Who?'

'Simon Matthews. He told you I was looking into you. Into your car.'

'He's a good lad, Simon. Knows which side his bread's buttered on.'

She looked at the door once more. Edged slightly towards it.

'Why?'

Beresford laughed. 'Oh, is this where I tell you my evil plan, is that it?'

'I don't know, have you got one?'

Beresford sighed. 'I'm not the bad guy here. Really, I'm not. I'm a bloody good copper. I'm not bent, I don't take backhanders. I catch villains. And I'm bloody good at it.'

'So why have you killed Roger Prentice?'

Another sigh. 'Too complicated to tell you.'

'And what about Phil Brennan? You kidnapped him, I take it?'

'Yeah, I did.'

'And you've been trying to derail the investigation. Your investigation. Why?'

'Like I said, you wouldn't understand. Complicated.'

'Try me.'

'She's got my kid. My wife too.' Traces of fear broke through the bravado.

'Who? The woman who has Phil?'

'Yeah. And I've got to . . . ' Another sigh. 'You do anything to protect your family, don't you?'

'But you don't have to do this,' said Imani. 'We're all on the same side. All the things you've discovered in this investigation, if you put it all together we could find her. Stop her. Bring your family back to you.'

A harsh laugh. 'You think I haven't considered that? Really? It was the first thing I thought. And the first thing she thought of too. That's why she said if I brought her in or stopped her I'd never see them again. She's keeping them somewhere that I can't get to. And if we brought her in she'd let them die.'

'She might be bluffing.'

'You got kids? Anyone?' Voice raised, shouting now.

'No, no I haven't.'

'Then you don't understand. You'd never say that if you had.'

'Look,' said Imani, turning away from the front door, making her way up the steps towards Beresford. 'Just stop it. Now. We can find Phil, bring her in. We'll get your wife and kid back. All of us. Together. Because we're a team. That's how we work, that's what we do.'

Another laugh, even harsher this time.

She moved further up the steps until she was right beside him. He was sweating, great droplets running down his shining head. His eyes looked like they'd been caught in headlights and he didn't know which way to run. He was twitching, desperate-looking.

'Come on,' she said, reaching out to him. 'We can sort this out. We can—'

The breath was knocked from her. Beresford picked her up, threw her over the stairs.

She didn't have time to think. Didn't have time to react.

All she had time to do, as her body hit the hard concrete floor, her head connecting with the corner of a metal workbench as it went down, nearly severing it, breaking her neck in the process, was die.

PART FIVE

LET IT ROLL

After The First

*A*fter Sean, killing came quite easy. Not that she did it straight away. Not at first.

She didn't go to university. Decided she didn't want to be with Fiona – couldn't be with Fiona. That was gone, broken. And with that, when she thought about it, there wasn't really anywhere else that she wanted to go. Or anything to study. So she left the children's home. Just walked out one day, never looked back.

She stayed in Chelmsford at first. Not because she had any particular fondness or attachment to the place, but because she still knew a few people. The gangs she handed the girls to from the home. She told one of the boys, Leon, that she wanted somewhere to stay. He found her a room in a shared house at the cheaper end of town. She knew it. She'd taken girls there for parties. It wasn't what she had in mind to live in.

It was OK at first, she thought. She quite enjoyed the parties, the access to pills and cocaine, booze and weed. And if she wanted to lose herself in sex there was always someone available: male, female, whatever. But it began to get her down quite quickly. Years of living in the home, sharing everything – especially space – made her want somewhere of her own. And she was also tiring of the whole scene. So young, she thought with a smile, so jaded.

But there was something else about the whole thing too. She could see herself falling down that rabbit hole, being swallowed up by the life she was living. Booze and pills and sex. She was hitting *all three hard. Harder than she had ever been. Especially the sex. She wasn't just fucking the girls and boys, she was hurting them. Couldn't get off until they were crying. And that wasn't going down well with some of the boys in the gang. Not because they didn't like what she was doing – objectively they couldn't have cared less. But just by doing it she was damaging their merchandise. And that wasn't on.*

Sometimes, when she was hitting one of the girls, really hitting her, until she was covered in blood, cowering and crying in a corner of some shitty room, screaming while she did it, she had a kind of out-of-body experience. She could look down on herself, see herself doing this. And she would see her face. No longer human. Just an animal baying and howling with rage, in pain.

Her walls were gone. Drugs, drink and everything else had battered them down. The sex was her only way of coping and that in itself wasn't enough. Because it wasn't keeping her controlled, it was becoming more and more excessive. And the highs were getting harder to reach, the comedowns of comfort harder to maintain, shorter in duration. She had to do something.

So she took herself off for a while. Went somewhere to think. Decide what she was going to do next. She had money. Or a bit of it, anyway. Saved from her years of pimping out girls. But it wouldn't last forever. She knew that. It didn't need to, though. Just long enough until she decided what she was going to do next.

She stayed in hotels. Meditated. That was something they had been encouraged to try in the home. A teacher had come in and tried to show them. It'll help you cope, she had said, show you ways to get through your days when it's all getting on top of you. Most of the kids had laughed, arsed around, predictably enough. But she had listened, taken it in. Practised it. On her own, of course. When no one was looking. And it did work.

So that was what she did now. In her hotel room. Looked inside herself, built that wall up again brick by brick. Told herself she didn't care about Fiona any more. And that she didn't care about what she'd done to Sean. That it was all in the past. That she was a new person.

The first time she confronted all that, the real first time, delving down, down inside her, she opened her eyes to find herself in floods of tears. Crying for her lost love. Crying because she had caused someone else's death. But she didn't carry that through with her when she came out of her meditative state. Quite the opposite. She felt calm, happy, even. For the first time in years, possibly the only time ever. At peace. All that had gone. And she could look forward to the future.

After that, her future came to her accidentally.

Despite not going to university, she still wanted to learn things. After all, her school had judged her to have an above-average intelligence and a temperament that would become easily bored and restless if not put to good use.

So she read. Widely and indiscriminately. Anything and everything. Devouring, accumulating knowledge, learning all the while.

It happened one night. A Holiday Inn somewhere up north. She couldn't remember where. Somewhere anonymous. That was the important thing. There was some kind of gathering going on in the bar. She sat there on her own, reading, drinking. Rebuffing offers from the local lotharios. Not that she was saving herself or had saved herself; there was just no one there she could be bothered to have sex with. They were all too boring. Also she didn't like taking them up to her room. Even though it was temporary, rented, it was still her own space. And she didn't like anyone to invade it.

She had just about finished her gin and tonic, ready to go up to bed, when this group of people came in. She couldn't make them out at first. They were mostly middle-aged, dressed in evening wear, a mixture of both sexes. All drunk or at least tipsy, all having had

275

fun somewhere and not wanting it to end. And the one surprising thing: they were all masked.

Some were simple Burt Ward as Robin types, some were elaborate creations. But everyone wore one.

She was intrigued. Suddenly she didn't want to finish her drink and go to bed. She wanted to know where they had all been. She went up to the bar. They were all clamouring to be served but she found a space for herself. A drunk middle-aged man would always allow a pretty young girl to be served first. Sometimes they would even buy her drinks.

I'll get that, said a voice.

She turned. He was tall, rounding out but she could tell he had been handsome once. Clearly he still thought he was. She had watched him as he entered with the rest of them. Some of the women obviously agreed with his assessment of himself. It was no accident she ended up standing next to him.

Gin and tonic please, she said, not even bothering to pretend she didn't want him to. No time for that lame trick.

He got her her drink. She thanked him, took a mouthful, letting him see the way she sucked on her straw.

So what's this all about, then? The masks.

You want one? he asked and produced one from his pocket, tied it on her.

Always carry a spare, he said.

She smiled, allowed him to tie it. It had a satin ribbon at the back. He stood back, admired his handiwork.

Lovely.

So what's it for, then? she asked again.

He smiled. A special party. You see that film Eyes Wide Shut?

She hadn't.

Oh. Well, like that.

You mean a sex party?

Now you're getting it.

She looked round at all the rest of them. So why come here?

This is where we're all staying. Or most of us. We've had our fun. If we want to continue, we do it here.

Must make breakfast a bit difficult.

He laughed, as if that was the funniest thing he'd heard all night.

She kept smiling at him. So, she said, do you want the fun to continue?

He did. He definitely did.

It was as easy at that.

She didn't know she was going to kill him. Not at first. She thought she would just fuck him. Maybe tie him up, keep him restrained while she went through his wallet. But one thing led to another . . .

He was a surprisingly good lover. He knew how to make her respond. Most men didn't, in her experience. And she enjoyed being with him. At times she even lost herself in what was happening. And that was dangerous. She had made that agreement with herself that she would never lose control of herself again. She couldn't allow that to happen. Not even with this man. Not even if she was enjoying herself. And, she was amazed to admit to herself, she was.

But all good things had to come to an end.

She was in his room, still wouldn't allow him back to hers. He had come well equipped for his night of fun. His bag contained all manner of toys. They had worked through most of them together. She now had him tied to the bed, face down. Ready to use on him the strap-on dildo he had so thoughtfully provided. But she stopped. Looked at his back.

She had read something in one of her recent studies. A blade, even a small one, a stiletto, perhaps, between the right vertebrae could paralyse a person. She had brought a long hatpin bought just for this. She'd been practising on an anatomical model that she'd bought online from a medical supplies shop. But just in case it didn't work first time, the Rohypnol that she'd slipped into his drink would have taken effect by now.

She got off the bed, crossed to her bag.

What you doing? he said. Making me wait?

It'll be worth it, she promised.

She found the pin. Counted the vertebrae. Slid it in.

Ow . . . have you . . . I can't . . . I can't move . . . Rising panic in his voice. What's happened? What have you done?

She stared at him, amazed that it had actually worked first time. All those hours of practice had paid off. Staring dumbfounded at him, smiling all the while.

What's happened? Why can't I feel . . . Oh my God, I can't move . . .

He was becoming hysterical. She couldn't let that happen. She knelt down beside him.

I want you to do something for me, she said to him, mouth close to his ear. I want you to give me your money.

What?

Give me your money, and I'll let you go.

He started shouting then, calling her names that she had allowed him to call her earlier but in a completely different context. She smiled.

I'd hurry up if I were you. It's reversible at the moment but it won't be soon.

Eventually her words penetrated and he calmed down. Getting out his iPad, putting in his passwords, transferring money from his bank account to hers was simple after that.

She stood up. Realised she was still wearing the strap-on, took it off. Looked down at him.

Right, she said, I'll take that out now.

She did so. But she was too late. The paralysis had spread. He had choked to death.

*

278

Back to her own room, checked out the next morning. No breakfast.

As she walked away from the Holiday Inn, a strange kind of calm came over her. She had been wearing a mask last night, along with everyone else. She had booked into the hotel under a different name. She had paid in cash. She had left her DNA in the hotel room but so what? She wasn't on file anywhere. The only thing that could be traced to her was through her bank account. She closed it that day, emptying all the funds, including his. It wasn't in her name to begin with.

His. She smiled.

She walked off, feeling like the next part of her life had just started.

43

The morning briefing. On the rare times he was part of a large-scale investigation like this, Matthews usually looked forward to them. Made him feel part of the team, an important component. But not today. He just felt terrible.

Beresford stood at the front of the room. But Matthews sensed a change in him. Usually he would be joking with the lads – or occasionally but very rarely the girls, but never in the same way as with the lads – but not today. He just stood apart from everyone else as they all filed in, looking at the floor. Shaking his head as if having a conversation either with himself or someone only he could hear.

Chatter and banter filled the room, the smell of takeaway coffee, paninis and pastries filled the air. Matthews studied Beresford. His eyes were red but not like they were the previous day. This just looked like lack of sleep. His usually immaculate dress sense – or if not immaculate, always neatly turned out to an almost military degree – was absent too. It looked like he had slept in the clothes he was wearing. Matthews looked round. No one else seemed to have noticed it. And there was something else too. Imani was absent.

Matthews had gone home the previous evening unable to relax. His wife had thought it was because of the case he was working on, had run him a bath and handed him a cup of tea. And he was grateful for that. But he couldn't tell her the real truth. He felt guilty. And, if he was being honest with himself, ashamed. Of what he had told Beresford. For what he had allowed Beresford to do to him.

He had given Imani his word. She had told him that she would be looking into Beresford because she found his behaviour suspect. Deep down, Matthews agreed with her. This was no way to run an investigation. If he had been in charge he would have done it differently. But he had rationalised it, thought that was just him being him, getting ideas above his rank and pay grade. It was only when Imani shared those suspicions that he felt justified in thinking such things. So what had he done? How had he repaid her? At the first opportunity he had covered for himself. Retreated behind Beresford's thinly veiled threats. Allowed himself to be intimidated. And given her up.

He had tried to rationalise it, claim to himself that he had done the right thing, that he was only looking after himself, that Beresford had been right in what he had said. But as soon as he had spoken, he knew he had said the wrong thing. And the more he thought about it, the more he was convinced that he was right.

And now Imani was absent. What was he to make of that?

He looked up at Beresford again. The man looked like he was unravelling. He started to speak.

'OK, thanks everyone for your, your attention.' Beresford glanced round the room. He didn't make eye contact, didn't seem to know why he was there. He closed his eyes and seemed to give himself a shake. Opened them again. Ready to go.

'Right. We've, er ... where are we today? How far have we got?'

He pointed at people, seemingly at random, asking for updates. There didn't seem to have been any. The same as yesterday, and the day before. No further information. No momentum. Beresford nodded at this news, as if everyone was giving the right answers to his questions.

Matthews waited patiently for Beresford to ask him for an update. Because he had made progress. Potentially, he had discovered other victims of the same killer. Or at least similar methods of death. Matthews was a cautious man. He wouldn't allow his imagination to run away with him.

Matthews had spent the rest of the previous day scanning the central police computer, looking for similarities in unsolved deaths. He didn't think he would make much progress since it was such a rarefied method of death but he had surprised himself. In addition to the three he had found when Beresford decided to have his little chat, he had subsequently discovered another two and potentially three more. He had then contacted local police forces, tried to speak to someone involved with the cases. From there he had attempted to build up a picture of the activity and a timeline.

The murders had all happened over a five- or six-year period. And, try as he might, he couldn't discern a pattern to them. They seemed to be random. And they were unevenly spaced out too. Two months between one, three years between another. Or at least that was what he had found. Maybe there were more, still waiting to be discovered.

Matthews, despite being a cautious man, desperately wanted to use the phrase 'serial killer' but knew he didn't dare. From what he knew – admittedly gleaned from films and the odd crime novel – serial killers worked in patterns. They had specific ways of committing their crimes, took trophies and always left some kind of signature. Besides the method of death, there didn't seem to be anything like that here. But the descriptions were the same. The victim had been seen talking to a woman in the bar the night before. Eyewitnesses could never agree on what she looked like. And then the victim, usually a middle-aged male, would be found dead. The same method of killing: a small hole several vertebrae down. Just the right place to paralyse. But small enough to be overlooked by a coroner not suspecting foul play. It was only later – if further investigation took place and it wasn't accepted as a heart attack – that financial irregularities were noticed. A large sum of money missing from his account. The trail would eventually dry up, the case would be left open. And that was that.

Until now. Until Matthews came calling, trying to link them all together.

And still he sat in the briefing, waiting for Beresford to call him to speak. And every time someone finished one of their pointless summings up, he would look anywhere but at Matthews.

Eventually the briefing broke up. Matthews felt that he hadn't been assigned a task. He waited until the floor had cleared, went up to see Beresford who was now sitting at his desk, looking at his screen, but not seeing it. From close up he smelt bad. Like something within him had started to go rotten.

'Sir?'

Beresford didn't look up. Matthews waited.

'Sir,' he said again, louder this time.

Beresford had no choice but to look at him. And Matthews found himself staring at a different man. The cocky, self-described alpha was missing. In his place was a tortured, even scared individual. He looked like the kind of devout Catholic monk that Matthews had seen in films who was terrified of God and wouldn't stop self-harming as a result.

'What d'you want?' Beresford sighed the words out.

'I . . . well I was wondering what you wanted me to do today, sir.'

Beresford shook his head, a teacher who couldn't be

bothered to talk to an unfavourite pupil. 'Whatever you were doing yesterday. Keep . . . keep doing that.'

'That's the thing, sir. I've been putting together potential victims that match the post-mortem on the three initial victims. I've found five more that match and another three that may do. God knows how many others there are.'

Beresford said nothing. Acted like he either hadn't heard him or didn't want to hear him.

Matthews felt compelled to continue. 'Surely we should be doing something about it? I mean, and I hate to use this phrase, but maybe we're looking at a serial killer.'

Again, nothing from Beresford.

'Well, surely that changes the whole complexion of the case, doesn't it? Shouldn't we be getting more people to work on it?'

Nothing.

'Sir, why didn't you ask me to give my findings in the briefing? I'm the only one who's made progress. Surely that should be shared with the team?'

Beresford eventually looked up. Stared at Matthews for a few seconds then looked away, seemingly unhappy with what he could see.

'Just keep doing what you're doing, Matthews.'

'But sir, I—'

'Just keep doing what you're doing. That's all.' Almost growling the words this time.

Matthews felt anger rising within him. And superior officer or no superior officer, he wasn't prepared to take this any longer.

'Where's Imani?' His voice was louder, angrier than he had wanted it to be. The odd head looked up from their work towards him.

Beresford tried to pretend he hadn't heard.

'I said where's Imani?' His heart was pounding. He had never spoken to a senior officer this way. Had never dared.

'Gone,' said Beresford, eventually.

'Gone where? Back to Birmingham?'

'Yeah. There. Wherever.' He looked up again. And this time there was something close to murder in his eyes. 'Now get back to work.'

Matthews walked back to his own desk.

Work was now the last thing on his mind.

44

Anni watched Marina sleep.

Exhausted from the night before, she had curled up and gone straight to sleep on the sofa as soon as she got back to Anni's flat. Anni had covered her with a duvet and let her sleep. Now, mug of coffee in hand, she sat and watched her. Watched over her, it felt like. Tried to make sure she didn't get into any more difficult situations. But, given both their track records, that was something of an impossibility.

Anni had eventually freed herself from Malcolm and his insistent questions and found there was a voicemail from Marina on her phone. She had listened. Heard what Marina said about Michael Prosser. Told her she'd left the same message with Imani too. Nothing yet from Imani.

Anni had jumped straight into her car after hearing that. She had planned to hit the gym for an hour or so, keep up the good work, but there was no way she could do that now, not after what had happened to Marina the last time she had been to Michael Prosser's. She must really want whatever information he has, she thought. Must want it desperately to go through that again.

Straight down the A12 to Chelmsford, trying to stay the right side of the speed limit as she went, not always doing so. This is when I miss being on the force, she thought.

Parked outside his flat, ran straight down the alley from the previous night, up the stairs, banging on the door. She waited, body tensed, coiled, breathing controlled, ready to leap into action again.

The door was opened. Michael Prosser stood there, his ruined face catching the weak light from the hallway.

'Oh. You must be Anni. Or Imani?'

'Anni.'

'Right. Come in.'

He stood aside to let her enter. She did so, noticing some kind of dressing on the side of his head as she did so.

She walked into the living room. Marina was sitting on the sofa, mug of tea in her hand.

'Hi, Anni,' she said, looking up. 'Kettle's just boiled if you want one.'

'I'm ... I'm all right, thanks ...'

This wasn't the scene she had been expecting.

Prosser came in, took his seat in the armchair, picked up his own mug of tea. Anni, looking between the pair of them, trying to hide her bewilderment, sat down next to Marina. She tried to give Marina a glance that said, Give it up, what's happened?

Marina took the cue, spoke in front of Prosser. 'Michael needed a bit of an adjustment in attitude if we were to have a conversation.'

Anni looked once more to the dressing on his head, saw the heavy metal torch sitting on top of Marina's bag. Understood.

Prosser sat with eyes downcast. 'I get ... sometimes I, I forget how to talk to people. I've got a lot of ...' He put his tea down, clenched and unclenched his fists.

'I know,' said Marina. 'Now let's move on.'

Anni recognised Marina's professional voice when she heard it.

Prosser nodded, seeming almost bashful.

Anni looked at the arm of Prosser's chair. A cheque lay there. She couldn't see the amount but she recognised Marina's signature. She knew what Marina was doing, why she was behaving the way she was towards Prosser. She had made an investment. She was being careful not to damage it.

'So,' Marina went on, 'you were telling me about the children's home.'

'Yeah,' said Prosser. 'Well, you know about . . . what they said about me. All of that.'

Marina nodded, said nothing. Very professional, thought Anni. Very controlled.

'It was the girl,' she continued. 'You mentioned her. She's the one we're interested in.'

'Right, yes.' He nodded. And in his ruined face, Anni saw that his mind had slipped back. Or he was thinking something he didn't want to share with them. That was fine with Anni; if it wasn't pertinent to the investigation, the less Michael Prosser shared with her the better.

'There was Fiona Welch. And this other girl. Thick as thieves they were.' He almost laughed. 'Pretty apt description.'

'Why?' asked Marina.

'Because that's what they were. They managed to get the vulnerable girls as they came in, befriend them, then pimp them out to the local gangs.'

'And why didn't you stop this?' Anni couldn't help it. Her voice rose as she spoke. She was aware of Marina flashing her a warning glance. She didn't look at her.

'What could I do?' Prosser shrugged. 'This was happening outside of the home, away from my jurisdiction. I had . . . there was nothing I could do.'

'So you turned a blind eye. Let these two girls abuse other girls when you had a duty of care to them.'

Marina turned to her. 'This isn't helping us, Anni.' She turned back to Prosser. 'Sorry, Michael. Please, continue.'

Anni knew what Marina had done, made an ally of Prosser, made an enemy of Anni. Good tactic, encouraged him to talk more to her. Confide. But she didn't like being on the receiving end. However, she kept her mouth shut, let him tell his story in his own way.

'Well, so these two girls. Ran the place, they did. Everyone was frightened of them. Everyone.'

'This other girl. What was her name?'

'Carol Woods.'

Marina and Anni shared another glance. Now they had it, something concrete. A name. They could work on it, make a breakthrough. Prosser's next words brought them down to earth.

'At least that was the name she was going by.'

Marina frowned. 'What d'you mean, Michael?'

'Well, when she came to the home, that was the name we were presented with. And she answered to it. Or she did after a while. Like she was getting used to it. Other kids thought she was deaf at first. But after a while they all called her it.'

Anni leaned forward. 'So what was her real name?'

Prosser made a helpless gesture. 'Dunno. We were never given it.'

'Is that usual behaviour?' asked Marina.

'Depends. Sometimes when kids are put into care they're given new identities. Like if they've been abused, so their abuser can't get a hold of them. Or they're sent to a different part of the country.'

'But you're always told about that? Given their backstory?'

'Usually, yeah. But not always.'

'Doesn't that stop you giving them help they need?'

'Yeah. Although with some of them, it's best not to know. In the child's best interests that as few people know about their background as possible. Gives them a chance to get over it.'

'And this was one of those cases.'

'Yeah. That's the theory, anyway.'

Another glance between Marina and Anni. Anni saw the sense of hopelessness in Marina's eyes. Like this big, concrete lead she had been counting on and paid for had suddenly turned to sand before her eyes.

'So you don't really know who she was,' said Marina, unable to hide the defeat in her voice.

Prosser nodded. 'And even if that was her name, I doubt she's going by it now.'

'You sound like you've seen her,' said Anni.

Prosser kept his head down. 'No. Not since ... no.' His voice dropped.

Marina was silent, nothing more to ask. Anni looked at her, aware of the weight she had been carrying for the last few days. It seemed to be pressing her down so much now that she seemed unable to move from underneath it.

'So,' said Anni, leaning forward once more, 'if you don't know her real name, d'you know anyone who would?'

Prosser looked up. 'Well, I suppose Caitlin might.'

'Caitlin?' said Marina, springing back to life. 'The woman I spoke to? The one who gave me your name?'

'Yeah, that's her.'

'And she would know her name? Her real name? Would she have photos of her? Or know of her whereabouts?'

'I don't know, but she's worth a try. She's got access to those files.'

'Come on,' said Anni, standing up. 'Too late to do anything tonight. That's for the morning.'

*

And now Anni sat there, watching Marina sleep.

She was sure Marina wouldn't have wanted her to, would have insisted that she get up, start looking for this woman. But Anni was content to let her sleep on. It was the right decision. Because one way or another, Marina was going to need all her strength for whatever lay ahead.

An Easy Life

If the tabloids had got hold of what she was doing, they would have called it a killing spree. Or worse. Her gender would have been invoked in as titillating a way as possible, there would have been a scramble to get photos of her, or background on her, and there would be lurid reconstructions of her seductions and murder methods. Because sex sells. And sex and death sells best of all.

But the tabloids would never get hold of what she was doing. She knew that. Never in a million years. Because she genuinely believed she wasn't like anyone else and she wasn't going to be caught. Serial killers got caught because they got careless. Because they thought they were all geniuses and couldn't resist letting their pursuers know that. Then they became sloppy, like they wanted to be caught. Then they were, eventually, stopped. One way or another. It was a cycle. She knew all about it. Had read up on the subject. And she knew that wasn't her or what she was doing. She had as much in common with them as she had with suicide bombers.

This was how she made a living. Nothing more, nothing less. And when she had enough to live on she would stop. Simple as that. Doing what she did was just like going to work every day. Well, not every day for her. Because she was so good at her job she didn't need to work every day.

She had honed her skills down to a fine art. But that didn't mean she had become complacent. Complacency was the enemy of creativity, she had once read. And she liked to think that, if nothing else, she was creative.

On the surface it seemed simple. Go to a hotel, wait, find her target. Take him back to his room, seduce him, paralyse him, clean out his bank account. Or at least skim an amount that was in itself sizeable but wouldn't be traced. Like an ISA or two. Something like that. She didn't get greedy. She worked within her system, her rules.

But beyond that surface simplicity was more complexity. She planned, watched. Targeted from a distance. Then when she was ready and only then, she would make her move. Conventions were best. Or business gatherings. She had become very proficient at spotting which of the herd was the most vulnerable. Or at least the most susceptible. Years of training had developed that skill. But that wasn't enough. She would then study her prey, his mannerisms, his likes, dislikes. His interactions with women, especially. Most important of all. And then she would see who he responded to, who he didn't and she would build her character, her look, accordingly.

This would all be done in the space of a day or so. If there wasn't anyone there who she thought her approach would work on, she left it alone. Went somewhere else, tried someone else. There was, she had discovered, no shortage of middle-aged married men ready to take a young woman to bed if they could get away with it.

When she had her target in sight, she would think best how to approach him. It wasn't always as easy as sitting on a bar stool waiting. She had to be cleverer than that. She did what needed to be done. She improvised sometimes. Other times she stuck to a rigid script of her own devising. But always with her focus on the eventual prize.

She went to great pains not to be noticed while she prepared, to be as anonymous as possible. She was good at that. What the Native Americans called hiding in plain sight. She had read about that too. And then she moved in on her prey. Separated him from

293

the rest of his pack, moved in for the kill. Literally. Upstairs to his room, the promise of sex luring him on.

Then the fatal, simple wound. Then she would tell him that he was paralysed and the only way he could get out of it was to give her a substantial sum of money. They always did. And they always died. Then she would pack up her iPad, wipe down any surface for prints, check she had made as little contact with the deceased as possible, and move on. Back to her own room, ditch the guise she had been in, sleep and leave the next day.

She would have the best night's sleep after doing that.

And that was that. Her glory years, she called them.

Was she lonely? Did she wish for comfort, companionship? Sometimes. Maybe. But the more she did this, the more she found herself pulling away from any other kind of contact with people. She was an attractive woman, and picked up admirers along her path. Men and women. But she rebuffed them all. Because, she rationalised, nothing would give her the thrill she got from her work.

Because it was a thrill. Yes it was a job, but what kind of life did a person have if they didn't enjoy their work? It was a cumulative thrill. Watching their excitement as they realised this woman was interested in them, the realisation that they were going to have sex with her and, most important of all, get away with it. Then back to the room, the nervous hesitation, or some speech about how they loved their wife but . . . She would listen patiently. Then the gasp when she undressed. She loved that part. It was her second favourite bit. She felt a huge surge of power through her body as the men gazed on her nakedness. Drank her in with their eyes. Stared in awe. She felt so alive in those moments. Like her body was composed purely of electricity. Immortal, beautiful, shining electricity.

And then came the killing. Her favourite part. Not because she wanted them dead particularly, but because it was an extension *of that power, that electricity. She had the power of life and death over these men. And they knew it. What could be better than that?*

And then that slow, lingering part when they would die. She would watch them, eyes wide and staring, as the life drained from them. They couldn't talk by this time, so complete was their paralysis, so she couldn't ask them questions. But she wanted to. What did they see? What were they feeling? What was there? It fascinated her. If she allowed it, it could consume her.

And then death. And it never ceased to be an amazing moment. One second there would be life. The next, nothing. Just dead meat. Incredible. And that just made her wonder all the more. Where had that energy gone? What was there to see? She was envious of them, in a way. They were having an experience that she couldn't share in. At least not yet.

So that was that. Her easy life. She had a home, a place she had bought, but she very rarely visited. And when she did she felt restless, wanting to be out on the road again. Home was where she went when there was nowhere else to go.

Yet she knew this couldn't last. For many reasons. She would get older, perhaps lose her looks, become less attractive to men. Or she might get bored. And if she got bored, she might become complacent. And she knew all about guarding against that. So no. It couldn't last. Best to make as much as she could right now. Go out on a high, while she was still enjoying it. And then let the future take care of itself.

That was the plan. And then she came back to Essex.

Was it out of sentimentality? She didn't know. Was it fate? Perhaps. Whatever the reason, she found herself back in Colchester, just up the road from her old home, if she could call it that. She didn't know how she felt. She had been expecting some kind of rush of emotions but she hadn't felt it. Instead it was like walking familiar paths but in an unfamiliar way. Like she was visiting places an old friend had told her about.

And then she turned on the TV. Saw the news.

Fiona Welch was dead.

And she genuinely didn't know what to think, how to feel. Stunned? Shocked? Yes, probably. But that was nothing compared to the news that followed. Because she saw the detective who was at the heart of the case, the one who had caught her.

Sean. Back from the dead.

45

'**B**ack from the dead then, are you?'

Phil opened his eyes. A woman's face floated before him. She looked familiar. In a good way. The best way. He smiled.

'Eileen?'

'That's right, Phil. It's me. Eileen.'

He blinked. Hope rose within him. Those last few days had all been just a horrible dream. No, not even a dream, a nightmare. But so real he could have touched it, felt it. Experienced it. But it was gone now, that face said. He was home. Safe.

He blinked again. Eileen's features shifted, rearranging themselves, coalescing from something familiar to something different, yet still holding enough of a seed of familiarity to make him catch his breath, believe what he saw. He kept looking. And with a groan of despair that echoed down at the bottom of his soul, he realised who she was and where he was.

This was no dream. This was real. If it was a nightmare it was a waking one.

'That was a long sleep you had. I thought it best to just let you. You seemed very tired last night. And agitated, too.' She sat down next to him. Reached out a hand, stroked his hair. 'But I calmed you down, didn't I?'

Phil closed his eyes, remembering. The feel of her body. His mouth on her breasts . . .

His mind was consumed by guilt, rage, embarrassment, pain. All there, running through him, triggered by the memory. And on top of all that were plenty more emotions too. Ones he couldn't so readily name. Ones that kept him down, stopped him from taking any action. He should have been up, off the bed, screaming at her. Telling him what he thought, planning all the while how he could get away. But something stopped him. He tried to work out what it was. Realised. He just didn't have the energy. The will. He couldn't even be bothered to move.

And with that revelation came another. He no longer knew what to think, what to feel. How to react. He didn't know what he was doing any more. Right and wrong, good and evil, order and chaos even, had gone, slipped away from him.

Resignation. That was his overwhelming, overriding emotion. Besting all the other emotions, hitting him like a train and laying him flat. He just wanted to close his eyes, let it all slip away. Let everything go. Forever.

This was his world now. This was his right and wrong. Whatever she said.

'You going back to sleep?' the irritatingly perky voice continued. 'No time for that now. But there'll be plenty of time for that later.' She laughed. 'Plenty. But not now. Now you have to be awake, get ready. Big day.'

Phil struggled to sit up. The room seemed lighter, as if it really was morning. It could have been for all he knew. But it could also have been the middle of the night too. Day and night, light and darkness, time itself, had all ceased to have any meaning for him. He was just here. Now.

His hands were still tied to the bedframe. He couldn't rise far.

'Whuh . . . why's it a big day?'

'Just is, that's all. Lot to do. Lot to get ready for.'

She stood up from the bed, walked round the room, examining things as if she should be doing something with them. Dusting or moving objects. But of course there was nothing there to move. Everything was only two-dimensional, so if she wanted to do that she had to mime at best. Which she did, humming to herself, smiling. Like she imagined a mother would do. The brightness of the overhead lighting just showed up how artificial the room was. The walls seemed even flatter than before. The blown up photo walls unconvincing, the life leached out of them. But for Phil the make-believe room didn't matter any more. None of it did. They had gone beyond all that now.

She sat down on the edge of the bed once more, still smiling at him, beatifically. Her eyes glanced at the two tablets, still on the bedside table. Her smile increased, then she returned her look to Phil.

'Are you hungry, love? Want some breakfast?'

Phil had to think about that. Was he hungry? When had he last eaten? What was his body telling him?

'I . . . I don't know . . .'

She laughed at his muddle-headedness. 'What are you boys like . . . Course you're hungry. You're always hungry. I'll go and get you something to eat, then. Would you like a bacon sandwich?'

Would he?

'I'll make you a bacon sandwich.' Another giggle. 'You can have it in bed. Like I said, special day. But watch for crumbs. And don't get sauce on the sheets. Bet you've heard all that before, haven't you? Sick of me saying that to you, nagging all the time.'

She stroked his hair once again. Kept stroking, staring into his eyes all the time. Her fingers moved from his hair to the skin of his face, caressed his cheek. Smiling all the time.

Her breathing increased. He was aware of her breasts, heavy, straining against her blouse, rising and falling with every breath she took.

Phil began to get an erection.

She moved her other hand down the bed, found it. Moved in closer. Mouth on his ear.

'You're a naughty boy, Phil Brennan, you really are. It's a good job I'm an understanding mother. But then . . . ' Her lips right on his ear now. Whispering the words, he could feel her soft breath against his skin, the feel of her hand on his face, stroking the faint scar that was there, the other on his growing erection. 'All boys want to fuck their mother, don't they? Really, deep down?'

She kept her hands, her mouth moving against him.

'And you're no exception . . . '

He closed his eyes. She was still calling him Phil Brennan, but he didn't feel like that person any more. This person still had the same name but he was now someone new. And he didn't know who – or what – he was.

Yes he did. He was whoever she told him he was.

She took her hands slowly away from his body. He opened his eyes. She straightened herself up. Smiling at him all the while. It was a different kind of smile this time, though. Gone was the previous indulgence, the mother almost neurotically smothering her child. Now it was like a different person was occupying the space she had previously rented. This smile was hard-edged, matching her eyes. This smile said one thing:

I win.

She stood up. Rearranged herself as if the mirror on the wall was a real one.

'Right,' she said, 'I'll get your sandwich. Then I have to pop out for a little while.'

Phil tried to clear the fog in his head. 'Why?'

'Just a few errands to run. People to meet. That sort of thing. And then I'll be back.'

She turned to him once more, smiled again. This time the meaning behind that smile was impossible to read.

'And then everything changes.'

Phil frowned. 'In what way? How?'

'You know how I said you have to embrace the darkness of your life, Phil? Go through the darkness, own it, then come into the light?'

He said nothing. Tried to remember whether she had actually said that. It seemed so long ago.

'Well, that's what we're about to do. You've got to go through the final phase. Into the final darkness. And then . . . Oh. So exciting.'

'What?'

'You're going to come into the light. And your life is going to change. In the biggest and best way ever.'

'How?'

'You're going to meet someone, Phil. Someone very, very special. And you're going to be so happy, that the two of you are going to be together forever . . .'

46

Matthews stared at his screen. But the words, images just moved about, like they were flowing over the surface, falling off the bottom onto his desk. He rubbed his eyes. No good. He just couldn't concentrate.

Imani. That was all he could think about. DS Imani Oliver. And what he had done to her. Or may have done to her.

He had phoned her several times. Nothing. No reply. Straight to voicemail every time. OK, he had reasoned at first, maybe she was on her way back to Birmingham. Driving, unable to pick up. But even as he thought that he knew he was trying to convince himself. What police officer would be unavailable, even when they were driving? Everyone he knew – including himself – plugged their phone in on entering the car, put it on hands free. Stayed contactable at all times. No. That was wrong. She wouldn't have done that. And also, he had seen how much she relied on her phone the day before, constantly trying to remain in touch with Anni Hepburn and Marina Esposito and making herself available to them in return.

No. There had to be a different reason.

He went over all their conversations from the previous day, tried to find some clue as to her whereabouts. And it all came back to one thing: she didn't trust Beresford. And she was going to look into his background. Starting with his car.

She had had a feeling that it wasn't in the garage as he had claimed. And Matthews had been listening, heard no mention from Beresford that his car was out of commission and he was borrowing a pool car or a hire. Nothing like that. So that just ramped up his suspicions.

He knew which garage Beresford had claimed to use. Imani had told him. So, furtively, checking no one was in earshot, he had called the garage. And received voicemail there too. Several times.

Now he was becoming uneasy. His unease was powered by guilt, he knew that, but he was starting to fear that something was wrong. Seriously wrong, perhaps. He glanced round the office. Beresford was nowhere to be seen, having disappeared after receiving a phone call. And that had been peculiar too. Whoever it was had seriously shaken him up. Matthews had watched as he listened to whoever it had been, his face getting paler all the time. Then, when he had put the phone down, he had looked round the office and left.

So now Matthews stood up and, without saying anything to anyone, left the office.

Prentice's Garage wasn't hard to find. Not in terms of direction, only in terms of size. It looked like a two storey lean-to on the end of a row of houses in New Town with a small sign and a large metal pull-down door. Which was currently closed. He parked opposite, crossed over to it. Tried it. Locked.

He looked round, bent down to the lock. A padlock attached to a ring concreted into the ground. Right, he thought. He crossed back to his car, opened the boot, brought out a crowbar. Looking around again, he bent down and, not without some effort, managed to break the ring and release the padlock.

Straightening up he felt dizzy, nauseous. His arms shaking from exertion. He took a moment, back against the wall, arms down at his sides, breathing deeply, trying to get his bearings again. It was the most exercise he'd had in ages. The most physical thing he had done possibly ever. But looking down at the broken padlock, he had to admit it felt good. Like the kind of police work most of the other officers would do and then brag about. He never usually felt part of that world, stayed out of those conversations. He smiled. If they could see him now . . .

He was sweating through his shirt, into his jacket. He loosened his tie, an unheard of thing for Simon Matthews to do. He was truly breaking new ground today.

Wiping his brow with the back of his hand, he looked round once more. Alert for anyone who may have seen what he was doing. If they had seen him they weren't letting on. But, he thought, it was that kind of area.

Bending down once more, he swung the door up and open. Stepped inside.

Light from outside hit the interior. He saw a light switch on the wall, reached for it. An overhead strip light came on. He turned back, pulled the door closed. Looked back into the room.

And stopped dead.

A car was resting haphazardly on the lift, one side higher than the other. He crossed over to it, looked down to find the obstruction. Found, in amongst a pool of congealed blood and oil, an overalled body, legs sticking out.

'Oh God . . . Oh God . . .'

He backed away, heart hammering. Nausea building up inside him once more.

He turned, put a steadying arm out to the wooden staircase.

And that was when he saw her.

She had been bundled into the stairwell, roughly, by the looks of it. Bent double and just stuffed into the space. He saw the jeans she had been wearing the previous day, her boots sticking out. He fumbled in his pocket for his phone and, with shaking fingers, turned the flashlight on. Her head was resting at an impossible angle to her neck. Eyes closed. Her shoulder and upper torso looked like they were pointing in opposite directions.

He backed away.

Shaking so much he felt like he just vibrated out of existence, heart pounding hard enough to jump out of his ribcage.

'Fuck ... fuck ... fuck ... Christ ... fuck ... '

He put his hand to his face, rubbed his eyes. It didn't help. He spun round, looking to see what else could leap out and surprise him. Didn't find anything. His arms flailed uselessly.

'Jesus ... Jesus ... fuck ... '

He felt his knees go, his nausea build. Knew he could sink to the floor at any second. He backed up to the closed metal door, leaned against it. His body slammed against it, the sound echoing round the walls. He closed his eyes, tried to regain control of his body.

'Fuck ... fuck ... '

He felt tears well within him. Tears of shame, of anger, of guilt. Of self-hatred at what he had done, at what he had allowed to have happened.

No. No. Not this. Not now. Later, but not now.

He fought hard, denying their release, regaining control of himself once more.

It took a few seconds – or perhaps minutes, he wasn't sure how long he had stood there – but eventually he managed it.

Straightening his tie, pulling his jacket back into place and fastening the button, he opened the garage door. Stepped outside. He walked across the street to where he'd parked his car, opened the boot, brought out a roll of crime scene tape. He always carried it with him, just in case. Be prepared. He had never used it. Until now.

He pulled the garage door down, attempting to close it once more with the broken padlock. Having done that, he unrolled the tape, placed it at either side of the door. He stretched another length across until it was resting in a huge X shape.

Then, still keeping his voice together, he made a phone call.

Once that was done, he pocketed his phone, straightened his jacket once more.

And vomited all over the pavement.

Detective Work

*D*etective Inspector Phil Brennan. That's what her TV screen told her. But she knew better than to believe what the TV screen told her. She knew his real name. Sean.

The name she had killed him under.

She watched the news, waited for the next news report, devoured that too. Got online, went to every news website that she could find. Read and watched everything. And the end result was still the same. Fiona Welch was dead.

She sat back. Tried to process that fact. It was going to be too much for her. She could feel it, was sure of it. All too much for her. Everything that she had kept hidden all those years, the suppressed emotions, the rage, the guilt and fear, all of it, was going to spill out now. Definitely.

Except. It never happened.

She experienced shock, disbelief. All of that. She couldn't believe what she was seeing and hearing. At least at first. But as the news sank in, she realised that the expected emotions weren't going to materialise. She waited for that rush but nothing happened. No mourning, no regret. No anger at her manipulation and eventual betrayal, even after all this time. Just . . . a kind of emptiness.

That was as much as she could acknowledge. Or her subconscious was prepared to acknowledge. After all, she wasn't exactly a stranger to death. Not the way she had been living for the last few years. And when she realised what Fiona Welch had been doing, how she had died, she was even less surprised. She had tried to prove a thesis she had written on the susceptibility of humanity, using murder and manipulation to demonstrate it. The fact that she had fallen – or been pushed, the news was vague on that point – to her death seemed kind of appropriate somehow. She couldn't explain how, but it just felt like it did. Fiona had been pursuing a different kind of murder to what she had been doing. More of a typical serial killer, no matter how many academic phrases she dressed it up in. How boring, she thought. How disappointing.

But Sean, that was another matter entirely.

Days went by and still she devoured the news. But her attention had started to wane where Fiona Welch was concerned. She was dead and gone now. No point in moping over her. But the detective, that was another matter. She wanted to know everything about him.

Detective Inspector Phil Brennan worked for Essex Police as a member of the Major Incident Unit. Or Murder Squad for short. He was married to a criminal psychologist called Marina Esposito who had until recently taught at Essex University. He was considered somewhat unconventional. His dress sense told her that. Most police officers were in uniform even when they were allowed to wear plain clothes. Not Phil Brennan. She had seen him interviewed on TV and he wore a tweed jacket and waistcoat with a plaid shirt underneath it. A tie had been slung round his neck almost as if in penance. He had a dressing on the side of his face. That, he stated whilst being interviewed, had been caused by Fiona Welch when she had kidnapped him.

A shiver of excitement ran through her when she heard that.

She had to find out more about the man. No, she had to find out everything she could about the man. She decided to stay in Colchester, at least for a while. She had been thinking of settling down somewhere and her own house was too far to get back to.

This would do fine. She rented an apartment by the river, in the same block that one of Fiona Welch's victims had lived in. She had hoped it was the same flat but she didn't think so. Although the rent was quite reasonable so she liked to think it was. Imagine to herself.

She began to haunt the library, checking out the newspaper library to find out everything she could about Phil Brennan. It was on one of her frequent trips that she became aware of the fact that she had attracted attention. Usually that would have been something she hated, and would have even actively – and possibly fatally – discouraged, but not this time. He was a librarian. And he seemed harmless enough.

Sorry for interrupting you, he had said one day after she had photocopied some old pages of the Colchester Gazette, *but I couldn't help noticing you're interested in crime.*

She turned to him, ready to . . . what? She didn't know. But then she looked at the man. Small, inoffensive. The overriding impression she got from him: loneliness. So she let him talk. Answered him.

That's right.

Are you a journalist? Something like that?

No, I'm just interested. Crime is a . . . hobby of mine.

His eyes had lit up at her words. Straight away she worked out why. He was an enthusiast. He thought he had found a fellow traveller. She smiled inwardly. If he only knew who he was talking to . . .

I'm looking into all the recent cases that Phil Brennan was involved in.

Really? This is your lucky day, he said.

She frowned.

I'm quite the collector. An enthusiast. I have, if I say so myself, amassed and collated a rather large collection of crime-related materials. All local, of course. I'm something of the historian.

Interesting.

309

Of course, I'd be happy to share it with a fellow enthusiast.

She fixed a smile in place.

And I'd be happy for you to do that.

And so began a quite unlikely friendship. Malcolm was as good as his word. His house had been turned into a filing system for his crime reports. She found the attention to detail that he had fascinating. He gave her total access. The first thing she did, of course, was look through his files for mention of herself. There was nothing there. Not directly. Just a couple of unexplained deaths of middle-aged men in hotels. She felt a familiar surge of power just reading about them. Knowing she caused that to happen, one less person walking on the earth because of her. And no one knew the truth of what had actually happened. Well, only two people. And one of them was dead.

But it was Phil Brennan she was interested in. And Malcolm had plenty of information about him. And it was a pleasure to devour it.

She also noticed something else happening while she was working her way through Malcolm's files. Malcolm was falling for her. He didn't come out and actually say anything, but she could tell. He began to take care of himself more. Washing his clothes more often, attending to his personal hygiene. He even tidied the house for her coming round, bought her expensive biscuits to go with her cup of tea. She tried not to notice but it was extremely noticeable.

This, she thought, presented her with a choice, do one of two things: walk away before he tried to get to know her better and began to see through the mousy disguise she had adopted, or fuck him.

She chose the latter.

It was easy. And it didn't take long. And Malcolm was so grateful. She had never experienced anything like it. And it was a new feeling for her too. The first time that she hadn't seduced a man simply to take his money and his life. It was a reciprocal agreement: she gave him what he wanted in return for him letting her have what

310

she wanted. No more, no less. And once that was out of the way she could get on with the important work, discovering Phil Brennan.

But fucking Malcolm came with its own set of risks. She had thought that he would be satisfied with that but he wasn't. She could tell that he was getting hung up on her, beginning to believe they were having a relationship. He had already started asking questions about her. Her life, her background. Her family. And there was only so long she could deflect them for. And given his skills at investigation he would try – and possibly succeed – to find out something about her.

So she decided to disappear again. Time to rest this persona. And she did. Walked away, disappeared from his life. And she felt nothing. Malcolm, she knew, wouldn't see it that way. She had broken his heart. She didn't feel too bad about it. The way she looked at it, he had been lucky. She could have done so much worse to him.

And she had what she wanted. As much information as it was possible to get on Phil Brennan. Now she just had to decide what to do with it. Why she was so obsessed with him, why she felt such an affinity with him. The resemblance to Sean wasn't enough. There must be something more.

A few months later she found out exactly what that was.

311

47

'Come in,' Michael Prosser called. 'It's open.'

He had sat in the same chair all day. Hadn't moved at all. Just thinking.

Thinking. And accepting.

He had made a phone call after Marina and Anni had left. His heart had been heavy but he had realised he had no choice. He knew what was coming. Expected it. Once he had made that phone call he knew that everything would change. He had just been trying to decide if it was for the better or not. That was all.

And, all in all, he decided that it probably was.

Respect. How fucking stupid. How pathetic. Respect. As if that would ever happen. Could ever happen. Not now. Not ever, really. Too much had happened to him. He had caused too much of it. That was the thing. And the visit of those women in the last couple of days just brought it home to him how pitiful the whole thing was. How pitiful he was. Because their visit had shown him just how far apart he was from what he wanted, how low he had fallen. Respect. Yeah, right.

It's the hope that kills you. He didn't know where he'd first heard that one. But it was so right. Those women, especially yesterday, especially Marina Esposito, had given him hope. And that had led him to make that call. Which in turn had led to this visit.

So yeah, that phrase was just about perfect.

'Michael Prosser?'

He turned, surprised. This wasn't the voice he had been expecting. It was male for a start.

'Who the fuck are you?'

The man stepped into his living room. Prosser got a good look at him. Tall, well-built, shaven-headed. Well dressed, too. Or at least expensively dressed. His suit looked like it had been slept in. His face, like his head, was sprouting stubble. He looked like an angry peach. And his eyes were red-rimmed.

Prosser recognised him. He was the man who had attacked Marina Esposito in the alley a few nights ago.

'Do you want my name?' the man asked. 'Would that make it any easier?'

'Sit down,' said Prosser, pointing to the sofa. 'You may as well.'

He sat down. Prosser noticed he was wearing gloves. Latex ones. He had expected something like that.

'I know who you are,' Prosser said. 'From the other night. And from the home. I remember you. And I know you remember me.'

His visitor seemed uneasy. 'Right.'

'She sent you, didn't she?'

He nodded. 'Yeah.'

'Well, then. That's all we need to say to each other.'

'Look,' said his visitor, 'I just want you to know ... I just ...'

Prosser waited. His visitor looked like a man used to speaking his mind but not explaining his heart.

'I ... Look, given the choice I wouldn't be doing this.'

'Choice?'

'It's my son, see. She's got my son. So I've got no choice. And my wife.' A huge sigh. 'She's got her too.'

'I see. And you have to do what she wants if you ever want to see them alive again.'

'Yeah.' He looked up, straight at Prosser as if he had just read his mind. 'That's . . . that's it. Exactly it.'

'So why not go to the police?'

The visitor stood up, looked about ready to explode. 'I am the fucking police!'

Prosser just stared. He didn't feel like he was in any danger from the man's outburst. He was just venting his own guilt, rage and impotence at her. And that was OK. Prosser could well understand that.

'So how did she get you?' asked Prosser, genuinely curious. 'I mean, I think I can guess. But I'd like to know.'

He said nothing. Just stood there staring at something that wasn't in the room. Or even the present.

'Did she fuck you? Seduce you?'

He nodded. 'Yeah.' He laughed. It was bitter and soon died out. 'Pathetic, isn't it?'

Prosser almost smiled. There was a word he could relate to.

He continued. 'She said at first that she'd tell my wife. And my son. Well, obviously I didn't want that, did I? So I tried to stop her.'

'Not easy, is it?'

He shook his head.

'Didn't realise what kind of person you'd taken on. At least, not until it was too late.' Prosser felt he could have been talking out loud about himself. 'You never win with her.'

His visitor nodded. 'Yeah. I found that out.'

'The hard way,' and before his visitor could answer, continued, 'I'm guessing this wasn't the first time you'd cheated on your wife.' Asking questions again. Intimate ones. He almost felt like he had his old job back again. Social work. Helping

314

people. He shook his head. A last hurrah before the end. Dignity. Respect.

Or self-delusion.

Whichever.

'No,' said his visitor. 'It wasn't. Not by a, by a long ... whatever.' He walked towards the window, tried to look out through the grime-encrusted glass. 'She found out, you see. My wife. About the others. Well, not all of them. One of them. And it made her think there'd been others. I mean, you would, wouldn't you? And there had been. So I ... I threw myself on her mercy, so to speak. Asked for forgiveness.' He turned back to Prosser. 'I feel I can tell you all this.'

'You can. Go on.'

'It worked. For a while, anyway. And we had Callum, my son. And he was supposed to bring us back together, make us stronger again. Change everything.'

'And then she came along.'

He nodded.

'And she was ... let me guess. The kind of woman you'd always wanted but didn't realise until you met her? Not to mention the best fuck you'd ever had, of course.'

He nodded. 'Yeah, I ... yeah.' Amazement in his voice at having his thoughts so neatly summed up.

Prosser nodded. 'She's good at that. Her unique talent, you might say.'

His visitor stared at him. Really looking at him, as if actually seeing him for the first time. 'What's your story, then?'

Prosser pointed to his ruined face. 'This. Her. All you need to know, really.'

He nodded once more.

The two men occupied the room in silence. Eventually, Prosser broke it.

'And then she wanted you for something. And to make sure you did it, she took your wife and son.'

'Yeah.'

'And said that you'd only see them alive when you'd done what she wanted.'

'Yeah.'

'And that was ... what? Covering for her? Killing for her?'

He nodded, head downcast. 'And the rest.'

'And you think that after today she'll let you have them back again.'

'Maybe not after today, maybe she still wants me to do something more for her. But I hope not. I just want ... want them back again.'

'Sure, she'll let you see them again. She might even let you have them again. But they'll both be dead.'

He looked up sharply, as if he'd been stabbed. 'What? What the fuck are you on about?'

'They're dead already. Or most probably dead.'

'No ...' He began pacing the room, hands to his head. 'No ... don't say that ... no ...'

'Sorry to disappoint you, but they're already dead.'

'No ... no ...'

'Yeah. They are.' Prosser sat back. 'So really, you've done all this for nothing, haven't you? Should have gone to police after all.'

He crossed the floor, stood towering over Prosser. 'I can't believe that ... I can't ... can't ...'

His anger peaked. He reached down, grabbed Prosser by the throat, picked him bodily off the seat. Squeezed his hands hard around his neck.

'Go on ...' said Prosser, through gasped breaths, 'go on. I'm ready. It's ... it's what you came here to do ...'

And then he was in tears. Rage giving way to something else, huge, flowing streams cascading down his face.

'I'm sorry ... I'm so, so sorry ...' Not talking to Prosser now, he was sure of that.

Prosser stared at him, tried to hold eye contact.

'Sorry ... I ... oh God ... sorry ...'

Prosser's eyes closed. Behind them it seemed like stars were forming and galaxies were bursting. He felt beyond pain, beyond stress. He began to feel at peace.

'Sorry ...'

His words gave way to uncontrollable sobs as he dropped the lifeless body to the floor. As it fell, he collapsed beside it, like a puppet with its strings cut. Sobbing his heart out.

That's when DCI Franks and Marina Esposito ran into the room.

Seconds too late.

Epiphanies

*I*t started with a boy in a cage of bones. It ended with Phil Brennan finding out just exactly who he was and where he came from.

She devoured the story of Phil Brennan's next high-profile case, even rekindling her affair with Malcolm the librarian to discover as much information about it as possible.

And what a wealth of information there was. Just by investigating the boy and determining both who he was and why he was actually in the cellar of an abandoned house, locked up inside a cage constructed of bones, led Phil Brennan to come face to face with his own past. Family secrets long since buried resurfaced and he was left to face a painful, shocking truth.

Phil Brennan, as she had discovered, had been brought up by a local couple, Don and Eileen Brennan. They had fostered many children over the years but Phil had been different. They had taken to him for some reason, eventually adopting him as their own and giving him their surname. And he had responded in kind to their gesture by following his adoptive father in his career as a police detective. Don Brennan was now dead but Eileen Brennan was still alive. Eventually she would make the move to Birmingham along with Phil, Marina and their daughter. But that was in the future.

Phil Brennan's biological parents, she discovered, had been members of a cult that was based on an estate out in the countryside bordering Essex with Suffolk. The Garden, it was called. They had become disenchanted with that way of life and wanted to leave, citing tales of hideous abuse. To this end, they managed to contact the local police who were already running an ongoing investigation into the cult, building a case against the leaders. Phil's parents, having risen to what was regarded as a privileged position within the commune, would be star witnesses against them, just the sort of believable couple who would enable them to make a successful prosecution and get the cult closed down.

Unfortunately, the potentially damning information they possessed made them too valuable to leave. But leave they did. Again with the help of the police. The leaders of the cult, sensing that the tide had turned against them, did everything in their power to track them down and silence them.

The family were in hiding, sent to a safe house only few people knew the location of. But the reach of some of the people behind the cult was long. Their location was given out and they were tracked down.

She remembered where she was when she read the next part. She would never forget. In Malcolm's house at his computer. He was hovering in the background, making tea or something, giving her one of those expensive biscuits he imagined she enjoyed. But when she read the next part it was like she left her own being, the planet, even, completely.

She experienced the most enormous epiphany ever.

She didn't believe in God, an afterlife or have a spiritual bone in her body. But after this she began to. There was no way this was coincidence. No way at all. This was the universe – or whatever – telling her what she had to do. Guiding her, showing her what to do with the rest of her life. It was the most powerful thing she had ever felt. Nothing – not even the thrill she got from holding power over those men – came close.

Because Phil Brennan's family were hunted down. His mother and father were murdered.

But their son and daughter were left alive.

And daughter.

That was the part she couldn't believe. As soon as she read that she imagined herself on her back, the cold seeping through her warm coat. Smiling.

Make a snow angel, he said. And showed her how.

A snow angel.

Yes.

This was it. She knew it. This was the defining moment of her life. Her whole existence had been building towards this moment. Every single thing she had done, or had done to her, or endured or even enjoyed had led up this. Here, now. In this place, reading this article.

Her childhood of not knowing who she was – really was – or where she was from. Moving from foster home to foster home, to adoption agency after adoption agency. To the children's home. From meeting Fiona to killing Sean to honing her craft on all those victims. To this. Here. Now.

Fiona coming back into her life was just the catalyst. Even if she was dead. No, that was better. She had to be dead. If she had been alive, she might never have got to know about Phil Brennan.

She smiled again.

And how had she got to know about Phil Brennan? Because he was Sean's doppelganger. And that was why she had such an affinity with Sean. Because, even though she didn't know it at the time, Sean was the spitting image of her long-lost brother. And that was why Sean had had to die.

It all made the most perfect, crystalline sense.

Malcolm just stared at her, not knowing what was happening to her, what he could do about it. She didn't care, didn't even notice him. Because from now on, she would only have eyes for Phil Brennan.

She read through it again, just to check she hadn't made a mistake.

She hadn't.

She left Malcolm's house. Walked away barely seeing the world around her. Back to where she was living.

This, she knew, was the defining moment of her life.

And she knew what she had to do next. Be reunited with her brother. Her long-lost brother.

She loved saying those words, kept rolling them around her tongue, all the way home.

Reunited. Yes. But properly reunited. Not just a letter telling him who she was and who he was in relation to her. He might just dismiss her as some sort of nutter. And she couldn't just turn up on his doorstep either. That approach wouldn't work. Because what would he do then? What would happen to her? He might just thank her and never see her again. And she couldn't take that. Not rejection. Not after everything she had been through to reach this point. No.

Another, more horrific, thought struck her. What if she did get to meet him and tell him whom she was and he didn't want to know her? What then? That was rejection on an even grander scale. A massive scale. A doomsday scenario. And what would she do then? No.

She would have to take her time with this. It needed careful handling. Delicate. Insightful. She would have to make him want to meet her. She would have to make him want to be with her. Forever. And ever.

It wouldn't be easy, she knew that. But nothing worth doing ever was. Life had taught her that. It might take years. Such careful plotting and planning. Years. But it would be worth it in the end. Because she would have him.

She smiled. Oh yes. She would have him.

Forever.

48

Malcolm Turvey sat in his usual place in his usual tea room on Sir Isaac's Walk. In a corner seat almost hidden by exposed beams and brickwork, he had his bag at his side, his files and papers spread out on the table, fighting for position with his teapot, cup and saucer.

Anni entered the café, saw him straight away. She had received a call from him earlier that morning, a sense of urgency in his voice, almost begging her to meet him, and as soon as possible. She had been ready to humour him, fob him off with excuses. He just wants to feel part of the investigation, she had thought, important and involved. But there was something about his tone that she hadn't heard before. And that told her she had to meet him.

He looked up as soon as she entered. Beckoned her over. No smile this time, no wide-eyed excitement. Just a serious, almost sombre, tone that she didn't recognise.

'I've remembered something,' he said before she had taken her seat.

'What?'

'Or rather someone,' he continued, then looked away, as if it was going to cost him something to go on. 'And I think it might be important. Very important.'

'All right, then. Tell me.'

He poured another cup of tea, just to have something to do

322

with his hands, it looked like. 'When I say I've remembered something,' he said, 'what I mean is I knew this all the time. I just didn't know how important it was. Or could be.'

Anni waited. Tea ritual completed, he went on.

'There was a woman.' He couldn't made eye contact with her, looked at the table as he spoke. 'She used to come into the library. She was a regular in the end. And interested in crime. Local crime.'

'When was this?'

He looked up. 'Well, that's the interesting thing. The more I thought about her, the more I thought she might be important. So I checked my records since I last saw you.'

'And?'

'From what I can gather from them, and from what I can remember, it looks like she came in just after Fiona Welch's death. In fact, I think that was the first case she was interested in.'

He had Anni's full attention now. 'So what did you do?'

'Supplied her with everything we had. Newspapers, internet access, the lot. It was . . . I was just happy to be sharing this' – he pointed to his bag, his files – 'my passion, with someone else. A fellow enthusiast. And . . . ' His eyes dropped once more.

'You . . . what? Developed a crush on her?'

'More than that.' Malcolm's face reddened.

'What, you . . . ' Anni smiled.

Malcolm nodded.

'You sly old dog.'

Malcolm reddened even more. It seemed as if he didn't know whether to smile or look embarrassed. He managed to do both.

'Anyway,' he said, waving his hand dismissively, 'it didn't really last long.'

'What happened?'

He shrugged. 'She just . . . disappeared one day. Like she'd arrived, suddenly as that.'

'And that was the end of it?'

'Not quite. I'll get to that.' Another embarrassed look, almost ashamed, then he continued. Sadness in his voice. 'She got what she wanted, I suppose. My files.'

'Which ones was she interested in, in particular?' Anni could guess the answer before he said it.

'Fiona Welch, at first. Then Phil Brennan.'

Anni nodded. Exactly as she had expected. She had that old cop buzz back again. This was important. This could even be a breakthrough. 'So what was her name?'

'Diana.'

'Not a real name, presumably.'

'No. Diana Monroe. The name was false. I checked it out.'

'Then what?'

'Like I said, she disappeared. Once she had everything she wanted. But then there was that case a few months later. Well, of course you remember it, you worked on it. The boy in the cellar. In the cage made out of bones.'

'Oh yes, I remember. I'm not likely to forget.'

He nodded. 'She popped up again then. Still calling herself Diana. All smiles, like she'd just popped out to the shops for a pint of milk, or something. Well, I tried to have nothing to do with her. Keep her at arm's length.' He sighed. 'That didn't last long.'

'You started seeing her again?'

Another nod. 'She seemed to know which buttons to push. And there was a . . . I don't know, I can't describe it. A wildness to her? She wanted to . . . ' He sighed, cast his eyes down once more. 'I can't say it.'

'You may as well tell me, Malcolm. You've come this far talking about her.'

He shook his head. 'She wanted to . . . have sex. At . . . at murder sites.' He couldn't look at Anni as he spoke.

Anni nodded. 'And you went along with her?'

Another nod. 'Like I said, she had a wild streak. She made you feel . . . transgressive? You know what I mean.'

'So getting back to the cage of bones case, what did she want to know about that in particular?'

'Phil, again. Not so much the case but him. His background, his family. All of that.'

'Why?'

He shrugged. 'God knows. She was obsessed with him. Totally obsessed with him. I mean, when we . . . had sex, you know, at the places . . . she would . . . it sounds stupid to say it. But it would be like she was doing some sort of ritual. Like she was trying to contact dead spirits or something. Or using Phil's name. Saying it out loud when she was, you know.' He sighed. 'That was why I broke it off this time. I couldn't stand how she was making me feel, what I was becoming with her. I mean, doing that was one thing, but the way she got during it? It was scary. And shouting out another bloke's name. That wasn't nice. Not nice at all.'

'So how did you get rid of her?'

'I just . . . pretended to be seeing someone else.'

'And that worked?'

He nodded. 'And I never saw her again.' A troubled frown creased his face. 'Well, until recently.'

Anni leaned forward once more. 'Recently?'

'That night. On the walk. By the riverside when I found the body hanging there in the old Dock Transit building. She was there. Or at least I think she was.'

'Didn't you recognise her?'

'Not really. Not at first. In fact, it's only because of everything that's happened since then that I started to think about it. And then she just popped up in my mind. And all of the memories came tumbling out.'

'So what was she doing? What made you remember her?'

'Well, you have to take into account the fact that this walk had been her idea, really. She'd suggested it to me. Do a murder walk, she said. That should drum up a bit of trade. And when I was made redundant by the library services, that's what I did. I wouldn't have done it without her putting the idea into my head in the first place.'

'Right.'

'I suppose ... ' Another shrug. 'Maybe I wanted her to see that I'd done it, come back to me. I know it sounds pathetic, especially after everything that I've told you about, but ... I did like her. A lot.'

'I'm sure.'

'Pathetic, really.'

'No, it isn't, Malcolm. Anyway, back to the story. You said you saw her?'

He nodded. 'Or thought I did. Even if she looked different. More ... I don't know, confident. She wasn't wearing glasses any more. Hair a different colour. She seemed taller, somehow.'

'From what I've heard, she's a great actress.'

'Yeah.'

'So what made her stand out? Why did you notice her?'

'Well ... for one thing she seemed to be looking the other way. When everyone was looking at the body, she was looking at the crowd, seeing how they were reacting. And another thing.'

'What?'

'She was smiling.'

Anni sat back, shook her head. 'So that was that? We've got no way of finding her?'

Malcolm almost smiled. 'Oh, I didn't say that ... '

49

'No. Definitely not. No.' DCI Gary Franks was not a man used to having his authority questioned. Especially not by a woman.

Marina held her ground, glared at him. All those old wounds were opening up between them. Reminders of skirmishes past. Matthews, watching, sensed that neither would give in.

After discovering Imani's body and recovering enough to be useful, he had called Franks, told him what had happened. Franks initially didn't believe that Beresford could be involved, but Matthews, coolly and calmly, opened up enough doubt in his mind for him to take action. Beresford had his phone with him. He could be tracked by that. Franks said to leave it to him, he'd get it sorted.

Matthews had then phoned the number that Imani had left him for Anni. No reply. He tried Marina. She was on her way to Chelmsford to talk to someone. He couldn't bring himself to tell her on the phone what had happened, only saying that he had to see her urgently when she returned.

And he had waited. The CSIs had arrived and began their work. Uniforms were cordoning off the street, beginning their door-to-door enquiries. Everything was under way for a murder investigation. Then Franks called him, told him to get back to Queensway as soon as possible.

He did so, found Franks and Marina together, Beresford in an interview room, and another body on their hands. He was speechless, surprised at how quickly things had changed.

And now, in his office, the door firmly shut but not enough to block the sound of raised voices, Franks was holding court.

'But Gary—' began Marina. Her sadness and grief at the death of Imani had given way to a righteous anger and she wanted to direct that anger at Beresford.

'No. I said no. And it's stupid even to ask.'

'Why?'

He looked at her as if she'd just asked the most ignorant question ever. 'What? You honestly need me to spell it out to you?'

'No of course not. But try to look at this from more than just your point of view.' She clearly wanted to add 'for a change' but stopped herself.

'Someone else's point of view? OK, then. How about the CPS, how about their point of view? If I let you wander in there and—'

'I wouldn't be wandering in. Don't be so demeaning.'

'If I let you go in there' – he stressed the word 'go' – 'and conduct the interview with Beresford, a good defence barrister, or even an indifferent one, would have your testimony torn apart in minutes. Seconds, even.'

Marina just stared at him, trying to come up with an argument but knowing that, as he saw it, he was right.

As he saw it.

'Look,' said Franks, continuing, 'you know what protocol demands in these kinds of situations. Someone unconnected with the case comes in and handles the interview. Especially when it's one of our own.'

'Exactly, and where are you going to get them from? Just about the whole of this station's working on this case. And everyone here, and a few other stations too, know Beresford. Who d'you suppose you could get to do the interview?'

'Yes, I agree it's difficult. We'll have to—'

'Exactly,' she said, cutting him off. 'So let me do it.'

'No. Definitely not.' Pointing at her now. 'You're too involved. It's your husband who's gone missing, remember. Who we're trying to find.'

'You think I've forgotten that? Seriously? Really?' She leaned forward until he could look nowhere but into her eyes. 'You're right. It's my husband she's taken. My husband who's gone missing. And that bastard in there can tell me where he is.'

Franks shook his head. Took a walk round his office to get away from her penetrating gaze. 'You see, there you go again. Calling him a bastard. You think that's going to make for a good interview? That level of emotionalism?'

'Of course not, that's for here, in this room. In that room I'm a professional. And you know that.'

'Yes,' admitted Franks, 'you are a professional. And very good at what you do. There, I've said it. A compliment.'

'Thank you.'

'But you're also wilful and strong-headed. And you put your needs for information first instead of the whole investigation.'

'What?' Marina couldn't believe what he had just said. 'My husband *is* the investigation . . .'

Franks shook his head once more. Took a deep breath, exhaled. Gave himself time to come up with counter-arguments against her words.

'You're not even staff,' he said eventually. 'You don't work here any more. You're just a civilian now.'

'Yeah, I am. But how many times have I been in that room, as a civilian? How many times have I questioned suspects and got a result? How many?'

329

Franks had no answer for that. Not without undermining his own argument.

'Thought not. But, Gary, this is what I'm good at. No, what I excel at. It's what I'm trained for. When I walk in that room I don't let my feelings get in the way. Ever. I'm there to do a job. And I'm bloody good at it.'

Franks said nothing.

Marina, sensing, or rather hoping, he was relenting, continued. 'Please. Just let me try. What have you got to lose? The custody clock's ticking and there's no one else here who can do it.'

Franks thought. It seemed like the room was holding its breath.

'I don't like the way you do things. You're anti-authority. Anti-discipline.'

Marina gave a small laugh. 'Of course I am. But I get results. Don't I?'

Franks sighed, rubbed his huge, paw-like hands over his face. 'All right, you've got first crack.'

Marina breathed a sigh of relief. 'Thank you. Thank you, Gary.'

'But I should—'

'Sir.' It was Matthews. The first time he had spoken for ages.

They both turned to him in surprise, almost forgetting he was there in their verbal sparring.

'Could I go with her, please, sir?'

Franks frowned, looked incredulous. 'Not you as well, Simon . . .'

'Please, sir.'

'Look, DC Matthews, I appreciate the offer. But as I was just about to say, as senior officer it should be me who accompanies Dr Esposito into the interview room.'

330

'Yes, sir, I know, but . . . ' He paused, gathered his thoughts, continued. 'As Marina says, this is an unorthodox case. An unorthodox situation. And DS Beresford lied to me. He made me complicit in the disappearance and murder of a fellow officer. I can't let that stand, sir. I want a crack at him.'

Franks stared at his DC. He was usually a reliable officer. Thorough. Neat. Everything by the book, paperwork always handed in on time and to a high standard. But Franks had never seen this fire in his eyes before. This passion.

'Sir.'

Franks sighed. 'I must need my bloody head examining.' He pointed to the door. 'Go on, get in there, the pair of you. Before I change my mind.'

50

For Anni it felt like déjà vu.

Down on the River Colne by the old Dock Transit building and the lightship. The first time she had met Mickey Philips. Watching him throw up as he found a mutilated body. Bless him, she thought. Then tried to take the smile off her face as quickly as possible. Not the time or the place.

The flat they were looking for was in a contemporary block on the waterfront. Directly opposite the building where Fiona Welch died. Just beside the lightship where one of her victims was found. Appropriate, she thought.

'So this is it?' she asked Malcolm as they entered the building, waited for the lift.

He nodded. 'The last known place that Diane Monroe lived at.'

They alighted on the fourth floor. Anni looked out of the window. 'Perfect view,' she said. 'If you like looking at old crime scenes.'

Malcolm didn't reply.

'D'you know whether she's still here?'

'No idea,' said Malcolm, producing a key, 'but we'll soon find out.'

He moved to the door, put the key in the lock. It fitted.

'Did she give you that?'

'Sort of,' he said, glancing up to give Anni a furtive look, then back to the lock again.

'Wait, so you copied her flat key without her knowing?'

He looked up. 'I realise how that sounds, but it wasn't like that.'

Anni raised an eyebrow.

'Honestly.'

'So?'

'She . . . took some of my files. To read, she said. Study. And I trusted her at the time because I . . . '

'Because you weren't thinking with your brain?'

He nodded, reddening once more. 'Something like that.'

Anni looked at him. She was struck, not for the first time, as to just what a creepy individual Malcolm actually was. She sometimes forgot that when she and him were talking, but something like this just reminded her. He was trying not to look at her, though, clearly embarrassed about his admission. Creepy, yet somehow likeable, she thought.

He opened the door, swung it wide.

'After you,' he said.

Anni looked into the darkened hallway. Suddenly felt nervous.

She stepped over the threshold.

51

The interview room door opened and in stepped Marina and Matthews. They both pulled up chairs, sat at the opposite side of the table to Beresford. He didn't look up. Sat with the chair pushed away from the table, his long body stretched out, legs crossed at the ankles, arms folded. He looked like he had been asleep. He barely acknowledged them as they entered.

'Where to start?' said Marina.

No response from Beresford.

'For the record,' she said, continuing, 'this is just a preliminary interview. And you've decided that for now you don't want a solicitor present, or your Police Federation rep. Is that correct?'

Beresford nodded, but only barely.

'Right then,' Marina said, voice bright and businesslike. 'Here.' She reached into her bag, brought out a file. Removed from the file a photo. Slapped it on the table in front of Beresford. He flinched, blinking, tried to pretend he hadn't.

'Michael Prosser. Dead.'

She took out another photo, slapped that one down.

'Imani Oliver. One of ours. Stuffed under a staircase at a garage.'

Another photo, another slap. Another flinch from Beresford.

'Roger Prentice. Garage owner. Anyone we've missed?'

Beresford stared at her. Eyes hard, defiant. He smiled. 'I've played this game longer than you, darling. Gonna take a lot more than that to get something out of me.'

Marina said nothing. Just continued to stare at him.

Matthews leaned forward, about to speak. Marina touched her foot to his. The message clear: don't. Leave this to me. He sat back again.

Marina kept staring, Beresford kept smirking.

'You were crying when you killed Michael Prosser. Remember? Crying while you strangled him. Did that make you sad? Did you not want to do it? Or did you think no one would be there to witness it? You crying like a baby.'

Beresford's face showed rising anger. Then, not without a struggle, he managed to control himself. Sat back again, tried to look as relaxed as possible.

'You'll have to do better than that. Like I said, I've done this before. I know all the tricks in the book. I invented some of them. You're really gonna have to surprise me if you want me to say anything.'

Marina gave a brief smile. 'We'll see.'

'We will.'

'You see, I only want the answer to one question. That's all, just one question. You know what that question is?'

Beresford shrugged.

'I want to know where my husband is. That's all. I don't want to know about all the people you killed, or how many, any of that. Oh, I daresay it'll come up in the conversation, it's going to be unavoidable. But I just want the answer to that one question. Where is my husband? That's all. And before I leave this room, I will have it.'

Beresford laughed. 'Give it your best shot, sweetheart.'

'Oh, I will.'

She tried to look confident. She only hoped she could feel as confident as she looked.

52

Anni entered the apartment, Malcolm following behind. They moved slowly, cautiously down the hallway, unsure what – if anything – was waiting to jump out at them. Anni listened as she went. No sound coming from in front of her. Either someone was doing an expert job of hiding, or the flat was empty. She didn't want to jump to conclusions just yet.

She reached the living room. The blinds were drawn. Weak light penetrated the slats, giving the room its only illumination. Anni looked round. It was open plan, with room for a dining table and a breakfast bar come kitchen along the rear wall. There was only a cheap fold-up wooden chair and a table in the centre of the room. Apart from that, there was no other furniture.

'Spartan,' she said. 'Very minimalist.'

The table had empty food wrappings on it. Microwave meal dishes. Lasagne, bolognese. Dirty forks still in them. One for Forensics, she thought.

'Try not to touch anything,' she told Malcolm.

'I won't. I'm wise to that.'

'Good.' Another look round. 'Did she ever invite you here? For dinner or anything else?'

'No. Never.'

'I can see why.'

She made a quick inventory of the other rooms. Checking

for activity, double-checking behind all open doors, fearful of a nasty surprise jumping out at them. Nothing. There was no one there but the two of them. She allowed herself to relax slightly then.

Anni had to admit, it felt good to be doing this again. She had missed police work. Not the form-filling and report-writing, none of that. But this. The detecting, finding things out. This was when she used to come alive. She could feel it happening again.

I just wish Mickey was here to share it.

She shook her head, banished that thought as far away as she could. She had work to do.

The bedroom was as empty as the living room. A mattress on the floor, sheets and pillows, a duvet. All plain, no colour. A cheap white self-assembly wardrobe. She looked inside. Full of clothes. Different colours, different styles. Nothing similar. Like they were all disguises for different personalities. She found make-up as well, wigs.

It felt hollow, empty. Like the person who slept there, ate there, had no personality of their own, thought Anni. They had to put these clothes on for them to be someone, just to leave the flat.

'Marina should see this. She could get a PhD out of this place.'

Malcolm called through from the living room. 'I think I've found something.'

Anni went to join him. He was standing behind the breakfast bar, a laptop on it, a sheaf of papers in his hands.

'A clue?' he said.

'Very probably. Let's hope so.' She looked at all the papers, the laptop. 'You any good with this kind of thing?'

Malcolm smiled. 'My department, I think.'

He opened the laptop, got to work.

53

'So why did you do it?'

Marina stared at Beresford who still sat smirking at her. She kept her unblinking gaze on him. He couldn't hold his but didn't want to let her see it, he rolled his eyes, stared at the ceiling instead. Blinking while he did it. She knew though. She saw him do it.

'So why did you do it?' she asked again.

He still said nothing. Marina continued.

'I'll tell you why, shall I? Or rather, I'll tell you what you would say, if you were going to reply to me. Right?'

No answer.

Marina sensed that his smirk was really hiding fear. Or at least hoped it was. She continued, mimicking his Essex accent as she spoke.

'She's got my wife and kid. That's what you're going to say, isn't it? Or what you would say. She's got my wife and kid. I only did what I did because of that. Am I right?'

Beresford shrugged, but the smirk was starting to fray around the edges.

'Yeah, yeah, yadda yadda. Wife and kid. Big deal. Yeah. That's the excuse. What you tell yourself. And anyone else who asks or questions you. Wife and kid. Yeah. Anyone else who would ask you to easily explain your actions. Wife and kid. Right. And you expect us to believe that, don't you. Wife and kid. You expect us to say, oh, poor you. What you have to do to protect your family. Poor, poor you. Don't you?'

Beresford said nothing.

Marina leaned forward. 'Bullshit.'

Beresford struggled not to, but registered surprise.

'Yeah. Bullshit. You see, that's your excuse. For what you did. Wife and kid. But it's not the reason, is it? Oh no. And that's what I want to know. The reason. Why you really did what you did.'

'Fuck you.'

Marina kept going. 'Because it's a big leap, isn't it? By any stretch of the imagination. I mean, there you are, a police officer, serving the public, upholding the law, and suddenly you're a multiple murderer. All in the name of protecting your family. Well that escalated quickly, as the kids would say.'

Beresford was looking round now, seemingly decidedly uncomfortable.

'I mean yes, obviously. You want to protect your family. I can understand that. Totally. Completely. I mean, what partner, what parent wouldn't? Of course.' She nodded. 'And shall I tell you something? I've done it myself.'

She sat back, waited for him to take that in.

'You've probably done your research on me. I should imagine so, anyway. And on my husband. When you realised what you were getting in to. So you might know this already. And forgive me if I bore you with it again. But Simon here might not have heard it.'

Matthews perked up at the mention of his name.

'You see, a few years ago, my daughter was kidnapped. And that was bad enough. That was a parent's worst nightmare. But that wasn't everything. Because the person who kidnapped my daughter also seriously injured my husband. And mother-in-law. And actually killed my father-in-law. My family. All the people I cared about and loved most in the whole world. So yes. I can understand what you must have been going through. I would have done anything – *anything* – to get my daughter back. Except one thing. D'you know what that was?'

Beresford tried to look disinterested. Failed. 'Why don't you tell me?'

'I will,' said Marina, not acknowledging that it was the first time he had actually engaged with her. 'Murder. That's what I wouldn't do. Murder. Oh, I wanted to. I really did. You see, I came face to face with the person who'd stolen my daughter and I was very, very close to killing her. God, I wanted to. I don't mind admitting it. But you can understand that, can't you?'

Beresford just stared at her.

'It wasn't a rhetorical question, you can answer.'

'Yes.' His voice was like a croak.

'Yes of course you can. We all could. Even Simon here, I'm sure of it.' She leaned forward again, eyes locked on to his. 'But what I never thought about, never even considered, was killing anyone who got in my way. And there were plenty of people trying to get in my way, believe me. Or ask DCI Franks, he'll tell you. He was one of them. But I would never – ever – think of murdering, of killing them. And you know why?'

'No.'

'No.' She gave a humourless laugh, sat back. 'No. You really don't know, do you?' She sat back, hoped he understood what he had just admitted to.

Obsession

Phil Brennan. Oh, Phil Brennan. But how to make him notice her, that was the question. But not just notice her. That would never be enough. He had to believe her, in what she had to tell him. Everything she had to tell him. Totally believe her. And go along with her. Really, he just had to fall in love with her. And then live happily ever after with her.

Eternally happy ever after.

She had giggled at the thought of it. Like trying to attract the attention of a boy at school, she thought. Not that she had ever done that. Well, not in that way, anyway.

So what was that way? Or this way? Phil Brennan was her brother. But the way she thought about him was ... more than a brother. Much more. Much, much more. He was becoming everything to her. Her obsession, her career. Her life. The feelings she was experiencing for him, they went much deeper than just brother and sister.

She tried to think it through, explain it to herself. While glorying in that sweet feeling at the same time.

Here was the man she had been separated from for most of her life. She had gone through her whole life not knowing who she was, who she really was, and suspecting that another part of her was out there. Another piece to make her complete. And she hadn't been able to function as a single individual with that in the background all of this time. She had always felt lacking as a person. Hollow.

Unconvincing. And now she had found him. That missing piece of herself.

It had to be him. Of course it did. How else could she have been led to him? First Sean then Phil. And then discovering Phil's family background. It had all fallen into place then. And she had become obsessed with him then. Knew they had to be together. In every way possible. On every level. It was inevitable.

She desired him, yearned for him. Lay on her own at night, imagining his body entwined round hers. Total. Complete. Soul deep.

La petite mort.

Le grande mort.

She knew that some people wouldn't understand. Obviously. A love, an obsession, like theirs wasn't the kind ordinary people could understand or were designed to understand. They were different, special. And the love she felt for him went beyond some stupid bourgeoise morality. All she had to do was show him, let him experience it for himself, and he too would experience that same love for her.

All she had to do was get to him.

She had to find a way. And she did. Again, it was so obvious that it must have been meant to be. Fiona Welch's work. Where else should she start except with her old friend, her old lover?

So she studied Fiona's work, her techniques, her ideas, immersed herself in them. And that's when the plan came to her. Again, like a gift, almost fully formed. Become Fiona. Assume her persona, her identity. Carry on her work. Finish what she started. Improve on it, even. Yes. That would get his attention. There was no way he would ignore her then.

But she couldn't just rush into it. This would take planning, scheming, plotting. It would take time. And money. Which was fortunate, because she had plenty of both things. Especially time. For this to work as well as it should, as it had to, she had all the time in the world.

Finding victims was easy. Almost too easy. They were just about lining up for her, no shortage of willing participants.

She had once witnessed a hypnotist at work. Close-up, backstage. One of her dates had worked in a theatre, so she had gone with him, interested in keeping him alive long enough to find out what went on there. And she had enjoyed herself. Sadly, he hadn't made it to the second act. But watching the hypnotist had been fascinating.

He had chosen his subjects carefully. They were all to be in the audience that night and all came to see him of their own volition. The interesting thing, she had decided, was not the ones he had chosen but the ones he had rejected. And the way he had rejected them, the reasons why. She tried to see it through his eyes. He had spotted something in the rejects that would cause a barrier to being hypnotised. Some lack of susceptibility. And it wasn't something that was apparent in physical form, either. Physically powerful people were accepted while smaller ones were turned away.

What he looked for was some kind of commonality, some kind of willingness to be hypnotised, a susceptibility. How he saw that, she didn't know. But she vowed to find out.

And she did. In fact, she had known it all along. And used it herself. It was how she chose her victims. How she managed to work out – usually in an instant – which male would make the best subject. And she had always chosen well so far. She had never made a mistake.

That went even more so for these victims.

She couldn't remember their names. She never could. Eye colour, yes. Smell even, yes. Names, no. They weren't important. Just like hers wasn't. As long as she spotted that susceptibility. As long as she could manipulate them. And she definitely knew men, and certainly knew how to manipulate them. More than that: how to make them love, honour and most importantly, obey her. How to make them kill for her. And not regret it. And still love her and want her all the more.

She followed Fiona's notes to the letter. And it worked. The three she chose were all willing to be led. And they all killed for her. Without regret, without qualm. But first they did something that she knew would get Phil's attention. They remade their girlfriends in Marina Esposito's image.

She couldn't have sent out a more obvious, unambiguous signal if she tried.

Eventually the men were arrested. And the trail led back to her. Or Fiona, as she was calling herself by this point. And doing a good job of it. Living like Fiona, dressing like her. She had adopted her speech mannerisms, her walk, everything. She was Fiona. She almost believed it herself, she was so convincing. And if she was being honest, if she hadn't done all this with the sole intention of getting noticed by Phil, she might have continued as Fiona. Become an enigma from beyond the grave.

But no. She had work to do.

They arrested her but found they couldn't charge her with murder because she hadn't actually killed anyone. And she was also claiming to be someone who was dead. So they freely admitted that they didn't know what to do with her. In desperation, they sent her off to a secure hospital in Suffolk.

And that was when the fun really started.

54

Anni watched Malcolm work. He was sitting on the folding chair at the table, the laptop open in front of him, papers spread out all around him.

'What are you looking for?' she asked.

'I'll know it when I see it ...' Not even looking up, his reading glasses perched on the end of his nose.

Anni kept watching him. Studying him. Poring over papers, following what was on screen with his finger, lips moving at the same time.

That man had sex with the person who killed my partner. The thought came, unbidden, into Anni's head.

Not just had sex with, but was in a relationship with, for God's sake. Cared for her. Wanted her, desired her. Thought about her, probably bought gifts for her. Looked forward to spending time together. Planned a future with her. Loved her, even. Yes, definitely loved her.

And now here was Anni, working alongside that murderer's ex-lover. And doing so in that murderer's apartment. How does that make me feel? she thought. She didn't know. Uneasy, yes. Definitely. Anything else? Yes, loads of things, loads of emotions. But not any of them easily quantifiable or identifiable. At least not that she wanted to explore at the moment. But there was one overriding emotion she was experiencing. Anger. She could feel it building up within her once more.

The man whose lover killed my partner is in this room right next to me . . .

That anger wasn't going to diminish any time soon. That anger was going to need an outlet.

'Found something,' said Malcolm, looking up.

Anni, pleased to have something to take her mind off her increasingly dark thoughts, crossed the room to see, stood over his shoulder looking down.

'Here,' he said, pointing to a stack of A4 sheets. 'It's a letting agreement. She's rented another property. A house, by the looks of it. I've checked on the map. It's down off the Avenue of Remembrance. Some new-builds there, a whole estate. By the leisure centre.'

Anni said nothing. Just stood behind Malcolm, looking alternatively between the papers he was holding and the back of his neck. That thin strip of skin between untidy hair and overdue-for-a-wash shirt. Naked. Vulnerable.

'And there's this,' he said, pointing to the screen. 'Another let, it looks like. A unit on an industrial estate, from what I can gather. Somewhere out by Elmstead Market, on the way to Clacton.'

He looked up, did a double-take at the expression on her face.

'You OK?'

Anni blinked, snapped herself back into the room. 'What?'

'I said are you OK? You were looking funny.'

'I'm fine,' she said, a little too quickly. She looked down at the papers he held in his hand. 'Let's try the house first.'

She swept out of the apartment, like she couldn't bear to be in it for a second longer.

Malcolm, folding the papers and bringing the laptop, followed her. Frowning.

And suddenly wary of her.

55

Marina was still interviewing Beresford, Matthews watching. She was still smiling at him. Beresford, not knowing why, was looking uneasy.

'Have you worked out what you just admitted to me yet?'

'I didn't admit anything.' Beresford frowned. His voice was angry.

'Think about what I asked you. Think about your reply.'

He said nothing. Just stared at her. It seemed like he had the feeling he had been bested in some way but hadn't yet worked out how. So he covered it up with anger and irritation.

'You killed anyone who got in your way, didn't you?'

Beresford gave a small shrug of acknowledgement.

'And you know what?'

'What?' His voice dead on the surface, trying to hide a genuine interest. Issued more like a challenge than a question.

'You enjoyed it.'

He gave a snort, shook his head, rolled his eyes. The whole repertoire. 'You haven't a clue,' he said, voice curled into a snarl. 'Not a clue.'

'Really?'

Marina sat back, regarded him some more. Unblinking. Seemingly making up her mind about something before speaking. Reading him.

'Have you ever apprehended a rapist?'

He stared at her, warily.

'It's not a trick question, it's just a question. Have you ever apprehended a rapist?'

He shrugged. 'Maybe.'

'What about a man who beats up women? Targets women, hurts them. Abuses them. Just for the hell of it. Ever arrested anyone like that?'

'Yeah, course.'

'What about a child rapist? Someone who preys on children, vulnerable little children, who can't fight back. Who forces them to—'

'What you on about now?'

'Just asking. It's just a question. Have you ever arrested a child rapist?'

'What d'you want to know for?'

'I just want to know, that's all.'

'So you can make some decision about me, is that it? Then come up with some bullshit theory.' Another snort.

'Is that a yes or a no?'

'Yes. Course I have.'

'Good,' said Marina nodding. 'Right.' She sat back, her academic, genuinely curious voice in place. 'And how did that make you feel?'

'What, you're a fucking psychiatrist now?'

'Psychologist. How did that make you feel? When you brought them in, booked them? How? Like you'd done some good? Got some scum off the streets?'

'Yeah, course I did.'

'And when you arrested them, these pathetic individuals, these child rapists, when you'd actually seen what they'd done, did you want to hurt them?'

Beresford thought for a moment, then leaned forward. Eyes

349

locked with Marina's. 'Yeah,' he said slowly, relishing the word and the emotions it evoked, 'I did. I really did.'

'I'm sure you did. Who wouldn't? I'm sure I would.'

'Yeah,' Beresford said, warming to his theme. 'Especially when they started crying. Because where they were going, prison, they'd get it easy. Put on the vulnerable prisoners' wing, kept apart from everybody else, protected. Because that's what we do. Worry about their human rights. Protect scum like that.'

'So before they got there . . . '

'Yeah. Before they got there I wanted a session with them. Anyone would.'

'What stopped you, then?'

Beresford froze, didn't answer.

'Fear of getting caught, was it?'

He shrugged.

'Were you worried that if you did it and word got out and there was a court case then you'd lose your career, was that it? Lose your job, your respect, your pension, even. Your family, perhaps. And all for some piece of shit like that, is that it?'

'Something like that, yeah.'

'So what if you didn't have that fear? What if you could do it and not get caught, what then? Would you hurt them? Teach them a lesson?'

'Yeah,' Beresford said, smiling and nodding. 'Yeah. Course I would.'

'You'd hurt them.'

'Yeah.'

'You'd kill them, wouldn't you?'

'Yeah.'

'And you'd feel like a hero for doing it, wouldn't you?'

Beresford smiled, like he was imagining the adulation that would go with it. 'Yeah, I would. Because that's what I'd be.'

'No you wouldn't.' Marina's voice suddenly icy. 'What you'd be is a killer. A murderer. That's all.'

Beresford blinked. 'What?'

'A garage mechanic. You killed him. An ex-social worker. You killed him.'

'Yeah, but they were—'

'Doesn't matter. A serving police officer. You killed her. A fellow officer.' She sat back, regarding him like he was something she had to scrape off her shoe. 'You're a killer. A murderer. That's all. You've made excuses, you've lied to yourself about what you've done and why you've done it but you're just a killer. Just another criminal who deserves to be sitting on that side of the table.'

'I was—'

'No, you weren't protecting your wife and son. You were using them as an excuse. And you were killing because you thought that excuse protected you. Because you thought you could get away with it. That's all you are.'

Something broke behind Beresford's eyes. 'I'm not . . . I'm not . . .'

There was a knock at the door. A uniform entered, said there was a visitor for Marina.

She stood up, irritated to be interrupted but knowing that it must be for a good reason.

'Well,' she said to Beresford, 'I'll leave you that little thought to be going on with.'

She left the room.

Silence fell.

Eventually Matthews unfolded his arms, leaned forward. He smiled. It wasn't pleasant.

'Now that she's gone,' he said, 'now we're alone at last, there's a few things I want to say to you . . .'

Ready For the Rest of Her Life

*S*o simple. So, so simple.

   Most people would have thought that being caught for a crime and enduring the subsequent incarceration would be the end of the story. But she wasn't most people.

   Yes, she wasn't in prison. That was a plus. She was in a secure hospital. And that was fine. That was also part of the plan. Her well-paid solicitor had arranged that. No. This wasn't the end of the story. It was just the beginning of the next chapter.

   As she had expected, her crimes attracted attention from Essex Police's MIS. Namely Anni Hepburn and Mickey Philips. This was part of the team who had taken down the real Fiona Welch. When she saw them walking towards her for the first time she was so excited she could have asked for their autographs.

   But no Phil. At least not yet. She would just have to try harder.

   She cast around for a way of attracting more attention and found it quite easily. Murder. Inmate on inmate, with the strong suspicion that she was behind it. Which she was. The killer she chose was so simple and susceptible that it was almost laughably easy.

   But it worked. It attracted more attention. This time it was Marina Esposito.

   It wasn't Phil, no, but she tried to look at the positives. It afforded her a chance to study the woman who called herself his wife close up. And that she did. All the time the woman was talking to her she was

*watching, trying to work out what – if anything – had attracted Phil
to her. She couldn't find anything. Marina Esposito had nothing
that she didn't have. She had smiled inwardly on discovering that.
She had no competition.*

*She could sense the next phase approaching. And it did. An
escort back to Colchester to be formally questioned about the murder
in the hospital. And the driver? Mickey Philips.*

Perfect. So perfect.

*He wouldn't fall for her charms. She knew that straight away.
He was too much in love with Anni Hepburn for that. But there
were other ways. She wasn't just some one-trick pony. There was
a more direct approach she could take. Much more visceral. One
that Mickey definitely wouldn't survive.*

And he didn't.

She had always been good with her teeth.

*And then she was free. And if that didn't attract the attention of
Phil Brennan she didn't know what would.*

*But she had attracted his attention. Especially after what she
did next.*

*It was a risk and at the time she was in two minds about doing
it. The cautious, pragmatic part of her, the part that had ensured
her continual survival and expanding bank balance, said don't do
it. The other part of her, the yearning, desperate and, if she was
honest, romantic part of her, wanted to do it. Had to do it. So that
side won out.*

*And in hindsight it turned out to be the best thing she could have
done.*

*She invited herself in to Phil's house when he and Marina
were out. She just wanted to be near to him, see what he saw,
feel what he felt. Be close to him. For hours she was alone there,
soaking up the atmosphere, touching things that belonged to him,
smelling his clothing. She drank a bottle of beer from the fridge.
His beer, it must be. Just to savour the taste, experience what he*

experienced when the cold liquid ran down his throat. She didn't like beer, never drank it. But this tasted like the most beautiful thing in the world.

She found a book of old photos from his childhood, was thrilled to go through them. And that's when an idea formed.

His childhood. That's what she had to do. Recreate his life in reverse. Take him from where he was now with Marina through to his adoptive mother Eileen, back to his childhood with her. And from there, spend their eternity together.

Perfect. That's what she would do.

She took the photos. And took some more, of the house where he lived. Every room. She noted down where the crockery had been bought, what brand of beer he liked to drink. Checked the dishes for what they had eaten. Built up as full a picture of Phil's life as possible.

Because that was the life she was going to dismantle. Piece by piece. And then rebuild in her own image.

But she couldn't let it go at that. She had to do one more thing.

She got undressed. And got into bed, waiting for him.

Eventually he returned, entered the bedroom. He saw her there, thought she was Marina. She didn't attempt to change his mind. Until he realised she wasn't.

Their first time together didn't go quite the way she had expected. She left him lying at the top of the stairs temporarily paralysed. Taking a selection of Marina's clothing, she left the house. And, as far as he was concerned, disappeared.

It had been worth it, though. Just those precious few minutes in bed with him, skin on skin, had given her the impetus she needed to carry on. The belief that everything was going to work out fine and they were going to be together. She couldn't wait.

She didn't disappear, of course. She kept very close to Phil. And when he and Marina separated she came close to stepping back in. Consoling him, making him forget his wife and daughter, starting *a new life with her. But she restrained herself. Concentrated on the long-term plan instead. It was better that way.*

She planned everything meticulously. She had to. She would get only one shot at this and it had to work. It would work.

First, she needed a base. There was an out-of-the-way farm renting out old outbuildings just outside Elmstead Market. She visited it. Found it perfect for her needs. The area around was flat, no one could arrive unannounced. The building itself was old, brick-built with a corrugated iron roof. No one was the slightest bit interested in why she wanted the building. She just knew she would be left alone here. Perfect.

Once inside, she had rooms built, like a stage or film set. The photos she had taken of Phil's house and his childhood home with Eileen were blown up and pasted on them. She sourced matching items from online for any three-dimensional objects that would be needed. And she stocked up on Phil's favourite beer. She couldn't forget that.

She noticed that the guy who sorted out the photographic enlargements looked a lot like Phil. And he also made it clear to her that he was available, should she be interested. She smiled. That was his fate sealed. All she needed was two others and the next phase of the plan could go ahead.

They weren't hard to find. And, as before, they were willing volunteers.

Three lookalikes. Three locations. Three murders.

She killed them the same way she had all those men in those hotel rooms. Then she arranged for the bodies to be hanged and left in locations that would definitely get Phil's attention.

But she couldn't hang the bodies herself. She was many things, but she just wasn't physically strong enough. So she enlisted help. Dave Beresford was an old friend of hers from way back in Rainsford Children's Home. He had risen to the rank of detective sergeant. Ironically, if Phil had not moved to Birmingham, they would have been working together. He would help her.

Except he said no. At first. She worked on him, fucked him, tried to manipulate him. He still said no. She was confused: this wasn't like her. She must be slipping. But she had told him too much now, she had to have him. Sensing he was wavering and that he would do it if the incentive was strong enough, she took his wife and son. Told him that he would only see them alive again if he did what she wanted. And got himself in charge of the investigation. Gave her the time she needed to do what she had to do. Seeing no alternative, he agreed.

As she had remarked before, she wasn't just a one-trick pony.

So it was all in place. She just needed one more touch. The tarot cards. At first she thought that was too much, gilding the whole thing slightly. But she decided to allow herself a theatrical flourish, not to mention slight misdirection. And it added an element of fun. What was wrong with that?

So it was ready to go. Phil was about to have his old life stripped away and replaced by his new one with her, the real true love of his life. Perfect. Nothing could go wrong. She wouldn't allow it to.

She almost spoiled it by going on Malcolm's tour that night. Poor Malcolm. Dear, sweet Malcolm and his love of crime scenes. Literally, as she had discovered. One slight misstep. She just had to see the reaction to finding the body, right where Fiona had died. She couldn't help it. Yes it was risky but she had to do it. And it worked out fine. He didn't recognise her. Didn't even look at her. And even if he had spotted her, what could he do? Nothing. He didn't know she was behind this. And he didn't know anything about her. There was nothing to worry about.

And now it was time to go and see Phil.

She rose from her seat. She had removed every bit of make-up from her face. Her hair was now its natural colour. She was naked. She was herself. Her real self. She looked in the full-length mirror. She didn't recognise herself. Didn't recognise the face looking back at her. Or the body she saw before her.

She didn't even know her own name. Her real one. She was wiped clean. A blank slate. She had no identity.

She picked up two small objects from beside her make-up kit and turned away from the mirror.

Ready to spend all of eternity with her brother.

Her love.

56

The house was a new-build, as Malcolm had said. Part of a development called Meander Mews. All different sizes and shapes, designed to give the impression of individuality, but all the same shapes repeating every so often. Some looked Georgian, some more rustic. The one they were interested in was beige brick. Small, insignificant. Not nearly as ostentatious as most of the houses on the street, and very easy to overlook. Just the kind of place you'd want, thought Anni, if you were planning something illegal and you didn't want to attract attention to yourself.

Again, the curtains were closed.

Anni had driven there and parked directly outside it. The street was quiet, almost like a toytown village. They got out of the car.

'You got a key for this one, then?' she asked Malcolm.

'No, I haven't.'

He looked warily at her. Uneasy around her since they had left the flat. Good, she thought. So he should be. Considering what he's done. Then, looking at his confused face she relented slightly. He didn't know he was having sex with a murderer, she thought. Give him the benefit of the doubt. But just as that was sinking in, another thought struck her: would it have made any difference if he had known? Or would that have made it even more exciting for him?

She cleared those thoughts from her head, concentrated once again on the job in hand.

'Right,' she said, looking up and down the street and taking a leather roll from her inside jacket pocket.

'What's that?' asked Malcolm.

'Lockpicks. Tools of the trade.'

Malcolm looked alarmed. 'But ... that's illegal. Breaking and entering.'

'I know,' said Anni, standing up against the front door, trying to finesse the lock to open, 'but I thought you liked crime? Got a thrill from it, a buzz, all that.' She hadn't meant her words to come out as harsh-sounding as they did. Too late to take them back now.

Malcolm just looked confused, hurt even. 'Well, yes, but ...'

'There you go then.' Anni stepped back. The door opened. 'After you.

He entered with Anni following.

The first thing that hit them was the smell. And Anni knew exactly what that kind of smell meant.

'Jesus, what's that?' asked Malcolm, stuffing his sleeve against his face.

'Upstairs,' said Anni, trying not to gag.

The air was rich with decay. Putrefying meat that had been left to rot in an enclosed, unventilated space for too long. The buzzing of flies, the air thick with them.

She moved upstairs, a reluctant Malcolm following. They swung open the main bedroom door. And there, on the floor, were the decaying bodies of a woman and a small boy.

'Oh God ... Oh God ...'

Malcolm turned and ran back downstairs.

'Malcolm, wait ...'

Anni turned and followed him.

359

He raced into the deserted street and fell to his knees, vomiting into the gutter. 'Oh God . . . Oh God . . .' Gasping between heaves until there was nothing left inside him, just dry heaves after that. 'I just . . . oh God, that . . . that sight, that . . . that smell . . .'

Anni stood behind him. 'Congratulations. Your first actual murder scene.'

He slumped back on the pavement, started to cry.

'Not like it is in the movies, is it?'

'Oh Christ . . . it's . . . it's awful . . . it's . . . oh my God . . .' He kept crying.

'Welcome to real life.'

Her back to the house, she took out her phone. Called Marina.

57

'Just you and me now,' said Matthews. 'Sir.' He frowned. 'Should I still call you sir?'

Beresford stared at him. A slight smile began to gather at the corners of his mouth. Matthews knew what he was thinking. Marina was gone. Little Simon Matthews was left. Little, easily manipulated Simon Matthews.

'Doesn't really matter, does it?' Matthews said before Beresford could reply.

He settled back, folded his arms. Studied Beresford.

Beresford spoke. 'All bollocks, this, isn't it? Eh? All bollocks.'

Matthews kept staring at him, unsmiling, not speaking.

'All bollocks.'

Still no reply from Matthews.

'You don't believe all her shit, do you? All that psychological shit?' He laughed. 'She's a right one when she gets going, though, isn't she? I bet her old man was glad to get away from her, eh?'

Nothing. Beresford began to look slightly worried. He still continued.

'Still, bet she bangs like a shithouse door in bed, though.'

Beresford laughed. Matthews didn't join in. Silence fell once more.

'You know,' Matthews said, eventually, 'I used to look up

to you.' His voice quiet. No drama, no histrionics. Just a small sadness, regret.

'Yeah? Well, thanks. You're a damned good copper, mate. Damned good.'

Matthews continued as if Beresford hadn't spoken. 'Really look up to you, you know? Admire you. I really did.' His voice quiet, compelling. 'Oh, I know you never noticed me in the office. Did you?'

Beresford made to answer, Matthews just talked over him.

'I just kept my head down, got on with my work. I wasn't one of your gang, didn't go drinking with the boys after work, didn't follow the rugby, none of that. I knew that. Not that type. Not me. Too quiet. Like I said, kept my head down, did my work, put my hours in. But I'm good at my job. I've always been good at my job. Bloody good. And that got me noticed. That got me promoted.'

Beresford nodded. 'Right, yeah. I see your point. OK. Well, don't worry, when we get out of this, I'll take you down the boozer. We'll sort it out. Don't have to feel left out, now do you? It'll be all right. You'll see.'

Matthews shook his head. 'No, no, you see, you don't understand. You don't get what I'm saying to you. Marina's right. You don't listen, do you?'

Beresford jumped at the mention of her name, like he'd been slapped.

'What I'm saying is, you used to be my hero. And now look at you.' He gestured dismissively at Beresford. 'Sitting there, the wrong side of the table. How the mighty have fallen, eh?'

Beresford tried to keep his face impassive, but it seemed to be a losing struggle.

'What'll the rest of the office say about you now, eh? Your old mates, the lads you used to go drinking with, talk about the rugby with, what d'you think they'll be saying about you? What kind of names d'you think they'll be calling you?'

It seemed to be the first thing that had been said to have directly penetrated Beresford's understanding.

'I'm sure you can guess, anyway. Not that they'll say them to your face. Because where you're going, you won't see them again.'

'No. No, no, no, you're wrong . . .'

'I'm not wrong. You're just like all the other bits of self-deluded scum we get in here. Got excuses for why they raped, or murdered. Just like you. Not wanting to face the truth about who they are and what they've done. Just like you. Well, you're going to get a long time to think about it. The rest of your life, I reckon.'

Beresford's head dropped. He shook it slowly from side to side.

'Oh, and another thing,' said Matthews as if it had just occurred to him. 'You know all those nonces and child rapists who get put away? The ones who you think it have it so bloody easy? Them? Well, you're going to get a chance to find out, aren't you? Because that's where they put the coppers, isn't it? The vulnerable prisoners' wing. There they'll be, all the kiddie-fiddlers and nonces, the child-killers and fuck-ups, and there'll you be. Slap bang in the middle of them.' He sat back, frowned as if another question had just occurred to him. 'I wonder if you'll think they have it so easy then? Maybe you can drop us a line, all the boys in the office, all your old mates. Maybe you could let us know.'

Beresford looked completely broken.

58

Marina walked into Franks' office, expecting to find Anni, perhaps. But there was only Franks.

Marina frowned. Then started to get angry. 'Why have you pulled me out of there? I was making progress, I had him about to—'

'Please,' said Franks holding up his hands in mock surrender, 'before you start just listen. You're making progress. Good progress. And I want you to keep going.'

The compliment moved Marina to silence. Franks continued.

'I've had an email. From Caitlin Hennessey. Rainsford Children's Home?'

'Right. What—'

'If I can get a word in, I'll tell you.' He handed her a print-out. 'This is the full report on Carol Woods. You can read it later at your leisure but I've read it and I'll just go over the bullet points with you. Time is of the essence, and all that. And I want you back in there.'

'Right.' Marina glanced at the papers, Franks read from his copy.

'Originally from the north of England, Yorkshire. Leeds, I think. Her father was a police detective. High-ranking, important. He pulled in a well-known gangster. Built up an airtight case against him. Naturally, this gangster didn't like that. So he put out a contract on Carol's father. And the rest of her family. They all had to go into hiding. They thought they were safe.'

'But?'

'But this gangster had deep pockets and people everywhere. The family were at a safe house. They were given up. Associates of this gangster tracked them down, killed the mother and father and the two police officers guarding them. The two children, a boy and a girl, were allowed to live. These two children were split up. Given false names, put into care. For their own sakes and for those around them, they never saw each other again. They came with as little information as possible to avoid any further repercussions. Carol, as she was now called, was sent to Rainsford.'

'What about the boy?' asked Marina.

'Doesn't say. Doubt we'll ever find him now.'

'And no one told her who she really was?' asked Marina, incredulously. 'Not even when she came of age? No one told her why she was there, who she was? Surely there was no threat to her by that time.'

Franks looked at the paper once more as if it contained all the answers to Marina's questions. 'Doesn't say.' He shrugged. 'Suppose we just have to assume that she slipped through the cracks in the system. Wouldn't be the first. Doubt she'll be the last, either.'

'Slipped?' Marina couldn't believe what she was hearing. 'She didn't just slip, she may as well have fallen through a crack in the Earth.'

Franks looked up at her. 'It's too late to help that little girl that we should have saved,' he said. 'But at least we can stop what she's become.'

Marina nodded and left the room.

On the way down the corridor, her phone rang. Anni. She took the call.

Stopped walking, listened. Almost on shock.

She ended the call, carried on walking.

A new sense of urgency in her stride.

59

'Look at me, Phil.'

He opened his eyes. Slowly, like they were stuck together. Like he was living in a dream he couldn't escape from. It took him several seconds, or even minutes, to realise that he was actually awake. His mind felt like it was lost in a mist; he waited for it to clear. It didn't, not fully. He had to concentrate hard to make out his surroundings, to differentiate waking from sleeping. His head spun, his stomach too. He didn't know where he was, barely who he was.

'Look at me, Phil.'

He tried to follow the voice with his eyes. Couldn't yet make anything out. Gradually things around him came into focus. His memory drip, drip, dripped back into him and he realised where he was, who he was with. Or thought he did. Everything had changed. The room he had been in – his childhood one? His home? – had disappeared. He was still in bed, that much was the same. But even the bed was different. Plain white metal, like an old hospital bed. And the linen had changed too. He blinked, looked round. The room was completely white, almost clinically so. The bed linen matched.

'Look at me, Phil.'

He looked. There stood a naked woman. He didn't recognise her. But the more he looked, the more he thought she seemed somehow familiar.

'You see me?'

He nodded. Or thought he did, his head was swirling so much he wasn't sure.

She smiled. 'See me for who I am. For who I've always been.'

He looked again.

'You know me, don't you?'

'Yes,' he said, somehow believing her words. 'Yes, I know you.'

'Of course you do. You knew who I was when I spoke those two words to you. The Garden. You knew.' She started to move towards him. Slowly and stately, so he could watch her, admire her, as she came. 'I'm the other half of you.'

He frowned. Tried to process her words. Didn't know what they meant. 'What ... I ... what d'you mean? The other ... what?'

She smiled at him. 'I'm me. Just me.'

She was right in front of him now. He could have reached out and touched her. He raised his hand. He was no longer restrained on the bed.

'You're free,' she told him. 'I've freed you.'

'Who ... the other half?'

'Of you. Come. Rise.'

She bent down, pulled back the bed linen. He was still naked. Slowly, at her bidding, he swung his legs out of the bed, placed them on the white floor. They were trembling, weak from disuse.

'You can do it, come on.'

She put her arms round him, helped him to his feet. Eventually he stood there before the bed, in her arms.

This is a dream, he thought. A dream within a dream.

She held him close, head buried in his chest. Breathing him in. 'You thought you'd lost me, didn't you?'

'Yes,' he said, because it seemed like the right thing to say.

'And I thought I'd lost you. Forever.'

She held him even tighter. He allowed her to. He would have collapsed back onto the bed otherwise.

He didn't know how long they stood like that. Time had lost all meaning for him now.

'Here we are . . . ' A whisper, a sigh. 'Here we are . . . '

'Yes . . . '

'Together again. And this time, we're not going to let anyone or anything pull us apart. This time we're staying together forever.'

'Forever,' repeated Phil.

She clutched him tighter.

He closed his eyes.

60

Anni had left Malcolm at the house, waiting for the police. Crying and vomiting into the gutter. She wondered what the experience would do to his love of true-life crime now. She doubted it would put him off, though. It would just – eventually, once he had recovered – become the jewel in his walking tour crown. The place he had bravely discovered the bodies.

Print the legend, she thought bitterly.

She had phoned Marina, given her an update. But one thing she hadn't told her was the location of the industrial unit on the farm. She felt slightly bad about doing that, especially since it was Marina's husband who was most probably being kept there, but she told herself it had been the right thing to do. Because chances were that the woman she wanted was there. The woman who had killed her Mickey. And if that was the case, she wanted her all to herself.

Yes, Phil would be safe. She would ensure that. But it was the woman. She was the primary target.

She was back in her flat now, making a quick stop before going there. She went into the bedroom, opened the wardrobe, knelt down. She reached in, right to the back, knocking over a stack of boxed shoes as she did so. She found what she was looking for, brought it out. Looked at it.

A metal box. She opened it. A Beretta M9 9mm semi-automatic. Illegal, of course. But easy to get if you knew where to look.

She had bought it after Mickey's death. At first, in the darkness that engulfed her, she was tempted to use it on herself. She had stood in the kitchen one day, over the sink, a photo of her and Mickey laughing and smiling propped up on the mixer tap in front of her. A near-empty bottle of vodka at her side. Her vision blurred with tears, bawling and crying her eyes out.

She had held that gun in her mouth, fingers on the handle, wrapped round the trigger. She could still taste cold metal when she thought about it. She had given a scream, willing herself to do it. But she couldn't. Eventually she had passed out on the kitchen floor, drunk. The next day she tendered her resignation from the police force.

And the gun had been put back in the wardrobe. Never touched again.

Until now.

Maybe this was what I actually bought you for, she said to herself. For her. She smiled. Nodded. That made sense.

She clicked a full magazine into place, chambered a cartridge. Put the gun in the back of her waistband, covered it with her jacket. She was ready to leave the house.

Well, almost.

Before she reached the door she bent down, picked up the large photo of Mickey and herself that she kept on the coffee table. Both of them smiling and happy, both looking like they had all the time in the world to be together. The same photo she had propped up in the kitchen that night.

She brought it up to her lips, kissed him, closing her eyes as she did so. Took it away. As she did so, she caught her own reflection in it. Saw her own face. It shocked her.

Jesus, she thought, when did I get so hard?

When Mickey died, she answered herself.

She put the photo back in its place, left the flat.

61

'So,' said Marina re-entering the interview room, 'did I miss anything?'

She looked between the two of them. Between Beresford's broken appearance and Matthews' angry one. She could tell immediately that the balance of power in the room had shifted dramatically. I don't need to know the details, she thought. Not at the moment. Just use it, keep going.

'Well,' she said sitting down, 'we've found your wife and son.'

Beresford looked up immediately. 'You've . . .'

'Yes. We've found your wife and son.'

A small light was lit behind his eyes. 'Are they . . . are they . . .'

'We'll come to that in a moment. Where's my husband?'

'What?' Beresford looked irritated to be asked the question. 'What about my wife and—'

'All in good time, I said. Come on, quid pro quo. Where's my husband?'

Beresford stared at her, suspecting a trick.

'Just tell me. Then we can move on. Then we'll talk about your wife and child.'

Beresford relented. He was running on empty, running on fumes. 'A lock-up. An old farm out Elmstead Market way. She's got a unit there. That's where she's been keeping him.'

'Postcode? Directions?'

'I don't fucking know . . . '

Marina turned to Matthews who was already out of his seat.

'On it,' he said, and left the room.

Marina turned back to Beresford.

'My wife and son,' he repeated.

'Yes,' she said, voice as brusque and businesslike as she could manage. She thought it would have to be, considering what was to come. 'We've found them. They're both dead, I'm afraid.'

Beresford sat there, his jaw open in shock. Staring ahead. Marina said nothing, let the news sink in.

'Dead . . . ' he said eventually.

'Yes. And I'm sorry. Sorry for them. Sorry that they had to die. Just for you. So you could justify your own actions to yourself.'

His head fell forward then wrenched backwards. Marina kept talking.

'They'd been dead for some time. Probably as soon as she took them. She had no intention of letting them live. And I think you must have known that, didn't you?'

Beresford screamed like a dying animal.

Marina sat unmoving. And unmoved. 'They say it's the hope that kills you in the end. Is that what happened to all those people you murdered? Did you do that in the hope of seeing your wife and child alive again? Is that the lie you peddled to yourself? Or did you secretly know that they were dead, secretly hope, even? Then you could behave the way you wanted to, and grieve later, telling yourself you didn't know when in fact you suspected it all the time. Is that it? Which one makes it easier for you to live with your actions? I don't know. But you have plenty of time to find out.'

She stood up, made for the door.

'We're done here. I'm going to find my husband.'

62

'Remember when you were a little boy?'

She held Phil tightly, wrapped him in her arms, enfolded him in her love. They had moved to the floor, sat in a corner of the room. The whiteness seemed to stretch away to infinity. Phil couldn't make out where the walls ended and the ceiling began. All he could think of was her calm, soothing voice, pouring into his ear, his soul, telling him everything was going to be all right.

'Can you? Can you remember that far back?'

He nodded, but it may have been because she was rocking his body slowly backwards and forwards.

'Before Don and Eileen, before the foster homes, before all that . . .'

He said nothing, tried to cast his mind back that far. It was foggy. Too foggy. Nothing was working properly in there. He couldn't even cast it back to before he had woken up. There was just that voice. That beautiful calm voice, pouring over him like liquid warmth, making everything all right again.

'You remember you parents, right?'

Phil nodded, not knowing whether he did or not.

'Your sister, even?'

'My . . . sister?'

'That's right.' She held him tighter, rocked him slightly harder. 'Your sister.'

He frowned. The clouds were back again. He was struggling to see through them, to make any mental images from the past rise up and form themselves in front of him. In their absence he just had her beautiful voice to guide him. It was the voice of an angel. A wholly truthful voice. He listened, followed it.

'Your sister,' she said again. 'Before your mother and father were killed, remember? There was you. And your sister.'

He nodded along with her words once more, not truly understanding their meaning but enjoying them all the same.

'You've worked out who I am by now, haven't you, Phil?'

He knew it was a question and questions usually demanded answers. Unless they were those other questions. He knew the word for that but it wouldn't come to him. What kind of question was that?

'Phil?'

'What?'

'You've worked out who I am by now?' she said again.

There was that question again. He didn't know the answer but he knew she wanted an answer and he didn't want to disappoint her so he gave her one. 'Yes.'

She hugged him tighter. It seemed to be the right answer. And that made him feel good.

'The day our mother and father were killed it was cold, remember?'

He nodded.

'And you and me were in the garden. And there was snow everywhere.'

'Snow . . .'

'And you taught me how to make snow angels in the snowdrifts.' She giggled. 'It was a happy day, that. Well, it started out happy anyway. And now we can continue. We can be happy again.'

375

'Yes,' he said. 'Happy again . . .'

She pulled away from him slightly, looking at him. Eyes to eyes. 'You do know who I am, Phil, don't you? You really do?'

Again there was that question. Maybe he'd said the wrong thing last time. He didn't answer this time.

'I'm your sister, Phil. Your sister. And you thought you'd lost me forever, didn't you? Well, you haven't. I'm here. And we're together again.'

She held him tighter once more.

'My sister . . .'

'That's right. I survived. And I found you. Oh, it's taken me years, but I've found you.'

She took her hand away from him, opened her palm, showed him what she had been holding. The two small capsules from the side of the bed.

She smiled at him.

'You're ready for this now. And now we're going to be together. Forever.'

63

Anni pulled up in the car, as quietly as she could, killed the engine.

The roadway onto the old farmland was cracked concrete coming off a gravel road. The land was flat, open. Both things acting as an early warning system should anyone turn up unannounced.

She sat in the car, unmoving, listening. All she could hear was the ticking and cooling of the engine. She looked up and around, checked the door once more. She was confident that she hadn't been heard. If she had, there'd have been some movement by now, some noise.

She got out of the car, closed the door as silently as possible. The building looked old, run-down. Brick walls and a corrugated metal roof. Blacked-out windows set into a perishing wooden frame. A once black door beside them. The rest of the buildings around it looked like they weren't in use. They were in various states of disrepair, some with temporary repair jobs that over time had become permanent ones.

She checked once more that the gun was still there and made her way to the building.

Night was falling. There were no lights outside the building. Or anywhere around. She stood for a moment, letting her eyes become accustomed to the gloom. She looked down the side of the building. Saw the outline of a car parked there. That was *her* car. She knew it. Must be.

And that meant she was inside now.

She walked all the way round the building. The woman's car was parked in front of two huge double doors. The main entrance, thought Anni. Probably not the best way to enter. She went back to where she had parked, tried the small black door.

Unlocked.

She smiled, holding the handle. Then pushed it slowly forward a few centimetres, ready to close it again quickly if it made a noise.

But there was no noise. And despite the door being and looking old, there was no resistance from it. Must be used often, she thought. Carefully, she pushed it all the way inwards until it was fully open. Then, with one last look around, stepped inside.

64

The circus was on its way.

Marina had heard that phrase once used by Phil and now always thought of it whenever the police rolled out in force on an operation.

She sat in the car with Gary Franks, the atmosphere tense.

'You did good work in there, by the way.' Franks looked out of the window as he said it.

'Thank you.' Marina smiled. 'Maybe I'm not so bad after all.'

'I never said you weren't good at your job. Let's just hope he gives his statement without any trouble and normal service can be resumed.'

'Yet here we are on the way to a potential crime scene. And you've let me tag along.'

Franks allowed himself a rare smile. 'You're cheaper than a hostage negotiator.'

Marina smiled at the backhanded compliment. 'Thanks very much.'

They left the single track road, hit the gravel one then made it onto the broken concrete road, the car rocking backwards and forwards as it negotiated potholes.

It had been a process of elimination to find the place. A simple Google search of the area provided them with the correct location. Simple, thought Marina, if you knew where to look and what you were looking for.

It was fully dark by the time they arrived, killing the lights as they did so. Marina looked at the car parked there.

'That's Anni's car,' she said.

'Anni Hepburn?'

'Yeah. What's she doing here? Let's hope she hasn't been taken as well.'

They exited their vehicles as quietly as possible. The armed response unit had parked down the road so as not to arouse suspicion. The backup team were similarly located and were getting into position.

Franks turned to Marina. 'You stay here,' he said, fastening up his stab vest.

'What? No. I'm coming in as well. That's my husband in there.'

'Exactly. And you can be the first to greet him when he comes out.'

'No,' she said, trying not to raise her voice. 'I've come this far. I got Beresford to confess which you were just praising me for a few minutes ago. I deserve to be in there.'

'Marina—'

'I've met her before. I'm the only one here who's spoken to her. I can be more help in there than out here. Cheaper than a hostage negotiator, remember?'

Franks stared at her, but eventually relented.

'Get a stab vest on. And stick close by me.'

'Thank you.'

He shook his head. 'The sooner you piss off back to Birmingham the better.'

They were ready to move in.

65

Anni crept inside the building.

It was dark, the only light coming around the wooden and card boards stuck in front of some old windows. She wanted to take out her flashlight but didn't dare. She could hear voices, or at least one voice, somewhere off in the depths of the building. She could also see light bleeding in from somewhere up ahead. Artificial light.

She waited while her eyes became accustomed to the dark. In front of her were large rectangular wooden frames, made into box-like constructions. There was a door leading into the first one. She went inside. Looked round. It was the photographic facsimile of a bedroom. She took out her flashlight, thought it was safe enough to use it in this box. She shone it round the walls. There was something familiar about this room . . .

She got it. Phil and Marina's.

The answer just opened the door to more questions.

Turning the flashlight off she moved out of the box room and walked onwards.

Cables snaked on the floor to a portable generator. That must be what's providing the light, she thought. She walked on.

Another box room, then another. The place was like a film set, she thought. Or a theatre. But she still couldn't understand why.

Eventually she reached the part of the building where the light was coming from. Wooden frames ran the width of the building. A doorway was inset in one of them. There was a small area on her side of the wall. A director's chair, mirror and make-up box. The make-up box open, the make-up used. The mirror with lights around it like she had seen in professional dressing rooms. The chair, judging from the depression in the seat, recently sat in.

She listened. Voices from the other side of the wall. She moved to the doorway, opened it a crack.

A woman's voice. Calming, soothing. She knew instinctively it was her.

Anger rushed up inside her at that. Her hand went for the gun.

No, she said to herself. Take a breath. Act rationally. Calmly. Think.

She looked round the door. Was quite taken aback. The whole room, about half of the building, was white. And there was Phil sitting against the wall, naked, cradled in the woman's arms. She stared at the woman. Didn't recognise her at all.

But it must be her. It must be.

She took the gun from her waistband, held it.

Took aim.

Ready to fire.

66

'Here,' she said. 'Take this.'

She handed Phil the capsule. He held his palm out, stared at it.

'Just put it in your mouth, bite down hard.'

He looked confused, frowned at her words. 'What . . . I . . . But . . . '

'Just bite down on it. That's all. Look, I've got one. I'll do the same. At the same time. And when we do it we look into each other's eyes. Right?'

Phil nodded, hoping again that was the right answer.

'Right. Look into each other's eyes. And smile. And then we drift away together. This world won't be able to hold us any more. We won't have to worry about anything any more. We'll never have to hide our love or let anything or anyone come between us again. We'll fly off into eternity. Together. Forever.'

Phil looked at the capsule in his hand. Then watched what she did.

She raised her hand to her mouth, transferred the capsule from her palm to her mouth. She smiled at him.

'Go on, then.'

Smiling, he raised his hand to his mouth.

67

Marina entered the building alongside Franks. The armed response team were waiting to be called. There were two other officers with them, both in full body armour. They all looked round, waited while their eyes acclimatised.

'Down there,' said Marina, pointing to where the light was bleeding at the end of the building.

She moved quickly, had spotted the outline of a figure at the door.

The figure saw her moving forwards, ducked inside the white room.

Marina reached the door, looked in. Whatever she had been expecting, it wasn't this.

Phil was over by the wall, naked, being cradled by a naked woman who was about to put something into her mouth. He was about to do likewise. Anni was standing at the far end of the room, pointing a gun at them.

'Stop,' shouted Marina. 'All of you. Stop . . . '

Phil looked up at her, frowned, head on one side.

'Anni? Anni, what are you doing?'

Anni kept her grip on the gun, pointing straight at the woman. 'She's mine. After what she did to Mickey she deserves it.'

'Wait!' Marina stepped forward slowly. Hoping that her friend wouldn't take a shot while she was there in front of her. And she didn't know what was going on between Phil and the woman so hoped her action wouldn't do anything to jeopardise getting him back. She needed to stall, time to think.

'What the bloody hell—' Franks had arrived.

'Stay back, Gary,' Marina told him. 'Please.' He started to speak, she held up a hand for silence from the centre of the room where she now stood. 'I'm going to do what you brought me here to do. OK?'

Franks understood, nodded, stepped backwards.

Marina turned to the naked woman who was now staring up at her. She looked feral, like a lion about to make a bid for freedom from captivity. Marina moved slowly. Cautiously. Respecting that feral, unpredictable ferocity.

'Listen,' she said, hoping that her voice would reach her, penetrate whatever layers of thinking she had. 'He's not who you think he is.' She pointed, kept her voice low, calming. 'Phil. He's not who you think he is.'

The woman snarled at her.

'You think he's your brother, right?' She swallowed hard, hoped the woman wouldn't catch the fear in her voice. 'He's not.'

'Liar!' she screamed.

'I'm not,' said Marina, still trying to keep her voice as calm and steady as she could. 'I'm not lying. He's not your brother.'

'You just want him back ... ' She clung onto Phil even harder.

Behind her, Marina was still aware of Anni trying to get in position to get a shot off at the woman. She turned, reluctantly drew her attention away from the woman.

'Anni, don't . . . please . . .'

Anni kept her sights on the woman, her gun held straight out. 'She killed Mickey, Marina.' Eyes never leaving the woman. 'She deserves it.'

'You'll go to prison, Anni. For her.'

'So? At least she won't be able to kill anyone else. I'll have done everyone a service.'

'But, Anni . . .'

Marina was aware of movement behind her. She turned round, faced the woman and Phil once more. The woman was trying to get her attention.

'You're just jealous,' shouted the woman. 'Yeah, you. Jealous of the love Phil and I share. Because it was never like that with you. Because you had nothing, *nothing* like it.'

Marina stepped forward slightly, hoped the woman wouldn't notice.

'It's got nothing to do with jealousy. Honestly. I told you before and I told you the truth. He's not your brother.'

'No . . . no . . . this is a trick. This what you've been told to tell me . . .'

'No trick. Just what I've learned, what I know. Phil is not your brother. Your brother's still alive, still out there somewhere.'

She started shaking her head wildly from side to side. 'No . . . no . . .'

Marina pressed on. 'Your parents were killed by a contract killer. Your father was a police officer. He arrested a gangster from Leeds who wanted him killed. The gangster got his wish.'

'No . . . no . . .' Even louder, trying to block out Marina's words with her own.

'Your parents were killed in a safe house. You and your brother were left alive. You were split up. Sent to foster homes, different ones. You weren't allowed to have any contact with each other. You were given a false name, so was he. You were never told his, he was never told yours.'

She was screaming now, incoherent, moaning and screaming.

'And then ...' Marina continued, edging further forward slightly as she spoke. She was aware of Anni making a movement behind her too. Held out a hand, gestured for her to stay back. She didn't know whether the gesture was successful.

'I'm sorry about this next bit,' said Marina, continuing. 'About what happened to you. But you were forgotten about. You slipped through the cracks.'

'No ... no ... lies ... liar ...'

'I'm sorry, but that's the truth. That really is the truth.'

'No ... no ...'

'Phil isn't your brother. He's my husband. And I'd like him back, please.'

The woman screamed once more, making the kind of sound an animal makes when it's been trapped. She turned to Phil, grabbed his face.

'Take it,' she shouted, 'take it ...'

Marina saw what was happening. She moved forward, tried to reach Phil before the woman could do anything. But as she did so, time seemed to slow down. The distance between Phil and the woman and Marina seemed to stretch out to the length of several cathedrals. The floor became molasses. Marina tried to run but it was like she was in a dream, couldn't move quick enough.

The woman pushed Phil back on to the floor, tried to force his jaws together. 'Bite, bite ... take it ... don't ... don't listen to her ... just bite ...'

Phil clamped his jaws tightly together.

'No!' Marina screaming now.

The woman looked up at Marina, triumph in her eyes. Then bit down on her own capsule, and slumped to the floor.

Marina reached the pair of them. But the woman's rapidly dying body told her she was too late.

Time stopped. The room froze.

Anni broke the silence.

'You bitch,' she shouted from behind Marina. 'You cheated me . . .'

Her gun still pointed ahead.

Marina reached down for Phil, who was lying on the floor. She tried to pull him into a sitting position.

'Phil . . .'

She was frightened to move him, scared to touch him, almost.

He opened his eyes, looked up at her. Smiled.

'Marina . . . It's you . . .'

'Yes . . .'

'I never made snow angels . . .'

He opened his hand. In his palm was the capsule.

'Oh, thank God . . .'

Marina hugged him. Felt tears run down her face. 'I've got you back . . . I've got you back . . . You're safe now, safe . . .'

He pulled away from her, so he could look into her eyes. Smiled. 'Marina . . . my . . . wife . . .'

She smiled back. 'That's me.'

'No . . . get off . . .'

Marina looked up. Franks had made a grab for Anni's gun. She was fighting him off.

'Don't—'

The gun fired.

A scream froze on Marina's lips.

The bullet hit Phil. It spun his body, drove him back onto the floor where he landed forcefully.

He lay there, eyes closed, the blood spreading out from under his body like angel's wings against the snow white of the room.

PART SIX

CLOUDS

68

Marina watched from a distance as the hearse arrived with the coffin and the pallbearers walked it up the aisle of the crematorium chapel. Birmingham Crematorium on Walsall Road was as peaceful and welcoming as it could be. But still Marina hated coming here. Not, she thought, that it makes me different from anyone else in that respect.

She saw a couple walk up behind the coffin, a woman and an old man. It looked like he was the woman's father but Marina knew it was Imani's parents. Her father was visibly shaken, walking with help from a cane and assistance from people either side. The man had taken the news about his daughter as badly as he could, having a small stroke when he heard it.

It was time for the rest of the mourners to file in. There were plenty of dress uniforms on display. Even Cotter was wearing one. They had nodded to each other, Marina declining her offer to come in with the force, sit among Imani's colleagues. She didn't feel she had the right, somehow.

Simon Matthews entered behind the police, also wearing dress uniform. Still not one of the gang, thought Marina. He didn't look at her. She told herself he probably hadn't seen her.

She waited until they had all entered then tried to slip in quietly at the back. A voice stopped her.

'Hi.'

She turned. Anni Hepburn stood there looking very uneasy.

'Hi,' said Marina.

It was the first time they had spoken to each other since that night in Elmstead Market. When Anni had shot her husband.

'I thought I'd find you here,' said Anni, looking down at the ground, finding the gravel outside the porch suddenly fascinating.

Marina nodded.

'I just wanted to pay my respects. That's all.'

Marina said nothing.

Anni sighed. 'Look—'

'Let's go in. This is for Imani.'

Anni nodded.

They entered together.

The service was humanist, which surprised Marina. The minster taking it seemed to have talked to plenty of Imani's friends and colleagues, and Marina found herself surprised that while laughing at some of the anecdotes she found tears on her cheeks.

Afterwards Marina spoke to Imani's parents, said how proud she was to have known their daughter. How privileged she had been to work with her. But she sensed her parents either didn't care or didn't want to know from anyone who had been connected with their daughter when she died so she started to walk away.

Anni caught up with her.

'Can we talk?'

Marina stopped walking, ready to hurl some invective at her old friend. Instead she just sighed. 'Yeah. Come on.'

They made their way to a bar in the city centre that Marina knew. The Old Joint Stock, a favourite of hers and Phil's. It was once an Edwardian bank and still had the ornate architecture and high ceilings plus a theatre in the back of the building. They found a table upstairs, took their drinks, sat down.

'I'm sorry,' Anni began. 'I suppose that goes without saying. Look, I didn't mean to—'

'I know. We wouldn't be talking now if you did.'

Anni nodded, took a sip of her gin and tonic.

'So what happened after that?'

Anni shrugged. 'They ran me back to the station, Franks had a right go at me. But since you didn't press charges, they let me go. And then I phoned you. But you didn't answer. Several times.'

'I was in the hospital. Seeing if Phil—'

'I know.' Anni sighed. 'I know, Marina.' She took another mouthful of her drink. 'Jesus, what a mess.'

They sat in silence for a while, Marina sipping her red wine, Anni her gin and tonic.

'Look,' said Marina, putting her glass on the table before her, 'I didn't take your call because—'

'You were with Phil. You said.'

'Can I finish? Yes I was with Phil. But I also didn't know what to say to you. If Phil had died because you'd . . .' She couldn't finish the sentence.

'I know.' Anni sighed again. Fell silent. 'Any news?'

Marina shook her head. 'Just the same.'

Anni nodded. Unsure what to say, what she could possibly say to make things any better.

She sighed once more. 'I just . . . it's grief. Grief does that to you. Makes you like that, makes you behave like I did. Anger. Revenge. All of that. I didn't mean to—'

'Did you mean to kill her?'

Anni opened her mouth to answer, stopped herself. 'I . . . don't know. Honestly? I really don't know. I mean, I stood there, pointing that gun, keeping her in front of me, knowing

I had the power to end her life. Boom, just one little pull of the trigger. And then she went and did that anyway.'

'And how did that make you feel?'

'Cheated,' said Anni, straight away. 'That she'd taken this showdown away from me. This power. I just . . . I don't know. I wanted to make her suffer, make her pay for what she did to Mickey. But she took that chance away from me. But when I've thought about it afterwards, I don't know whether I'd have actually done it. I think I just wanted to make her feel fear.' She nodded, as if hearing her words for the first time. 'Yeah. I think that was it. Fear.'

'But it all went wrong.'

Anni sat forward. 'You think I don't know that? You think these last few days, what is it now, a couple of weeks almost? You think that hasn't been hell for me? Really? Course it has. Worst time of my life since . . . '

They both acknowledged the name in the silence. Anni continued.

'It meant I was a killer. A killer, no matter how accidentally. And I'm sure Franks would have had something to say about that. I'd have done time. And I'd have deserved to. And I would have spent every day paying for it, like I should have done. Because then I'd have lost two of the best men I'd even known. And I'd have caused one of them to go.' Her eyes were blurring with tears. 'I would have deserved every kind of hell I got.'

She sat back, spent.

Marina couldn't look at her. There had been so much she had wanted to say to Anni. That was why she hadn't returned her calls. She had had imaginary conversations in her head, day and night, throwing every kind of accusation at her, hearing every excuse in return, then countering it brilliantly with another accusation until Anni was broken.

But sitting in the bar, looking at her friend and seeing how much hurt her actions had caused to herself, she knew that nothing she could say would make any difference. If she berated her, Anni would accept it. If she forgave her, Anni would accept that, but, Marina knew, not feel deserving of it.

So instead she thought of Imani's father at the funeral, remembered what grief had done to him. The real cost of it.

'What?' asked Anni.

Marina tried to smile. 'Drink, up, my round. Just got to nip to the ladies on the way.'

She went downstairs, locked herself in a cubicle. Once inside and sure there was no one around, she let out all the rage, fear, anger and grief that had built up inside her. Let it consume her until there was nothing left, or she felt there was nothing left. Until she felt ready to move on.

Then let herself out, checked her make-up concealed as much as it could, went to the bar and ordered more drinks.

69

'Iknow it's a bit of a hike, and you're probably puffed out, but it's worth it, believe me.'

Malcolm's tour was back on. And business couldn't have been better.

Numbers had doubled, trebled, even on weekends. And he had been on hand to happily accommodate everyone's needs, rewriting the script to bring it right up to date. Of course, being elevated to status of local celebrity with a direct involvement in the latest crime didn't hurt. Didn't hurt at all.

'Here we are. Meander Mews, the latest Colchester crime scene.'

The crowd had gathered round him. What a difference a few weeks had made. He still couldn't believe it. They no longer talked during his speeches, or giggled, texted, whatever. No. They now hung on to his every word. Took the whole thing in. Oohed when he wanted them to, aahed when he wanted them to. Just like he had imagined it would be.

'It was here,' he said, pointing up to the anonymous little house, 'that the witch, as we call her, killed two people. The wife and son of the police detective in charge of the case. To make him cooperate. To make him do her bidding, ladies and gentlemen, yes. The witch had power over him. Real power.'

They had read it all in the papers, of course. Seen it on the news and the internet. But they still wanted to come, look at the places for themselves, touch them, even. See if they could feel some of the evil seep through the house's walls, experience it for themselves. Some did. They told him.

'I could feel this, like, presence when we were there,' a woman had said afterwards. 'Like an evil presence ... didn't you?'

Of course he had. Anything to oblige. And she hadn't been the only one.

Self-hypnosis, he thought. What a wonderful thing.

'So yes, ladies and gentlemen it was right here. The witch took the woman and child and killed them. How, you may ask?' His eyes roved the crowd as he spoke. It got a good response when he did that. Upped the drama a level. 'Poison. She told him he could see them again when he had done her bidding. But he never did. All those people he killed on her behalf for the sake of these two. And they were already dead. Shocking. Shocking.'

He waited while that little nugget sank in.

'And how do I know all this?' He smiled. This was the bit he'd been waiting for. This bit had actually got him laid a couple of times. Oh yes. 'I found the bodies. Yes, me.'

Another dramatic pause while they took that in, then he continued.

'Yes, I found the bodies. And I'm sure you have plenty of questions about that, so let me speak first and then if I still haven't answered them, fire away.'

And he did speak, giving a version of what happened that night that bore no resemblance to the truth. There was no mention of the tears. Of the vomit in the gutter. Of the sleepless nights that had followed. Of the questioning of everything he had ever done, everything he was. None of that. There was just the heroic companion, the stoic friend who volunteered

399

to stay and greet the police while his companion went to stop another murder.

'Any questions?'

Plenty of hands shot up. And he took his time answering, embroidering each fact as he went, tailor-making them for the questioner. Bespoke answers. They should pay extra for this, he thought.

He also had his eye on a woman. She was standing off to the side. Not as attractive as the one from last week, but not bad. She'd do. Wasn't like he was going to turn her away, was it? Oh yes. He knew that look. Could spot it now.

This was who Malcolm was now.

And he couldn't have been happier.

70

Marina sat by the side of the bed. Waiting.

Time was measured by the machines' regular beats and pauses. Hooked up and wired into Phil, keeping him alive, giving her hope.

Hope. The cruellest of emotions.

He had woken up once, while initially recovering from surgery, before falling back into unconsciousness. During that short period of time he had grabbed the sides of the bed, shouted that he couldn't move. Marina had been sleeping in her chair, the same one she was in now, just waiting for such a moment. Hoping for one. She ran forward, took his hand in hers.

'It's all right, it's all right, Phil. You're OK. You're OK . . . '

She grabbed him, tried to calm him, comfort him. Looking round all the while for someone or something that wasn't there. She pressed a button by the bed.

He stared at her. 'Is it you? Really you?'

'Yes, Phil, it's me. Really me.' She tried to smile. Tried to let relief win out over all those other emotions.

He kept staring at her, his anxiety gradually subsiding but never fully disappearing.

'It's all right,' she said. 'Just lie back. Don't try to move. You'll hurt yourself.'

He did so, still staring at her. Not totally trusting her but taking her word that she was telling him the right thing to do, telling him the truth. Unable to move for the dressings, wires and tubes attached to him. But in his mind it seemed there were different things keeping him incarcerated.

'You're in hospital,' she said, trying to smile. 'You've been out for a couple of . . . '

Her head dropped, she started to cry.

'Oh God, Phil . . . oh God . . . '

His eyes closed once more.

She held on to his hand like she was drowning.

The bullet had penetrated his left lung which had collapsed and flooded with blood. Luckily the police officers were trained in triage and had held him together until the ambulance turned up. A second piece of luck was that the bullet hadn't directly hit his heart. It was touch and go whether he would make it or not and he spent over seven hours in surgery. The drugs in his system didn't help his body to fight back and although the surgeons had done their best, he had lapsed into a coma. Marina had looked at the prone, unresponsive body of her husband and tried to pretend that was a good sign, a necessary step for his body to heal itself. She had to tell herself that.

She had spoken to the consultant, had that dreaded but necessary conversation about Phil's chances of recovery. Fearful to hear any answer.

'Hypothetically, there's no reason why he won't come round,' the consultant had replied. 'He's sustained a serious injury but we seem to have caught him in time. No cardiac arrest, no brain injury so hopefully there's every chance he'll make a good recovery. Fingers crossed.'

Hopefully, she thought.

'What about a full recovery? Mentally, I mean?'

The consultant shrugged. His plastered-on smile faded somewhat. 'Well, he's been through a significant trauma. It just depends on his resilience, now. How well he wants to get better.'

Marina nodded. Looked again at the unconscious figure in the bed before her.

Sat down beside him once more. Waiting.

And here she was now, keeping her vigil by his bedside, wanting to be there when he woke up. *When* he woke up, she emphasised to herself once more. Not if. She had already been here once with a previous partner, keeping vigil at his bedside while the consultants asked if she wanted to give their consent to turn off the machines keeping him alive. She wasn't ready to go through that with her husband. Not now. Not ever.

Josephina was safe back in Birmingham. She hadn't wanted their daughter to see her father in this state. Part of her feared it might be the last time she saw him and she didn't want her to remember him this way.

No, she told herself. Don't think like that. Ever. He's coming back. She was sure of it.

It would be difficult, she knew that. What had been done to him was unspeakable. Most people would have snapped under the strain. But she took hope from a couple of things. The first was that he had woken up already. The second? Snow angels. He had remembered, or rather not remembered, snow angels.

Phil, no matter what he had been through, how tough and unbearable his ordeal, had kept that small part of himself intact. He must have done. He had realised he wasn't with his long-lost sister and wasn't going to take a suicide pill alongside her. And he had recognised Marina. How else would that recognition have stopped him from taking that capsule?

At least that was what she told herself. Had to tell herself. Because that was the spark that kept her believing, that convinced her that her husband was coming back.

She talked to him during the hours she sat there. Made up his answers, answered them in turn. Kept a conversation going. The one she hoped to be having soon.

'D'you sometimes get tired of all the death, all the heartache?' she said to him after returning to his bedside from Imani's funeral.

Course I do, came his voice in her head. *But it comes with the job. It's what we do.*

'Really?' she had said. 'But what did we achieve? Really achieve?'

No answer.

'I mean, we've been through hell, we've put our daughter through hell, and for what? What have we actually achieved? We've got a damned good officer killed. We've got you in a coma.'

She knew what his answer would have been. He would tell her they had got a psychopath off the streets, one who had killed countless people.

'Yes, but she'd done most of that before we stopped her. So the question is, did we do any good this time? Really do any good?'

She didn't know what his reply would have been. Not any more.

So she sat there. Kept her vigil. Waited for that spark of hope to fan itself into a flame. Waited for her husband to come back to her.

The days were blurring into an unremarkable mass. Hope had become as routine as everything else. She had just been to the coffee machine in the hall. Stockholm syndrome, she thought. I'm getting to like the taste of this stuff. She sat back in her bedside chair, the novel she had been trying to interest herself in splayed like a grounded flying bird on the bedside cabinet next to her.

She looked at Phil. No change. Picked up the novel. Tried to interest herself in it.

She didn't notice him move at first.

She sighed, took the novel away from her eyes. Thought of checking her phone.

That was when she saw it.

Just a finger, twitching. Then another finger moving with the first one.

She stared, unable to move, not daring to breathe.

Then a third finger. Then the whole hand.

She looked round, wanted to shout, wanted someone else to bear witness, to share this with her. She pressed the button to summon a nurse.

His whole hand was moving now.

'Phil . . .'

She held his hand, clutched it hard to her. As she did so, his left eyelid flickered open.

'Oh God, Phil . . .'

She felt tears starting to form in the corners of her eyes. Felt something real and tangible rise within herself.

Hope.

Acknowledgements

Time for some long haul thank-yous for this series. Starting with David Shelley, the man who initially commissioned (and played a massive part in the naming of) Tania Carver. Then all the subsequent editors at Little, Brown: Dan Mallory, Emma Beswetherick, Lucy Malagoni, Cath Burke, Katherine Armstrong and especially Jade Chandler who kept me on track for many years. And the rest of the team at Little, Brown too: the redoubtable Thalia Proctor, the ever-on-the-ball Jo Wickham, the fierce Andy Hine ... it goes on. I'm sure I'll miss people out if I continue so I'll just say thank you to everyone on Team Tania.

To my agent Jane Gregory for having my back all these years and the rest of the agency too: Claire Morris, Terry Bland and especially Steph Glencross for all her sterling work on getting Tania started.

To all the publishers abroad who've taken on Tania. Again too many to name but I appreciate everything you've done. Likewise all the booksellers, reviewers, tweeters, bloggers and friends who have been enthusiastic about this series. I can't tell you how much I appreciate it.

For Chrissie and Beth. Always. And to Jamie Lee, for putting up with my moods and madness on a daily basis.

And finally, thank you to the readers. To everyone who picked up a Tania novel and became invested and involved in the lives of Phil and Marina. I can't thank you enough. You made everything worthwhile.

'If you haven't discovered this talented newcomer yet, hurry.
She's on her way to the top' Richard Montanari

A sickening killer is on the loose – a killer like no other. This
murderer targets heavily pregnant women, drugging them and
brutally removing their unborn babies.

When DI Phil Brennan is called to the latest murder scene,
he knows that he has entered the world of the most depraved
killer he has ever encountered. After a loveless, abused
childhood, Phil knows evil well, but nothing in his life has
prepared him for this.

And when criminal profiler Marina Esposito is
brought in to help solve the case, she delivers a bombshell:
she believes there is a woman involved in the killing – a
woman desperate for children . . .

*

'With a plotline that snares from the off, and a comprehensive
cast of characters, Carver's debut novel sets the crime thriller
bar high. A hard act to follow' Irish Examiner

'Keep the lights on for this one. Carver has delivered another utterly terrifying, yet believable chiller' *Mirror*

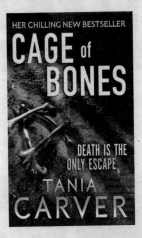

HER CHILLING NEW BESTSELLER

CAGE of BONES

DEATH IS THE ONLY ESCAPE

TANIA CARVER

Into the house. Down the stairs. Through the dripping dark of the cellar. Someone is there. Someone that shouldn't be there.

As a building awaits demolition, a horrifying discovery is made inside the basement: a cage made of human bones – with a terrified, feral child lurking within. Unbeknownst to DI Phil Brennan and psychologist Marina Esposito, they have disturbed a killer who has been operating undetected for thirty years. A killer who wants that boy back.

But the cage of bones is also a box of secrets – secrets linking Brennan to the madman in their midst. With the death toll rising and the city reeling in terror, Brennan and Marina race to expose a predator more soullessly evil than any they've ever faced – one who is hiding in plain sight.

*

'For thriller fans, *Cage of Bones* is a must, but be warned, it ain't pretty' *Irish Sunday Independent*